Carrie Lofty

. . . who knows how to blend "a skillful chemistry of intrigue and suspense with just the right touch of sugar and passion!" (*Fresh Fiction*)

Don't miss her first novel of the Christies

Flawless

Featured on Barnes & Noble's Romantic Reads as a super hot romance pick that is "as hot as July . . . [it] will take you out of 2011 and into the good ol' romantic past."

Book reviewers and romance bloggers adore *Flawless*. . . .

"I cannot express in my own words how gifted, how utterly magical, this author is with words. She paints a picture rich with emotion, struggle, and passion."
—Smexybooks

"I always look forward to a Carrie Lofty book because I know I'm in for an emotional love story with a rich eye to detail."
—The Book Pushers

"[Lofty's] prose is exquisite, her characters are extremely likable and genuine, and the setting was one that I would actually like to read more about."
—The Romance Dish

"A different and intriguing setting makes *Flawless* stand out, but Carrie Lofty's lush descriptions and evocative language bring the story to an even higher level."
—Reader to Reader Reviews

"An innovative historical story filled with diverse characters and a creative plot."
—CATA Network Single Titles

"[T]he chemistry between Miles and Viv was off the charts. Their interactions were heartwrenching at times but always so honest and raw."
—Books Like Breathing

"A sensual journey for the characters and for the readers."
—Australian Romance Readers Association

"Lofty delivers a near flawless story that kept me turning the pages."

—SOS Aloha

"The fireworks between the two are zingy hot. And the dialogue deliciously cutting."

—Drey's Library

"Exotic and intriguing. . . . Hot and passionate with sizzling chemistry. . . . *Flawless* had me hooked. This was my first historical romance by Carrie Lofty but it won't be the last."

—Book Lovers Inc.

"Miles was like Indiana Jones . . . rough, tall, handsome, and even carried a whip."

—Cheryl's Book Nook

"Now I can't wait for the rest of the Christie family to get their stories."

—Heroes & Heartbreakers

"The sensuality was exquisite."

—The Romanceaholic

"Viv's and Miles's characters are well-developed against a fascinating background of people and events that are reminiscent of the Wild West."

—Just Another New Blog

"When it comes to writing historical romance with sizzle, Carrie Lofty knows how to keep you reading."

—Coffee Time Romance

Don't miss the first historical romance
in the Christies series:

Flawless

Also by Carrie Lofty:

His Very Own Girl

An eBook Original
Coming September 2012 from Pocket Star Books

Starlight

The Christies, Book Two

CARRIE LOFTY

Pocket Books

New York   London   Toronto   Sydney   New Delhi

Pocket Books
A Division of Simon & Schuster, Inc.
1230 Avenue of the Americas
New York, NY 10020

This book is a work of fiction. Names, characters, places, and incidents either are products of the author's imagination or are used fictitiously. Any resemblance to actual events or locales or persons, living or dead, is entirely coincidental.

First Pocket Books paperback edition July 2012

POCKET and colophon are registered trademarks of Simon & Schuster, Inc.

For information about special discounts for bulk purchases, please contact Simon & Schuster Special Sales at 1-866-506-1949 or business@simonandschuster.com.

The Simon & Schuster Speakers Bureau can bring authors to your live event. For more information or to book an event contact the Simon & Schuster Speakers Bureau at 1-866-248-3049 or visit our website at www.simonspeakers.com.

Designed by Jacquelynne Hudson

Manufactured in the United States of America

10   9   8   7   6   5   4   3   2

ISBN 978-1-4516-1639-2
ISBN 978-1-4516-1641-5 (ebook)

To Keven
Because we both like cake.

Acknowledgments

Words cannot express how often my creative process was stimulated by correspondences with Zoë Archer and Lorelie Brown, both of whom influenced aspects of plot and characterization. I'm saying all of that with a straight face. Thanks to Ann Aguirre, whose dare in late 2010 skyrocketed the first draft into existence, and to Fedora Chen for her eagle eyes.

As always, Cathleen DeLong has been the caretaker of my crazy. You are the rock to hold down my helium balloon. *waves*

Camaraderie is essential in a business where insecurities make trouble like pesky gremlins. I'm glad to be part of the Circle Divas, the Broken Writers, and the Loop That Shall Not Be Named. I am also grateful for my friendships with Sarah Frantz, Jenn Ritzema, Karen Martin, Rowan Larke, and my ever-supportive family: Keven, Juliette, Ilsa, and Dennis and Kathy Stone.

Kevan Lyon and Lauren McKenna remain professionals without peer. I admire your individual skills as much as I appreciate your validation and encouragement. Thank you both.

Author's Note

Alex and Polly make me smile whenever I think of them. Class conflict that matures into a happy ending has always been one of my favorite romantic themes. I'm happy to have had the chance to bring these two disparate characters together.

During the Victorian era, Glasgow flourished. With a population that topped one million, it was the fourth largest city in the world. The milling industry that had been the mainstay of its early success was replaced, as demonstrated within these pages, by heavy maritime manufacturing. The need for a powerful seafaring presence was a key component of Britain's expanding empire.

The possibility of love across societal boundaries was far more likely in Scotland than in England. Self-made men were respected for their contributions to the city's prosperity, and the aristocracy did not hold as much sway. As a result, class confines were not as difficult to surmount as those separating the Protestant and Catholic faiths.

The difficulty of life in urban areas such as

Glasgow cannot be denied. But the Victorian era also offered remarkable potential. Because Scottish legislation has permitted access to classrooms for both boys and girls since 1696, I like to think a woman as clever and independent as Polly could have prospered—even when confronted with the most challenging circumstances.

As always, I look forward to your comments! Please contact me by email at carrielofty@gmail .com. I also welcome you to visit www.CarrieLofty .com and to follow me on Twitter (@CarrieLofty).

Prologue

Alexander Christie slumped into a supple leather armchair. With that artless collapse, his elbow struck a stack of papers on the nearby desk. A dozen star maps dumped onto the floor. Almost dispassionately, he watched them fall and scatter. He had intended to work upon returning from the will reading at his late father's brownstone mansion, but even the most engaging astronomical puzzles would not capture his attention now. The drama of the long afternoon made higher thought impossible.

Sir William Christie had been dead for three weeks, his stout brawn laid low by months of crippling pneumonia. Yet his influence, even from beyond the grave, remained undeniable.

"Glasgow," Alex said aloud, as if testing the word—the very idea of it.

From the other room came the sounds of a baby's cry. Alex looked up, his neck aching and stiff against that sudden movement. On a burst of restless energy, he shoved up from the decadent chair and crossed to the larger of the suite's two bedrooms.

"Is anything the matter?" he asked Edmund's nurse.

"No, sir." Betsy, a quiet Irish widow with two grown children of her own, glanced at him from where she stood over Edmund's bassinet. "Just a touch fussy this evening. But better than he has been, the poor little mite."

Still so small, so fragile. Delivered four weeks early, Edmund had been beset with health problems since the birth that had taken his mother. This recent bout with the croup was only just relenting.

Alex wondered if fatherhood would ever get easier. The edge of fear that cut under his skin never dulled. He walked to the bassinet. Betsy had swaddled Edmund in a length of pale green cloth, concealing his arms and legs in the tucked-in way that seemed to offer him comfort.

"I'm sure you could hold him, if you like," Betsy said softly.

Another slice of fear. Five months on and Alex still found no surety. No confidence in his abilities. The prospect of doing something wrong pushed like bricks against his chest.

"No. The boy needs his rest. We'll be traveling on with my brother and sisters to Newport tomorrow midday. You'll all be ready by then?"

"I'll make sure of it, sir. Esther is just down to fetch supper for us both," she said, referring to Edmund's young wet nurse.

"Good."

Betsy could not travel to Scotland. A trip into New York or to his father's palatial summer home in Newport was one thing. Prying her away from her family in Philadelphia was quite another, although Esther had family in London. He would not ask such sacrifices of either woman, even if he were of a mind to consider Sir William's ridiculous challenge.

No matter his internal strife, Alex could not resist touching the silken down of Edmund's dark, wispy hair. He knew that texture and he knew that precious scent.

Throat tight, he pulled back before he truly woke his infant son. Then there would be no rest for anyone.

"I shall retire," he said to Betsy. "Awaken me if you require assistance."

The nurse nodded and resumed her place in a nearby rocking chair, where a tangle of colored yarn spilled out of a carpetbag. Within seconds she had returned to her knitting. Alex nodded once, offering the approval she obviously did not need, and left the pair in peace.

He poured a slight drop of whiskey and retrieved the leather portfolio he'd brought back from the reading. As if doing so might change the contents, he unfurled his copy of the will.

"Alexander David Christie, son of Sir William Christie and the late Mrs. Susannah Burgess Christie, shall assume management of Christie Textiles in Glasgow, Scotland, for the period of two years. The demonstration of a profit at the end of that tenure will result in the award of a one-million-dollar bonus. Failure to do so will nullify any additional financial bequests beyond a single payment of five-hundred dollars."

Rubbing the back of his neck, he saw the machination for what it was—his father's petty revenge. Of Sir William's four offspring, only Viv had deigned follow in his footsteps as a pioneering entrepreneur, and even her acumen had been constrained by her marriage into the aristocracy. Now they all faced the individual choice of whether to play one last game of chicken with the old man's ego.

Alex was having none of it.

His life and his teaching position were in Pennsylvania, where he was due to be granted tenure within the year. A textile mill in the heart of Glasgow's industrial district was someone else's responsibility. He and Edmund would be fine.

Nevertheless, he dug through his attaché of personal belongings and found a picture of Mamie. She had been so young then, her hair severe and her eyes perpetually worried. But for the daguerreotype, she had managed a patient, nearly defiant expression of calm. Alex traced a thumb across that hard-fought smile. The guilt of her death remained difficult to bear.

What would you want?

The words formed on his tongue, but he was not the type of man to ask his dead wife for advice. She had always been so careful in her replies, often coaxing the solution out of him with a few quiet words. Knowing from the outset that no reply would ever come kept him silent.

A knock at the door roused him from his dolor.

He shoved the photograph and the will into his attaché, and then smoothed the lapels of his ink-black suit coat. A second knock sounded before he crossed the suite.

"Yes?"

Dressed in the hotel's rather pretentious green-and-gold uniform, a young bellboy held out a slip of paper. "Message for you, Mr. Christie, sir."

Alex opened the brief note. Ice laced his veins, freezing him out to the skin.

"Sir? He's downstairs in the reception room, sir. Awaiting your reply."

"Tell him I'll be down presently."

The bellboy pocketed a coin and disappeared down the corridor. Alex only stood in the doorway. As the nearest gas fixture softly hissed behind a glazed sconce, he reread that single line of writing: "Did he bequeath you enough to keep your son?"

Alex crossed to the fireplace in the living area and knelt before its trivial flames. The petty satisfaction he found in burning his father-in-law's taunt did not last long. Anger—a pure, blinding rage—was quick to screech back to life. As it always did. Hands bunched into fists, he ground his knuckles against the hearth's neat spread of marbled stone.

Josiah Todd deserved those fists in his face. Repeatedly. Until the man suffered as much as he had made Mamie endure. Until he begged for the forgiveness it was too late to offer his dead daughter.

Alex looked in on Betsy, who had fallen asleep in her chair. He penned a note rather than disturb her, leaving it on the message table. After appraising his appearance in a nearby mirror, he ventured into the empty corridor. At that hour, most of the hotel's patrons would be dining or taking in the city's many attractions. The Grand Central was a place for the very rich and the very influential. The stipulations of Sir William's will meant that Alex was no longer either. In the future, he would be better served by simpler accommodations.

But Josiah Todd blended in with that opulence and wealth.

In the reception room, he sat on a bench padded with colorful brocade upholstery. Ankles crossed, his face was buried in the evening edition. A full head of silver hair glinted beneath the light of a massive crystal chandelier. The smokestack trail of his ivory pipe circled up toward a ceiling replete with white and gilt crown moldings. A familiar gold signet ring glittered on his right middle finger. Mamie had hidden the matching burn mark on her inner ankle for two years before finally admitting its existence to Alex.

"What are you doing here, Mr. Todd?"

"Alex." The newspaper folded into itself, revealing a wiry mustache and muttonchops to match his silver hair. "Won't you have a seat?"

"No, I don't think so."

"You Christies so enjoy being bombastic."

Spine soldered, Alex kept his expression calm. Letting Josiah Todd see proof of how he riled an opponent was the quickest way to lose to the man. Mamie had never quite mastered the trick of letting his words slide over her, around her, past her.

They had hit her square every time, smashing whole chunks of her soul.

"You have me confused with my father, I'm sure." Alex clasped his hands behind his back. He dug his thumbnail into the meat of his palm. Any tension he felt would find expression there, out of sight. "Now, if you please. The evening grows late and I have no intention of humoring you much longer."

Mr. Todd stood with grandiose slowness. His paunch sat heavily at his waistline, concealed only marginally by the cut of his very expensive suit. Bright green eyes shone like the hard shell of a beetle. They briefly narrowed beneath his shiny silver brows before he once again found that ingrained hauteur. "You speak rather sharply for a man who only just learned he will inherit nothing."

Surprise registered in Alex's body as a slight tremor, like remembering the impact of a punch rather than receiving one. His prominent father-in-law, a direct descendent of one of the framers of the Constitution, had always been clever. Cronies and spies lived for his next dictate, greedy for how well he paid. That he might have learned the contents of the will, even before its divulgence to Alex and his siblings, came as no great shock.

"Mr. Todd, rest assured that I would speak to you just as bluntly, no matter the details of my father's estate."

"Ah, so nothing has changed. My daughter dies and you remain as arrogant as ever."

"She stopped being yours the moment she married me."

"Then she's in a better place now."

Alex dug his thumbnail deeper. "You are repellent, sir."

"What I am is of no concern to you, but could mean a great deal to my grandson."

The ice that had lined Alex's veins tightened until no blood pumped to his heart. Edmund was Josiah Todd's only surviving grandchild. Mamie's younger sister had been unable to conceive before her husband convinced a crooked bishop to annul their marriage, and their brother had died of cholera just before his eighteenth birthday.

Mr. Todd handed over an envelope. "This is notice from my attorney and from Judge Keller of Portsmouth that, from now on, I am to share custody of Edmund."

"Like hell."

"Such language. And Mamie always claimed you were a gentleman." With lifted brows, Mr. Todd regarded Alex as if looking upon a pile of rotting garbage. The feeling was mutual. "But perhaps that gutter talk is unavoidable considering your . . . lineage."

Alex ignored the insult and quickly gathered the gist of the legal summons. He couldn't stop the faint tremble that made the thick legal parchment shake at its edges, a show of apprehension that Mr. Todd surely caught. The reaction couldn't be helped. No matter that he'd likely been bought, Judge Keller made his interpretation of the law very clear. Edmund would be raised in Alex's care, but significant decisions about his place of residence, education, and even a potential stepmother would be subject to Josiah Todd's counsel.

"This is a farce," Alex said with a sneer. "Whoever this Judge Keller is, he'll be overruled by appeal."

"Well, now, that is a worry." But his tone and the slimy snake's smile he wore said that Mr. Todd was not worried in the least. "Let me get this just right. You're an astronomy teacher with no tenure, whose legendary father left you absolutely nothing."

No. Not nothing.

Sir William Christie, who'd dragged himself up from the gutters of Glasgow, had given Alex a chance. In just that moment, the axis of his world tipped. The tremble in his fingers stilled, and his blood pumped with strong resolve. Forget games and forget old grudges. Dead in the ground, his father was hardly his enemy—not when faced with the rich, influential beast who had abused Mamie.

Alex would go to Scotland. He would earn that million-dollar bonus and protect his son. Or die trying.

"You will never see Edmund again," he said. "Let alone possess the slimmest measure of control over his future."

Their gazes locked. And held. Until Mr. Todd turned to tap his pipe in a marble ashtray—a subtle retreat that further strengthened Alex's resolve.

"My boy, be reasonable. Do you really believe you have the clout to contend with me? Or the financial means?"

"I will, Mr. Todd. I guarantee it."

One

Glasgow
March 1881

*P*olly Gowan had never heard the sound of a cannon shell ripping open, but the blast that rocked the rear of the textile mill must have been a small taste of combat. The south wall caved inward under the explosion. A blinding plume of smoke and debris slammed toward the looms below. Three giant machines disappeared in the wake of that chaos of powdered brick. Shocked, screaming workers stumbled and ran in all directions, as flames licked their heels.

Eyes wide, taking in every horrifying detail, Polly didn't move. Her hands were still poised above the warp and weft of her own loom, the threads tangling from her lack of attention. She should move. Her thundering heart demanded flight. But she was consumed by one nauseating thought—one thought that meant the end of peace and safety for her people. And her family.

Tommy had gone through with his threat.

She held her aching stomach. The lightning-quick slam of that hideous realization gripped her hard, but not for long.

She kicked off the firing mechanism that powered the loom's arms and pulleys. It was instinct; if the place didn't burn to the ground, she might at least be able to salvage her work. Then she grabbed the hands of the nearest two little sweepers, Ellen and Kitty. They were sisters of only eight and ten, both as redheaded as Polly. At the next loom, Agnes Doward did the same with nearby apprentices. Together they gathered the children who worked the mill, most of whom had been scared into paralysis or equally useless screams.

"Come on now, lassies," Polly shouted over the din. The harried calls of the other workers competed with the burn and crash. "Out we go. Out into the street. The fire brigade will be here in a wink."

She doubted her own words. The fire brigade might eventually hurry to the scene, but only once they learned which building blazed. The chiefs knew how furious the mill masters would be if the factories were destroyed. The rest of Calton was simply not a priority.

"Polly," Agnes called.

Looking back to where Agnes had nodded, Polly saw that a hole the size of a horse had opened in the south wall. Its near-circular shape was visible now that some of the dust had settled. Flames still crawled over the wool stores. Male workers did their best with water from an outside pump, working a chain of buckets and swatting the fires with overcoats.

What in the bloody hell had Tommy been thinking?

She tugged the girls' hands a little too roughly. She'd sort out the culprit later, feeding him to the families of whoever came away from this sabotage with injuries. There were bound to be some. The explosion had been too large to leave everyone unscathed.

The crush toward the front and side exits was sizable and frenzied. Polly handed Ellen and Kitty to another worker, Constance Nells, and elbowed her way past a half dozen people. She hoisted her skirts and climbed atop two crates; an advantage of height made her feel as brave as she needed to be. The panic wanting to break free would just have to wait. She needed to keep calm and set an example for the others.

If the factory burned . . .

Cupping her hands over her mouth, she shouted at the top of her lungs—which her ma had always said were the equal of a booming dockworker's twice her size. That was not exactly flattering, but her strong voice was most useful today.

"Everyone, listen up!" For emphasis, she shouted it again in the Lowland Scots dialect they all shared. "Keep panicking if you want to burn alive. Whoever did this will win the day. They'll be glad for it, knowing we reacted like animals. I, for one, would rather breathe clean air again. Now, you'll bloody well calm down, keep care of the young ones, and behave like the Calton survivors you are!" She hooked a thumb back toward those who worked to quench the flames.

"And men, if you have any meat between your legs, you'll help save our livelihoods!"

For the span of a breath, there was no human sound. She had silenced them all. Nods and strong words of agreement followed. And, to her astonished pride, the seventy workers at Christie Textiles found their civilized minds. The men hurried back to help the efforts against the fire. The women hoisted children onto their shoulders and gripped their small fingers. Doors parted under the push of unseen hands, letting in a stream of misty spring sunshine. The smoke sucked out into the street, and Polly could taste the coming rain.

Two hands reached up to help her down from the crates. It was Les MacNider, a tall, skinny firebrand who talked as well as any professor—but only on the topic of workers' rights and the oppression of their people. Otherwise he was just as likely as any man to grunt vague replies and talk sport, gambling, and women. He was a loyal friend.

Polly accepted his aid in descending. "It was Tommy," she whispered.

Les shook his head. Although he was only in his late thirties, he was mostly bald. "I won't believe it. Not of Tommy."

"There's no time. Go help the other men. I'll make sense of whatever awaits us out in the street."

Les nodded again and added a grunt of agreement. He worked his lanky frame back through the factory to take up a position in the line of buckets. In the distance, the clang of the fire brigade's bells offered some relief, bringing with it a familiar flare of indignation. Polly wondered how quickly they responded to emergencies in Blythswood Hill. But she didn't indulge in bitterness. That way lay melancholy and a dependence on strong drink.

Or, in Tommy's case, a yearning for violence.

She rushed out after the last of the escaping workers. The streets were full of people, from both the Christie mill and across the street. Her fellow workers wore soot and ash like an actor's face paint, while those from Winchester's appeared curious and concerned. Every building on the street was vulnerable if the winds shifted.

Already the scent of hot water and wet ashes permeated the air. Maybe they had a chance. The fire brigade had taken position in the alley, back near the stables and where deliveries of wool were stored. Whoever had planned the attack knew the establishment's weakest place, right where the equivalent of dry tinder waited to erupt with the smallest spark— let alone actual explosives.

Rough hands grabbed Polly from behind. She yelped. Reflex helped her fight, but the hands were strong, implacable.

"You think you're unstoppable, don't you, Polly?"

A shudder ripped across her upper back. She stopped fighting, if only to process her shock. Although his sneak attack had been a surprise, Rand Livingstone never failed to single her out as a scapegoat. Winchester's overseer held a grudge against her as deep as the River Clyde. That she'd nearly made him a falsetto for the rest of his life had something to do with it.

The shock passed, and she fought. Tooth and claw had nothing on a Calton girl in the grips of unspeakable anger. He was a reptile. Positively inhuman. A factory could burn to the ground, and he would rather enforce baseless accusations or grab at her breasts.

"Let me go, you pile of vomit." She grunted and twisted in vain. Something in her shoulder gave way with a little pop. She cried out at the sharp pain. "Bloody let go!"

Livingstone held fast, and with all the men indoors, Polly could not rely on the scared, stunned women, who huddled to keep the children safe—especially the older lads who wanted a closer look at the blaze.

"You were warned," he growled, giving her arm another painful jerk. "You and your lot. You know any hint of violence would mean no mercy."

"As if *any* member of the Gowan family has ever advocated violence! Now, let me go. You're not a pig in a uniform—just an overseer! You just want to maul me like a doxy."

Leaning close, he breathed against her temple. "You're little better, you uppity bitch."

Polly had used the moment of stillness to recover her breath and to lull the dullard into slacking his grip. She twisted away, turned, and landed a hard punch to the underside of his chin. His head snapped back with a sick grunt. Her satisfaction didn't last long. Livingstone brought up his knee and slammed it into her stomach.

Polly dropped to the ground, gasping. "Evil son of a bitch," she whispered.

By now other men had gathered, including two constables. They looked brutish and wan in the thin sunlight. Distantly she heard Connie shouting for help, calling men from inside the factory to come to Polly's aid. She feared they wouldn't be fast enough.

"Get the others we want," Livingstone told his cohorts. "The usual: MacNider, Larnach, Nyman. Even that old woman. What's her name?"

"Agnes Doward," came a firm voice. Agnes stood just behind Livingstone. Polly, looking up from the pavement, wanted to wave her off. But her friend's posture was resolute. She wore a shawl around her thin shoulders, and her disheveled hair flipped and twisted in the breeze. "That's me."

"At least one of you scum has good sense. Not eager for a beating, old woman?"

"Not exactly. Which is why I'll refrain from saying anything more to you."

Agnes's age was completely indeterminate, a contradiction of smooth skin and gray hair. All Polly knew was that she had four grown children and had lost her only grandchild, a wee baby girl, to cholera during the previous autumn. Like many of the most active union members, she had little to lose.

Polly fought to her feet, supporting her stiff shoulder. She glared at Livingstone. "You won't have this unjust right much longer," she ground out, for him alone. "Look around. One day they'll realize how powerful they are. Nothing you do will hold back that tide."

He sneered. "They're sheep, and you know it."

His activities had attracted some attention, but as

Polly glanced up and down the street, she silently admitted the truth. Most people didn't want to get involved, especially against those two looming constables and their fierce truncheons. Fear created the inertia she had fought for years, and her father before her. Not that she blamed her fellow workers. There was pain to be found in fighting the way of things. Pain and danger.

But most days she just wanted to shake them all, to rile them to action, to prove what they could accomplish if they held together. Wasn't fighting worth making sure a gutless rat like Rand Livingstone no longer had the unchecked power to bully?

His hard-faced accomplices dragged two men out from the mill. Les, with his angular, spindly body, was easy enough to spot, as was Hamish Nyman's flaming red hair and full beard.

"Where's the other one?" Livingstone asked. "That young nuisance, Larnach."

"Nowhere to be found, sir." The nameless enforcer shoved Les along. "Even a few punches got nothing out of nobody. He didn't show up for work."

Polly's heart sank. Tommy Larnach had been one of her father's most loyal and trusted young allies, practically as much a son as were Heath and Wallace. Tommy's limp was a testament to that day when, a decade earlier, at the mere age of fifteen, he'd taken a terrible beating so her father would be spared an unjust punishment.

Yes, Polly had more than one reason to hate Rand Livingstone.

And Tommy had been Polly's first and only lover.

To think him capable of this destruction added an extra layer of agony to the place where Livingstone had kicked. Had Tommy been in the mill, he would've had at least something of an alibi.

One brute crossed his bulky forearms. "To the police station, boss?"

"Oh, no. We got special orders from Winchester. He wants the new mill master to know their faces. It's Christie's property. His charges to press. But he needs to meet them first." Livingstone glanced at the men in uniform. "Either of you got a problem with that?"

Neither objected. Hatred curled in Polly's gut. Once again, she and her kind were on their own. But she needed to stay calm despite the abuse of power— at least for now. Being the eldest child of Graham Gowan meant notoriety. His peaceful dedication to workers' rights spanned three decades. Polly's youth and gender would not protect her forever, especially if the masters discovered that she now served as her father's right hand.

"Come on, then." Livingstone prodded her in the lower back, always touching her more than was necessary. Little pinches and grabs reinforced what more humiliating damage he could do if the moment appeared.

Polly kept her eyes forward, her jaw fixed. "You remember that time I connected the toe of my boot with your bollocks?"

He growled and twisted her sore arm. The pain was worth it for his infuriated expression. "You pompous whore."

She kept her voice pleasant. A real smile shaped her mouth. "Next time I won't make that mistake. I'll rip them clean off."

"Shut up."

He shoved her into the back of a police wagon. She was joined by five more suspects. Her tartan shawl offered little protection against the slinking late-winter cold. Once inside the wagon, seated on a hard, shallow bench, she huddled closer to Agnes. The older woman's closed eyes silently proclaimed her boredom with this routine, even as ash still colored her hair.

"It gets a little tedious, being so popular," said big, gruff Hamish.

"You just wish you got as much attention from one of the MacMaster sisters."

"No, that's the wish of a spindly know-it-all like you." Hamish stroked his full beard. "I get my hands plenty full of the pretty lassies."

Polly grinned. They could be unruly, thick-headed, bitter people, but they were her people. Even in the midst of this crisis, they found ways of holding the fear at bay. And they were loyal. Les, in particular, would lie down in front of a team of galloping draft horses if it meant protecting union secrets.

Holding her aching arm, she squinted through the bars of the wagon's lone window, assessing the pewter sky. The temperature had dropped. Calton was hardly a pretty area on the most brilliant of days. In fact, the eventual sunshine of late spring and summer would only accentuate every crack in the tenement sandstone. But when licked by March's drizzle and cold, the buildings stood as dark, hulking shadows amid the ghostly gray. No color.

Their only hope was what they made for themselves.

Livingstone's aim gave her just the hope she'd needed. No one from the union had yet to meet the new master of Christie Textiles. Union committeemen collected information like birds building nests. What they had gathered about Alexander Christie did little to round out his image. Indeed, he was Sir William Christie's eldest child, born to an English noblewoman who had died during his infancy. Raised in London for a time by his mother's family, the boy eventually moved to New York City after Sir William remarried a Welsh commoner. Now he taught astronomy at an American university in a place called Philadelphia, and was widowed with one child.

But his personality, politics, and plans—even his appearance—were as opaque as the clouds. How could she strategize against someone she'd never met?

Now she would. Polly would know her enemy, just as she would discover the identity of the saboteur.

The wagon chugged to a stop. Livingstone jerked the double doors open, his hand on Polly's upper arm faster than she could have imagined. She stumbled to the pavement, where flint-sharp ice crystals chapped her cheeks. Agnes emerged last, as Les helped her down—more of that gentlemanly behavior that seemed so out of place. It was just his way.

The office of Christie Textiles was a modest affair when compared to some of the masters' grand places of business. Situated halfway down toward St. Enoch's Square, the squat, four-story building resembled in shape the dull bricks used for its construction. Heavy overcast clouds leached the walls of their deep red. A modest sign hung over the front door.

"The sign's been painted anew," Polly said to Agnes.

"New master. It's little Will Christie's boy, come home."

"Home." Polly whipped off her head scarf with a sharp flick. The breeze played keep-away with loose strands of her hair, but she hardly cared. She was just too riled. "He was neither born nor raised here. If you expect to find familiarity in him, my friend, you'll be hurt and disappointed."

Agnes shook her head. "He's got Scottish blood in his veins, though. No denying."

"I'll give you that. But masters are masters. They're never truly new."

Alex wanted a break from the expense reports and informational pamphlets spread across his desk. Numbers of a distinctly commercial variety clogged his thoughts. There remained so much to learn. Not for the first time, he wondered how his father had successfully insinuated himself into so many varied businesses. Had he really learned each industry as thoroughly as Alex was trying to learn the textile trade? Or did enterprises eventually come to resemble one another, so that the commodity no longer mattered?

He shrugged out of his coat and tugged at his ascot, so cross that he finally yanked off the silken noose. No matter how well his father had managed, Alex was not a businessman. The only way he knew to approach a topic was to study it from the ground up to the limitless sky—an aim made more trying because of Edmund's health. His minor illnesses and occasional fevers wore on Alex's stores of patience. Esther, Edmund's wet nurse, would leave in three weeks to join her extended family in London. He would need to find another woman to care for him. Soon.

The break he'd imagined was quiet and still, a moment to collect his frustrated thoughts. Instead, he endured the arrival of a police constable called Andrews and the mill's overseer, Howard McCutcheon.

For ten minutes, Alex listened as the men related the events of the late morning. Each passing description stiffened his ligaments and fused his bones in a combination of distress and outrage. McCutcheon went first: an explosion, a fire, a complete work stoppage. The mill's workers had spread out onto the streets or gone home. Some might even be in hospital with burns from fighting the blaze.

The constable's words were even more alarming. Sabotage, he said. Union agitators.

Alex took a deep breath and glanced at the papers, charts, and figures littering his desk. The time for studying was over. If agitators threatened his business, he would go to war.

"You're certain it was intentional? No accident of any kind?"

"Explosives were used, sir," Constable Andrews said. "No accident at all."

Alex slammed his fist against the desk and glared at the men until their gazes lowered. "I will not have my mill jeopardized and loyal employees endangered!" Only when he recognized his burst of temper did he force his voice to quiet. "What about suspects?"

With unkempt hair and his upper lip encumbered by a large mustache, Andrews did not fit Alex's image of an efficient officer of the law. But the man's posture and determined expression offered some comfort. "My officers will bring in the usual collection of riffraff and union whips."

"I'll want to see them personally—the union people, I mean. Intimidation is not a strategy they will utilize to any good effect. I guarantee it."

"Yes, sir," said both in unison.

Alex almost did a double take. He was unused to men snapping to his commands with that combination of unease and obedience. Many had responded to his father in a similar fashion. Never to Alex. Yet he appreciated the moment for what it was: expedient, uncomplicated. He would get results.

A banging noise downstairs in the lobby caught Alex's attention. "See what that's about," he told McCutcheon.

But by the time the overseer reached the door, a knock sounded from the other side.

"Who is it?" Alex shouted. A headache had burst

across his brow. His factory. His chance at beating Josiah Todd and protecting his son—literally in flames. He would see the damage himself, if only to make granite out of his firm resolve.

"Constable Utley," called a voice.

Andrews raised his brows, which were nearly as thick as his mustache. "See? My men."

Alex was unconvinced, because Andrews appeared equally surprised. Something was not as it seemed. He resented the deception, but it was not his most pressing concern. He nodded to McCutcheon.

A tumble of people spilled into Alex's office. The room was not exactly small. It was, in fact, larger than his father's library in that distant New York mansion. But as it quickly filled with roughly a dozen people, the office became a noisy prison cell. Two? Maybe three constables? Plus men who looked like hired muscle, and a few ragged, thinner folk covered in ash. Factory workers?

Then . . . red hair. The exquisite red hair of a young lady who would barely stand as tall as Alex's chest.

"Now that's more like it," Constable Andrews said. His mustache contorted into a sneer as he stared at the same woman. "Should've known we'd see you behind this. Mr. Christie, this is Polly Gowan. Graham Gowan's girl. She's the first I'd have personally dragged down to the station."

Alex blinked. The redhead had a name as lyrical as her hair was remarkable. He found himself staring. Outright staring. His heartbeat was a steady hammering in his chest—not because of the anger he'd only just stoked, but from a rush of sensual awareness.

Before he could remember his mind, his manners, his office full of strangers, he strode toward the little woman. Standing over her made him feel like a towering giant, powerful and strong. That feeling did not dim when she jerked up her chin. If anything, the blood in his heart raged even faster.

The shaky, eager way his body took note of her soap-fresh scent and trim waist was only going to complicate matters. Already he knew that he'd take thoughts of her to bed that evening. Pick over them. Analyze them. Relish them.

She wrenched her arm away from the brute who held her captive. But she didn't run or flinch or weep. Her bright green gaze collided with his. She stared him down with as much force and certainty as any man. Alex fisted his hands against a rush of pure, primal excitement. Sudden combustion.

He had never felt its like.

That she was a suspect only added an edge of violence to his body's dizzying response.

"Who are you?" he snapped. His voice was so low and curt as to sound wholly unfamiliar. "And what the hell did you do to my mill?"

Two

Polly stared up at the man Constable Andrews had referred to as Mr. Christie. She had expected some equivalent of a desk clerk, stooped and thin. Or just the opposite—a fat man with heavy jowls and a pocket watch worth more than her parents' tenement flat. Instead, Mr. Christie was the worst sort of challenge. He had caught her off guard.

Where was his coat? And his neckcloth? She couldn't remember the last time she had seen a gentleman so informally dressed—if ever. The shock of finding a hint of chest hair poking out from the collar of such a fine, expensive shirt was dangerously distracting. The contrast of wild and civilized was as pronounced as the stark white cloth lying against his tanned neck.

And despite her indignant temper, she had to admit that Agnes was right: he was a man born of Calton stock. Tall and broad-shouldered, he had a hard jaw designed to absorb life's toughest punches.

That didn't mean he knew how to fight. Could he bully, cheat, terrorize? Oh, yes. Of that she had no doubt. No one became a mill master without some sort of underhanded ambition and trickery.

But to win against her? She wouldn't allow it.

"I'm Polly Gowan. The policeman in your pocket said as much. And I sure as hell didn't try to burn down the place where my family's worked for three generations." She lifted her brows. "I believe that's longer than the Christies."

He scowled. Good. She enjoyed her victory if only to distract herself from his coloring. Tanned skin, yes. Hair like aged gold with bright tips the shade of ripe wheat—just the length to invite a woman's eager hands. His eyes were amber and green swirled together in a permanent whirlpool, deep and wild. The perfect hazel.

She crossed her arms, disgusted with herself, especially when the sting of her injured shoulder reminded her exactly which interests he represented. The distress of the day's events had tossed her concentration to the four winds.

"You'd be right," he said, his words clipped. "But the Christie name hangs above the front door."

"Thanks only to your workers. Without the men manning the buckets, you'd have lost the entire mill today."

For the first time since striding toward her like a bull charging a red cape, he broke eye contact. "Is that right, Constables?"

"Save your breath," Polly said. "They won't take a piss without Livingstone's say-so." She hooked a thumb back toward the man's looming bulk.

Mr. Christie raised his brows. Was that nearly . . . amusement? Of course not—not under those circumstances. She was looking for hope where there was none to find.

The constable named Utley threw Polly a sharp glare, then replied with a shrug that proved her right. "No telling, sir."

"All very helpful," Mr. Christie said dryly. Maybe he realized how little he'd pry from their useless mouths, because he quickly returned his attention to her. "You must be a union girl. I've heard of your father."

"No accomplishment there, master. Even a man who's been in textiles but a few weeks must've heard his name."

A whisper of a smile tipped his mouth. Again, she felt a shiver of something unexpected. His obvious anger was tinged with a strange humor, like that of a conspirator rather than an enemy. "Don't make that mistake, Miss Gowan."

"What mistake is that?"

"You seem to believe that I need more than a few weeks to know my business."

She leaned in, chin still raised. From that proximity, she could smell him—all warm, freshly bathed skin and downy cotton cloth. "If you knew anything, you'd realize Graham Gowan has never advocated violence, nor does anyone who stands with the union he leads."

Except Tommy, whispered a niggling voice in her mind. She pushed it away. No sense telling men with such deeply held prejudices about her suspicions. She would deal with Tommy soon enough.

"You sound proud of your father's reputation," he said.

"Rightly so. And I plan to surpass it."

"Freak she-devil," Livingstone muttered at her back. "She needs a husband, not explosives and a grudge. A firm hand would keep you in line, girl."

Les and Hamish cursed his churlish accusations, but Polly found herself curiously unaffected. Quite the wizardry Mr. Christie's eyes could produce. He needed a haircut, although to tamper with those sandy-blond strands would be an injustice. They added just enough softness to a hard, sturdy face. Brow, cheekbones, nose—all as precise as an architect's lines, but with the burly toughness she'd expect of a workingman.

He was a deadly handsome man. Her need to suck in a quick gulp of air proved as much.

Polly forced her attention to him. "So, Livingstone, you would be the one to—what was it? Keep me in line? Apply a firm hand?"

"Bet on it," the overseer said coldly.

"Not a bet I'd take, actually. Odds are I'd have your skin for curtains before sunup." Polly smiled sweetly, still watching her real opponent. "Now, then, Mr. Christie, you seem ready to act as judge and jury. Shall I fetch an ax and reveal my neck?"

He blinked so hard it was nearly a flinch. "Excuse me?"

"You might as well be my executioner, too."

And, good Lord, he could be. A quick glance down revealed hands bunched into fists like mallet heads. He wore that beautiful white shirt and finely tailored woolen trousers, yet the simmering anger pulsing from his robust body was anything but elegant. More like . . . brutal. There was no mistaking how his baser instincts would resolve matters.

How odd. Most masters left their dirty work to men like Livingstone. This Mr. Christie looked ready to knock heads. Polly shivered and returned her gaze to his face. But that was no help either. Breathtaking hazel eyes stared back at her, narrowed, fierce in his disconcerting blend of ire and intelligence.

She cocked a hand on her hip. "No bloodshed today, then? No beheading? Just rampant accusations and brute force, instead of a proper investigation. Typical, I say. If this is how you do business with your workers, especially after an emergency, I've all I need to know about what sort of master you are."

His deep assessment was nearly more than she could endure. She would've rather suffered more of Livingstone's jabs and pinches. At least she knew how to deal with that slimy creature. Standing before Mr. Christie, waiting, holding her breath, with the whole room silent after her taunt, she felt terribly exposed, as if he could peer past her bravado to the place where she hid moments of doubt.

But they were just that. Moments. She never let her doubts last long.

He broke eye contact again, releasing her from his magnetic hold. "Who are the rest of you?"

The constables introduced themselves straight-away, but the hired muscle remained silent. "I'm Rand Livingstone, overseer at Winchester Fabrics. And these are the suspects we brought in."

"Let me get this straight," Mr. Christie said quietly. But something warm and exciting shivered up Polly's backbone. The new master was anything but calm. "You're the overseer at *Winchester*. Yet you're handling the apparent detention of *my* workers. Under the authority of these constables?"

Livingstone exchanged a furtive glance with Andrews. Hamish, Les, and the others offered sharp protests. Their voices layered over one another until all that remained was the blurred sound of accusations and masculine shouts. Polly would've joined the fray, but she was too busy watching Mr. Christie. His eyes flicked back and forth between Livingstone, the constables, the workers, the brutes, and finally to Polly.

"He has personal reasons for ensuring I learn my place," she said evenly, although she felt no such ease beneath her breast. "Even after these accusations, he could have left the matter to the authorities. But I have no doubt he relishes the opportunity to see me punished. Personally."

His gaze stayed, but it did not rest. She could feel his attention like a touch. His expression shifted. Apparently all that searching and probing led to a conclusion, but his features did not soften. If anything, he appeared even harder. He unfurled those big hands, shook them as if to return the blood to his fingers, and turned away from everyone. Beneath his fine white shirt, the taut line of his back seemed hewn of iron.

Briefly, he stood at the lone, wide window and looked out to the darkening sky. Gray shadows and the blue light of a fading afternoon competed for dominance over his strong brow and sharp cheekbones. Only then did Polly notice the coat he should have been wearing, tossed over the back of his chair. Her rebel mind insisted on playing out that moment. How had his body moved as he shed an encumbering layer of civility? Even now, poised in that tense moment, she admired how the revealing cotton stretched between his shoulders. Her gaze followed where twin shirttails disappeared into the snug waistband of his trousers.

She shut her eyes. Not that closing them would stem the rush of images. She feared what her mind would conjure come nighttime. Although she secretly led the union in her father's stead, she was still a young woman in the presence of a stranger who fired her blood. He was the master of Christie Textiles. Her adversary, if not her outright enemy. But he was also a precious novelty in her tiny world: a strong, handsome, intelligent gentleman.

"I want all of you out," he said at last. His odd American accent, so low and rough, invaded her darkness.

Polly opened her eyes on a shiver, oddly disappointed that their introduction was already at an end. She had hoped to glean much more about his character.

"Pardon, sir?" asked Constable Andrews.

Mr. Christie swiveled away from the window. "Out of my office. I'm going to chat with Miss Gowan."

"You don't know what the hell you're doing," Livingstone snarled. "She bats her green eyes and wraps every Calton man around her finger."

"You are radically out of place by speaking to me in such a tone. I'm no Calton man, Mr. Livingstone, and I'll manage just fine." At another bare syllable of protest, Mr. Christie strode around his desk. Polly shrank back, out of his way and nearer to Agnes, as he went straight for his target. He stabbed an angry finger against Livingstone's sternum. "I don't want to see you in my building ever again. If you interfere with business that relates to Christie Textiles, I will have you arrested for trespassing and harassment."

"The law doesn't work for you."

A callous smile shaped Mr. Christie's firm, wide mouth. Polly hadn't been able to imagine him smiling, and that cold expression did little to help. It was too . . . calculating. "No, I suspect the law works for the highest bidder. I will ensure they're well compensated for putting you in your place. Get out."

Raw hatred flickered through the overseer's eyes, but Mr. Christie stood his ground. His big fists were back, curled and primed for a fight. Polly covered her mouth with unsteady fingers. To see Livingstone get his comeuppance at the hands of this new master would be the making of her wildest fantasies.

Hit him, she found herself chanting. *Hit him.*

But the coward didn't give him a chance. Livingstone took a step back, his expression still twisting around powerless fury. "I won't forget this."

"I should hope not," he said. "Now, Constables, keep the other workers in the clerk's office down the hall. I'll meet with them later."

After Agnes and the various men filed out, Mr. Christie shut the door behind them. The tension around his shoulders and neck had eased. Truly, he had been ready to brawl. Only now did his body relax, having won the round with words and threats. She released a breath laced with an esteem he didn't yet deserve.

Once again, Polly found herself pinned by his unerring attention. "Sit," he said.

"I'd rather stand."

"I suspect you'd argue with the door if the mood suited you."

She said nothing, so as not to prove him right. Instead she lifted her eyes. *Challenge them,* her father had always instructed. *Men never expect a direct challenge from a woman.*

"Why me?" she asked.

"Because you know more about that explosion than the rest of them combined."

Polly scowled. "I don't know a bloody thing. Had I been by the south wall, I could've been killed today."

"Instead you're here in my office, and we're going to have a conversation. Union, business, sabotage—the topics shouldn't come as a surprise."

He crossed the room. The thinning rug swallowed the sounds of his footsteps. The solid wall of his body pressed into her space. Polly did her best to keep away from him while giving no ground. Her throat closed. She found nowhere to look but toward the little thatch of hair that poked up from his open shirtfront.

After a hard swallow, she found her voice again. "I don't know anything."

"I don't believe you." Mr. Christie's hazel eyes narrowed. For a moment, so near, they shared the same air. Polly was almost dizzy from the unexpected intimacy. "But if you'd rather, we can let the subject drop."

Relief swept through her lungs like the scent of flowering hedges. Unexpected. Sweet. She rubbed her sore arm. "I'd like that, yes."

He bit his back teeth together. Muscles bunched along his jaw. For a moment, he actually looked pained. Then an expression of firm resolve hardened his sharp features once more. A resolved warrior in half a business suit. "Then you have a choice, Miss Gowan. You can stay here with me and talk, or I can give you back to Livingstone. He won't stand up to a man, but I have no doubt what he's capable of doing to a woman."

You'd give me over to that beast, even suspecting what he might do to me? What kind of monster are you?"

Alex needed to back away. He *needed* to, or he would touch Polly Gowan. For the past fifteen minutes, he'd fought that urge as he had rarely fought any battle. Not to caress her or seduce her. No, he just wanted to prove she was real. Like a tiny, angry valkyrie, she was almost mythic in her strength and the righteous burn in her bright green eyes. Her accent was as strong and unfamiliar as that of any Glaswegian, an exotic brogue with its oddly clipped consonants, but she added an impish brightness.

Alex gripped the edge of his desk, with yet another war brewing behind his breastbone. He was honorable in his heart and soul—a quality that in many ways had been the making of him. Threats were nearly too much to stomach, especially against a woman. The alternative, however, included losing his business to an unidentified saboteur and handing Edmund over to Josiah Todd.

That would never happen.

He had no doubt Livingstone was a beast. In fact, it was from Josiah Todd that he had learned to identify such a covetous, proprietary look. The brutal overseer believed, for some reason, that Polly was his to manipulate. And maybe worse. Just as Alex's father-in-law had believed Mamie was his. In every way. Forever.

She would have been, had not Alex intervened.

Yet had he ever desired a woman with such swift, infuriating speed? Polly Gowan had been in Alex's office for only a quarter hour. Still, he was compelled. Fascinated. Drawn to her. The reaction was so fierce as to remind him of his long years of celibacy—throughout his marriage almost entirely, and certainly since Mamie's passing. Despite his body's aching insistence, however, he wasn't in the habit of drooling after every pretty new female. Polly appeared infinitely resilient, as if she could take the full force of a man's desires, and demand as much in return.

"I'm no monster," he said as evenly as he could manage. "After all, I am giving you a choice."

"It's no choice, and you know it. Out on the street, he practically pulled off my arm. When that wasn't enough, he kicked me in the gut. Take those facts and choke on them."

Alex stilled. "He kicked you?"

"What does it matter to you? Still ready to toss me to him?"

No, he thought bitterly. More like he regretted not popping the man's jaw when he'd had the chance. "You'll be the one to decide, as I said."

Polly swept that fiercely red hair back from her temples, her hands quick and agitated. "And here I'd almost thought you gallant."

"Gallant?"

"For standing up to him that way. No one ever does."

"And now?"

"I take it back."

"Can you take back a thought? I don't think so." He leaned against the desk and crossed his arms, well clear of temptation. "You thought I was gallant. The idea was there. It existed in your mind. Now you've altered that thought by adding new data. Happens all the time. For example, I thought you were beautiful."

She pulled her chin back on a quick intake of air. Alex hid a smile as he watched the words sink in, like water quenching dry summer soil. Her lips parted. She touched her hair again, and then dropped her hands.

"Thought?"

Such uncertainty in her voice. Perhaps her position in the union and among the mill workers had stripped her femininity. With a rare flash of intuition, he suspected that men would desire her without truly appreciating her singular beauty. Her pretty, sprightly features and bewitching red hair were obvious enough. Although her mud-brown gown's boxy shape and worn fabric did much to conceal her physique, she had lush breasts, a neat little waist, and hips designed to be palmed by a man's eager hands.

Something inside him, buried deep, surged to wakefulness. He didn't feel like himself. He was rougher, somehow. His temper was stretched and frayed. He would've brawled in his office had Livingstone done so much as scratch an itch.

"Yes, I thought that," he said tightly. "But then I learned you could've been part of this plan to destroy my factory. I'm sorry to say such knowledge has tempered my opinion."

"Fickle man," she said with a huff.

"No more than you deeming me a monster rather than gallant."

Her lips curled in disgust. "That's because your behavior changed. The same cannot be said about my appearance."

"Well, you have me there."

"*Such* a gentleman."

Although Alex could not say as much—nor could he indulge in the smile her waspish tongue inspired—she was even lovelier now. Indignation, fury, and maybe embarrassment had flushed cheeks already colored with abundant freckles. Eyes the color of bright spring grass snapped. A habit of chewing her bottom lip had made it both fuller and pinker. She tempted him to dark places with nothing more than a cagey sideways glance.

Beyond her disconcerting effect on his control, Polly Gowan was priceless. He certainly wasn't going to give her to a brute like Livingstone, but she wasn't leaving his office until she accepted her new role in his life. Research alone had been unsuccessful in finding a way past the locked door of secrecy that protected the Calton textile union.

She would be his key.

"Time's up." Quicker than Polly could react, he wrapped an arm around her lower back and shoved her none too gently toward the office door. He'd meant to keep her from further injury after hearing how Livingstone had abused her. Now he was forced to intensify his threat. He pulled her hip to hip with one hand and reached for the doorknob with the other.

He was touching her. And she was very, very real.

"Out there with him, Miss Gowan, or in here with me."

"I won't! Throw me to that wolf if you must, but I'm not talking to you."

Alex only gripped tighter, despite how his throat had closed and his lungs ached. "What is so bloody hard about talking?" he said past gritted teeth. "Sharing information, for God's sake. You act like I'm already prepared to dismantle the whole system, when you don't know a damn thing about me."

"Such language. I wouldn't have thought you had it in you."

Alex cringed inwardly. When was the last time he'd cursed at all, let alone at a young woman? Very rarely before that afternoon.

Polly tilted her chin. "But the fact remains that you're a master. Jesus knows you'll use anything I say against us."

He stopped her at the open doorway. The hands at her waist were not caressing. No. Just holding her in place. She looked ready to dart for the Highlands.

"So that's been the way of it?"

"Don't play dumb," she snapped. "I know you're not."

She crossed her arms beneath her breasts, dragging him back to thoughts he had no history of indulging—the weight of her flesh in his hands, the heft and the softness. He smiled softly, simply enjoying the strong, unexpected buzz of anticipation. Her gaze caught on his mouth before darting away.

"There's only so much a man can learn from books," he said at last.

He pulled her aside and shut the door. Although he had been the one to place her in danger, he enjoyed the flush of relief on her freckled cheeks and the deep breath she exhaled. Good Christ, he really had been alone too long if such manipulations aroused him.

But she didn't thank him. She didn't even back away. Had she known he was bluffing? He traced the fast beat of her pulse where it throbbed along her neck. Maybe he'd made an impression after all. She certainly had turned him inside out, and so quickly, too.

"Well, I see that you have plenty of books, Mr. Christie. Good luck, then. Perhaps a little more reading will do the trick while the rest of us load bricks, fix looms, and start again." She pushed away and sauntered toward the door.

Sauntered . . . as if he would let her go.

He caught up with her, easily, eagerly. He'd found another reason to touch her. With his hand trapping her wrist, he turned her to face him. During the initial fracas, he hadn't given thought to his state of undress. Now he could think of nothing else. His cravat gone. Her mouth so close to his bare skin.

Alex channeled his surprising, almost overwhelming need. He *was* a good man, but the pressure building in his veins knew no limits.

"You don't seem to understand," he ground out. "You'll tell me what you know and do everything I ask."

She raised her free hand, perhaps to strike him, but he caught that, too. They stood body to body in the middle of his office. Alex stifled the rough breath that would've given away his arousal.

"If you don't," he continued, "I'll do worse than threaten you with the likes of Livingstone. You have a job you'd like to keep, yes?"

"Ha!" The fury was back in her eyes, pure and cold—the most provocative shade of green he'd ever seen. "You need a woman of my experience more than I need your company's name on my pay packet."

"And who else would hire you? A woman with

your reputation? It would be a very easy thing to turn the other masters against you. You're already a prime suspect."

"You fit in with them seamlessly. It's in your nature. You sit behind a desk when the rest of us break our backs and little girls of only four years put in a full day's work."

Something made him protest. Gamblers would've railed at him for tipping his hand, but at that moment, as Polly Gowan vibrated with anger, he could not be the ogre she believed. He released her wrists and resisted the urge to apologize for the red marks he'd left there. "I'm not like every master," he said softly.

"Now, *that* you'll have to prove."

As if standing outside of himself, he bridged the scant distance between their faces and touched a lock of her fiery hair. Silken. Alluring like nothing he'd ever known.

She stiffened. Her full mouth flattened into a sharp line. "But you are like every other *man*. May I go?"

"Yes," he said with an exhale. From somewhere deep inside, he found his resolve once more. "I must question the others."

"And what about the factory? I'm not so optimistic as to hope we won't be held accountable for our weekly quotas, even working among shambles."

"We'll discuss it tomorrow, Miss Gowan. I'll be there for the first shift."

Three

"How bad is it, girl?" Da asked.

Polly exhaled from where she finished the last of the washing up. Her da sat at the tiny dining room table. Ma had settled into a chair nearest the fire, with a sack of lacework in her lap. She would continue to knit until she made her first mistake, perhaps knotting a strand of the delicate floss or dropping a stitch. On some nights that meant she stayed up later than anyone.

Heath and Wallace, Polly's younger brothers, had already snuggled into their pallets. They arose so early to work the docks. Their young bodies needed all the sleep they could manage, and more food than their combined wages could afford.

The thought of food tightened Polly's stomach, but there was no more to be had. Ma had eaten even less. Complaining would be a disrespectful waste of breath. She focused instead on the crisis at hand. A grumbling belly was nothing to the troubles they faced.

"Except for Mary Worth's crushed hand, there were no terribly bad injuries. A few burns and nicks, and men who'll have trouble breathing for a few days. It could've been so much worse. We'll take up a collection for the wounded at our next assembly."

That was another reminder to stem her scant complaints. For the most part, they had been very lucky.

Da chuckled softly. "There's my lass. Always people first. And the mill?"

Her cheeks heated at her father's understated compliment. "Any building can be repaired. Why wouldn't I think of the people who can't be replaced? The masters may think we're as interchangeable as belts on a generator's engine, but I refuse to."

"Mrs. Gowan, I do believe we've raised this girl right."

"No thanks to you," Ma teased.

Da's brief bout of coughing cut their banter in two. Thankfully it didn't last long. Looking on his withered features and crooked back pinched Polly's heart. The disease in his lungs was very bad. No one could breathe cotton strands for so long and emerge from the mills unscathed.

Some facts were unavoidable, and more painful for it.

After recovering, his watery green eyes sharpened. His body might be ailing, but his mind remained as clever as a fox. "Now, the mill."

"Liam Ferguson says there's hope, but I haven't seen for myself. Once I finished in Mr. Christie's office, I waited for him to question the others. That's why I was late. I wanted to know what they'd learned and what he'd asked."

"And?"

And . . .

That was the puzzling part. The strange, dangerous man had barely questioned Agnes and the others. Instead he had taken down their employment histories, current residences, and the names of their kin. He'd tried to pry union information from their stubborn Scots lips, but they'd held the line. "Not a word," Les had said, his bony chest puffed up. He was proud and deserved to be. Not every worker could stand up to a master, let alone one as changeable and compelling as Mr. Christie.

Compelling was too gentle a word. Throughout her long, chilly walk back to Calton, with stops to gather news from other factory families, she had returned to him in her mind. His surprising blend of roughness and elegance continued to surprise her. Yet his sturdy, stubborn jaw with a shading of blond stubble looked at home on an otherwise aristocratic face.

And his clothing! A workingman in Mr. Christie's state of undress was something to take for granted. They abided the dictates of toil, not fashion. To see a man of means so disheveled was nearly the same as seeing him naked. He possessed the same hard lines, dense muscles, and limitless power of any laborer. Darkness lurked in him, caged and wary.

Polly took a deep breath to regain control of her addled mind. He was just a man. She set the last tin dishes on the shelf. After she dried her hands and removed her apron, she turned to sit with her father.

"Mr. Christie only asked what one might suppose," she said. "Details about who's in charge of what. But you should've seen him, Da. Constables, Livingstone, me and Hamish and the others, all piled into his office like chickens in a coop. He looked like he was trying to read another language!"

Except when he'd looked at her. Then he had been so intensely focused, watching her with a piercing interest. It remained to be seen whether his intelligence would be a threat or an asset.

She was determined to turn him toward her cause. His brief moment of hesitation . . . *I'm not like every master.* She had almost believed him. It was the earnestness in his voice, and the way his hazel eyes had softened. As if he genuinely cared.

At the very least, it suggested an opening—if she proved brave enough to barge through. The stakes were too high for her to turn coward.

"Livingstone was there? What did he want?"

"He said Winchester sent him with the constables." Polly shrugged. "Maybe they couldn't trust that Mr. Christie yet knows his up from his down. And you know Livingstone uses any excuse to smack heads and grab girls."

"I should've killed that bastard years ago."

"Da! Don't talk that way. I appreciate the sentiment, but what would we have done with you rotting in a jail? Or worse?"

Her father's slack features took on the determined sternness of a man half his age. "He'd have got what he deserved for touching you."

"I came to no harm. And he won't hold rich

men's favor forever. Brutes like him never do. They get greedy."

"So who did it, Polly, girl? The mill fire? You must have some idea."

She looked away. "No one we trust is talking. Makes me nervous."

"Don't hide from me, lass."

With a shaky breath, she wrapped her hand around the tin cup that held the last of the day's coffee. Already the stove cooled. The room was losing its warmth. At such a late hour, Ma wouldn't put another hunk of coal in the fire. Da's hands curled around a mug of his own, where his knuckles stood out as swollen lumps. Polly briefly closed her eyes.

"Tommy wasn't at work today," she said quietly.

"Tommy Larnach? That doesn't prove anything."

"Worse than that, Da. He was so angry last week down at Idle Michael's. He'd tipped back a few too many whiskeys and started going off about burning down the whole mill. How it would serve the masters right if they lost everything."

She shuddered at the memory of his cruelly twisting lips. He was so different from the young man he'd once been. Whip-thin and roughly handsome, he used to grin at her with carefree abandon. They shared the same neighborhood, the same friends, the same past. But they would never share the same future. Shortly after their one and only encounter as lovers, when she'd refused his request that they marry, he'd beaten a man half to death in the taproom of Idle Michael's pub. No explanation. No apologies.

A year in jail had changed him.

Nothing had been easy between them since. Yet Polly refused to take the blame on herself for refusing him. Two years had passed since his proposal. She had been too young, too full of ambition, and their brief flirtation hadn't warranted such a commitment.

Tommy's bitterness was his own to swallow, not to foist on everyone else.

And if he had sabotaged the mill . . .

"I can't believe it of Tommy," Da said. "Hamish, maybe. He has that much backbone. Tommy might be full of piss and wind, but he doesn't have it in him to take so much responsibility on himself."

"I hope that's true, Da. But as soon as Mr. Christie finds out who he is, what he said, and how he wasn't at work today, what else will he think?"

"We need to find out first. No matter if Tommy did it, we'll all suffer if the saboteur isn't found. The law will step in and crack random heads." He reached out and squeezed her hand. "I rest easier here, even trapped as I am, knowing you'll be my eyes and ears and voice in this."

Hot pride swept through her. She nodded once. She was her father's right hand for a reason. Yet that had always been her trouble. She enjoyed guiding the union. Those men and women accepted her, perhaps more easily because female laborers dominated weaving. That also meant her expectations were very different from those of other Calton girls. Had she been anyone else, she might already be married, with a family of her own. Tommy's proposal would have been the start of her life as a young missus.

Another strong cough overtook her da. He clutched his chest and high up on his throat. Air wheezed as he finally dragged in a steadying breath. "Well, give it to me, then, child. What's the new man like?"

"I haven't made him out yet, Da. He's different. That's all I can say."

"Different how?"

"He . . ."

She let her voice trail off rather than say anything too hastily. Da needed concrete impressions of Mr. Christie, not her wispy, dizzied feelings. The tone of his voice—the strange, clipped American accent that still held a touch of English grace—would not leave her be.

"He's very smart," she said, staying with the facts. "Our boys tell us he teaches astronomy in America."

"Astronomy, eh? So he has his head up there with the stars?"

"At times, it seemed that way. He lurches between thinking things through and appearing ready to come out swinging—as hard as any blustering master. He threatened us if I refused to help in his investigation."

"Threats you take seriously?"

"I don't know."

"He got an eye for you, girl?"

Ma spoke up. "Graham. Enough of that."

He turned in his chair. The rickety wood creaked beneath his slight weight. "It's a question that needs asked. Polly's a pretty lass, and he'd be a blind man not to take an interest."

"Da, stop now." Polly sipped her cool coffee, wishing briefly for a spot of sugar. It was a nicer thought to remember how Mr. Christie had touched her hair. That had been the most surprising moment of their encounter. Surprising and . . . electrifying.

She cleared her throat. "I think he sees me as someone he can prod for information."

"Well, then that's what you do. If he's as smart as you suspect, maybe the facts will get to him. He'll see the sense in working with us rather than against us."

"How would I do that?"

"You're a woman. You'll think of something. Or he will." He winked.

"Graham Gowan," Ma said. "You'll turn your only girl into a trollop for the union."

"I'll do no such thing, woman."

"Bad enough you have her mixed up in the whole circus." The pace of Ma's stitches never slowed.

"I do it because I want to," Polly said to them both.

"So he's a handsome devil, then?"

"Da!"

He squeezed her hand. "I'll watch my tongue, girl. You know I wouldn't have you walking this line if it wasn't important. Just . . . be careful."

"I know, Da." She swallowed. "I'll do my best."

Her mother scowled. "None of this will be fitting for much longer. You'll be one-and-twenty soon and in need of a husband. You can bet your wages no man in his place will want a wife from Calton."

That hard, true assessment stung under Polly's

skin. So dismayed, she was almost thankful for her father's next fit of coughing, if only as a distraction. But not really. This time his face shaded toward purple and his rough hands gripped the edge of the table. Ma rushed over from the fireplace to rub his back, while Polly drew water from a pitcher.

Agonizing minutes later, Da finally regained his breath. Ma helped him to their pallet, both of their backs slightly bowed.

Fifteen-year-old Wallace turned over on his mattress. Hair a shade brighter than Polly's deeper red stood out from his scalp in disheveled spikes. His pale, freckled skin fairly glowed in the dark. "What happened?"

"Go back to sleep," Ma said softly.

Polly watched the scene as if outside of herself. A single room for five people. Kitchen and living space and a bedroom, all smashed into one space. The familiar, age-old sense of indignation fizzed under her breastbone. No one on the planet worked harder than her family, unless you counted the neighbors next door and the neighbors beyond them. They were happy together, content and full of easy laughter.

But they deserved more. Justice, at the very least.

"Polly," called her father.

She met him at the wide pallet he shared with Ma. The gasping purple had faded, leaving him nearly as wan as the gray-tinged sheets. Wisps of silver hair stuck out from his head, which was otherwise bald. "Yes, Da?"

"Do what you can to bring Christie round to our

ways. If that means letting him take a closer look at our lives, that's what you do. Keep him occupied while you learn who did this. You need to find out before he does, or there'll be no holding the police at bay."

"Wouldn't that be like letting a spy into our midst?"

"It's either that or let a grand chance slip away. If he feels we're being accommodating, maybe he'll keep from getting the constables involved, and work to change the other masters' minds." He coughed again but repelled Ma's attempt to keep him still and quiet. "I'll sleep once I've said my piece, woman. You listening, girl?"

He wore that quirky expression that always made her lighter inside. He teased her while putting all his faith in her. Polly smiled. "Can't help it with you shouting so."

The merriment in his eyes was brighter than she'd seen in weeks. "That's my Polly. It's been four years since the last change in management. We have a chance with a new master. Do what you can."

"I will, Da. I promise."

Julian Bennett was a very large, very uncouth man with more money than sense. In the modest library in Alex's leased home, Bennett sat on the other side of the desk and sipped his second Scotch. He cleared his throat after each swallow. Perhaps a nervous condition? But he hardly seemed nervous. Born to a disgraced baron and a Welsh whore, he was proposing to buy out Christie Textiles.

"Yours is a small operation, Christie, and suddenly caught in dire circumstances. With so few looms to start with, you'll have no means of keeping up with the output of larger competitors."

"Such as yourself," Alex said evenly. He was quite proud of that evenness, to be honest, because what Bennett proposed absolutely could not occur—at least not until the two-year contract was concluded. Selling the business was strictly prohibited by Sir William's will. Not that Alex had the power to do so. He merely served as a manager in the employ of a board of directors.

The board could decide to sell, however, especially after the sabotage. The cost of rebuilding might outstrip the benefit. They were under no obligation to ensure that Alex turned a profit. Their only genuine obligation was to the shareholders.

"Yes, such as myself," Bennett said. "My backers are prepared to pay cash within the week, not stock or options. Cash. What do you say to that?"

"That it's a very generous offer, one the board will most certainly hear. But I have no intention of giving up my inheritance without a fight. I haven't had time to assess the damage," he said, pointedly referring to the clock on the mantel. Bennett had appeared unannounced on his doorstep at half past seven, demanding an audience. The first of many such meetings Alex was likely to field.

Vultures on a carcass.

He understood professional competition. Truly he did. Yet clamoring over a tenured position at a prestigious university proceeded with quite a different timbre. Polite exchanges at dinner parties. Comparing others' accomplishments against one's own. Subtly negotiating into higher circles of influence. Alex had not played the game particularly well, but his steady work led to good opportunities, no matter the politics.

The frenetic pace of industrialism was a very different animal. Little peace to be had. Little time to reflect and contemplate. He was swimming against the currents of so many streams. Steady work would not be enough in Glasgow.

"But why resist, Christie? You could be done with this place and home before summer."

"I have my reasons."

And he had no reason whatsoever to reveal them to the likes of Bennett. The terms of the will had never been made public, not beyond the necessary board members. That by no means ensured total secrecy. Anyone could be bribed, as Josiah Todd had demonstrated. News of a million-dollar bonus would only cause trouble. Suddenly people might agree to Alex's proposals only in hopes of earning a piece of it. The cost of securing consent would be determined in dollars rather than negotiations.

Bennett finished his breakfast of Scotch. "You're a bloody fool if you think you can chase your father's legacy. No one can fill Sir William's shoes, not even his firstborn."

Alex hid an inner wince. He knew that as surely as he knew the sound of his son's soft cry. But damn it all if he wouldn't try. Although he had never shared his father's lust for business, he had observed every trick, every tactic. Sir William Christie had insisted, and Alex had always been a quick study. He had never applied that latent store of knowledge. Now he would.

"I'm well aware of my limitations with regard to trade," he said without false modesty. "That does not mean I'll change my stance. From now on, deal directly with the board regarding these matters. They may want to sell, but I do not."

Pulling to his feet meant Bennett led with his copious stomach. He swallowed a belch. "I'll do that. In the meantime, you have a duty to stand with us masters when it comes to those union agitators."

"Oh?"

"We won't let them pollute our industry with violence. The ringleaders *will* be brought to justice. Maybe your misfortune has been a blessing in disguise," he said with no attempt to hide his satisfaction. "With the union discredited, we'll dismiss their wage demands and calls for safety improvements."

Alex's temper pulsed beneath his ribs. He did not like Julian Bennett. The magnate's opportunistic smugness reminded him not of his father, but of Josiah Todd. Such a bully believed everything was his. He just hadn't claimed it yet.

Instead of indulging in his burgeoning anger, Alex pulled a meticulous note from a stack of papers he had culled. "Speaking of safety improvements, I feel compelled to point out two facts. Since the installation of the fans at Christie Textiles, instances of illnesses and absences have dropped dramatically, and employee turnover has been halved. Quite the return on an investment, you must admit."

Bennett actually laughed—a wet, grating sound. "You won't need me to buy the factory from you, Christie. You'll give it away to the union whips instead!"

"So, you know how they think?"

"Think? They're animals. They want as much as they can snatch from unwary men. I'll see you in a few weeks. Tell me then your opinion of those maggots." He set the empty tumbler on the desk with jarring force. "Good day."

The chuckle in his voice did nothing to alleviate Alex's disquiet. He had worked alongside unions in Philadelphia, hoping fairness in legislation would promote a better society. Fewer children working. More people educated. Mamie's passion for fairness had obvious origins in her father's abuse, but that did not mean Alex believed in it any less passionately.

Yet the sabotage was undeniable. He needed to find the culprit, all the while keeping men like Bennett at arm's length and proving his authority to the board.

For a moment, needing to quiet his agitated brain, he leaned against the wingback chair. His brother and sisters had all been assigned similar tasks, with Viv sent to Cape Colony and the twins, Gwyneth and Gareth, to equally unfamiliar locales. Although busy lives meant few opportunities to spend time together, they had corresponded frequently. He'd known all about Gwen's latest auditions and opera performances, as well as Gareth's stylish friends and his string of female admirers. He'd shared sympathies with Viv as her marriage teetered on the verge of collapse, just as she'd pulled him past his dark sense of failure following Mamie's death.

Even his father had written once a week, as regular as he was gruff. He had been a hard man to understand and even harder to love, but Alex missed him with a sharp ache. He missed them all. Surely word would come from them soon, and he would be able to report his successes.

Yes. Success.

It was just past eight. He stood and inhaled deeply as anticipation heated his skin. Time to see his factory . . . and to track down his key to understanding the weaver's union.

Polly Gowan.

Four

$\mathcal{A}$lex skipped the cab, preferring to work the tension out of his limbs. Spring suited Glasgow well, layering a bright shimmer over the harsh industrial architecture. The citizens remained as spirited as ever, with their steps quicker and their smiles wider as the day stretched its legs. That robust spirit reminded him so much of his father that it almost hurt to watch them. Rough people. Hard. Crude, even. Yet they lived with an abandon he envied.

A half hour later, he arrived at the factory, where the first shift was already busy and loud. Employees operated what looms they could. Thirty such looms bordered the large square building, poised beneath windows to keep their gears and engines cool. The clamor of whisking machinery was equal to that of a barreling locomotive.

A haze of white fluff was being sucked toward where steam generators powered massive fans. The blades dragged cotton fibers out of the air in a steady river of minuscule white specks. Over their hair, women wore kerchiefs, which were made pastel by fibers and lingering ash. Most of the male workers sorted through the rubble of the back wall. A hole as big as a hackney offered an unnatural view of the rear delivery area. Charred black places licked up along the bricks.

But most of the looms had survived. Hundreds of threads. Thousands of movements per minute. Alex remained impressed. Before this mill, he hadn't stepped foot inside a factory since his youth. The success of the mill would be owed to the many hands working so many machines.

Another thought came unbidden. Had his father been anyone other than stubborn, resourceful, dubiously immoral William Christie, work in a factory would've been his best opportunity. Otherwise, a life on the streets would've been brief and violent, leaving no more lasting impact than a strike of lightning. Instead, he had clawed free. This factory was only one example.

Pride welled in Alex's chest. He had never quite put those pieces together.

News of his arrival swept over the factory floor like the wind swirling in through that gaping hole. The work did not cease, but idle chatter did. What attention could be spared was directed at him. Rarely had he felt more conspicuous.

Howard McCutcheon met him at the door. "Sir, good to see you here."

"Thank you for directing the cleanup so soon. How does it look?"

"We'll need to hire an engineer to be certain, but

the local men with building experience say we were beyond lucky. The structural damage doesn't extend to the ceiling. The supports weren't affected." He shrugged. "For all the fuss and bother, the explosion did less damage than the fire."

"How so?"

"We lost two looms to the initial blast, but the belts of another five were melted beyond use. The fire also cost several shipments of wool and three days' worth of finished product. Two horses suffocated. And Mrs. Worth, a weaver, may lose the use of her right hand."

Alex nodded. The stink of wet ash and burnt wool still lingered. "Thank you, McCutcheon. I authorize you to hire an engineer to confirm that initial assessment. *Today.* I won't have these people working any longer than they must in an unsafe building. And I'll discuss with the board what can be done to compensate Mrs. Worth."

McCutcheon tipped his head, wearing a slightly puzzled look. "Yes, sir," he said slowly. "That's . . . decent of you, sir."

"And I want a progress report delivered to my office at noon and at the close of second shift every day. Now, bring me Polly Gowan."

The squat, dark-haired overseer was good enough to squelch his flicker of surprise before turning away.

Alex looked over his new domain, alive with hope. Although the damage would be costly, they could rebuild and repair.

Technically, he was a manager, and he had never been further out of his element, yet the factory *felt* like his. He had first thought his father's will absurd, just another attempt to goad his children toward the family business. Then, later, Alex had considered the assignment a means to an end: banishing Josiah Todd from his life.

But this was elemental. This was a chance to prove his mettle, in a way academic success had never quite offered. To make this place *his*. To stamp it with hard work and ingenuity. What would that be like?

He watched McCutcheon's progress past dozens of machines as the overseer beelined toward Miss Gowan. She stood before her loom, but the work was far from stationary. Activity twitched down her spine in quick jerks. A plain gold-brown frock hugged her rib cage and flared over animated hips. Her lithe yet sturdy body moved nearly as quickly as the machine, but her elegant neck remained graceful, held at a proud angle while others stooped.

McCutcheon tapped her on the shoulder and nodded back toward Alex. Her jaw dropped. Apparently she hadn't believed that he would arrive so early at the mill. He enjoyed taking her by surprise.

She took up a tartan shawl that she wrapped around her shoulders and, to Alex's frustration, obscured the flow of her curves. Silvery light caught the flecks of cotton that salted her clothing, glittering as she walked. Like snowflakes. Or stars. Alex had yet to catch sight of the stars over Glasgow, what with March still so overcast and the air smoky—proof of Glasgow's commitment to industrial success. Maybe that explained his mind's turn toward whimsy.

Snowflakes and stars.

He shook his head.

As Polly neared, she smoothed her expression to placidity. Only when she met him face to face did she reveal true feelings; a fierce scowl ruined the line of her auburn brows. "Do you have any idea what this will do to my reputation?"

"Your position within the union offers safeguards few women can claim. You know a lot more than you've told me, Miss Gowan, and you *are* going to help me."

"You're cracked in the head, Mr. Christie. No one here did that damage. Why would we have reason to? Your search needs to start across the street at Winchester's, or down the road at the Bennett factory, or McGovern's."

"In time. But for now our goals are in alignment. You need to clear every member of your union." He leaned in close, catching the scent of some sweet floral soap—a fresh morning smell. "If you don't cooperate, I'll tear it to tatters by the end of the week."

"You're a bastard."

Polly's insult was almost swallowed by the grumbling factory, but she looked around anyway. She could only imagine what everyone must think of her—perhaps conspiring with the new master, or even flirting with him.

That they might think she was sticking up for their interests, as she always did, was her only hope. She had worked for years to build a solid reputation among her peers. Her word was worth a lot more than that of a master fresh off the boat from New York.

"Name-calling, Miss Gowan? I thought you'd be above such pettiness."

"And why's that?" she asked, hands on her hips.

"Because your tongue's as sharp as your mind. Calling me names seems unworthy."

She blinked. The mill master was paying her compliments on her least ladylike habit? What manner of trickery was this? But, silly girl, she enjoyed his unexpected words.

He crossed his arms. His suit was more modest than the one he wore at their first meeting—although arranged with proper decorum now. Shouldn't someone of his profession be leaner, with his muscles wasted away by days spent over books? Or made portly by too much rich food and not enough sweat? Underneath the tailored garments lurked a man with the strong bones of the heartiest Scotsman.

The set of his mouth suggested that he rarely found humor in the world. Feathery creases stretched out from his eyes and lay in furrows along his brow. Frowns. Not laughter. Too bad. His shapely lower lip was made for smiling.

"I told you yesterday that I'll have no part in betraying my own."

"Maybe not voluntarily." Mr. Christie surprised her by grabbing her upper arm. "McCutcheon, where is your office?" he shouted over the din.

The overseer frowned at Polly's struggles. Then he tipped his chin to the far corner of the mill floor. The door to his tiny box of an office was tucked between two massive looms.

The master of Christie Textiles tugged her across

the factory floor. Polly literally dug her heels into the plank wood floor, using the fingernails of her free hand in an attempt to pry free. Nothing stopped his determined march toward the office.

Only when Les and Hamish materialized did Polly cease her struggles. They looked ready to do violence. The last thing the weavers needed was a brawl with Mr. Christie. She shook her head at the pair.

"Back to work!" Mr. Christie shouted. The proud height of his stance did not ease. If she hadn't been so offended by his bullying behavior, she would have admired it. She enjoyed men who knew their minds.

In the Lowland Scots dialect they shared, Polly shouted her orders to Les and Hamish. They nodded with obvious reluctance and restrained anger.

Once inside the office, Mr. Christie slammed the door and pushed her shoulders against it. Polly gasped. Just that quickly she was caged by his wide chest, and held fast by wide, strong hands. She looked up to where his eyes blazed.

Should she be scared of him? Lord, she prided herself on being able to read people. But, distressed by the man's quick rush of anger, she was afraid. Did he really possess the resolve to carry out his threats? Her da's instruction to curve Mr. Christie toward their ways fled from her mind. She gave little thought toward bending his will—only to surviving it.

No. She did *not* give in.

Livingstone had crawled his hands up her skirts in an attempt to make her cower. But he hadn't succeeded in anything other than limping away, his manhood intact but his pride in tatters. Mr. Christie would fare no better.

"You *will* help me," he said again, giving her shoulders a shake. "Because this is my command."

"Well, well." No matter the noisy pulse of alarm in her ears, she forced bravado into her voice. "You truly can behave like a master. And that's not a compliment."

"What did you say to those men?"

"That if I wasn't out in fifteen minutes, they should assume the worst and feed your carcass to their hounds."

"You believe me capable of . . . ? Jesus." He shoved away from her and thrust agitated fingers through his hair. A twisted expression said he was appalled by what his behavior might imply. *Good.*

"Then tell me what I'm supposed to think," she said.

"I think you're damn infuriating." Tight, stiff paces marked his progress across the tiny office. "How hard is it to see that cooperation suits us both?"

"You're right, actually, but I don't trust you." She clearly punctuated each word. "If you find the culprit first, you'll use his identity to your advantage—dismantle the union, dock our pay. Don't think it hasn't happened before."

He glared and cracked his thumb. "Whereas you'll hide whoever it is from the authorities."

"Don't think that means he'll escape punishment. We take care of our own, and we discipline our own."

"How positively clannish."

She huffed and tightened the Gowan tartan

around her shoulders. "You may as well have been born on one of the planets you study. I cannot imagine why you don't just go home."

"Because this is my future on the line!" He strode across the room and slammed his fists against the door, on either side of her head. Polly gasped.

"It's my business," he continued. "*My* responsibility. And if you don't help me, I'll make sure that the constable arrests someone you hold dear."

"You wouldn't know where to put the blame if you had a compass."

"I'd wager Livingstone has an idea. Perhaps one of your brothers? Heath and Wallace, are they?"

Polly blanched. He was so incensed that she believed him without doubt. His civilized exterior was little more than a ruse. She inhaled in an attempt to find some serenity. Mr. Christie must have noticed, because his gaze arrowed down toward her bosom.

"I underestimated you," she whispered.

He leaned in. Their contentious mouths were so close now. "The textile industry isn't the only thing I've been learning. Look at me, Miss Gowan."

Polly could only obey, caught in the spell of his chilling magnetism. His sharp features were just as stern as they had been the afternoon before, only now, heavy circles colored the delicate skin below his eyes. Manic energy blazed from those darkened hazel depths.

A gentleman would back away. A tyrant would press his advantage. Polly would lay no odds on either.

"Do you see that I didn't sleep last night?" The huff of his question warmed her forehead with his breath. "Because I didn't. My son was restless. I studied in his nursery. My topic for the night included how best to make you cooperate."

"*Make* me?"

"I think you've just realized that I can," he grated. "Your turn. What do *you* see on my face?"

She swallowed. He was simply . . . overwhelming. Yet Polly fell back on her old faith. She began with man's most obvious weakness: desire. The occasional glances at her body—he knew she was a woman, just as she was affected by his masculinity. Had he wanted to attack her in a manner more suited to Livingstone, he would've done so by now. Instead, his wrath was leashed.

His limit was the fairer sex.

She was ready to bet her body on it.

"I see fatigue, yes." He held perfectly still as she lifted her hand. Not even his eyes moved. She dared trace the throbbing vein at his temple. Only then did he gently flinch. Surprise registered in the slight lift of his brows. "I see fury. And I see you're in deadly earnest, Mr. Christie."

He closed those troubling eyes. "I am."

Polly touched the golden-brown locks that occasionally fell across his brow. In his office, he had done the same to her hair. That echo felt important. As if fated. She tucked her fingers deeper into roughened blond silk.

"Alex, you don't want to do this any more than I do." His name felt strange on her tongue, but she earned the desired effect: it was his turn to shudder. "Yet we're both caught in this mess. It's made you ready to rip out a man's kidneys . . . or ready to kiss me."

Polly had hoped her dare would be enough to rouse some sort of passion, just enough to guarantee that this particular gambit had a future.

But she had not expected a kiss—hard and swift and certain.

He swept his mouth down over hers and delved inside. No prelude. No breath of hesitation. Warmth coiled through her chest and trickled down her spine. Alexander Christie kissed like a man. A real man. And she had never before felt its like.

Arguing with him had been a test of wills. This was another sort of battle. She fought his hold, bringing her hands into the fray. His hair, his scalp, his nape. He groaned into her mouth when she tugged. His grip trailed along her sides before he boldly palmed her arse.

Polly squeaked. His tongue plunged in, sleek yet rough. Minty, salty tooth powder added layers to his natural taste. Both of them inhaled with rough, quick breaths. The strong hands on her backside pulled their bodies flush. Another gasp from Polly as she realized exactly how their kiss affected him. Alarm edged her pleasure like a too-bright halo.

His mouth was too persuasive. He kissed as if the next seconds of his life depended on turning her bones to liquid. Polly dropped her heavy head back against the door. Alex followed, kissing down her jaw and throat. Only the prim, buttoned collar of her working gown kept him from venturing further.

A hard pounding at the door shattered their blend

of mouths, hands, eagerness. Alex pushed back. His hair was a scrambled mess. He must have realized the direction of her gaze because he pushed his fingers through those unruly strands.

Polly smiled softly. "Your hands are shaking."

The pounding continued, followed by Hamish's deep bellow. Alex glared daggers. "And you look as if I deserve what punishment they're here to dispense."

She tilted her head to one side. "Well kissed, maybe. But not accosted. Surely you know the difference."

"I know the difference," he said grimly. His expression assumed a stoic detachment. Smooth, tan skin. Icy distance. The seriousness in his words made Polly frown. For a moment he appeared . . . haunted. Old ghosts in dark places, deep in those gold-green eyes.

She took a deep breath and smoothed her gown. The tartan she pulled over her shoulders felt like a shield. "Well, then, we're merely back to matters of my reputation. Luckily Hamish will behave himself." She winked. "I hope."

Polly opened the door to a very angry man. His face was nearly as red as his beard and curly, curly hair. "What the hell has he done?"

"Talked." She could not help but run her tongue over her lower lip, where her skin still tasted of Alex. "We've begun negotiations, haven't we, Mr. Christie?"

Only after another moment did Alex loosen up enough to speak. "Miss Gowan is correct. You have nothing to fear from my intentions, Mr. Nyman."

She could see it on Hamish's face: surprise that

the mill master had remembered his name. It only added to Polly's belief that Mr. Christie could become an asset, if she could keep him from realizing her suspicions about Tommy.

"Off with you then, boys," she said.

Alex—did kissing a man entitle her to thinking of him by his Christian name?—stared after them.

"They just . . . left," he said. "As if you were a queen dismissing servants."

"I have a commanding personality."

He rubbed his jaw. Maybe he was incapable of making a jest in return. He certainly was straitlaced. Until he kissed. Then he was an animal unleashed.

"Distractions will only knock me off track for so long, Miss Gowan." The gold in his eyes shone like bronze in sunlight. His gaze settled on her mouth. "Delicious though it was."

War. Battle. Combat. She was not going to let him take this moment from her. "And you'll stop at nothing?"

A muscle along his neck twitched. "Nothing."

Polly straightened the ends of her shawl, where the gold, green, red, and purple strands formed a neat fringe—a reminder of her family and her community. "Very well. You've talked me into it. I'll help you, and that means learning everything about the people who work for your profits."

She grinned, surprising even herself. *Let him think the idea was his.*

"Just be ready to keep up, master. I intend to show you the *real* Glasgow."

Five

Polly smiled to herself as she watched the church congregation disband following Reverend McCormick's two-hour sermon. Not all congregants wore their relief so obviously, but she felt what could only be described as a collective sigh. Six-day work-weeks and an entire morning in church meant few hours to breathe on one's own time.

Voices came out to play. Laughter. Chatter. Although their planned picnic would be moved indoors because of a light drizzle, the congregants were abuzz with the welcome change of pace.

Polly was not as relaxed as she might have hoped. Following another conversation with her father, she was even more confident about the role she needed to play with Mr. Christie. She certainly hadn't told Da about what took place at the factory. The fight. The kiss.

Her blush was even hotter in church.

The strategy remained sound. She would show

Mr. Christie their ways, convince him of the union's validity, and use what wiles she possessed to distract him while her people searched for the saboteur.

And she'd have a good time.

That particular goal had come upon her in the wee hours before dawn. She'd lain in bed, eyes wide and unseeing in the pitch darkness, as her family shuffled and snored. That kiss had been the most wickedly sensual moment of her life. To do it again would be no hardship. The man was simply too handsome and too intriguing for words. He was also infuriating, which made her want to fight harder.

Now she knew where all that fight could lead.

Passion.

Indulging in passion for a few weeks would be like frolicking in a dream world. She could have her fun, help the union, and collect a sweet, flirtatious batch of memories to keep with her until she was old and bent.

She snapped back to the busy church by quickly sidestepping a pair of boys in their Sunday best. A young widow called Justine O'Lachlan huffed after them with a determined expression. Polly hoped Reverend McCormick didn't catch the lot of them, or their picnic would be replaced by a scolding. The old man was notorious for his upstanding view of the world—all black and white. He was the compass that pointed their small congregation toward Heaven.

But by Polly's estimation, losing a husband at the age of eighteen, with two babes born of that brief marriage, was more earthly punishment than Justine deserved.

Wives and mothers prepared the tables, which stretched before the altar. Huge piles of sausages, fresh bread, boiled cabbage, and soups made from every root vegetable known to Britain were laid out in an array that spoke more of cooperation than bounty.

Her stomach rumbling and her mouth watering, Polly helped where she could. However, she was constantly interrupted by Calton citizens eager for news. Some asked for union assistance regarding illnesses, hardships, and scrapes, and she addressed each person with a hopeful heart. At events such as this, she truly believed they could make something better of their downtrodden little community.

"I'll do what I can, Mrs. Hounslow." She patted the old woman's hand, which was gnarled by work and countless years. "Many are out of their winter stores of coal, but surely someone can spare a few until the warmer weather returns."

"God bless you, my wee lassie."

Polly hugged her before asking, "Is that a new shawl? It's lovely."

"Since Christmas last. My niece, Elaine, made it for me." Mrs. Hounslow's expression sobered. "Such a dear girl, with her little ones."

She knew why the old woman hadn't mention Elaine's husband, John—a nasty, hard-fisted man. That Elaine wasn't at church came as no surprise. Polly would need to send Doc Hutson around to their place while John was on the factory floor. The pattern was always the same, but it always weighed on her heart.

Ma had been lucky, because Da was just about

the gentlest man in Glasgow. While healthy, he had worked tirelessly and always brought his pay packet home on Friday night. Other women stood outside the factory doors, hands outstretched, just to rescue the precious funds before their menfolk took to the pub. For saving their babes from starvation, such women were labeled nags and crones, their fears derided.

Polly wanted nothing of marriage if it looked like that.

Others came and went until she was finally able to gather a bit of the luncheon for herself.

"What looks good?"

So shocked by that unexpected accent, she nearly dropped her china and silver. Holding a plate and fork, Alex Christie stood beside her at the head of the banquet table.

Sunlight through a nearby stained-glass window pelted his face with dots of color. He was attired simply in a dark blue suit that complimented his sandy-blond hair and pleasant tan. But the suit strained to accommodate his height and baffling brawn. Had she known no better, she would've assumed him just another Scottish laborer dressed in his Sunday best. He was so roughly, undeniably male.

"Rising to my challenge, eh?"

"That's right," he said. "I go where you go until we both get what we want. If you wish to argue again, we certainly can. Surely, your church is the *best* place to make a scene." His expression revealed exactly what she had expected to find: a quiet threat. "You'll recover from that spectacle in no time."

"I hate that you know you're so clever."

The radiant gold in his hazel eyes could melt glaciers. "Don't expect me to find anything objectionable about that."

The men Polly knew led with their fists. Although Alex Christie seemed capable of such, he led with those beautiful eyes. Every corner needed to be examined. Every face cataloged. She could almost see his mind working as he assessed what must be a wholly unfamiliar scene. She felt herself drawn deeper into his influence. He turned the ordinary new. All of a sudden, she had something that no one else in Glasgow could claim.

She had Alex Christie's complete attention.

Alex. She was losing her mind over this man.

"Everything's good," she said at last. "Calton women can make a feast out of three potatoes and a piece of smoked ham." She leaned in. A deep breath filled her nose with his freshly shaved scent—a bit like pine, a bit smoky. "Just avoid Mrs. McDonough's pie."

Alex's mouth quirked into a near-smile. "You'll have to stay with me." His words were a low rumble, like hearing a distant train's rattling speed. Powerful, yet still out of sight. "I wouldn't want to make that mistake."

"Too many other, more important mistakes for you to make. But none would taste so foul."

He pushed down along the table, so close that their hips brushed. "You say that, yet I've already been talked into trying blood sausage."

"Before or after learning the name?"

"After. Decidedly after."

"Fine. Have a go at Mrs. McDonough's pie, if you like. We seem to be the sort who thrive on dares, so consider this my gift to you. It's right there." She indicated what appeared to be something made of blueberries, then leaned in to whisper. "I swear she bakes with soap flakes rather than flour."

"I'll pass. But next time there's a dare in the offing, do let me know. "

He was even more handsome when he simply . . . loosened up. The line of his lower lip swelled to a pleasing fullness. His gaze stopped poking and prodding. While not grinning—*yet,* she vowed—he wore an expression of contentment. Not as desperate as the drunken lads who grabbed at happiness before falling face-first in the gutter. She quite liked it.

Despite her smile, Polly couldn't help but acknowledge the sharp undercurrent to their conversation. He was a master. They were using one another. Time to remind them both of those bare facts.

"You left bruises, you know."

Alex stopped in the middle of ladling gravy over fried potatoes. "I . . . what?"

"Bruises," she whispered. "On my shoulders. And my hips. Barely there, mind you. But I thought you needed notice that our actions have consequences."

"You're just saying that to rile me."

"Is it working?"

"Yes. I'm asking you politely to stop."

"Oh, no. Not until you believe me." She found a clear spot on the table and set down her half-filled plate of food. Without ceremony she reached for the lace trim that hugged her collarbone. "I could show you, if you like."

He caught her hand. His jaw clicked as he gnashed his teeth. "Don't."

She shrugged and continued down the line of food, as if she hadn't just knocked the daylights out of Alex Christie's tranquility. The beast was back. Quietly, stealthily, the entire line of his body changed. The gold overwhelmed the green in his eyes, like those of a wildcat on the prowl. Clenched back teeth accentuated the hollows beneath his cheekbones. The mouth she had tasted but a few days previous flattened into a smooth, colorless skin.

Oh, she enjoyed that. Just a few words and she could send the clever master to his knees. She liked being on a more even footing.

"I should apologize," he said hoarsely.

"*Should?* Interesting. Because that certainly wasn't an apology."

"Maybe because you don't seem to be asking for one."

Polly raised her brows. "A woman needs to *ask*? Is that how you Yanks do it?"

He sidestepped a cluster of lads, all of whom eyed him with the suspicion of youth on the hunt for trouble. Color deepened the tan along the back of his neck. Strong tendons stretched into his neck-cloth, and down to where a familiar stiffness had invaded his shoulders. Polly had the oddest impulse to ease his muscles.

"Here or in the States, that's not how a man should behave." He turned the earnestness of his eyes to meet hers. For Polly it was like being hit by the full force with a cannonball. "Can you forgive me, Miss Gowan?"

How could she play dirty if he insisted on being gentlemanly?

"We'll see."

"That's it?" A frown overtook his earnest concern. Just a glimmer of temper underneath. And who would react differently? He had offered his sincerest apology, and she had left him to twist. *Good.* She could understand a man of pride.

"Yes," she said as she turned away. "We'll see if I let you do it again."

Using a hunk of dark bread, Alex sopped up the last of the juices on his plate. He sat with the mystifying Miss Gowan on the backmost pew. She gracefully balanced her dish on her knees. He wondered if society women in New York could've managed such a feat. And in their Sunday best, no less.

Yet "Sunday best" was a relative term. Polly's dark blue gown, although of very good muslin, did no favors for her pale skin and auburn hair. She looked nearer to mourning than a young woman on the verge of springtime. The cut was also woefully out-of-date, perhaps fitted when she had achieved her figure.

And what a figure. Vulgarity was not an impulse in which he indulged—until meeting Polly. Her petite frame only accentuated a high, rounded bust. Already he'd held her hips and her round, firm backside. Those memories made him ache. Had he truly left bruises? To believe he'd behaved in such an ardent manner was too new to process, as if looking inside himself and finding a lion.

Why he wasn't touching her again, when they sat side by side on the church pew, was even harder to understand.

Alex cleared his throat and set aside his dish. "Have I met all of the major players?"

"Who?"

"Your union allies."

"It's not *my* union," she said with a shake of her head. *Auburn* was too tame a word. She was a redhead, pure and simple. Only the poor lighting and perpetual Glasgow haze stole its vibrancy. He wanted to see her in the bright light of a full summer sun. "It's the weavers' union."

"And your role in it?"

"Just another member."

"I don't believe that." He sat back against the pew and crossed his arms. "Come clean so we can stop the bickering before it begins."

"Aw." Her wide, guileless smile was almost too much to resist. "You're no fun. The bickering is the best part. Otherwise we'd have nothing to say and nothing would mask how much we dislike one another."

Was that true? It didn't feel true.

He had the most splendid view of her profile, with her rounded cheekbones and full lips. Her willful nose had a bump on the bridge, which was the only feature even approaching a flaw. The curve of her jaw was delicate, but not so much that she appeared childlike—just graceful and very feminine. Skin without flaw.

She had the face of a woman who had never known softness, but who courted laughter. The combination was so novel as to be perplexing. He had never dealt well with snap decisions. New information took him days, sometimes weeks, to process. Rather than admit what manner of man she could tempt him toward becoming, he fell back on the role of master.

"Tell me," he said solemnly.

"My father is the head of the weavers' union, in a day and age when skips are king of the Clyde. We're long past the glory days of the Calton Martyrs."

"The Calton Martyrs?"

Her gaze floated across the rumbling bustle of the church. So many bodies packed into one space. At least they kept the late March chill at bay.

"During the time of my da's father. Ordinary weavers faced off against an armed regiment in a fight for fair wages. They're heroes to us all. But now we're more likely to starve to death or die of typhus in a one-room tenement." She shrugged—a habit she demonstrated when she skirted too near uncomfortable subjects. "Used to be good money for skilled workers. These days, the weavers are mostly women. Able menfolk have moved to the docks and the shipyards."

A shade of bitterness spoiled her lilting words. Perhaps that was unavoidable. What she did was difficult and tedious, as worthy as anything a riveter or steelworker could manage. That didn't change the timbre of Glasgow. The ships brought the money. The ships brought goods from all over the world. And the ships fostered an arrogant attitude that only men were hearty enough to contribute to the city's prosperity. He'd learned that much within hours of his arrival.

"Does that explain why a woman leads their union?"

"My da's still the union boss."

Alex called her bluff by standing. "Perhaps I should talk to him instead. Maybe he'll know more about the saboteur than you've revealed." He reached for her arm but was beset by a moment's hesitation. Would she really have tugged the edge of her bodice to show him proof of his ungentlemanly ardor?

The flicker of knowing mockery lit her eyes—their most vibrant green. Resolve shot through his limbs. "Come then," he said. "Off to see your da. I won't waste my breath on some feisty but useless lackey."

Polly stood but did not fight his hold. Even her eyelashes were that same vibrant red. They seemed to glow beneath even the palest light. He could see every freckle across her stubborn nose. She smelled of lilacs. Some tonic to tame her unruly curls? He wanted to pull her close and lose himself in perceptions he rarely indulged. The senses were for analysis, not pleasure.

Even without the experience to know for certain, Alex knew she was a woman who could provide pleasure.

"My father is unwell."

Alex stilled. "Truly?"

"Yes, truly. Sometimes there are things the heart accepts less readily than the mind."

A wave of sympathy swirled through his chest. He knew that feeling. He'd known it every time he touched Mamie and felt her flinch beneath his slow, cautious fingers. That hadn't stopped his hopes from envisioning a day when she would accept the affection he'd fought to keep gentle.

His mind, however, had known the truth. Josiah Todd's perversions had ruined her forever.

"You have my sympathies, Polly."

A wobbly grin shaped her lush mouth—a pouting lower lip, and an upper lip prone to curling with amusement. "So it's Polly now? Speak to the weaver's union boss with a little more respect, master."

"About time you admitted it."

Her grin was full and cheeky. "You flirt rather well when you don't think about it."

The realization that he *had* been flirting was difficult to reconcile. What else could he call it when he'd spoken with the hope of seeing her smile? How long had it been since he'd felt such an impulse? With Polly, the teasing came as naturally as quarreling and lust.

He would need to watch himself. His goals were simple, as if written on a list: find the saboteur, keep the board from selling Christie Textiles, earn his inheritance, protect his son. Polly Gowan figured in as a source of information. Nothing more.

Considering how he'd behaved the last time they were alone, that was for the best. Never had a woman affected him so strongly. He had been almost . . . *bestial*. Reliving those moments hit him without mercy—the shame and shock of knowing he was capable of sinking to such depths. Yet, quick on the heels of that disbelief, came a very different sort of shock.

He wanted to kiss her again. Just as he had. Without reservations—and this time, without regrets. That would mean ensuring she craved the passion as much as he did, but that was blasted unlikely.

Polly glanced back toward the pulpit, where the congregation's women began to dismantle the remnants of the feast. "Now what, master?"

She didn't offer the polite courtesy of letting him hide. She poked and prodded as if she had a right to know his every thought, no matter how unsavory.

"You tell me, Miss Gowan."

Playful sparkles shone in her jewel-green eyes. "I think it's time you found out what it is to be a real Scottish man." She nodded toward the rear of the church, where Hamish Nyman and his cronies bunched together. They had changed out of Sunday suits, into much rougher fare. Their voices grew rowdy. "The boys will be wanting to blow off steam. Even with the mist, my money's on a match of some kind. Probably footy. You have any experience with sport?"

"I played rugby at Harvard. Polo. Rowing."

She looked him up and down. "Very posh. But at least it explains your body." Before Alex could choke back his surprise at her bold comment—and the hot warmth that bathed his skin—she continued her baiting. "You'd better be good enough to put up a show. If you lose face against these men, you'll never get anywhere with them."

He had never been a stranger to competition or the masculine politics inherent in a good grudge match. A full decade older now, he still participated in the sports of his youth, as his only means of alleviating the physical frustrations of having been married to Mamie.

This would be harder. Tougher. With workingmen out for blood against their employer.

"No worries," she said. "I'm sure you'll survive a few minutes of running the ball around."

"You're enjoying this."

"All by your command, master. Don't fault me for enjoying the spectacle."

Les MacNider strolled over. His lanky posture and slow gait were at odds with his quick manner of speaking. He looked like a balding scarecrow but with less stuffing. Ragged. Hard-boned. Always moving. "Well, then, master. You up for a game?"

"Les," Polly said. "The pitch is probably so rain-slicked you'll knock out what few brains you have."

He offered a toothy, unabashed grin. "Got that right. Nothing up here to damage."

"That's for certain, you mongrel."

She smiled. At Les. Just the way she'd smiled at Alex. What he felt wasn't jealousy so much as the disappointment of becoming just another man. For a few moments he had been someone almost . . . intimate.

He wanted that again. No. He *needed* that again.

Hesitation disappeared like a puff of smoke. Alex

would stand as a man among these rough people. He would impress Polly Gowan. She was lightning and ragged impulses. The jeering in her eyes would transform into surprise and frank approval, or he'd be left like a fallen soldier on a field of battle.

He clapped Les hard on the shoulder. "I'm in."

Six

Sarah Fitzgibbons met Polly at the church doors. "You're going out there, too?"

"Would you rather stay in here and have Mrs. McCormick convince you to finish cleaning?"

"But it's so cold! All to watch the men we see every day roll around like pigs?" She gave a disdainful sniff. "I'm sure I won't bother."

"Suit yourself."

Polly grabbed her shawl off a hook at the back of the church, happy to be free of unwanted company. When she worried that others might see her as an ambitious climber, Polly thought of Sarah Fitzgibbons. The young woman talked of little beyond her list of potential well-heeled suitors. With her classically beautiful face, fine body, and unusually blond hair, she would probably succeed in snagging a prosperous husband.

Polly understood but could not relate to those ambitions. Did such an attitude hold merit? She had been working with her father so long that every thought, every action, tied into a better future. If forced to sit patiently and endure the present as it was, Polly would've gone mad a long time ago. The security of an advantageous marriage held appeal, but the cost of giving up what she valued would be too high.

And not even for the grandest mansion would she miss the chance to watch Alex Christie attempt to kick a football.

She spotted Agnes Doward and Connie Nells. That the latter was also heavily involved in union activities probably would have surprised the likes of Livingston. Tidy and quiet, with her two wee babes tended by an elderly grandmother while her husband worked the ship hulls, Connie hardly seemed the type. But not every advocate was a firebrand. Perhaps that was how they'd managed to keep the peace for so long. The weavers were lucky for the presence of so many clearheaded women, whose concerns boiled down to security for their children.

"Are you up for the match?" Polly nodded toward the male parade filing out of the church.

"They'll bust their fool heads," Connie said.

"That's what I told them." She leaned closer. "But Mr. Christie is playing, too. Tell me you're not the least little bit curious."

"Sure I am. And you seem doubly so."

"Hardly!"

Connie shared a grin with Agnes. "And just who did you eat lunch with, Polly Gowan?"

"Oh, no. Don't start painting me with that foul brush. It's union business and you know it."

Agnes put a calming hand on her arm, her smile more indulgent. "Connie's only teasing. Aren't you?" She arched an eyebrow at the other woman.

"Of course I am. As if the mill master would take a fancy to any of us beyond a quick tup!"

Despite her sudden flush of embarrassment, Polly forced a chuckle. "Are we allowed to say 'tup' in church?"

"Probably not," Connie said. "Outside we go."

They stepped beyond the threshold, into the struggling afternoon sunlight. The temperature wasn't quite so biting, and the wind had dwindled to nothing. She might actually enjoy this.

Alex Christie was going to have his head handed to him. She was edgy and almost giddy at the prospect of seeing the mill master forced to swallow mud.

"Has either of you seen Tommy?" Connie asked. "I thought for sure he'd be here."

"Not for days," Agnes replied.

Polly inhaled past her nerves. "I wonder if we should be worried."

Agnes leaned in close. "Do you think he had anything to do with what happened?"

"I don't know," Polly said. "But I'd like the chance to talk to him. He's caused trouble before, but he's never bald-facedly *hidden*. It'll make him look even more suspicious."

"He must be lying low with someone." Connie's cheeks looked even paler beneath the silvery spring sunlight. Mist sparkled in her dark hair. "I'll ask around, especially his auntie. She has a fondness for cake and my wee girls. Maybe we'll pay a visit."

Polly nodded. "Thank you."

Across from the church, in the park known as Glasgow Green, a score of men had bunched into two teams—one side red, the other side blue-and-white stripes.

"Oh, my," Polly breathed.

She and the other women joined Justine O'Lachlan at the base of a towering monument dedicated to Lord Nelson. Justine's young lads were running through a particularly large mud puddle, but her eyes were on the assembling teams. She cupped bone-white hands around a steaming mug of tea.

"I'm not having very Christian thoughts right now," she said by way of greeting.

Neither was Polly. The men had stripped off their shirts. Although the slanting afternoon sunlight offered no warmth, it gilded those masculine bodies. She had seen as much before. Curiosity and boredom meant there was little about the male body she didn't understand.

Her gaze, however, was drawn to one man in particular. Alex had yet to change out of his suit. He still wore a modest yet fine pair of woolen trousers. He shrugged out of his coat with particular grace. How could a man of such robust health have so little regard for what his body did? What it was capable of?

His stomach was flat, his shoulders wide and rounded. The narrow channel of his spine was flanked by wide ribs and sinuous ligaments that flexed and twisted as he warmed up. The graceful movements of his arms were underlain with powerful muscles. Long, study bones and potent flesh. Rough and raw. Coarse. Yet never common. The aristocratic line of his strong jaw would never let anyone forget that he came from good stock. Only, Polly hadn't expected so much of his father's hearty Scots build—a bear of a man underneath his finery and respectability.

Energy shimmered off of him, all around him. Or maybe that was just the steam of hot skin meeting cold air. He looked like a pagan god of war descended to Earth for a contest among mere mortals. He scrubbed one hand almost lazily through the swath of hair spread over his sculpted chest, as if it were the most natural thing in the world to stroke such primal masculinity. Polly flexed her own fingers. She wanted another opportunity to touch and explore, this time finding her way to that virile torso.

What would his body feel like beneath her palms? Against her cheek? Beneath her tongue?

Although she knew how dangerous such thoughts could be, she did not censure her imagination. She was offered so few chances to be anything other than sacrificing and good. This moment, absorbing the sight of defined muscle across a wide, solid back, was just for her. Even a blink would discredit such a gift.

He knelt to grab a shirt. Even his rear had a taut firmness she hadn't thought to find. His trousers stretched across trim hips and hugged his sleek lines with perfect definition. Polly couldn't remember the last time she'd admired a man's arse. Perhaps because no other man's arse made her want to claw deep and hold on tight.

The cold grabbed at her nerves. She licked her bottom lip, then dug her teeth into the meat. Deeper inside her belly, and lower between her legs, a glorious heat kept her immune from the March chill.

"I told you," Connie said, her whisper meant for Polly alone. "Disinterested. Ha!"

"Shush!"

Alex tugged a blue-and-white-striped shirt over his head. She was disappointed to see his brawn so demurely covered once again, but the spell was not broken. Scouring fingertips down to his scalp, he gave his hair a good undoing. Sunlight set every blond strand alight. His expression practically shouted his resolve—the grim set of his mouth, and the way his eyes rocked from man to man to man, gauging opponents and teammates alike.

"Come on. Let's see this if we're going to see it."

Polly led the women to the edge of the pitch, where another dozen people had gathered. She recognized wives and girlfriends, fathers and mothers. A sense of belonging eased over her once again.

When Alex strode onto the slippery, half-frozen pitch, her peace evaporated. In its place pulsed a tension that she hadn't expected. What if he didn't do well?

What if he did?

Luckily, he wound up being on the same team as Les and Hamish. Perhaps that would keep Connie from teasing her anymore. But probably not. In their neighborhood, teasing was a prime pastime.

Justine bounced once on the balls of her feet,

clinging to Polly's arm. "So exciting. The winter has been so dull."

Perhaps that also accounted for some of the excitement. It was simply good to be outdoors again. They spent so much time cooped up in noisy factories and cramped tenements. Now the afternoon was quiet except for the happy talk of those standing around her. All was expectation and eagerness.

A retired riveter called Jules MacDonald took his position as referee. At his signal, two players walked toward the center of the pitch. The battered round football waited there. Its dirty stitched leather had seen better days, but it would serve for this test of manly wills. Polly stamped the cold out of her feet, locating where Alex had taken his position at the right rear of the pitch. It was a good place for a beginner, because few men could attack using their left foot to strike the ball. He could certainly survive the next ninety minutes, although his chances of eating muddy turf were diminished.

The whistle sounded.

Cheers shot out from the sidelines. More people had arrived, bringing the total to nigh on fifty. Polly grinned as the pace of play picked up and good-natured insults began to fly.

"Oooh, Walt's in good form," Connie said of her husband.

And he was. Walt tore up the right wing toward the opposing goal. His usual slouched expression had transformed into one of concentration. He dribbled the ball past the first defender, then another.

His shot on goal was deflected. The stout goalkeeper shouted at his players to resume their positions.

Play continued for several minutes before Alex tasted any hint of action. But when it happened . . . A quick-footed attacker swerved past Les and collided straight into Alex. Both fell to the ground amid groans of sympathy from the crowd. Polly winced.

Alex elbowed his opponent in the chest and scampered to his feet.

"He must be running on pure stubbornness," Connie said.

Agnes grinned. "It's not like he knows what he's doing, the poor dear."

They weren't wrong. Although Alex was quickly stripped of the ball, he put on a fantastic chase. Sweat slicked his face and neck. Exertion darkened his skin. Every quick exhale became a white plume in the chilly air.

That initial contact marked how he continued to play. All muscle. No skill. Polly couldn't help but admire his tenacity. Unlike what he must be like while studying or teaching or tabulating accounts, he was a fighter now. His body was the instrument, not his intellect, and he overcame every opportunity to wade into the fray.

Les lost the ball, which sailed past their keeper and through twin goalposts.

"Damn," Connie whispered. "We're one down."

Justine elbowed Polly. "Hamish looks upset."

Sure enough, Hamish was screaming at Les and another player, who waved a dismissive hand. Alex stepped in to keep Hamish from going after his teammate. For a moment it looked as if Hamish would pop the mill master in his grim, determined mouth, but Polly was able to breathe again when the men parted and play resumed.

Once again, Alex's team was on the back foot. They bunched too quickly along the defensive line, leaving a gap for another attack. This time the keeper was able to deflect the ball, but the damage had been done. Polly could almost feel morale cool and collapse.

Their team was down by three when halftime was called. After switching sides, the lopsided battle forged on. Alex was on the near side now, where Polly could better read his expressions. More resolve. His sandy brows dipped low on a frown. He licked his lower lip and clapped his hands to rally the defense.

"Come on now, men. We have this. Buck up and fight these bastards!"

A rush of hot admiration whisked through Polly's veins. *Do that again.*

Alex even grinned at Hamish, apparently enjoying the hard competition. "Don't tell me you're tired, Nyman. Would bust your pride something fierce if I'm still standing while you're flat on the ground."

"Piss off, Christie. You'll get yours!"

Justine stilled. Agnes gasped. Polly's knees went soft and wobbly.

Yes, Alex was a different sort of man, but he was still a man. He only grinned. "Not until we bury these smug gents up to their eyeballs."

Hamish clapped his hands, too. "Let's go, boys. You heard the master."

The air was charged with potent energy. Alex

looked ready to eat the competition for an afternoon snack. Teeth bared, he bent over and braced his hands against his thighs. Blue-and-white fabric stretched across his back.

"Here comes Lennox again," Justine said.

She jerked her eyes away from Alex. "Is that his name? The little quick one?"

"That's right. He's Anne-Margaret Lennox's youngest boy. You didn't recognize him?"

As the lad ripped past the midfield line, Polly tried to get a good look. He was just too fast. She hadn't seen Paddy Lennox in at least ten years, not since his da had gone to prison for killing a man. After that, the family disappeared from good company. Even in poverty, her people had lines that would not be crossed.

Young Paddy had nearly made it past Les when he tripped. Polly didn't see exactly how it happened, only that he flew through the air and landed hard against the unforgiving ground.

How it happened didn't matter. Tempers made short by the unbalanced play sparked to life. Les, who stood over young Lennox, was the first to be mobbed with accusations of having tripped the lad. He was jumped by two of Lennox's side. Then Hamish barreled into the skirmish.

And to Polly's surprise, Alex Christie—covered in mud and sweat—joined in, too.

Alex distinctly remembered the last time he'd thrown a punch. On his wedding day. Josiah Todd had deserved his head cut from his body, but a crack across his mocking mouth had made the point:

Mamie was Alex's wife, and Josiah would have nothing more to do with her.

Bloody hell, it still felt good. Just cutting loose.

He'd seen Les trip the fast boy, just as he'd clearly seen a dozen other bad calls. None of it mattered. He only knew that supporting Les, Hamish, and the men in blue-and-white stripes was the right thing to do. They were his teammates.

And after a rough hour of intense physical exertion, all the while losing in front of Polly Gowan, he was in the mood to bloody a few noses.

He hauled a skinny man off Hamish, then spun him away. He'd barely time to offer Les a hand up when he was jumped from behind. One minute standing . . . the next minute knee-deep in the mud. Slippery grass slid beneath Alex's palms. A fist connected with the back of his skull. The blows kept coming. He grabbed his attacker's hand, using the leverage of his low position to hurl him to the ground.

Alex used the moment's distraction to jump to his feet. He spun into the crack of another punch—this one to his cheekbone. That blaze of hot, red fire freed him from any further niceties. He twisted and dodged, facing his opponent behind raised fists. Two quick jabs came to nothing, but he landed a third against the man's kidney. The punch Alex took to the gut barely registered, so fast and hard did his blood beat. His uppercut snapped back the other player's head and sent him staggering.

Alex rode high on the rush and flow of the fight. The whistle blew again and again. People at the edge of the playing field barged forward. Men were restrained. Alex turned at the feel of a hand on his shoulder, only to find Hamish standing there.

"Enough for now, Christie, unless we want to spend the night locked up."

"Until the next time then." Alex certainly couldn't afford to be caught by the authorities.

Les, too, arrived to offer his thanks. "Wouldn't have thought a man like you had it in you, friend."

Alex spat blood and wiped his lips. "Maybe I like surprising people."

"Now if only you could learn to dribble and pass," Les said with a laugh.

They turned to walk off the pitch, but another Scotsman wearing blue and white stopped Alex with a hushed call. "Mr. Christie, a moment?"

"Yes, what is it?"

"I'm Walt Nells, sir. My wife, Connie, works your looms."

"I know Constance, yes. What can I do for you? Other than give you better cover next time."

Walt smiled, but the reaction was fleeting. "Sir, there's something you should know about what happened at the mill."

"Oh?"

"I didn't want to share it with Polly Gowan because I know her. She'd go off half-cocked." He glanced toward where Polly waited with the other women. "I work at Gallagher's Shipyard. Different men frequent those pubs down by the docks—with different information than she'd be able to find here in Calton."

"What sort of information?"

"Just what you'd need to know to solve your

mystery. Please don't make me say much more, Mr. Christie. It's a tricky spot. I don't want to be labeled a snitch, but neither do I want my wife to lose her job. Our family needs the money."

"How many children do you have?" Alex found himself unaccountably curious. With every passing hour, they were becoming people. Names first. Then grins and the sounds of voices and the quiet details of their lives. He might regret that closeness if hard decisions came down the line, but he hadn't changed so much as to become completely insensitive.

"Two, sir. Girls too little to work the factory."

Young, then. Under five or so. Walt looked barely old enough to shave, despite his burly frame. "Just a pub and a name, Nells. Can you give me that?"

"Jack Findley at Old Peter's on the Clyde."

"I won't forget this. Thank you."

"Just . . . keep Polly safe. We need her more than you could know."

Left to ponder the implications of that remark, Alex turned—and walked right into a wall. That's what it felt like. Sudden loss of momentum. Bright shots of pain. The strike of a fist landed dead center of his chest. The world spun backward.

When the spots cleared from his eyes, he blinked and coughed. "What in God's name happened?"

Les knelt over him, as did Polly Gowan. "A bruiser named Kilgore," Les said. "He didn't take kindly to you hitting his brother."

"Apparently not."

Alex slumped against the ground, with the wet, cold grass as his pillow.

"Come on, master." Les tugged on his arm. "Fun's over."

Polly said nothing as she helped Les lift him from the soggy ground. Alex felt every bone in his body, and all of them protested. When he next focused, he found himself in a darkened room where several of his teammates chattered with a good-natured spirit. He could even make out members of the opposing team, greeting one another while exaggerating the afternoon's events.

Alex pushed into a sitting position. A wince revealed yet another injury across his cheekbone.

Polly slipped into the booth next to him. She carried two steaming mugs of coffee. "This will help."

"Where are we?"

"Idle Michael's. He opened the pub for us after the brawl, to get something warm in the men before they head home."

"Idle Michael?"

She smiled. "Doesn't sound like he'd make a very reliable innkeeper, but he's a good man. Still going strong at sixty."

Alex reached for his mug. Warmth seeped through earthenware, instantly relaxing the tension in his arms. His first sip, however, caught him by surprise. "What is that?"

"Just some whiskey. You don't like it?" Eyes made smoky in the dim lighting still glittered with laughter. Another tiny dare.

"No, I like it just fine." He took a heftier drink. "Women are allowed in the pubs?"

"Let's just say I'm allowed in this one. My da's

rules are a lot more important to me than anyone else's."

The comfort of the small tavern and the heady warmth of the whiskey-doused coffee eased Alex's pain. He settled gingerly against the booth, sinking into worn leather.

Her brows drew together. "Are you badly hurt?"

"I'll be fine."

Without ceremony, she swept the hair back from his nape and whistled. Alex was caught between surprise, an acute awareness of her gently probing fingertips, and pain. "That's a nasty one," she said. "And I know you took a bruiser to the chest. Come on. Bring your coffee."

She helped him out of the booth.

"Hey, master." Les held a bottle of whiskey by its neck. "How's your face?"

"Hurts like hell," Alex replied evenly. "How's your arse?"

"Thoroughly kicked, sir."

Trying to follow Polly's practical lead, he shuffled after her, back to the taproom of the pub. She wore the scent of rain in her hair. Thick red curls had escaped her pins to cup freckle-dusted cheeks made beautifully pink by the spring winds and the pub's warmth. Practically wild now, she looked just as she had after their kiss—deeply, thoroughly ravished.

"Sit," she said, waving to a wooden cask.

She returned moments later carrying a tray of supplies: bandages, iodine, a needle and thread, and a kettle that proclaimed its boiling contents by the steam it sloughed.

"The doctor, Mr. Hutson, is out delivering Shea Lockney's baby. We've waited long enough to see if he would make an appearance." She knelt before him, balancing on the balls of her feet. The hand she used to steady herself was only inches from his thigh. "I'm afraid you're stuck with me."

"Have practice at this, do you?"

"I have two younger brothers," she said with a grin. "Off with your shirt, now."

"It's freezing in here."

"You're able to take punches full-on in the face, but you cannot stand a wee bit of cold?" Her accent intensified when she teased him. He only wanted more. "You have none of my sympathy, Mr. Christie."

Tugging the sides of the jersey, she stripped him from the waist up. There she remained. Motionless. Their gazes held fast. The breath he'd meant to exhale stayed trapped in his lungs. Green eyes made dark in the shadows moved as haphazardly as a butterfly's flight. To his shoulder, his hip, his throat—dancing over every inch of his bare skin. But the tilt of her lips made each ripple of awareness even more intense. She was smiling. Softly. Her approval of his body, woman to man, was an elemental burn.

Alex had not felt so vital in a very long time.

"Now," she said softly. "Let's see how badly off you really are."

Seven

Just like Heath. Just like Wallace.

Although Polly tried to reassure herself with those words, her hands wouldn't stop shaking.

Alex Christie was a beautiful man. And he certainly wasn't one of her brothers.

She'd thought she knew the lay of his body when watching him change clothes earlier that afternoon. But such a distance did him little justice. Now she absorbed as many details as possible. Maintaining the guise of a disinterested helpmeet would not last long. Surely he could hear her heartbeat; it was an endless peal of thunder.

His chest was sprinkled with blond hair a shade darker than the thick locks still edged with sweat. Rather than repel her, that startling, purely masculine hair fascinated her. Firm, well-shaped, almost graceful muscles used the flickering lamplight to cast appealing shadows across his skin, and those same shadows lent a dreamlike quality to his strong lines and hard edges. Hardly trusting her eyes, she wanted to touch—to feel and keep feeling until she knew exactly how he was made.

Maybe she could do both.

"You're a mess," she said. "A nasty scrape here on the boot mark along your ribs. See? They broke skin. The base of your skull looks like mince. And here, hold this cloth to your cheek."

The wounds she'd listed did not include the bruises marring his lovely flesh. Dark patches of purple and blue were interspersed with nasty red welts. She would need to run her fingers through the hair on his chest to check for more cuts and scrapes.

Yes. That sounded like a fine idea. She could touch *and* be his nurse.

Alex gingerly held a damp cloth his cheek and grimaced. "Good Christ. What was I thinking?"

"I doubt thought had much to do with it. Instinct. Reflex. But I bet it felt bloody good while it lasted."

"How would you know that?"

"Not even girls escape a Calton childhood without a scrape or two."

He tongued a minor cut on his lower lip. Polly ran a thumb just below that sweep of wetness. His eyes darkened yet again, followed by a quiet hiss. Affecting him was a potent drug.

"Does it hurt?"

He shrugged. "Not bad. Unless I smile."

"Little chance of that," she muttered.

"What did you say?"

"I said . . ." She debated the usefulness of a lie and discarded the idea. Poking him with the unexpected was the surest way to sneak under his skin—just where she wanted to be. "There's little chance of you hurting your lip with a smile. I've yet to see one."

"I smile. Sometimes."

She fisted her hands on her hips. "Dare you."

"Aren't you supposed to be cleaning me up?"

"Consider this a bargain. One smile in exchange for the attention of an unskilled nurse."

The smallest quirk touched his lips. How could he express himself with so little actual movement? She was used to overblown, half-crazed men who never let anything get in the way of shouting every coarse thought at the world. Subtlety was not an art form known to her people.

"My side of the bargain does sound reasonable," he said. "But you don't make your services sound very appealing."

"Oh, I intend to make this experience *very* appealing."

His surprise was unmistakable. Raised eyebrows. A quick inhale. How could a man who'd been married seem so surprised by passion? She hardly enjoyed how they stood at odds regarding their goals, yet she'd certainly enjoyed their kiss. He turned harder and more certain when consumed by desire. Polly indulged in a private smile. She was the one to drag the wildness out of him, and she relished that special power. Perhaps too much. Just as she craved making him smile, she was toying with explosives and an open flame.

Alex's expressive, watchful eyes were almost unreadable in the pale orange of the lamp's cozy flame. "You're looking at me as if I were a supper of steak and potatoes."

"Mmm. I do enjoy a good steak. Can't remember the last time I bit my teeth into a really good slab of beef."

His jaw tightened. "Biting, eh?"

"That is how one chews, yes? And we are still talking about supper?"

"Of course."

"Of course." She leaned close, her breath against his temple. "So what do you say, master? You owe me a smile. Or you'll lose all the admiration you gained on the field of battle."

"Your admiration?"

That was dangerous territory. She had practically invited it. Teasing and touching were far preferable to something so . . . personal.

With her hands sliding down his chest, she whispered, "I could always tickle one out of you."

He grabbed both wrists in one of his iron-strong hands. "*Your* admiration, Polly?"

A tight swallow barely worked down her throat. How was it possible for him to be so powerful and robust? His job was to study the stars. Yet he was both posh and rough. That combination was outright sorcery.

"Yes. My admiration."

"There," he said, releasing her. "That wasn't so hard, was it? Pride still intact?"

She tilted her head to one side. "You're . . . *teasing* me. Aren't you?"

Another twitch of his fine lips. "I am."

"Good God, master," she said with a laugh. "I didn't think you had it in you."

"That's a line I've heard more than once this afternoon. Miss Gowan, I'm capable of more than you assume. Including dares. Now come wash my back, lass."

Polly stood still, astonished, breathless—not just because of his brash words, so out of keeping with his staid personality. Not just because of the unexpected endearment. But because of the wide, stunning smile that accompanied his mischief. He had lovely teeth, straight and white, and dimples that came out of nowhere. Where had he been hiding those? The lines at the corners of his magnetic eyes deepened. All the tension he carried across his stern brow just . . . lifted. He appeared years younger when caught by the impish humor that belied his station.

"Now you owe me."

Ah, the sound of his voice, with those strangely accented words, so rough and low. If anything, his smile intensified.

She bent at the waist, near enough to kiss that beautiful gift. "And *that* sounds like another dare."

"I was right," he said, removing the cloth from his cheek. "It does hurt when I smile."

Polly laughed, long and loud, as she wet the cooling washcloth again and wrung out the blood. Starting with his back, she washed away splotches of mud and dull green grass stains. The flex of his expansive muscles dried her mouth. He was only shifting, perhaps to find a more comfortable position on the cask, but the supple movement held her mesmerized.

He jerked away with a slight hiss. Bringing the light closer, Polly found a nasty bruise the size of a small apple just below his right shoulder blade. The flesh had knotted into a lump.

"Och, that's a nasty one." She leaned around slightly to see his expression. "Fist shaped. Or maybe a rock?"

"Wouldn't be surprised." The smile had been replaced by a pain-laced grimace.

Satisfied that Alex's back was as well tended as she could manage, she licked her lips in anticipation of her real prize. His chest.

Polly knelt between his legs and looked up. From that vantage, his broad, long torso took on exotic proportions.

Something ominous lurked in his eyes. Dark and hungry.

"Do it," he rasped.

She nodded. Suspecting that Alex Christie could convince her to eat a hat, she did as he commanded. With the washcloth, she carefully washed his chest, down his ribs, and around to what she could reach of his thick shoulders and sinuous sides. Rather than detract from his blunt male beauty, Alex's bruises lent him a shockingly potent strength. He wasn't just smart, wasn't just big—he was tough, too.

The hair on his chest was just as intriguing as she had imagined. Even there in his office, with only a glimpse of it at the open throat of his shirt, she had been curious. Springy and fine, it gave way beneath her fingertips as she traced each muscle, all the way down to his taut stomach. Goose bumps followed in the wake of her touch. She edged around to the elegant sweep of his ribs, petting more than washing.

"Lift your arms, please."

He looked ready to protest. The words were right there, trapped behind his sleek lips. But he complied as he offered another of those teasing little smirks. Despite having started this game, Polly's cheeks flushed hot at the sight of hair under his arms, and the way his pectorals changed shape as he lifted and stretched. Heat sizzled across her scalp. She washed beneath his arms—probably the most intimate task she had ever undertaken.

Suddenly he hissed, following with a low grunt. He wrapped his left hand protectively around his ribs.

"Let me," Polly said gently.

Alex took a deep breath and let her touch that tender spot. "Careful."

She probed very softly with two fingertips. The skin along that particular rib was hot and swollen. "Bruised it badly. Or a small fracture."

"Damn it all."

Straightening on her knees, Polly brought her face within inches of his. "You'll live."

After she finished cleansing his upper body, she used iodine and bandages to dress each wound.

"Now for your face and nape." She dumped the filthy water and poured new.

"Seems minor by comparison."

"But bleeding still."

A shout of laughter from the pub froze Polly mid-motion. Someone pounded a table, while another pair of men broke into song. She had left the taproom door open on purpose, but she still wondered how it would look if someone walked in on her and Alex. After all, she was still unmarried and he was still naked from the waist up.

No. She was not doing anything wrong. Worst case, she had her father's instructions and his word as her defense. No one of importance would dare contradict him.

But if she'd thought washing his back and his chest was intimate . . . that held not a candle to repairing his face.

He had nowhere to look but at her. Bold, earnest hazel eyes traced her hairline, the ridge of her nose, the arch of her cheekbones, and her jaw. That intensity burned her skin as she wiped away the dirt and blood. He made her feel both warm and exposed, illuminated for him alone.

She cleared her throat. "This one above your eye will need stitches. It's deep."

"You've done this before?"

"Like I said. Two brothers." She threaded a needle. "Tip your head."

He led with his eyes, as she was beginning to anticipate. He looked up. The tilt of his chin followed. A thick swallow bobbed his Adam's apple.

With a steadiness she didn't feel, Polly carefully sutured. The taut strength of his body, so controlled, pushed against her legs and her stomach.

To distract herself, she said, "Heath is seventeen and Wallace fifteen." Again she sounded odd—not herself at all. "They work down on the docks. Have done for about five years. Factory work isn't something men can boast about, unless they've achieved a position of leadership like Les and Hamish and Mr. McCutcheon."

She paused, wondering if she should continue. Only when she realized she had nothing to lose did she press on. "That makes the union all the more important, you see. Women and children are powerless enough as it is. Without bargaining, we don't have a hope of being treated how we deserve." She tied off the last of the sutures and stepped away, needing distance from what dream they'd created together. Dreams ended. "And I think a smart man like you sees that. It's a matter of justice."

An unfamiliar dizziness had stolen over Alex from the first moment he entered the taproom. That watery-slick feeling in the pit of his stomach hadn't eased. Pain, lust, and an unexpected compassion layered over and over, sinking him into an unhealthy state of mind. Any state of mind that excluded logic was not where he liked to be.

And at that moment, almost every thought had to do with stripping Polly until she was equally exposed.

He focused on a faux pearl button at the base of her throat. Above the hem of lace at her collar, her pulse fluttered with reassuring speed. She was not unaffected. He needed that. Finding himself alone within such a moment would be pure cruelty.

But he was not in Scotland to indulge an irrational attraction to a local girl. He was in Scotland to secure his son's future. That meant doing his job.

"Justice or not, I have a business to run," he

said, the words emerging more harshly than he'd intended.

Polly's lips twisted briefly before she let out a soft exhale. "You're finished, sir."

She had walled herself off, much as he had. An eerie blankness stole over her expression. But from the first moment of their introduction, she had been too proud to keep her quick mind under wraps. He had seen that spark and the cagey calculation too often for him to believe this ruse.

The technique must be useful. He could imagine any number of strangers taking a quick look at her calm, bright green eyes and assuming the least flattering scenario—that she was a simple young woman whose value began with a docile nature and ended with a fine figure. Whereas with men she trusted, and even with Alex, she challenged them with an uncompromising gaze. He much preferred the latter. At least then he better understood where he stood.

Mamie had employed very different defenses against her father, and to a certain extent against Alex. She simply . . . disappeared. Separate bedrooms after their disastrous honeymoon had been inevitable. The only time he'd held her through the night was when she crawled into his bed, with tears streaking her cheeks after a nightmare.

Which was probably why he felt like his kisses with Polly were the first of his life. He'd never felt their like. Molten lava and chills and a sweet, welcome homecoming.

He stood and stretched. The pain in his back and along his ribs was stronger now, but nothing ached so badly as the constriction around his heart. It was being around this woman. Even innocent contact with Polly had his body tense, buzzing and edgy, let alone the kiss he had claimed in the factory office. He'd behaved like a barbarian. Yet she had returned it with equal greed.

Why her? Why a factory girl who stood opposed to his ambitions? Why a woman so complicated as to scramble his mind?

"Thank you," he said gruffly. "I appreciate what you've done for me. All of it."

"No favors, Mr. Christie."

"Would you do me the favor of calling me Alex?"

"Trying to soften me to your intentions, master?"

He stepped near enough to touch. "No, because you've washed and stitched me. Give me that much, Polly."

She chewed her bottom lip, followed by a grand show of returning the washcloth to a basin tinted with his blood. "Only when we're alone."

He couldn't help another smile, despite the grab and pinch at his cheek. In turn he watched her mouth. So delicate and teasing. He wanted to kiss her. Whereas flirting with her was a bad idea, kissing her again would be disastrous.

Hewn of tension and sharp edges, he grabbed his jersey.

She snatched it away. "It's filthy. Stay here."

His blood was still a tempest in his veins when she returned from the main room of the pub.

"Here you are." The coat and shirt she extended were his own. "I think Idle Michael was going to keep them if no one came forward. Come on, then. You'll catch your death."

She tugged the shirt over his head and guided his hands through the sleeves. Her fingers slipped through his to complete the task. The private, almost wifely deed shook him down to his soles. He hadn't been so well tended in a very long time.

Maybe ever.

When she couldn't get a button to poke through its hole, Polly stepped closer. A tiny frown folded over her eyes. She licked her bottom lip, as if this opponent, along with any other, would not have the better of her.

Then she looked up.

The mood between them had been thick, slow, charged with a static hum he didn't trust. All of that changed when their eyes met. He breathed as if sucking air at a high altitude.

He cupped her cheek and slid his fingers back toward her hairline. Silken strands teased his palm.

Although he knew Polly Gowan was perfectly capable of taking the lead, he wanted to. Just to prove he could—this time without shoving and bullying.

He kissed her. Relief and a sweet rush of longing soaked into him past the pain, numbing it with the dizzying rush of his mouth against hers. He swept his tongue between her lips, and she met him at the barrier of her teeth. They coiled together, arms entwining, pulling body to body. Gasps matched, as did quiet, low moans. Smiling, Polly tipped her head back. He kissed her jaw, her neck, down to her graceful collarbone. She only gasped for breath. Alex growled with the satisfaction of giving her such plea-sure, even as he took his own.

The cold air in the taproom whisked across damp skin. Such a contrast with the fire in his blood. She shivered. He pulled her closer, sheltering and claim-ing at the same time.

"You're going to make your lip worse," she said on a shaky laugh. But still she held his shoulders.

"I find I don't care."

Another of her delicious feminine moans spoke to him on a gut level.

More, it said. *More, until I'm satisfied.*

She tasted of whiskey and coffee and eager female. Alex angled his head, kissing her harder. He slipped his hand around her waist and flattened his palm at the base of her spine. The cadence of their breath-ing matched—some rough gallop of air. Teasing nails across his shoulders made him groan, half in pain and half in pure pleasure. She went to his head faster than any alcohol. He slid his hand farther down until he cupped the perfect rounded slope of her ass. He'd done so in the factory office, but this was more deliberate. He took his time, relishing, memorizing.

Because he didn't trust they would ever share such a moment again.

Alex fought the momentum of their desire. He released her body, abandoned her mouth. The hot burn in his lungs was a worse torture than the ache along his brow—although the throbbing fullness of his erection trumped both.

He wanted this woman.

And he had never wanted a woman so badly.

Eight

*P*olly walked through the next three days in a fog. She woke and dressed, worked and ate. The wall of the factory was nearly repaired. Almost everyone was back to working at full capacity. But part of her mind was always in that taproom, with Alex's hands on her bum and his tongue thrusting deeper. Hours in front of the looms provided no distraction. In fact, the lulling monotony tempted her back into his arms.

She had gone further than any good woman would go.

She hadn't gone nearly far enough.

Yet the man who had left that taproom was the master of Christie Textiles. He was a privileged, man-nered gentleman, no matter what bruises, stitches, and abused clothing he wore.

On the fourth day after the picnic, she awoke before dawn to the rustling clamor of a morning already in full swing. Heath shouted at Wallace, Ma rattled a pan over the stove, and Da coughed, although not so badly. In light of her restless thoughts and electric dreams, she smiled at the sounds of her life. Her family. Her safe, familiar place.

Although she loved the security, a small part of her wished for some quiet—a place of her own. Then she imagined how lonely such a life would be. She needed the vigor and purpose and brazen, devil-may-care happiness of her community. She pushed out of her pallet and headed behind the curtain to change into her gown and apron.

After a quick trip to the communal bath at the back of the line of tenements, she returned to help Ma fix the morning meal. The family living space was a hazard of rumpled blankets that needed to be layered in the corner. She picked her way over her brothers' boots.

While Ma helped Da dress for the day and situated him in his chair next to the fire, Polly continued breakfast. She stood over the stove, idly stirring a pot of oatmeal. A few skinny pieces of bacon fried on the second burner. Cooking meant an odd respite of sorts, because no one could call her away from her duties. Otherwise the food might burn. So she took her time with steady, unhurried movements, letting her mind drift once again.

Why did I do it? Why do I still want to?

Because she did. That simple. There were no deeper explanations, no decisions about politics and the union. She had wanted to touch him and watch him ease into her touch. When was the last time she had contemplated doing something so selfish, let alone followed through with it?

A spatter of fat landed on the back of her hand. She muttered to herself and served the bacon onto a plate, which was promptly snatched away by Heath.

"My thanks, Sis," he said.

"Aye, not bad at all." Wallace's mouth was already stuffed full.

She ladled up bowls of oatmeal and laid them on the table with a pint of milk. "You two would eat raw horse if it meant filling your bottomless stomachs."

Wallace grinned—such a shiny, skinny young rascal. "But your cooking is so much better than raw horse."

"So that's what you boys do down at the docks? Dare each other to eat uncooked draft animals? Hardly seems worth the pay you bring home."

Heath stroked the ginger fuzz that constituted his attempt to grow a full beard. Polly figured he would be married and the proud papa of his second child before that happened. "Whatever we do, it beats minding a mechanical knitter all day." He feigned a shudder. "I don't know how you stand it, Polly."

She set the kettle on a burner and cranked up the fire. "Because I have the patience of a saint and the mind of a faraway dreamer."

Heath grinned. But an unusual sobriety overtook features on the verge of manhood. "The new mill master is Christie, right?"

Polly blinked back her surprise. It was no idle question, if she knew her brother. Wallace was a scamp who never meant any harm, but Heath was canny and popular with the young ladies of the neighborhood. He had the devil in him, as Ma often said.

"That's right. What of him?"

"Any reason he'd be down at Old Peter's on the docks? Mick Shaunessey saw him down there Monday evening. Just having a drink, mind. But it seemed odd."

Before Polly could respond, Ma bustled through the kitchen on a flurry of activity. She carried a basket full to overflowing with laundry. "Don't let these boys eat your breakfast, Polly love. And lock up when you go. Make sure Da has enough firewood nearby."

Ma's reminders were always the same on laundry day—the only day she left Da for any length of time. She donned her shawl and headed to the common laundry at the top of the street. Polly tried not to notice the way her shoulders stooped under the weight of the heavy basket. Yet still she bustled on with the energy of two women.

Heath shoved the last hunk of bread into his mouth. "Well, I'm off. Try not to get into trouble down at that hoydenish factory. Probably sin everywhere and we're missing out."

She reached over and flicked him behind the ear. "Think what you like if it'll keep you working. I'll just be standing at a loom, like you said."

She threw together a pot of tea for her brothers, and added milk and a scant ration of sugar for each. They shrugged into their coats and scarves, grabbed the steaming earthenware mugs, and disappeared into the dawn on a flurry of farewells. The little tenement rooms always sounded especially quiet after their boisterous departure.

Only after he finished his breakfast and Polly cleared his dishes did Da take out his pipe for the first smoke of the day. He puffed once or twice before clearing his throat. "Meeting tonight. Hamish is responsible for gathering the men. Do what you can to gather the women. You ready?"

"Aye." She nodded but felt compelled to state the obvious. "You know how difficult it is for the women to meet during the week. They have husbands and babes whose bellies know little of solidarity."

"If their husbands had any sense, they'd attend right alongside them." He coughed twice. "Damn fools have no notion what's good for them."

"We do what we can, Da. That's all we can do."

She stared into the fire, where the memory of Alex's eyes watched her right back. She had not seen him in three days. What, exactly, had he been doing down by the docks? Sniffing out some information she should've found? Already she took two hours longer than usual to walk home from work. Asking for information. Cajoling reluctant workers to give up what they knew. Looking for Tommy. Not even Connie's blandishments to his aunt had produced results.

With a decided effort, she pulled her gaze away from the mesmerizing flames. "I'm worried none of this conniving will come to anything. Mr. Christie doesn't seem to care for business at all. Then he behaves as if the mill is the most important thing in the world. I can't figure him."

"Do your best and keep at it, my girl. Then at least we'll have fought. We'll have looked this life in the face and said it's not enough." He turned his regard to her. He took her hand. "Because it isn't, Polly dear. This isn't enough. Not for you."

Polly clutched his hand, giving it a good squeeze. "Why are you telling me all of this, Da?"

"Because you're going to the meeting by yourself tonight. I no longer can. You'll speak for both of us."

"Alone?"

"Aye. And don't you let Hamish or Les upstage you. You hear?"

He waited for her nod. He expected so much from her, even when she didn't believe herself ready to bear those expectations. And yet, she always had.

"Yes, Da. I won't let anyone down."

"There's my girl." After putting out his pipe, he tugged the blanket across his lap. "Now, be gone with you. You have a long day ahead."

Alex arrived at a community hall in Calton at just after nine that evening. He hadn't gleaned much from his trip to the docks except for the time and place of the next textile workers' union meeting. In fact, all he'd earned through a day of hard work, frustration, and arguments with the board of directors . . . was a letter from his father-in-law.

The sharp evening cold had nothing on the cold in Alex's heart. The letter had outlined the exact measures Josiah Todd intended to take in order to retrieve his grandson. Additional legal actions. Punitive measures. A campaign in the papers. The threats sounded rational enough, but beneath the flourishing vocabulary and condescension was fury. Impotent rage had practically vibrated off the page as Alex read it in his study.

Your offense to my family will not go unpunished. I will have my grandson returned to me at any cost.

Alex had needed to sit down, and he'd needed a drink.

Rather than burn the letter, as was his temptation, he had carefully secured it in the top drawer of his desk. A reminder. He had come to Calton for a reason. The fulfillment of that reason meant attending a union meeting. He had done so on several occasions while supporting Mamie's reform efforts, but he'd never stood by as an interloper. A businessman. A father who would do anything to win security and safety for his son.

The winds swirled away as he walked through the heavy double doors and down a long corridor. Voices and laughter streamed out of a room at its end. He tugged the flat cap lower over his eyes. Although he would be recognized if approached directly, he hoped to cling to the shadows. The identity of the saboteur was, of course, drastically important. But he also needed to know more about Polly's involvement in what the other masters called *agitation*.

The atmosphere inside the small hall was far more festive than he would've imagined for such a function. He expected . . . snarling? Restlessness? Maybe a sense of violence to justify what had happened at his mill.

Several dozen men and women, perhaps sixty in total, mingled in loose clumps. More than a few mothers carried babies on their hips. Young children of all ages dodged around and through their parents' legs. The assembly was almost as much a party as the Sunday luncheon. Only here, some still wore the detritus of their professions. Flecks of cotton. Strands of weft thread. Perhaps they had come straight over from the ends of their shifts.

Thinking of his own son, he wondered if the children had eaten. Or their parents. Just what was it about this meeting to make burdened workers relinquish their precious free time?

He slowly moved to a rear corner of the room. From there he could see a small stage where a lectern awaited the man of the hour: Graham Gowan. Alex crossed his arms and leaned against the wall, still sifting through what scant information he'd gathered since Sunday.

Sunday.

Christ.

He rubbed two fingers along his bottom lip, where the memory of Polly beat the strongest—even stronger than the cuts and bruises that lingered from the football match. Four nights of erotic dreams revealed what he could no longer deny. What he felt for Polly Gowan was pure, undeniable lust. Funny, he had thought himself immune to that potent drug, as if he had simply . . . disconnected. He had done so for Mamie's sake, and for the sake of his own sanity.

He had come to love Mamie, but his initial impulse toward courtship had been chivalry. Their youthful friendship had blossomed softly along the beaches of Cape Cod—the summering place for wealthy families. Her slow, slow moves toward trust had provided clues enough to understand what life meant under her father's roof. The man had taken liberties. Ungodly liberties.

By the age of sixteen, Alex had planned to marry Mamie when they were grown. No passion beyond their shared political causes had ever been part of their union. Instead, they had forged on with mutual respect, common tastes and pursuits, and the wish to honor years of companionship.

He had nothing in common with Polly, nor had he known her long.

Yet there he stood, scanning the room for a glimpse of her bonfire hair.

Connie Nells stepped forward to the lectern. She was a solid woman, hearty and stout, with blond-brown hair swept back in a bun. Her husband, Walt, stood toward the front of the crowd. He had crossed his arms in an intimidating way, but the encouragement he offered Connie in the form of a smitten smile belied his posture. He didn't seem upset with his wife's position in the union, just protective of her place.

Alex stayed close to the wall, curious. He still couldn't see Polly. Made sense, since she was so short. In a lot of ways she reminded him of his dear stepmother. Same fire. Same surprising strength in a small package. But whereas Catrin—the only mother he'd ever known—had used subtle tactics, Polly charged at the world with browbeating smiles. He didn't understand where she pulled up such reserves of optimism. But it was infectious. Her brightness was slowly, furtively sneaking into his bones.

Connie raised her hands and tried to quiet the crowd. After a try or two, she looked to her husband. Walt cupped his hands and shouted, "Shut up!"

The assembly quieted enough for Connie to offer her welcome. "As you know, Graham Gowan suffers from white lung and has been housebound for some time." Many nodded, their expressions brimming with sympathy. "But I am pleased to say that he remains strong enough to advise his chosen second. Part of our purpose here today is to approve or reject his choice."

Alex frowned and stood straighter. Murmurs blanketed the crowd in a buzz of expectation.

Connie raised her hands again, which achieved her ends this time. "You probably suspect who I mean, but let me introduce her formally. She'll speak for a moment, and then we'll vote."

Alex spotted Polly making her way toward the front of the crowd, then right up to the lectern. The jump his heart made was as annoying as it was predictable. Her gown's dark forest color accentuated pale skin and vibrant hair. Red flushed her cheeks and brightened her freckles. She kept her keen eyes level and her chin up. If the rules of Society were written down somewhere, Polly Gowan had never received a copy. She did as she pleased.

"I want to thank you all for coming out tonight," she began, beaming as broadly as Alex had ever seen. "And thanks again to Hamish for reserving our space here in the common hall. It's just small enough to ensure none of us will feel the cold."

Laughter met her remark, which had been delivered with just the right amount of sweetness. Even Hamish grinned, his body language as formidable as Walt's. Polly glanced across her people with obvious satisfaction. Then her gaze caught on Alex. He kept his expression as neutral as possible.

She blinked. Her bright eyes widened only a fraction. Quickly, she looked away.

"And on a Wednesday, no less," she said with a laugh—that one slightly strained. "Forgive my father for forgetting what a challenge it can be to feed and bed children in the middle of the week. Obviously my brothers and I have become far too independent." She nodded to two young men standing off to the left, both of whom shared Polly's distinctive coloring: pale skin, green eyes, and hair like flames. "Although I'm doomed to continue my independent ways, Heath and Wallace will be more than happy to burden our da for as long as humanly possible."

Slowly, Alex began to relax. She was a marvel. Often he had stood at the front of a lecture hall or, more recently, at the head of a boardroom. But that was not his forte. Polly's example was one of confidence, cheeky humor, and some untenable magnetism. He could not help but be pulled in. She had the whole assembly in her power.

"Of course you know why we're here." Her voice took on a serious timbre. "No one has yet come forward to claim responsibility for the destruction at Christie Textiles, which resulted in permanent damage to Mary Worth's right hand. That reminds me— Heath has the collection for Mary and the other victims. Please donate what you can."

The taller of the two brothers, who sported a ragged young beard, held up a glass jar that rattled with coins.

"But even more seriously, our failure to find the saboteur risks our reputation as lawful citizens. We have an opportunity to prove to the masters that we can, indeed, police our own. We can show them that we are not the mindless droves they believe us to be. My da has clasped that dream close to his heart for nearly three decades. I intend to continue his policy. Whether you wish that to happen depends on your vote."

"We're behind you, Polly," Les called. Shouts of approval followed his.

"Thank you. All of you. So please . . . do this for your community. If you know anything about the explosion, talk to me. Talk to my father. We seek only a fair resolution to this chaos."

Alex listened, transfixed. What sort of childhood had inspired her current position in life? So many questions, each chasing fast on the heels of his fascination.

"And if someone comes forward to press for violence?" came a voice from the crowd.

Scowling at Polly was a tall, skinny young man with dark hair that poked out raggedly around his ears. He had the face of an attack dog. The hairs on Alex's arms stood straight up. The union had gathered for measured debate, but the skinny lad was a provocateur.

Polly's stare was a direct challenge. "Air your grievance."

"Why bother? No one fights the Gowans."

"Watch yourself," she said. "You're speaking out of line and you know it."

Polly flicked her eyes toward Alex. For three heartbeats, they clashed.

She's hiding something.

In particular, she was hiding something with regard to that young man.

To conceal the fists he could not help tensing, Alex crossed his arms. Then he nodded to Polly as if to say, *Continue.*

By all means, continue, Miss Gowan.

Nine

Although Polly felt her smile slipping, she forced her expression to remain bright and encouraging.

Alex had come. And so had Tommy.

The two were as volatile as the explosives used to rip a hole in Christie Textiles. And, with a shiver of recognition, she realized that she'd kissed both men. The only other man who'd ever touched her was Rand Livingstone, but that memory evoked a very different shiver. No pleasure. Only the fear of having been completely powerless, even just for a moment—until she had grabbed back her control with a swift knee to his bollocks.

Alex had the potential to control her. She felt it as her body leaned forward at the lectern. Greed. Curiosity. A hundred emotions, none of which agreed on a course of action. He wore a flat cap that nearly concealed the angry red slash above his eyebrow. His garments were practically those of an ordinary laborer, yet something about his posture gave him away. Not so combative. Just more *assured*. For some reason she'd never realized how tall he was. The assembly hall held no power to diminish his height.

He'd snuck in. Blunt on occasion and so clever underneath it all, of course he had. Polly could not help her sense of having been duped. She would've invited him had he asked.

But she couldn't concern herself with Alex right then. Tommy looked as if he'd spent the last week in an alley. Perhaps he had. Others in the crowd clapped him on the back and smiled at his return. She only prayed Alex wouldn't overhear some incriminating remark. Given the right clues, he could easily put two and two together. She wanted a moment alone to brain Tommy before anyone else had the chance.

Yet the whole of the room awaited her next remarks.

"We all know that there may be difficulties in the future," she said, voice clear and even. "With the arrival of Alex Christie as our new master, we have reason to hope that our expectations will be satisfied. We deserve to be heard."

"Bully to that," called a man with a raised fist. "How do you know he's any different than the rest of the scheming masters? They take us for all we're worth."

"We haven't had a raise in over a year."

"The only concessions we've had are the new fans. But they use that as an excuse to dock our pay packets."

"How many of us must be sacked before we strike back?"

"The new master won't be any different. Don't you make that mistake, young lady."

Polly's head spun with the anger spewing forth from so many mouths. The timbre in the room had shifted. Her authority was slipping away with each new angry comment.

"Unless tending the new master's needs has given you special insight," came another voice.

"Is that true, Polly?" A smirk of satisfaction shaped Sarah's perfect lips. "Taken up with His Highness?"

Polly wanted to utter the first retort that came to mind. *No more than you've taken up with George Winchester.* But she kept quiet.

"Few of you have made the effort to know him," she said. "Whatever I do is on behalf of our interests. Any who doubt that can take it up with me personally. Just remember how well I can swing a punch." She aimed that last directly at Sarah.

The adults were scowling now. They were as frustrated as she, needing answers, needing guarantees. And they were spoiling for a fight. She had to end this. Now.

"Do you remember those moments in the mill?" she shouted. With an angry swipe, she tossed back curls made unruly by the dampness. "Men, have your wives told you how scared they were for their lives and for the lives of your children? Do you remember how we ran for the doors and nearly gave that unknown villain what he wanted? There'd have been seventy dead, charred to a crisp. And what would the papers have said?"

"Animals." Hamish's voice was low, but it carried well. "We'd have been dubbed animals."

"That's right. I said it then and I mean it still. They'd have painted us as dumb Calton scum who hadn't the sense to escape a burning building. The blame would've been pinned on one of our ranks, with all the sympathy directed at the masters who endure our agitation."

Her head with throbbing with a heavy pulse. Her people were scared, and she could set them right. She could calm them when everyone else panicked, even if that meant no calm for her.

"So I ask you," she continued, her voice harsh. "Is that how you want to be remembered? Because I refuse with all my strength. I will not be *defined* by others. I will not be *bullied* by others. And if you can't stand with me, then I cannot be your leader."

Silence greeted her words. Eyes flicked around the room, meeting other hostile, discouraged expressions. For her part, Polly found the only safe haven in the room. It should have been one of her brothers. Perhaps Les or Hamish. Her allies in this fight.

But it was Alex.

Again, she recognized his talent for communicating so much with so few alterations to his features. Just a shift of his eyes, a different set to his firm lips. She only felt . . . warmed. Supported by what she took to be admiration.

Whether or not it was true had no importance right then. She needed the fantasy. He was a harbor amid the ever-strengthening voices that debated her future.

Among the men, Tommy postured and raised his fists. Hamish and Heath slipped quietly through the group and restrained him, using just enough force to hold him back without riling him further. She wondered what they said to ease the tension that twisted his back. She wondered what the others had said to rile him in the first place.

Bloody hell, she needed to corner him. Soon.

"So what say you, Calton weavers?" Her throat scratched and ached with the force of bellowing over so many opinions. "Will you give into this goading? Or will you follow me as you followed my da, toward a place of respect no one will deny?"

Some shouts of approval gave her hope. She lowered her voice. "I need you, my friends. So do our neighbors and families. Mrs. Dervish is out of work again because of her hip. Will we abandon her? Sammy Higgins. Are you here, man?"

"Aye, lassie."

"Sammy's eye is gone, an injury he suffered at Locksman Woolens. Will we abandon him, and his dear wife, Patrice? Because if we choose the path of violence, that is our fate. The strongest among us will be jailed, our voices stripped. The neediest among us will be left without aid. Then look at the babes you carry and imagine them orphans. I swear to you, *that* is the darkness we court."

She paused, with another quick glance back to Alex. "And if we don't find the culprit behind the damage at the Christie mill, we *will* be blamed for it."

Talking could only take opinions so far. Da had always said as much. Eventually, one needed to step away and let minds come to their own conclusions. Those conclusions stayed firm.

So she exhaled and opened her hands. "It's time to vote. I leave it to you, friends."

She stepped down from the lectern and strode through the crowd that parted for her. After grabbing her tartan shawl off a hook, she left the hall. Only when out of sight did she lean against the nearest wall, close her eyes, and breathe.

The door opened, then closed just as abruptly.

She looked up, half expecting Alex to have followed her. What would he say? She couldn't begin to guess. But it was Tommy Larnach.

Alex stood rooted. His shoulders dug into the wall at his back.

He wanted to go after Polly, but he would be too conspicuous. Even watching the skinny, dark-haired lad follow her into the corridor was not inducement enough to make him move. He needed to see how this group of angered, scared people reacted to Polly's measured plea. Her words had raised goose bumps along his bruised and aching nape. In the United States, her skills as an orator would've been a marvelous asset for those advocating workers' rights.

Here, she could be the most potent threat to his business, his success, his future. And yet she had so eloquently advocated negotiation and finding the saboteur.

Finally, after minutes that dragged like weeks,

Connie Nells returned to the lectern. Interesting that a woman took control of the vote. Maybe it was another tactic to soothe the multitudes. Alex knew full well that had his father stood in her place, he wouldn't have been able to refrain reiterating his position—and threatening those who disagreed. The man had charged through life, half brute and half cagey tycoon. Whether that was to be admired or frowned upon had depended on the moment.

However, the union needed even tempers.

Walt Nells only needed to clap his hands a few times. Everyone quieted and looked with mixed expressions toward his wife. Some anger. Some resolve. Some fatigued resignation. Alex had no guess as to the vote's outcome.

"No more deliberations, I think." Connie's words carried about as much punch as she could muster, but with a peaceful Lowlands lilt—nearly a lullaby. "All in favor of opening the floor at the next meeting toward the purpose of suggesting new leadership, raise your hands. Hamish and Walt will take the count."

Tense moments passed.

"Twenty-one," called Hamish from one side of the room.

"That's what I have," Walt replied.

"The count stands at twenty-one. Now for Polly Gowan." Connie wet her lower lip. She handled herself well, but public speaking was obviously not her strong suit. "As a reminder, Polly's position would be known only to us, for her own safety and our combined success. The police will not respect a woman at the head of our union. And the masters may not take our demands seriously. Graham Gowan would retain the official title. All in favor, raise your hands."

Again Hamish and Walt circled the room. Alex tried to count, but his place against the back wall allowed no clear vantage.

"Thirty-six."

"Aye."

A whoop of approval surged up from the crowd. Alex breathed out. She was a tricky devil, but at least Polly Gowan was the devil he knew.

As people shared congratulatory smiles and handshakes, and as mothers roused their sleeping children, Alex slipped into the corridor. He did not want to be spotted. Polly's success might be completely undone if anyone knew he had attended.

He stopped short. The dark-haired lad stood entirely too close to Polly. Detained by wiry arms, she fought with the wall at her back. They shouted at each other in unison. Their strong Glaswegian accents were incomprehensible when spoken at the same time, blending into a messy brogue, but their argument contained as much of the Lowlands dialect as English. There was no deciphering any of it.

Alex slammed the door to the meeting hall.

As one, they turned toward him. The lad grinned, nasty and severe. Polly showed no hint of reaction. How did she do that? Without preamble or apology, she shoved the young man's bony chest. Then she hissed something Alex couldn't understand—maybe more of that Scots language.

The lad only laughed. His eyes remained sharp and dangerous.

Alex's scalp throbbed with an oncoming headache. "What the hell is going on?"

Polly didn't look back as she strode past. "Not your business, master."

He caught up quickly. But he didn't touch her, not with a pair of dark, keen eyes upon them. "Aren't you curious how the vote came down?"

"I won. There would've been a brawl otherwise. All that violence unleashed in the guise of celebration. In the meantime they must to be civil." She shook her head, as if remembering her present company. Then she huffed a sharp breath—her only sign of relief. "I'm going home."

"No, you're not." He opened the door for her and forced her to meet his gaze. "You're going to take me to Old Peter's."

"You need no direction. I've heard tell you visited already."

"Fine," Alex said tightly. "Let's frame my instructions with more precision. Tonight, Miss Gowan, I want answers."

Alex walked through the darkened city with Polly at his side. Her pace was everything reluctant. Slouched shoulders. Slowed steps. She kept her eyes on the cobblestones, and tipped the crown of her head against the gusty winds whipping down the street. Frenzied hair trailed out behind her.

She was a creature he'd never thought to imagine. A woman unlike any he'd ever known. Rough-hewn and cheeky, resilient and stubborn. Her boldness called to him.

That boldness tempted him toward thoughts he had no business thinking. Hard thoughts. Charged with sex and expectation. His nighttime fantasies made real. Primal and powerful, his hands shook with his effort to maintain some reserve.

He wanted her, yes. But nothing about her could be trusted. Those kisses . . . All in service of the union? His stomach turned over at the idea. That would make her a prostitute and him a complete and utter fool.

"I still don't understand where you get the right to haul me down to the docks in the middle of the night. I worked twelve hours today. I just fought to keep the union peaceable, which will benefit us both. And now we're back to you and your ham-handed demands." She scowled at him from under her thick lashes, which clumped together in the damp, heavy air.

"Who was he?"

"What?"

Alex didn't relent. Her guileless nature was about as innocent as that of a naughty little sprite. Whatever interaction they sustained from now on would mean keeping that fact front and center in his mind . . . especially as he caught hints of her scent. That pervasive machine oil, layered over a woman's feminine, floral perfume. The combination addled his senses.

"The young man. Dark hair. He spoke against you at the meeting—was the first to advocate violence, in fact. Then to find you in the hallway, arguing? What am I supposed to make of that, Miss Gowan?"

"Back to Miss Gowan, eh? Well enough. We were getting a little too chummy."

Chummy. Alex shook his head at her understatement.

The streets became narrower and murkier as they walked down from Gallowgate. Dockside tenements huddled like rain-soaked soldiers in a muddy trench. No warmth to the fires and scant lights. Upon his first, fruitless trip to Old Peter's, Alex had hoped to find conditions better than his grim imaginings. If anything, they were far worse: desolate and worn, pitted by the rot of dank harbor waters and clouded by the poison of countless smokestacks. That didn't take into account whatever hid behind closed shutters and shadow-strewn stoops.

Polly walked on with no apparent notice of her surroundings, until she veered down a slim alleyway.

"A trade for a trade," he said to her stiff back.

She stopped. Turned. Tilted her head. "How so?"

"I tell you something of importance to you, and you tell me who he was."

"How do I know that what you have to tell is of any importance?"

Alex looked straight ahead. He had reclaimed her curiosity, her attention. He needed both, on complicated levels. Fisting his hands behind his back, he said, "I'm meeting with the other textile masters on Monday."

Polly passed beneath a window that glowed softly from the inside. The faint light cast her skin in orange and darkened her eyes. "So soon? Something's changed."

"Well, my mill was nearly destroyed."

"Maybe."

"Fine, I'll bite. What do you fear?"

"No, I don't think I'll say. You'll go in with opinions formed already. I want you to see those vultures for what they are." She grinned for the first time since they began walking toward the docks. "I promise not to say I told you so."

"You're excessively confident for a . . ."

She jerked her gaze up to meet his. "For a what?"

Good Christ, he was trying to impress her again. The deepest recesses of manhood demanded it. He smiled, pleased when her brows lifted and she inhaled sharply.

"For a woman, Polly. You're excessively confident for a woman."

She recovered quickly and shot him a saucy look. "I'll take that as a compliment, master."

"It was meant as such."

"Then you have more taste than sense."

He laughed at that—hearty and full. His smile had widened her eyes, but his laugh left her slack-jawed. "Ah, for my colleagues or my family to hear that sentence. They'd wonder whom you were talking about."

"Are you so different here, Alex?"

The mad beat of his blood, which had started the moment he stepped onto Scottish soil, would not quiet. "Very different. Now, your turn. Trade for trade."

Polly smashed her lips together. "Old Peter's is right around the corner."

Continuing her stride down the alley, her boot heels kicked out from beneath her hem. The mist of a late evening nearly concealed her as she turned the corner. He followed and kept an easy pace, just watching how she moved. Gracefully, but with the artlessness of a girl. Had she any idea how she affected men? Even her speech at the meeting hall had seemed heartfelt rather than flirtatious. He couldn't think of another woman who might accomplish such a feat without a heavy dose of coquetry.

Where did that air of majesty come from? She should barely know what it was, let alone how to use it so effectively.

"Polly, I'm not going to let it go."

"So I should give up what I know before you make more threats against my livelihood and my family?"

"Yes."

"One of these days I'll call your bluff."

Alex's mind flashed to his young son's face. "And you'll lose."

Polly sighed, which emerged as a vaporous white cloud. "That was Tommy Larnach. He and I were . . . close."

A pinch in his gut told him exactly what that innocuous little word meant. "And tonight?"

"He's still angry that we're not as close as he wants."

Her voice was flat and unremarkable. And yet the young man, Tommy, had been the first agitator at the union meeting.

"I don't believe you," he said quietly.

"Believe what you like." She shrugged, but the motion was anything but dismissive. Almost *defensive*. Again Alex experienced a tickling sensation. She was hiding something from him. "Tommy's a wild lad," she said, "but his heckling was about getting my attention. He proposed two years ago. I refused. Ever since, it's been a test of wills."

"Why did you refuse him?"

"Because if he had said I possess too much confidence for a woman, he wouldn't have meant it as a compliment."

Ten

Polly led the way along the dockside boardwalk. The mist was heavier so close to the Clyde. Mysterious curtains of rain transformed the air into swirling ghosts. So vital to the city, the river was deep and wide—just the right sort of harbor for receiving the biggest vessels in Britain. It had turned a little town into a thriving city. Dozens of ships shot masts and steam stacks into the heavily overcast night. They melted into the fog. Farther out, beyond anything she could see in that gloom, would be another hundred ships—warships, passenger craft, and transport vessels that brought new people to Glasgow every day.

Some stayed. Some, like Alex, might even see a little of its beating heart. Only those who lived and breathed its air from the first seconds of life could know it like Polly did. The good and the bad.

Old Peter's was part of the bad.

"What did you learn the first time you were here?"

"I didn't stay long enough to learn much of anything," Alex admitted. His eyes roved up and down the walkway, where even the hissing gaslamps no longer offered their orange imitation of warmth. "I was here to ask about a man named Jack Findley, but was given a distinct impression I should leave."

She chuckled. "You're lucky that's all they gave you. A master showing up in a dockside hole like that?" With lifted brows, she indicated the dilapidated little building on a corner just across from a jetty. "Frankly, I'm not sure how you're still among the living."

"Let's just say I drank my whiskey very quickly."

"Whiskey, eh? I knew that was the right spirit for your coffee at Idle Michael's."

"Very good. You win. Happy?"

"Always." She grinned. "Let's do this or don't. Are you sure you insist?"

"You tell me. Is Walt Nells a trustworthy man?"

"Walt told you to come here?" She kept her voice low but could not mask her surprise. "Whatever for? He should have come to me."

Alex took her hand and threaded it through his crooked elbow. "For some reason, he had this strange notion you'd pursue the lead on your own."

She scowled, but she did not pull away. Or protest. Damn them both, Walt had been right. Old Peter's looked like an assault waiting to happen—or worse.

"Don't smirk," she said. "It ruins the line of your mouth."

"You were looking at my mouth?"

"I always do. Checking for any intent to kiss me

again." She peered up at him. "Well, master, any such intentions this evening? Is kissing me among your plans?"

"No. But then, that sort of plan seems to catch me by surprise."

"Then it's not a plan." On tiptoe, she whispered against his throat, "That's called a whim. You enjoy them when you stop thinking."

"Show me how to do that."

"Oh, you know."

His arm tensed beneath hers. "Can you be serious for three minutes? I need you to be my cultural interpreter. Maybe you can retrieve answers to questions I didn't even get the chance to ask."

"Sometimes being serious is the surest way to stand out. But I know how to do what needs be done." She stood on tiptoes again and kissed his chin. "Now all you have to do is say please and thank you."

"How about, 'Let's get this over with'?"

"Very well. I wouldn't have agreed if you were dressed any other way. You might *almost* pass." She nodded to the door. Behind it thumped drunken male laughter and off-key singing. "Just don't say anything, Yank. Can you manage that?"

He offered a little bow. His smirking smile was back in place as he held the door for her.

Old Peter's was an intimidating place. On a Wednesday evening, the only patrons were single men eager to drink the rest of their pay packet before Friday, and married men who'd rather join them than go home to their families. A couple dozen dockworkers crowded around the scuffed tables and the long bar. Smoke hung like a cloak just above their heads. The ceiling had likely been white at one time. Now it was dingy yellow. Paintings of Scotsmen in kilts and their elaborate clan regalia lined the walls.

Polly left Alex in the doorway and hurried out again. She ditched her shawl behind a thicket of wasted shrubs, the buds of which had not yet found their springtime blood. At Alex's curious look, she took his arm once again. "My shawl is cut from tartan of Clan Gow. I don't need enemies from the first moment I step in."

"Whose are these?"

"Cameron. Just know nothing of the Chattan Confederation and we'll all see the sunrise."

"I can certainly do that without talking."

"Good," she said with a nod. "I thought you had it in you."

"And I thought you were beyond clan associations."

"Me? For the most part. My family climbed down from the Highlands a few hundred years ago, seeking work and opportunities." She winked. "Not everyone is so enlightened."

Skirting around a few tables, Polly guided him through the drunk, hulking patrons. She kept her pace even. Not striding, but not mincing along either. She was pleased to see a few women, at least, although she wondered as to the source of their income. Dockside girls were plentiful. If she could pass as one for only a few hours, she wouldn't mind being ogled so blatantly—if Alex could keep his temper in check. Waves of indignant anger pulsed against her back as she led him to an empty booth.

"It's like a whole other world," she whispered. "Even for me."

"Oh?"

"I'm used to walking into Idle Michael's and being able to greet everyone by name. I know they must look as burly and unapproachable as this lot, but that's not how I see them. Just my friends and family."

"You don't know much of life outside Calton, do you?"

"I've been across the Clyde once or twice."

He blinked. "That's astonishing."

She set her jaw. "Never mind. You promised to keep your fine mouth shut. Give me two bob."

He handed over the money, but his eyes were busy trying to poke into her hidden places. Again. She didn't need to fight two enemies at once. The men in this pub were enemies in the making.

"Now make a show of fondling my backside as I walk away."

Oh, but she wanted to laugh. His expression was worthy of a daguerreotype, something to save for the rest of her life. "You want me to . . . ?"

"Fondle my backside. Grab for my tits. Pretend you've already bought and paid for my body." She gave him a patient look. An exasperated look. Anything to lessen the anticipation her words shocked to life just beneath her skin.

His hands on her. Lightly. Just a little playacting, certainly.

"Be practical, Alex. Look around. What sort of woman might enter an establishment such as this?"

"Prostitutes," he said quietly.

"Aye. You ready?"

Their eyes met. He appeared as insulted as if she had called his honor into question.

She leaned closer and licked the outer curve of his ear. The tremor that shook down his body was almost visible. "Treat me like you did in the mill that day. Like you own me. Anything else will be suspect. If I don't order drinks soon, we'll need to leave before we even start. Got it, master?"

"Aye, lass."

"No, don't do that. Just terrible!"

She stood and threw a saucy glance over her shoulder. A fake laugh bubbled from her mouth. Alex had given up exasperation in favor of frank, robust interest. If *he* was faking it, he was doing a bloody good job. But she felt his interest—that genuine hum—too strongly for his hazel-eyed stare to be a ruse.

"I'll do what I want tonight," he replied.

Large, strong hands wrapped around her waist. Alex pulled her close, but he didn't sit her back in the booth. His taut fingers pulsed up to her breast, as aggressive as an invading army. He cupped her flesh and gave a hard squeeze. Polly squealed. His other hand slipped down toward the apex of her thighs. Heat burst to life right there, right where it seemed he would touch. Instead he bent her down for a quick kiss. Tongue. Rough stubble. And a farewell swat to her bottom.

"Whiskey," he rasped. "And don't dally."

Polly stumbled a little as he gave her a shove. Her knees didn't quite work. Nothing did. In the flash of a few seconds, Alex Christie had turned the tables. She much preferred setting the terms of their flirtation. But with a pair of grasping hands and a shocking kiss, he had spun her in heated circles.

She recovered quickly—at least on the outside—and made her way to the bar. "Three whiskeys, and a pint of bitter."

The bartender looked like walking gristle. His black hair was streaked through with gray, but the pub's odd smoky light made it seem like smudges of ash. "You're new." The suspicion was impossible to miss.

"Down from Wreston way. Jobs have gone." She shrugged. "Girl's got to make a living."

"No denying that. Just watch yourself. New girls don't last long with . . . well, without protection."

Polly glanced back toward where Alex sat glowering. With his shoulders hulked forward, elbows on the table, he seemed massive. Potent. "I'll fare well, thanks."

He grunted something and handed over her drinks. Polly took the opportunity to make a more forceful impression, crossing her arms beneath her breasts and leaning against the bar. The man's eyes flared. No mistaking that he appreciated what he saw, although in her plain dark green dress—one she'd been wearing since sunup—she didn't feel particularly attractive.

Funny, that hadn't been the case when Alex watched her so closely.

"I'm actually here looking for a man. He owes my da money." She looked up through her lashes. "Been on the lam ever since. If I find him, I can make sure it's worth your while."

Again that greedy look toward her bosom, her hair, her plastered smile. "In coin or . . . ?"

"Whichever means more to you. My da needs his money, and Jack Findley needs a good thumping. With that one in the booth, frankly, I was hoping to manage both tonight."

"Findley, eh?" The bartender's eyes became as glassy as marbles. Completely unreadable. A shiver chased up Polly's back. "Didn't realize he was in the habit of bilking gutter trash of imaginary fortunes."

"Imaginary? More like our life savings! We're Mac-Clerichs, a sept to the Camerons," she said, nodding to the tartan on the wall. "We're practically cousins. You wouldn't turn your back on one of your own, would you?"

The bartender made a face. "I don't believe a word out of your pretty little mouth, girly."

"At least tell me where he's from. I won't bother you again." She hooked a thumb back toward Alex. "And I'm sure I can make it worth his while to leave an extra fat tip."

The barman leaned in. Their mouths were almost near enough to touch. With a quick nod, he indicated her bodice. "Three buttons. Right now."

Her face flushing hot, she straightened. She didn't dare look toward Alex. If he knew what she was about to do, he would pound the bartender to a sick pile of meat. Polly had no doubt.

A jaded smile shaped her mouth. She *felt* jaded. That such a man would make a request shouldn't have surprised her beyond a flush of embarrassment, but she had been of a mind to think the best of people too long. Swallowing her disappointment and contempt, she unbuttoned one, two, three buttons. Not too quickly. She put on a nice show.

The bartender poured a shot and swallowed it quickly. "Squat man. Not much taller than you. From one of the textile mills. An overseer, I think. He won't be interested in the likes of you, my doxy."

"Ach, no more for you, then, if you're going to be so prickly."

Polly buttoned her gown, picked up the three shot glasses in one hand and the pint of bitter in the other. Not that she hurried back to the booth, but she certainly didn't dally. The bartender's words had curled a nasty ball of dread in her stomach. With the barest of details, she and Alex were suddenly back on opposite sides.

If an overseer was responsible for the sabotage, who would believe Tommy over his word?

She had barely set the drinks on the table before Alex resumed his eager façade. The hands that always surprised her—strong, capable, yet without a single callus—grabbed her around the waist. Momentum plunked her squarely in his lap. She straddled him face-to-face, with her skirts rucked up to her knees.

He palmed her jaw and cheek. Another kiss. Hotter still. His lips had barely finished a quick plunder before moving down to her throat. Polly shivered, and shivered again. His enthusiasm was undeniable, right beneath where she burned hot and wet.

"What did he say?" he whispered against her skin.

Polly forced a laugh, which was tinged with giddy excitement. She probably sounded half-drunk already. He had that effect.

She turned and grabbed one of the whiskey shots. It burned down her throat, all liquid fire and instant relaxation. The tension seeped out of her bones. She pushed fully against Alex's broad chest. "Your turn. Then I'll tell."

He didn't hesitate, nor did he let go. Restless fingers cupped her breast. He swallowed a shot with a single gulp. That muscular throat deserved to be kissed. She licked from his collarbone to the dimple behind his ear.

Alex's shoulders shook beneath her hands—just one hard shudder. Then he, too, eased back into the booth's warped leather. Her quick glance toward the bartender and a few other men revealed what she had hoped: interest without suspicion.

"Now," Alex grated out. "Tell me."

He was sounding more brutish by the minute. She chuckled against his cheek. Knees spread wide, she fit herself more snugly against his thick manhood. "Or what? You'll kiss me again? That's hardly a threat."

He caught her loose bun in his fist. Fire blazed hot and shocking in his gentleman's eyes. "Don't make this a wasted trip when I have to haul you out of here by your pretty red hair."

Alex was breathing hard. He ached, and Christ, he was tempted.

"I don't doubt that you would," she whispered. "And wouldn't that make for an interesting time?"

"I saw what you did at the bar." His voice was a low growl. He bared her shoulder and kissed her there—anything to ease the need to mark territory he did not own. Yet each touch urged him to risk more. "You unbuttoned your gown for that stringy waste."

"I did. And now I know Jack Findley is a textile overseer. I'd give you a description of him, but I doubt you'd be able to keep the details. Not right now."

She wiggled her bottom. Alex moaned in her hair.

Somewhere deeper, where his thinking mind still resided, he wondered how far she was willing to go. With regard to *anything*. She was either very skillful or very brave.

Alex held more of Polly than he knew what to do with. His body operated on vital, pumping instinct. He squeezed both of his hands: one at her breast, one buried deep in her hair. Her little wince shot straight to his cock, as if he needed a stronger reminder of his raging arousal.

"Easy now, master." She smiled sweetly. "I'm done teasing, and so is the bartender. He seemed doubtful that Findley would owe a dockside girl any money. Called him too posh for a doxy like me. That was my ruse, you see."

"I'm enjoying our ruse."

At the thump of a door being thrown open, she gasped and turned in Alex's arms. "But all good things come to an end. We need to go."

Out of reflex, Alex had tightened his hold on her waist. Four constables had entered the pub. Their scowls and assessing stares meant they hadn't stopped in for a drink. "Are they after you?"

"Polly Gowan specifically? No. Women strewn across the laps of paying customers? Yes. We must protect our fair city from vice, you see."

"Christ," Alex whispered against her neck. "I'll do what I can to influence them."

"And reveal that you were here at all? Not much of a secret investigation, master."

"Back door, then?"

"Let's hope."

Alex popped her off his lap and gave her a little shove. He was out of the booth in a flash, but not fast enough to escape shouts from the front of the pub. A quick look back revealed the bartender pointing them out with his gnarled finger.

"Go!" Alex said sharply.

Polly hitched her skirts and ran. Dodging tables and chairs, she used her shoulder to burst past a single door at the rear of the smoke-laden room. Alex stumbled after her, through the doorway. A taproom similar to the one at Idle Michael's was filled with the usual boxes and crates, along with the foul stink of urine and mold.

His hand protectively at her waist, Alex kept his body between Polly and the door at their back. He stopped, turned, slammed it.

"Wedge it shut!" she called over her shoulder.

Using his back, he pushed a huge wooden delivery crate inch by inch toward the door. Fists slammed against the other side as soon as he shoved it into place. Sweat lined his brow.

"Quick now," he said again. "We don't have much time."

"Oh, no, master. I think I'll take my time and have a chat with the nice lads." Polly picked over the crates with her skirts bunched in white-knuckled fists. "What do you *think* I'm doing, Alex? I'm going as fast as I can!"

"You would argue with a storm cloud in the middle of a hurricane."

"And I'd win." She reached the back door. "Padlock. Damn."

Alex spotted an ax in a cobweb-strewn corner. "Get back."

She complied with gratifying speed by ducking behind a large crate. After a grip to position his hands, he took swing after swing against the rot that surrounded the lock. Chips flew. The wood splintered beneath his successive strikes.

He used his heel to kick their way free. The lock flew out into the night, along with part of the handle. Polly scampered out from her hiding place just as their escape door swung open. Cold, wet air smacked Alex in the face, a welcome relief after the tight heat of the taproom and his hard-earned sweat.

He took Polly's hand without thought. They rushed to freedom.

Two more constables stood not five feet away, holding black, intimidating truncheons.

What use was thought when faced with an immediate threat? He swung high, but nearly lost his balance on the slippery cobblestones. The ax slipped from his fingers and slid behind a cluster of shrubs.

Polly rolled low against a constable's knees, then produced a slender knife from out of nowhere. A masculine bellow shredded the night as Alex struck the other constable—kidney, sternum, chin. With his palms flat and taut, he slammed them against the man's ears, then punched him twice in the face.

"Go, Polly!"

But the man she'd stabbed caught Polly's skirts. She grunted as she landed on all fours. The sound of skin and bone hitting the pavement unleashed a tide of violence from deep inside Alex. He kicked the constable square in the bollocks, then yanked Polly up with his arms around her waist. Neither looked back.

She hissed but her pace never flagged. "That way," she said. "Left down that alley."

The tight, high walls created a passage with no visible end. Darkness and fog swallowed the way out. Angered voices and heavy footsteps hurried close behind. With nowhere else to go, Alex followed her into the alley's smoky black mist.

"Do you know where we are?"

"Not exactly." She was breathing almost as heavily. "But I know which direction is home."

More voices. This time at the top of the steeply descending alley. Letting the constables catch Polly was out of the question. He wasn't through with her yet.

Her directions took them left, then right, then back to the right again. Alex was completely lost. He only hoped she wouldn't lead him headfirst into a wall.

"Are you sure?" he asked.

"I *am* looking for something."

"Could've fooled me."

"That'd be too easy."

Alex grimaced. "*Polly.*"

Limping slightly now, she felt along the brick. No gaslights graced such a place. No shining reflections from the Clyde. Not even a hint of illumination from the tenements that surrounded them like sullen giants.

"Yes, here it is."

She probed a little notch in the side of a brick building. A trick door opened beneath her fingers and closed them into a space no larger than two feet square.

Her breathing mingled with his, both in warmth and in sound. "Not to say they were designed for escaping constables . . . "

"But they were actually designed for escaping constables," he finished with a grin.

Footfalls pounded along the cobblestones outside. The sound was wet and indistinct when heard from inside their little shelter.

The threat eased. Polly felt around on the floor. "Take off your coat," she whispered.

More rustling noises as she stripped him, not even waiting for permission. His knuckles burned from those punches he'd landed. He clenched swollen fingers into fists, relishing the burn. She seemed to be . . . kneeling?

He let his head fall back against the wall. *Her* head would be . . .

Bloody hell.

A match flared to life. She lit a nub of a candle and wedged it in a corner. He began to protest—the light would be seen—but she'd shoved his coat along the bottom seam of the door. The tiny candle barely offered enough light to blink clear of the darkness. He could see her now, not just hear her breathless gasps.

And now, out of immediate danger, he could *blame* her.

He took both of her shoulders in hand and hauled her to a standing position. Pulling her close, taking her mouth—the most primal instinct. Her little cries edged him on. Whiskey, followed by unbridled aggression, had blunted his senses. Her kiss burned through that fog. The sweep of her tongue across his busted lip hurt like hell.

"More," he rasped. "Give me more."

"Yes, master." She kissed him with matching ferocity.

He drove his fingers into her thick, damp curls. "Jesus, Polly. What the hell kind of man have you turned me into?"

Eleven

A *dangerous* one," Polly whispered. "I like it."

Alex cinched an arm around her lower back. Their upper bodies came together in a rough crash. With his other hand he captured the base of her skull. If he meant to be gentle, he was failing completely. But she didn't want gentle. She angled her head to one side and plunged into his hot mouth. His moan vibrated against her tongue.

She felt it happen, when his control slipped as if coated with oil. Needing something solid, she edged against the brick. At least there she wouldn't fall. Only his strength would rival the wall at her back.

Bunched and humming with tension, his body was solid and strong beneath her hands. Nothing about him was quiet or contemplative now. He attacked her mouth, matched her need, jerked it higher. The sugary tang of whiskey flavored his tongue. He drank deeply of her kisses, over and over, taking all she offered.

He worked his hand more deeply into her hair. Sharp spikes of anticipation and pleasure nettled her skin. She couldn't get close enough. Pins pinged onto the cobblestones as he plunged his wide hands into her disheveled curls. She sighed when he scraped down to her scalp and tugged her head back, just as he had in the tavern. Only this time, it was no act. He was taking over. Polly sank into the miracle of making this fine man lose control.

Nimbly, she unfastened the top three buttons of his shirt. His fingers, not so sure, worked at her bodice. He dipped his mouth, kissing her cheek and her jaw. They had kissed before. Each had escalated with growing passion. Now her neck became new territory, a new expanse for Alex to explore, to lick, to graze with his teeth. She shivered and sank her fingertips into the hard caps of his shoulders.

He *pulsed*. All energy and need.

He pulled harder on her hair. She fought back just enough to chuckle softly in his ear. "You think I'm going somewhere?"

"If you had any sense."

"Do you, when it comes to me? To this?"

His answer was a full-on growl. He bent low and sucked the crook where her neck met her shoulder. Garish colors spiked behind her closed eyes. His hands sank down, down, until he grasped her backside. *Hard.*

"Oh, but you do like my arse, don't you?"

"Perfect."

Unbuttoning the rest of his shirt, Polly dove beneath the fabric and dragged blunt fingernails across his nipples.

"Just as good . . ."

He broke off. She could just barely see the bob of his throat as he swallowed. The light cast from the lone candle swathed his features in stark, strong shadow.

She scraped his nipples again. "What were you going to say?"

"Just as good as I imagined."

Before Polly could make sense of that curious sentence, he ground his hips against the softness of hers.

"You want this?"

"Very clever, master," she said with a quiet laugh.

"Polly, think— I don't want to . . ."

She nuzzled his neck. The stubble sprouting from his jaw rasped her cheek. She nipped at his collarbone, then down, down, to trail her tongue through his chest hair. "You'll regret it for the rest of your life if you don't."

She nuzzled deeper, found one nipple, and swiped it with a slow, wet lick.

"Damn it, Polly. Make me stop."

"You'll have to stop yourself. And neither of us wants that."

"You deserve better."

"And you're still able to talk," she said with a chuckle. "I'm impressed."

"Is that a problem?"

She stood on tiptoe and nipped his earlobe. "No, a goal for myself. I'll have you speechless before we're through."

As if to make the point unmistakably clear, she

slid a hand down his torso and grasped his stiff rod. Alex's inhale deepened into a low moan, which affected Polly like nothing else could. His satisfaction wet the skin between her legs. He bucked against her palm, then clenched the flesh of her ass, as if in retaliation. Another crushing kiss. Her head spun when he was right there, again, slipping his tongue between her lips.

"You're right," he whispered. "Regret it for the rest of my life."

"Then make it good."

He grasped her skirts and bunched the thread-worn fabric in his hands. With the skirt out of the way, he found her drawers and plunged beneath her waistband. Polly gasped against his mouth as he slipped his hand between her legs.

"Christ."

"Wet for you, aren't I?"

"Yes."

She noticed the change almost at once. He slowed. He breathed. The rhythm of his fingers inside her became deeper and more deliberate. Each subtle change said that he would see this through. He found a spot inside her wet folds, deeper inside. Hooking his fingers, he pulsed against a place that blazed tingling sweetness out toward her belly and upper thighs.

"Touch me," he said. No hesitation. Only a command that shivered down to where he pulsed and teased. "Grip me."

Weaker now, even as he grew more determined, Polly fumbled with his trouser buttons. His distractions weren't helping: fingers tickling inside her quim, mouth at her throat. Her palms felt hot, but they were nothing to the raging heat of his shaft. She worked him with a firm, rhythmic caress. Curiosity pushed her as fast and far as desire. There in that corner of darkness, she wanted nothing but to be claimed by Alex Christie.

Delving inside his waistband with her free hand, she found the taut muscles of his buttocks. And squeezed. Hard. Each thrust displayed his body's hard, unexpected power. Little filaments and sparks radiated out from where he caressed her. All the while she stroked the heft of his solid weight. Hot and huge. His pulse was so strong that she should've been able to hear it.

The slick wetness against her thumb caught her by surprise. She swirled it over the head of his cock. He thrust and grunted. Still taken aback, Polly froze.

Is that all?

She only had Tommy to go by with regard to experience. Already Alex had lasted longer, teasing her and kissing her in ways Tommy had never attempted. But she knew a man was finished when his body released its liquid.

With a shaking exhale, her limbs trembling, she let go and pressed her hands flat against the brick.

Alex stilled, too. He lifted his mouth from hers and peered through the dim candlelight. His chest shook. *Strange.* He didn't look slack and restful as Tommy had. No, Alex looked even more tense and eager.

The cast of his mouth could have been carved

from solid rock. His heavy exhale was nearly a shudder. "Polly, have you changed your mind?"

Alex studied forces of nature, how the stars could burst into awe-inspiring displays of color and grandeur. That was how she kissed him, with the vigor of a storm in heaven. Glorious Polly Gowan with her bonfire hair and unrelenting charisma—wide eyes glittering in the faint light, skin glowing iridescent white.

But she didn't move.

If he needed to play the gallant gentleman . . . how did a man step back from such a precipice?

Because it was the right thing to do. She must think him some crazed beast. He felt like it.

No matter his hard, shaking muscles, he pulled free of her body, his fingers slick with her sweetness. "I won't guess what you want."

"It doesn't matter now."

"Bollocks to that. Tell me."

The puzzlement on her face and along the shadowed ridge of her delicate brow only added to his confusion. He'd thought her throat elegant—her most elegant feature, in truth. As she swallowed past some incomprehensible worry, it was simply erotic. He adored her resilience and fervor, but even more, he needed proof—proof that she desired his attentions as much as he craved hers.

"You . . . you were done, yes? You were wet."

"Done?" He laughed, as if that might do something to release the steaming passion trapped beneath his skin. "Oh, Polly, we haven't finished."

With his free hand, Alex smoothed a caress along

the inside of her wrist and twined his fingers with hers. Then he guided her back to his shaft.

"Touch me again. Like you did."

Polly gripped him. Her mouth gaped open. "Oh, my."

"See? Harder than ever." He'd thought her cheeks unbearably soft, but her pert arse was smooth perfection. "I'm incredibly excited," he said, his forehead pressed against hers. "That was just the beginning. A little like how wet you are. It's just another way to ease the joining."

"I *have* done this before. I wasn't lying."

"Oh, I believe you. But I wonder how well you enjoyed it. Did you climax, Polly?"

"Did I . . . ?"

"Climax." He found her wet sheath again and dove deeper, increasing his speed. "All of this beautiful tension—did you find its release? Or did he leave you wanting and frustrated?"

"Frustrated," she said with a shudder.

"Not tonight. Tonight you will know how passion should conclude." He kissed her softly. "And so will I."

Questions quivered across her lips. Questions he wasn't prepared to answer. Instead he flicked his fingertip against a place at the apex of her thighs. Her body jerked. "Oh!"

He did it again, then again, building the pattern into tense circles. With one hand she grabbed his waist. Burrowing inside the open flaps of his shirt, she smoothed a rough touch along his ribs. The cadence of his pulse jumped.

Before Polly, when was the last time he'd been touched?

I can't remember.

When was the last time he'd been gripped and stroked?

Never. Never like this.

As if accentuating her power, she flicked her thumb over his swollen head in faster circles. Alex fought the arousal she stoked. He had goals, too. The way he'd given over to the moment didn't mean he was a completely selfish bastard. He wouldn't have his full release until she was sated.

And that, too, was new. To satisfy a woman . . .

She was ripe and eager and entirely his for the taking. That he could have such an effect on this passionate creature made him feel invincible. So when Polly reached down to cup his balls, he ground his molars together and steeled himself. In all the chaos of the last few weeks, hours, minutes—at least having a goal made sense.

A blazing light behind his eyes became brighter. Yet he saw everything with unnatural clarity, down to her individual freckles and eyelashes. Desperate noises filled their tiny refuge, as did the humidity of shared exhales. She gasped his name.

He leaned in close, lip to lip. "Quiet now."

The few inches between their bodies shrank to naught. He nudged his thick shaft against her inner thigh.

"Breathe, Polly."

She did as he told—a heady rush of power. And on one deep breath, he filled her.

She groaned softly against his neck, then shivered. Alex hooked his forearm underneath her thigh. So wet. So completely open to him. His rod stretched and pressed and oh, Jesus—he just *thrust*.

Polly held on to his shoulders and tossed her head back. She trembled with each plunge and measured withdrawal. Her breath became erratic. And even in the midst of that gathering pleasure, she found a smile. "You're not talking anymore."

Alex wrapped his forearm under her backside and drove deeper. Relentless now. She'd stolen his voice, but he would steal her breath, her very mind. The beat of their bodies matched the thump of his heart. Head down, chest heaving, he claimed her with relentless force. Her little noises intensified, noises like crying and begging and rapture . . . until she pressed her mouth against his chest to muffle her ecstasy.

Alex was an animal now, some night creature crying to the moon. Only the very last vestige of chivalry provided strength enough to withdraw. He found her hand, bringing her back to his swollen cock. Their fingers clasped as he showed her the rhythm he needed. He didn't need long. After a few hard strokes, he tensed and groaned. Heaving a powerful tremor, he collapsed with his forehead resting against the brick wall, just over her shoulder.

Polly's grin tickled his neck. "Well, now, that was embarrassing."

He stiffened, except for his lungs—still heaving. "Oh?"

"Not you, silly. *Me*. How could I mistake the two?"

She licked along his jaw, then kissed him almost chastely. "I'll know for next time."

Next time. Jesus.

After retrieving a handkerchief from his coat pocket, Alex did his best to clean up the mess. His chest burned as if he'd inhaled flame. The feel of her body clamping over his cock—the vital, unmistakable proof of her satisfaction—had been more than he'd dared dream.

"Damn," she said, teasing. "I shut you up too much."

He shoved the handkerchief in a pocket and fastened his trousers. Polly had already straightened her clothing—the miracle that is woman. Only the tangled wildness of her unbound hair gave her away.

And, God, her smile. A little shy. A lot dumbfounded.

He could relate.

Without thought, he simply reached for her. Crisscrossing his arms around her back, he held her close. She tensed at first, then melted against him. A ragged exhale eased out of her chest.

"Thank you, Alex."

He grinned against her hair, where he caught traces of smoke from the bar. With no more pleasant distractions, he was left with the pain in his lip, his brow, his ribs. The effort required to forgo those misgivings was not so Herculean as he would've imagined. He only nuzzled deeper and breathed her in.

"I was going to say the same thing," he whispered. "Thank you."

She giggled even as she straightened his collar.

"I'm tempted to tell Tommy what a poor showing his efforts have proven."

"Don't. God, please."

"Hush, master. There's no chance I ever will. That was . . ." Eyes bright, she would not let him look away. She even caught his chin in her hand to force their gazes together. "That was amazing. And unbearably private. For me and you."

"For me and you."

Slowly, she rose up on tiptoes and pressed a soft kiss against his mouth. He wondered at her hesitation until he realized how many doubts *he* harbored. Surely she must have as many. So he kissed her back. Not as roughly or with the same fevered intensity, but the power of that unhurried touch of lip to lip shook his bones.

"Let's get out of here," he said.

"Amen. You would not fare well in jail."

"You've been?"

She shrugged. "For an hour or two at a stretch. It's mostly for show. But I can't imagine the esteemed Mr. Christie standing before a judge."

"I wouldn't be the first Christie to do so."

They intertwined their fingers, just as they'd done when stroking his rigid shaft. Alex blinked past the sudden resurgence of his arousal. The thought alone, only a few moments on from the act itself, was enough to quicken his breath. He'd become a man possessed.

After a quick check of the deserted alley, they walked away from the private little hiding place. He had shared one of the most intimate encounters of his life, but he would never find that secret cubby again. A place as ephemeral as fog and memory.

The sky remained hidden behind a silver slime of clouds. The cold was fierce now. They joined hands. Their shoulders brushed and bumped with every step. Her magnificent hair was an unbound cape that caught flickers of light from the hissing gaslamps. She looked every inch the wild woman who could ravage and be ravaged, but her naïveté about the act itself reminded him that she was no practiced harlot.

"When do your parents expect you home?"

"I don't think they do."

"Your life here. It's . . . let's just say it's different."

With a quiet laugh, she hugged his arm. "Might as well be the moon, I suspect. But they trust me to stay safe and not cause trouble."

"What about what we just did?"

"Well, I wouldn't brag about it, that's for certain. Though I could. It was well worth bragging about."

Alex grinned. "Another compliment. Better watch yourself."

They walked in silence until they reached a street that curled along the river docks. Every shipbuilding contract with the British military establishment supplied thousands of jobs, the effect of which wove down to the woman at his side. Only, scraps and hand-me-downs weren't good enough. Not for Polly.

He had no notion of what to do about the situation. All he knew was they had come too close to irrevocable trouble. No matter their differences, he would not allow her to be hurt. Any harm visited upon Polly would be some unfortunate soul's last mistake.

"What did Livingstone do to you?"

"The man you threatened me with?"

"That seems like . . . a long time ago."

She touched his cheek. "Yes, it does. And it's probably not what you're assuming. He wants me willing, I think, because he's had opportunities where forcing me would've been an easy thing."

She said it so nonchalantly, but Alex forced his throat to relax and his fist to open. "Then what?"

Polly glanced toward the river, where boats bobbed in the night quiet. A gentle but steady wind whistled through the ropes and moorings. "About five years ago, Da's health was just beginning to fail. He'd organized a strike that turned sour. The masters claimed he'd told the strikers to use their fists. But the police were the ones to wade in with dogs and truncheons."

Outrage added volume to her words, no matter the time separating past and present. Alex found himself caressing her upper arm.

"They held the so-called ringleaders in prison for five days. Da was sick. Livingstone was there, working for Winchester as always. Even then, Livingstone was a surly cuss with no decency. He threatened to beat Da unless he confessed. Rather than see that happen, Tommy stepped up and said *he'd* started the riot. That he'd done it on purpose. So Tommy got the beating instead." She shivered. "That limp of his? Livingstone did that."

"That's part of why you protect him, isn't it? Tommy?"

She mashed her lips together. Alex had learned enough about her to know when she was done sharing.

"I'll find out what I can about this Jack Findley person," he said. "I can observe how the other masters react to his name. We're close, Polly. Nothing about either of our endeavors will be safe until we solve this."

She sighed in a way that lent him no confidence in her cooperation. "Very well."

"Will you do me a favor?"

"Oh? Now you have me curious. But before you say a thing, know that I have something very specific in mind as to how you'll repay me."

"Does it have anything to do with what we just shared?"

A mock pout curved her sensual mouth. "Alas, no. You'll meet with the masters. You'll search for what you can about this Findley bloke. But I also want you to listen. Use that brain of yours and consider what you've seen of my people—and what you hear of the masters' greed and suspicion." She took a deep breath. "I know we're on opposite sides, but perhaps it doesn't have to be that way."

Alex put an end to their stroll and studied her heart-shaped face. Such wide eyes. High cheekbones. Luscious mouth made for kissing. All the right shapes to suit a devoted, trusting woman. But she was as clever as ever, just as cagey.

"I will," he said. "I'll listen."

"Then ask what you will."

"My son's wet nurse is leaving for London in a matter of days. I think he's about ready to move on to solid foods. So what I really need is a reliable nanny. I'd appreciate recommendations, a few names." He stroked her jaw, touched her lower lip. "I know you wouldn't mislead me on this, Polly."

"No, I wouldn't. Just as I know you'll want to find out all you can about any woman I recommend. So I'll give you that name now: Agnes Doward. Perhaps I can bring her round on Saturday." She grinned and slanted those bright eyes toward him. "Do what digging you must before then. Agreed?"

"Yes."

They shared a hackney back toward her neighborhood. The looming brick form of her tenement was no different than the dozen flanking it. Polly Gowan lived there. Every night, she climbed those crooked steps toward some squalid set of rooms. Alex's sickened sense of outrage was nearly as strong as had been his desire. She deserved better. Pure and simple.

She turned to leave, but Alex caught her wrist. He kissed her there, along skin that thumped a sweet, steady pulse. "Good night, Miss Gowan."

Her hesitant smile wasn't near enough to the real Polly, but it was still beautiful. "Good night, Mr. Christie."

Twelve

Polly had never known such a treacle-slow day.
Not only did a raw edge of fatigue scratch beneath
her eyelids, but she kept glancing toward the nearest
timepiece. At breakfast, it was the small mainspring
clock on the mantel. On the factory floor, it was the
large, stark Roman numerals on the wall above the
exit. The second hand loafed and the minute hand
moved as sluggishly as a miser opening his wallet.
The hour hand didn't move at all.

She would see Alex that evening, as an escort to
formally introduce Agnes. And two days hence, he
would meet with the other mill masters on Monday.

That thought would not leave her mind, always at
odds with their reckless night together. What would
he do or say? Would he listen, as she'd asked? Or
just inquire after Jack Findley? She liked to think
Alex was above the greed and ease with which the
masters could strip so much of what the union had
gained. She liked to think that, but he was obsessed

with making the mill a success, for reasons she had not yet figured out.

Apparently a man of science and learning, he certainly hadn't behaved that way since arriving in Glasgow. She had a hard time picturing him as studious. Severe, yes. Grim at times. For the most part she had witnessed his potential for a quick temper and violence, and had been on the receiving end of delicious, overwhelming lust.

Good God. She still shivered and ached, no matter the blaze of satisfaction she had relished. Nothing of logic helped her understand what making love to Alex would mean for the future. In thinking back on their shared passion, however, she didn't want to be logical. In a world of rote traditions and few options, he made her *feel*. For now, that was more than enough.

She finished her quota just after lunch, in the vain hope that working harder would speed time. Her efforts only left her without a suitable distraction as the day dragged. With as much cheer as she could muster, she helped a relatively new hire untangle the lead threads of her loom—a tedious, time-consuming task. She accepted an incoming delivery of dye and raw cotton, then directed the heartier women in sorting bundles.

Christie Textiles was nearly back to full capacity, and in only two weeks. The engineers and a dozen hired masons had already done wonders to repair the damage done by the explosion.

Only when she sat on a large crate did drowsiness catch up with her. She nodded off twice, awoken the first time by Connie's gentle hand on her shoulder.

The second time . . . Alex had pressed her up against that brick wall, his eyes full of a desire she'd never known. But the wall crumbled. She slipped out of his grasp, falling backward, her arms pinwheeling—

She jerked awake.

With a quick glance, she realized that the others must've let her sleep. She was alone in the sorting room. Composing herself, she stood and stretched. She was edgy at the prospect of seeing where Alex lived, as well as meeting his young son. It was more proof of their growing connection—a connection she could not afford to indulge. Making love was practically recreation. Any deeper intimacy, so much nearer her heart, needed to be stopped.

The shift whistle blew, nearly stripping Polly of her skin. She pressed her hands over her startled heart.

Free.

The second shift workers began to arrive. With more speed than grace, she collected her belongings, which did not include her tartan. The fact she'd left it behind at Old Peter's was an annoyance. She loved that piece of cloth. The history of her family. A reminder of why she fought.

There was nothing to do about it. She certainly couldn't return to that grimy pub. With a sigh, she resolved to replace it. One day. Maybe she could save enough money.

In the meantime she had borrowed her mother's shawl. She filed out the door with the rest of her colleagues. Forcing a smile, she took Agnes's arm as they walked into the bustling afternoon. The clouds were as stoic as ever. Workers streamed out from the factories lining that industrial thoroughfare, while others arrived to take their places.

"I have a question for you," she said.

Agnes's eyes twinkled a bright, watery blue. "I may have an answer."

"Mr. Christie needs a nanny to care for his young son. He asked me to make a recommendation, and I offered your name. He would like to meet you as soon as possible. I thought maybe now."

"When the weather is so fine for walking?"

"Exactly." While sidestepping a slushy mud puddle, they avoided an overburdened wagon and its feisty, skittish draft horse. "He's willing to offer a private room in his home."

Agnes's gray hair, swept away from her face, was sprinkled with mist and a few stray cotton fibers. A faraway look softened her features. "That would be . . ."

Her voice broke. Polly kept her eyes forward to give the woman the privacy she deserved.

"I'd like that, Polly. Do you think he's the sort to keep his promises?"

"I'm hoping he does." She hesitated.

"Hold nothing back, my girl. This is too important for things left unsaid."

"What if I've completely misread him?"

The skin at the edges of Agnes's eyes crinkled as she smiled. "When was the last time that happened, my dear?"

With a blush to warm her chilled cheeks, Polly returned the grin. "He's not from Glasgow. I hardly know the language he speaks."

Her glib words hid a deeper fear. She did not enjoy the idea of making such an error, especially with Alex. If Polly made such a colossal mistake, burdened by inappropriate emotions, her da might be less trusting of her judgment in the future. Her mother's suggestion that she marry and settle down would become more forceful.

They turned the corner toward Dennistoun.

Tommy Larnach leaned against the wall of a bargain haberdashers. His ankles were crossed and he smoked a thin cigarette, all calm nonchalance. Polly tensed. She let go of Agnes's supportive hold and rushed toward him. Grabbing his grimy collar, she hauled him into a nearby alley.

"You never answered me, Tommy." Tension burst into a mean temper. "I need answers. Now. You know what's at stake."

"I do." He exhaled smoke, which blended into the early evening mist. "But I wonder if you do. Making time with the master seems to have slowed your urgency."

She slapped him. Her palm stung, but Tommy only grinned. The boy she'd once adored had turned into a much harder man. She cataloged his features and found no trace of his younger self. Dark brown eyes were narrowed and suspicious. An otherwise fine, thin mouth curled with animosity. And the hardship of life—perhaps made worse by time spent on the lam—was etched across his skin in tiny lines and too many scars. He led with his face, believing every punch was aimed right at him.

She'd only added to it.

"You have no right." Her voice scraped out of her throat. No matter what had happened between her and Alex, she was still the same woman. To be accused of letting Alex take the place of those ambitions was one insult too many. "I have sacrificed my entire life to improve our lot. You once did the same. How can you have fallen so far?"

"I never had far to fall," he said, his words quiet.

"Don't play that pity game with me. So, you were born a bastard. But your aunt and uncle were good to you. I *know* you, Tommy. Now, tell me once and for all. Did you set off the explosion at Christie Textiles?"

He snuffed out his cigarette. Crossing his arms, he took a few steps away from her. Maybe he would run again. She would have to share her suspicions then. Tell her da. Leave Tommy's fate up to the union membership. Instead, his limp was more pronounced than ever. Sleeping rough had taken its toll. Polly was reminded of what he, too, had sacrificed. But anyone could reach a moment when they'd had enough, when impatience and frustration lashed out quicker than thought.

Finally, he turned. His expression displayed none of his usual morbid humor. He was tired. The deep circles beneath his clouded eyes forced her to step forward and take his roughened hands.

"Tommy, please."

"I didn't do it, Polly."

Relief forced an exhale from her tight chest. "Swear it."

"I swear it on what we had. The good and the bad.

Nor did I have a hand in planning it—nothing of the sort."

"Why weren't you on the floor that day?"

He looked down at their joined hands. To Polly's surprise, his ears were tinged with red. "I was sick with too much drink, found myself in a prostitute's bed. And Lord, girl, my leg has pained me so fierce. I couldn't face another day loading crates and feeling lower than shit. The union meeting riled me all over again, even though I know what you said is true." His smile was lopsided. "I'd voted for you, lass, if that makes any difference."

A lightness filled her heart. She did not doubt him. Not now. But she still needed facts, if only to refute those who would not believe him so readily. "And hiding?"

"Even you doubted me."

Polly's eyes glazed with tears. She blinked them back. Agnes walked toward them, her face composed and her gaze watchful. No judgment there.

"We'll make it right, Tommy. I promise." Pulling away, Polly gave him the strongest smile she could manage past her unhappiness. "Do you believe me? Will you trust me on this?"

He nodded once. The hardness had returned to his mouth, but his eyes were none too sharp. Even his shoulders had relaxed.

"Good," she said. "Then take refuge with your auntie. Tell her I sent you. Until we figure this out and can clear your name, I'll keep anyone from searching for you there."

"Thank you." His gratitude was but a whisper, and

his ears had tipped red once again. A man's pride was a hard, prickly thing. "And Polly?"

She had begun to walk with Agnes, but turned to face her previous lover. "Yes?"

"I'm sorry for what I said about you and the master. I know you wouldn't betray us that way."

The bones in her neck rusted. She said good-bye, but a pit opened in her stomach. That pit didn't swallow her burdens, only opened a wider chasm of doubt. She steered her people with no such doubts.

The question was whether she could steer her desires with equal strength.

Half an hour after talking with Tommy, Polly and Agnes arrived at Mr. Christie's residence: an unassuming two-story detached home on Circus Drive in western Dennistoun. The brick exterior had seen better days, with chipped paint on the front door and on the trim of a small bay window. An overgrown garden had suffered the worst of the winter, leaving behind only withered vines and warped evergreen hedges.

Polly peered down the narrow little street, surprised to realize that the master of Christie Textiles counted such a modest home as his castle. Although, comparing it to the cramped quarters she shared with her family, she couldn't help a twinge of envy. To have her own room would be like a welcome from Saint Peter. The temptation of starting her own household—no matter the husband who made that possible—stemmed almost entirely from that desire. A little space of her own. To breathe. To think and to be.

She and Agnes walked up a crooked flagstone path. Polly used the creaking brass knocker to make their presence known. The cold had seeped into her fingertips, leaving them numb and clumsy. She huddled into her mother's wrap.

A man answered the door, dressed in a uniform coat that had also seen better days. The sleeves were frayed at the hem, and the braid sagged at his collar. His face was oddly triangular, with the distinctive ruddy coloring of a Highland man. No potential for friendliness could be found in his expression. "Yes?"

"We're here to see Mr. Christie. He's expecting us."

"I can offer you tea while you wait."

She had pegged him correctly. His Highland brogue revealed that Alex had hired him locally rather than bringing him from America.

Following him into the foyer, Polly slipped the kerchief off her head. Her eyes were drawn to the ceiling that lifted high above a wide front staircase. Her family's home was tight and small like a warren. Sometimes she felt she'd go mad from the close press of those four walls, but at least they kept warm.

"May I ask your name?"

"Mr. Griggs."

"Mr. Christie's butler?"

"And valet, coachman. As he requires."

Again Polly was puzzled. She had assumed Alex to be of means. How could he be the son of the famous William Christie without inheriting a fortune? Yet he lived in a modest part of town, and his butler attended to the tasks of three men. Was

Alex miserly? Or was there yet another mystery to be solved? That prospect whacked a headache across her brows. She couldn't stand being in possession of so few answers.

"Seat yourselves," he said upon reaching a small parlor. Its lone, wide window faced the street where children had come out to play, likely after hours spent working. The vigor of youth. "I'll ask Mrs. Percy to fix the tea."

With that, he disappeared between a pair of pocket doors.

The smell of vinegar and lemon told of a room recently cleaned. No pictures adorned the walls, and no mementoes decorated the mantel. Only shelves and more shelves, all lined with books. At what cost had he sailed so far with such a collection? Were they so very important to him? Again he trod that line between a street tough and an academic. Polly didn't know which to trust. She had no faith that any man could be both.

Minutes passed as tea was served. She and Agnes talked in hushed tones about the house, their families, and the way the factory had so quickly recovered from its wound. Their chat was so companionable and relaxing, despite the unfamiliar surroundings, that only the opening of the parlor's pocket doors alerted her to Alex's arrival.

His thick shoulder pushed casually against the dark wood frame. In the fading light, his hair shone deep, deep gold, and the green was bright and strong in his hazel eyes. Her mouth dried.

Again he wore simple garments. Although neatly

pressed and well crafted, they were assembled without care. He had shed his coat, which revealed dark blue suspenders pulled taut along his chest. She imagined how easy it would be to slide them down his arms, unfasten a simple row of buttons, and gaze upon bare skin.

She clenched her hands in her lap. "I've brought Mrs. Doward."

"As I see." He turned his eyes away from hers, then greeted Agnes as the older woman stood. "Good of you to come. I'm looking forward to finding the right woman to guide Edmund through the next year and a half."

"Year and a half?" Polly asked in surprise.

"Yes. That's how long we're staying in Scotland."

The bluntness of his words struck her in the chest. She hadn't ever thought to ask. He would leave.

How did one simply . . . *leave*?

What would that be like?

A girl like her never left Glasgow. Not only was it terribly frightening to consider, but it would mean turning her back on her family and her entire community. Not good enough for them, they'd think—worse than a climber like Sarah Fitzgibbons.

Even if the desire to see more of the world sometimes dug holes in her chest and ripped at her heart, she knew it was never meant to be.

"Mrs. Doward," Alex said. "I hope you won't be offended when I say I've already inquired after your family and background."

Polly marveled at how solicitous and kind he sounded. She'd heard very different tones. Suddenly she was greedy for that degree of softness. To be spoken to with such courtesy by a man she fancied. It was as unknown to her as the thought of leaving Glasgow.

"I wouldn't expect no less," Agnes said. "Not from a father worth his salt. And you seem steady enough of mind to be such a man."

If anything, Alex stood a little straighter. Some of the tautness around his mouth eased. "You're welcome to stay here in the house. I have a spare room off the kitchen that is adequate, very snug and warm. The pay will be double what you make at the factory."

As Agnes's eyes widened, he eased into the parlor and stood near a faded yellow brocade settee. The wallpaper over his left shoulder was beginning to peel along the doorjamb.

"I would enjoy that, sir."

"Then consider my offer official. And now it's time you met Edmund."

Alex led the women into Edmund's nursery, where Esther, the nursemaid, was just changing his nappy. Mrs. Doward bustled forward to take over the chore.

Esther only shrugged at the silent dismissal, offering him a graceless bob. "Good evening to you, sir."

Edmund let loose a satisfied belch. Mrs. Doward swaddled him in a way that proclaimed expert levels of practice, then took a seat in the rocking chair near a gentle fire. A soft lullaby barely reached Alex's ears, though they stood but a few feet apart. She appeared as if she'd been sitting in that chair for ages, not a few moments.

"It's good to hold a little one again," she said, almost to herself.

Polly stood against the wall closest to the door. Her gaze had gone soft, an expression he had seen once before. Mamie had often worn such a look of confused yearning. Her inability to tolerate even Alex's gentle touch meant they would never have children, although her longing for one had never ebbed.

Then came Mr. Todd's threats. He challenged the legitimacy of their marriage on the grounds it had not been consummated. That it had been, only once on their wedding night, was no business of his. Mamie's hope was that a child would prove the validity of their union. They would again escape Mr. Todd's machinations, while satisfying her longing to hold a babe in her arms.

Now the fruit of that difficult time was Alex's sole charge—all of Mamie he had left to keep safe. His steady purpose.

The strangeness of seeing Polly in this environment rather than in a place of toil and noise twisted a place under his ribs. With rosy coloring and lively eyes, she looked far too soft to belong anywhere other than places of comfort. That she had removed her kerchief upon entering his domain, revealing her fire-red curls, was a familiarity he craved.

She could relax here. Be at home here.

He tore his attention away from her unexpectedly tender expression.

Mrs. Doward smiled, still rocking Edmund. "Why, this wee one is no fuss at all."

"He's ten months old and already experimenting with solid foods. My hope is that he'll be able to do without a wet nurse very soon. But I would consider your advice on the matter."

"Small for a lad of ten months, if you don't mind my saying, sir."

"He was born four weeks early."

"Och, but he'll be hearty soon enough. Too much of his da and grandda in his bones."

"You knew my father?" Alex asked with a frown.

"Everyone knew little Will Christie. He left, just as he should've. Such a soul could never stay in a place as tight as Calton." She sighed and touched her nose to Edmund's forehead. His eyes had drifted shut. Such contentment. "But those are stories for another time, I think. This wee one needs his sleep."

"If we're in agreement, I'll send you home in the carriage with Griggs to collect your belongings."

"And you say you'll pay me double the factory floor? That hardly seems fitting."

"His safety is paramount. His mother is no longer with us, and my attention must remain focused on the business."

Polly tipped her head to one side. "Have you *no* family to tend him? Her people or yours?"

The idea of the Todds tending to his son had driven Alex to Scotland in the first place, but he was not at all eager to share those details. "No, I'm afraid it's just the two of us."

Mrs. Doward gently laid the infant in his bassinet, then sat beside it to continue the gentle rocking. "Thank you for the opportunity, sir."

"No, thank you. Now if you'll excuse us, I have matters to discuss with Miss Gowan."

With Mrs. Doward's nod, he led Polly into the corridor. Only a few days before, he'd fondled Polly in a rough tavern as if she were a prostitute, beaten and escaped from four constables, and experienced the most potent sexual experience of his life.

It seemed too banal to offer her more tea.

"Come with me," he said.

"Where to?"

No more playacting. She was deep inside his world now. Having known him only from the factory floor, his office, and ribald encounters, he wanted her to see him in his element. Something true, even if he felt that truth warping and changing with each waking day.

But the stars still made sense.

"To my observatory."

Thirteen

Polly didn't follow him straightaway. She studied his wide palm as if she had never seen *any* man's hand. Her mind was still in that nursery. The affection and concern shaping Alex's expression had stolen a small piece of her heart. She could hardly think of something as abstract as an observatory when her questions were so basic. Who had been this frail child's mother? What had she been to her husband? What did he feel now that she was gone?

Even after what had transpired between them, she could not imagine broaching such a personal subject. Perhaps because, in her heart, she knew her motives were not pure. She fancied Alex Christie. Whatever he felt and continued to feel for his late wife were potential complications.

Her body and her ambitions didn't want complications—no more than she'd already conjured.

Finally she took his hand and they ascended the stairs. Creaky floorboards gave away every step. Her pulse sped. Being near him pricked needles under her flushed skin.

He led her through the darkness, beyond the landing at the top of the narrow stairs. After rummaging in the dark Alex lit one lamp, then another, until the room in which they stood was filled with a warm glow. She slid moist palms along her skirts.

Silly, she thought. *You're being silly.*

"Come in," he said from beside the window.

He was standing by the largest telescope she could have imagined. With only a vague impression that the machine was used for stargazing, she'd pictured it more like a spyglass. This device was stabilized on three stout legs. The barrel was wider around than a beer stein. Nothing cluttered the floor around it, as if the space had been cordoned exclusively for its use. Only a small writing desk with a spindle-back chair waited nearby. A few rows of books and another chair covered in blue brocade could not compete. The telescope was the centerpiece. She was drawn toward it just as she was drawn toward Alex.

"It's the largest one I own," Alex said, almost reverently. As if he'd changed into a whole other man. To complete the transformation, he retrieved a pair of wire-rim glasses from among charts and papers on the little desk. "But for weeks now, I could've had it pointed toward a pile of muck for how often I've seen the stars."

Polly smiled. "Glasgow isn't exactly known for clear skies."

Alex stooped over the eyepiece of the telescope.

He squinted, adjusted a few dials, and made notes on a chart of some kind. A half-full cup of tea served as a paperweight atop an inch-thick stack of papers.

He glanced backward. On occasions he appeared positively aristocratic—all strong lines and finely wrought symmetry—but that had clashed with his more brutal impulses. Now his glasses lent such an academic air that Polly momentarily questioned her sanity. What would the likes of him want with a girl like her? When he had treated her more . . . *roughly*, she almost believed him capable of forgoing everything in order to claim her.

On that evening, after having seen his son and his more composed nature, she despaired. A craving she hadn't realized she possessed sank through to her heels. They had no more future than was permitted by their overlapping, occasionally conflicting interests.

And in a year and a half, he would be gone.

She swallowed and tried to find a light voice. "Are you looking for something in particular?"

"My hope was to write a paper to further examine the origin of the Orionids. I haven't had much time of late."

Polly nodded, although her understanding and a big chunk of her confidence were tumbling away in a sloping rush. "Care to explain, Professor?"

"I'm not a professor. Just an instructor until I earn my tenure. I'd hoped my paper would make that happen." His quirk of a smile appeared a little forlorn. "It'll have to wait."

"Some dreams must," she said quietly.

They watched one another for a long moment. The cut on his brow was healing well; he'd removed the stitches. But no matter how scholarly the glasses made him appear, she did not like them. They caught the lamplight and reflected the details of the room. The eyes she so anticipated studying were almost entirely obscured.

He returned to the telescope. "The Orionids are an annual meteor shower. When Earth's orbit takes the planet through the path of a comet, particles from that comet enter our atmosphere. As they plummet to the ground, they catch fire and streak across the sky."

"Shooting stars."

"Exactly." Another adjusted dial. Another note with his nub of a pencil. "The current debate regarding the Orionids has to do with which comet. I hadn't thought to get involved because my opportunities to observe them back home were scarce. The latitude is all wrong. But here . . ."

"Here?"

He straightened. His smile broadened, electrifying Polly down to her soles. What a different man he was when he spoke about astronomy—not so reluctant as when he discussed business, not so rough as when he didn't get his way.

"Have a look. We're in luck tonight."

Polly scraped her teeth across her bottom lip, then smiled back. "Very well."

With more nonchalance than she felt, she stepped toward the telescope. He smelled wonderful. Warm. Clean. A hint of shaving soap still lingered. The scent would be so much more satisfying if she nuzzled the crook of his neck.

He turned both lamps down to near-darkness. "They're just for recording notes. But it's best to let the eyes work without so much contrast."

"Such a ready explanation, master. As if you thought I'd suspect you of less academic motives."

He sighed, still smiling a little. "You're teasing me again."

"Nicely spotted. Now, what am I looking for?"

"You'll see."

Polly leaned over the eyepiece as she'd seen him do.

"Close your other eye," he said.

She did—and gasped. A dozen pinpricks of light seemed near enough to touch. Then they were gone, like sparks climbing out of a bonfire. Another two took their place before fading. Then four more. Pieces of light came and went across the deepening backdrop of night. A sense of floating outside of herself overcame Polly, as if she were watching quick, silvery sprites. So hypnotized was she by their fleeting performance, she nearly forgot about Alex.

But his voice . . .

"Beautiful, aren't they?"

So low and so close.

"Beautiful," she echoed, not knowing what other word would do. She hadn't his breadth of language.

She was surprisingly moved by what she witnessed. A longing lodged in her chest, much as she experienced when thinking about faraway places. A girl like her should be content with knowing such wonders existed, if she ever learned about them at all.

"They're best seen out away from the city," Alex said. "Factory smoke and electric lights obscure their true grandeur."

She straightened, reluctant to leave those stars but knowing her place was on the ground. "Tell me, why did you want to show me this?"

He took off his glasses and set them next to the cup of tea, which could have been days old. His hazel eyes took on that darker, probing directness. Nearly all of the green was stolen by night shadows. His mouth, generally set toward some stern purpose, remained relaxed. A gentle smile held his lips in a soft caress. The dimmed lamplight made a thousand possibilities . . . possible.

"Lord knows what you must think of me after . . . after everything. I wanted to show you who I really am."

Polly impulsively kissed his cheek. "I know what sort of man you are, master."

"Please, don't call me that again."

The distant sound of Edmund's cry jerked his gaze toward the door.

Too overwhelmed by that intimacy, she needed out. Edmund was the perfect excuse. "I'll be leaving now. My family will expect me for supper. And you have your boy to attend."

"True." He stuffed his hands into his trouser pockets. "With Griggs having taken the carriage, I'll hail a hackney to get you home. The hour is late."

Although she wanted to protest, she recognized his determination and relented. "Aye. I'd like that."

It was Monday morning, the day of Alex's second official meeting with the mill masters. His first had been mere days after arriving in Glasgow, and he'd known nothing, held no opinions.

So much had changed since then.

He knew his mood was poor when he welcomed the distraction of Edmund's cries. After heating a bottle, he sat in the nursery rocking chair and held his son.

His thoughts glanced toward Mamie, but perhaps not in the way a widower should regard his late wife. He should feel more guilt about how much he enjoyed Polly's company, not to mention his undeniable sexual response to the young woman. However, Mamie had never been the sort to indulge in jealous fits. Quite the opposite. Her insistence that he take a mistress had been one of the more difficult conversations they'd navigated. Alex had refused. With consideration for his needs alone, taking a discreet mistress would've been the obvious solution.

He'd still held out hope that she would come around. One day.

Holding their son, with the sun angling through the eastern windows, Alex craved her level mind and keen sense of empathy. He wanted to understand Polly Gowan, which might be beyond his capacity. Mamie had been his emotional barometer. Social engagements, dinner parties, casual picnics on the beach—the trivialities of human ritual made sense when she was there to help interpret. He'd gauge her mood and her reactions, then pattern his replies accordingly. They had become friends that way, with weaknesses offset and comfort supplied.

On his own, he had no North Star to guide him.

Worse than that. He had young Edmund to raise up to manhood, without the steadying care Mamie would've applied. Although fragile, maybe even broken, she had been such a generous woman. Fatherhood would not seem quite the terror with her to steady their little family.

"You tell me, Edmund. What do I do?"

Seeking advice from his infant was only slightly less desperate than talking to his dead wife. He closed his eyes. Images of Polly assaulted him almost immediately. Red hair. Wide eyes. Mischievous comments. He'd tasted her ardent kisses and pulsed inside her welcoming heat, but he had yet to see her body. That was a brutal truth.

He could not indulge again, not while keeping his perspective. Why hadn't he left well enough alone?

Dawn found him before sleep did, with Edmund dozing in his arms. Arising, his back stiff, he settled his son into his crib. Agnes met him in the doorway, already dressed. Her salt-and-pepper hair was covered in a floral kerchief. Only two nights on from moving into Alex's home, the woman was already a blessing.

"Good morrow, sir. Just come to check on the wee lad."

"He was fussy during the night. Feeding him did little."

She nodded and softly smiled. "Then I shan't wake him now."

He turned to go—and saw a note slid under his front door. Although he sprinted forth and faced the cool smack of a spring morning, he saw nothing of the message bearer. This was no ordinary postal delivery.

He recognized the handwriting. Josiah Todd didn't even feel the need to disguise his threats anymore. Yet with each new letter, the scrawl was becoming more difficult to read. This was the fourth Alex had received. Always the same threats. Always the same "proof" that Edmund belonged to the Todds.

After ripping open the missive, Alex quickly scanned its contents. Dawn lit the heavy ivory paper, yet nothing could completely illuminate its meaning. Disjointed sentences were interspersed with quotes from Shakespeare and the Bible. Alex swallowed the taste of bile. If the raving words were any measure, Todd was going mad.

Time shrank around Alex in that little foyer. He'd been allotted two years to make Christie Textiles profitable—if only he kept his head and learned quickly. But the mill fire and the threats from his father-in-law chipped away at that luxury of time. His gut told him he had far fewer days.

Damn. Time. He checked a wall clock. The meeting would begin in less than an hour.

He quickly washed, dressed, and shaved. As for the letter, he tucked it in his suit coat. Perhaps he needed a potent reminder of what the meeting meant for his son's future.

In the building that housed the offices of Christie Textiles, he strode past a line of clerks who busily attended their masters' greatcoats. Alex climbed up to the meeting room and dropped his portfolio at the head of a large table surrounded by eight chairs. The boardroom took up most of the second story; its construction dominated by a wide bank of windows that overlooked the street below. The view was impressive, but Alex knew enough about the movement of heat to realize what a colossal waste of resources those windows entailed.

Eventually all of the seats were filled.

"Gentlemen. Good morrow to you."

A selection of replies filtered back, from George Winchester's spoiled Etonian elocution to Frankie McGovern's broad Highlands brogue. The seven men represented Alex's competition and his closest equals in Glasgow society. None had been born to status. All were self-made or the sons of self-made men.

The meeting started politely enough, although plagued by conflicting reports and agendas. Alex kept his temper. Initially. He was too busy taking notes when the odd tidbit fell from careless lips: production quotas, wages, absentee rates. He was still a newcomer to the industry, and conflicting courses of action demanded data. After sorting through the figures, he would make his decisions. Later.

As the hours progressed, however, the resonance of the conversation slid toward hostility. Even belligerence. Insults against the union. Disdain for lazy, corrupt constables. And the beginnings of an agreement to lower wages.

Alex's skin prickled. Yes, he had worked with Mamie for social justice. And yes, he was honoring Polly's entreaty to listen on behalf of the union. But those concerns conflicted with one stark fact: the son he'd held that morning was not safe. He touched the place where Josiah Todd's letter burned like a reminder of hell.

His mill *would* earn a profit. It was well behind in fulfilling orders because of the sabotage, and reserve cash stores had been drained because of the repairs. The board threatened him almost daily. Julian Bennett's and George Winchester's polite words around the meeting table didn't erase the knowledge that they wanted to pick the bones of his failure.

The bickering increased. Grew louder. Became even more insulting. The barely civilized fervor grated over his skin and dug into his brain, until it was too much.

"Enough! You sound like lads fighting in a park. This is supposed to be a business meeting, for Christ's sake."

"Well, then, talk business." Bennett leaned forward over his sizable paunch. "Any progress been made on the sabotage at your factory?"

"I'm not at all of a mind to have such vandalism revisited," said Frankie McGovern. The hard Highland accent matched the sharpness in his eyes. Even Alex's father had not revealed such a cutthroat expression. "Neither, I believe, does your board of directors."

"My investigation is proceeding. In fact, a lead has given me hope I'm growing closer to discovering the man's identity."

"Lead?" Bennett raised his eyebrows. "Do tell."

"I have reason to believe a man named Jack Findley was involved."

"That's ridiculous," Bennett said with a laugh. "Findley is my overseer. Where did you get the idea he was involved?"

"Where do you get the idea that his position at your mill exempts him from suspicion?"

The hulking man leaned his elbows against the table. His tight, beady little eyes were swallowed by his cheeks when he smiled. "It doesn't. But perhaps you'd like to know that Findley was at Idle Michael's the night Tommy Larnach threatened to burn down your mill. He said it right there in front of Findley, bragging to anyone who'd listen."

"My sources within the police regard him as the prime suspect," Winchester added. "Ask that Gowan girl you're so close with these days. See what she says about how Larnach has no alibi for the morning of the explosion."

Tommy had been at the union meeting. What had he and Polly really argued about? Perhaps Alex had got it wrong from the start. Walt Nells could've told him about Findley for reasons other than protecting Polly. Maybe he knew that, as a shipbuilder, his suspicions about Tommy would have been received poorly by the weaver's union. His reference to Jack Findley may have been a roundabout way of indicting Tommy without betraying anyone outright.

What did that say about Polly? She'd been willing to risk a great deal at Old Peter's. Had she been duped by Tommy? Possible, given their long history. Alex thought she would keep hunting for the saboteur, even if the guilty party proved to be her first lover. About that, however, he had no proof—only the hope she was as good as her word.

"I *will* ask her," Alex said at last. His throat burned and his head throbbed. "Many tasks occupy my time, but none rivals bringing the responsible party to justice."

"Unless it's tupping a certain union girl." Winchester's posh tones added an extra layer of filth to his words.

Alex stanched an impulse to choke the bastard. "We can remain civil, or we can step outside. I don't appreciate baseless accusations. And surely it would make sense for the rest of you to help solve this mystery. All of your factories could be at risk."

"That's true, Christie," Bennett said. "And Larnach is our man. The constables are on constant lookout, but he seems to have vanished. We'll breathe easier once he's locked up for good."

Alex stood. The building bore his family name, and his patience had been scraped raw. He spread his hands flat on the table and leaned into his stance. He'd seen his father affect just such a pose over his huge mahogany desk, which had been intimidating as hell even as an adult.

"Make no mistake," he said. "When discussing matters that involve my business, I *am* the final word."

"You'll check that attitude right now, if you know what's best for your bottom line." Fat, frustrating

Julian Bennett did not blink when he challenged Alex. "Shall I explain why?"

"Do try."

"The eight of us represent the last holdouts of textiles in Glasgow. If you cannot align your interests with ours, then Christie Textiles will fall outside of the protections that come with collective bargaining. You'll be at the mercy of the union, rather than the other way around. Then God help you, man. Your board of directors will eat you alive."

"The union has yet to approach any of us with demands, concerns, or ultimatums of any kind. Why borrow trouble?"

Bennett smiled. "Because of the pay decrease."

"I still don't see why it's necessary," Alex said, repressing his growing frustrations.

Frankie McGovern opened a cigar case and set about lighting one. "My dear Mr. Christie, the price of our goods is slipping, especially now that the Americans compete on such a massive scale. To save costs, we're cutting wages by ten percent and reducing staff by an equal percentage. In four weeks."

Alex's gut coiled. How much would ten percent affect Polly and her family? Or anyone in his employ? He couldn't begin to imagine what a ten percent reduction in the workforce would do to Calton. Were these reasonable cuts or petty punitive means of imposing the masters' authority?

"We had it mistaken, gentlemen," he said. "My failure to discover the saboteur does not stand as your biggest threat of violence. They'll strike."

Bennett banged his meaty fist on the tabletop.

"Then we'll crush them until they *cannot* strike. The police will be involved. The ringleaders in jail. They must understand the consequences for standing in the way of progress."

Or profit.

That word had the power to shock Alex to stillness. What was he doing arguing against such measures? He was in Scotland to earn a profit. Nothing else mattered.

Or at least, nothing else *should* matter.

He gathered his hat, greatcoat, and attaché. God, he was angry. He wanted just one man in the room to look at him the wrong way. No one did. The decision was his to make.

"Very well. Have it your way. With the consequences on all our heads." Alex tipped his hat. "Good day, gentlemen."

He strode out of the room, needing air and time to calm down. His true colors—bloody and dark—yearned to take control. There in an austere meeting room, his first instinct had been toward violence. Findley and Larnach. Winchester, Bennett, and the specter of Josiah Todd.

What the hell was happening? When had the thought of disappointing a factory girl become tantamount to a criminal act?

After all, he'd just agreed to the masters' cost-cutting scheme. Against all logic, his legs grew heavy and his chest tensed around each breath—the feeling that he'd just agreed to something very, very wrong.

Fourteen

Outside Polly's tenement, Alex climbed into the carriage behind the swish of her skirts. The air between them was thick with tension, although that was mostly his doing. He kept a great many secrets from her now, just as she likely kept a wide variety to herself.

Then why the impulse to see her? He'd started the morning with the intention of dragging the truth out of her. But the sky had cleared unexpectedly, even if his thoughts remained overcast and gray. No matter the masters' opposition and Alex's renewed distrust, he wanted to show her something beautiful before her ambitions and hopes were crushed.

After all, he was one of those masters.

When the wage decrease became known, she would never speak to him again. Yet he hoped that one day she could look back on something of their time together and think it worthwhile. He would give her an experience that had nothing to do with unions or mills or even sex.

"Griggs," he called. "Alexandra Park."

Polly angled him a curious look.

He returned her confusion. "You've heard of it, yes? On Cumbernauld?"

She crossed her arms beneath her breasts and looked straight ahead. "I thought we were going for a drink. But maybe it's some sort of test. How much of my own city don't I know? How small is my world?"

"Nothing of the sort. Just more of me showing off. We don't always have to be at odds."

"You still haven't told me what happened at the masters' meeting the other day, and I don't think you will. How *can* it be any other way?"

Guilt hit him like a blow. He defended his reasons as doggedly as he would've defended his own body.

"I enjoy your company, Polly. And I like to think you're not with me just because of union ambitions."

"Are you flattering yourself?" Her smile returned. He could always breathe easier when she smiled, even if a tease propelled it into being.

"Yes," he said. "Yes, I am."

He unfurled her tight hands and took one in his own. Asking her about Tommy—and receiving a true answer—remained his intention. Maybe he could do that without arguing. She no longer looked on him with suspicion. If Polly trusted him with the truth, they could avert disaster on all sides.

The lamps along Cumbernauld Road tinted the air pale orange. Soon they would be out of reach of those artificial beacons. He had thought to bring his telescope, but what he intended to show her was amazing enough when seen with the naked eye.

"Would you tell me about his mother? Edmund's mother?"

Her question jerked his gaze away from the carriage window. Forget the politics of Glasgow. Her question dug straight into his heart, dragging him back to the moment Mamie died. Polly couldn't know the flood instigated by her question. Mostly he felt guilt. He'd never been able to do enough, with her death as the ultimate failure. Only Edmund remained—a slim hope of redeeming himself to the woman he'd sworn to protect.

To endure that crush of emotion, as he always had, he turned to logic. A recitation of facts.

He let go of her hand and cleared his throat. Then again. "Mamie was never a robust woman. I think . . ." Training his eyes on a distant pinprick of lamplight, he said, "I think her body couldn't stand another moment of pregnancy. She died three hours after his birth."

"Alex, I'm sorry."

"I am, too. She didn't deserve what happened."

"But, if she was so frail . . . ?"

The question was obvious, even if she didn't finish. "She wanted a baby. It was the only time when she truly put her foot down and insisted."

"How long were you married?"

"Just over six years, but we'd been friends since I was fourteen. Our families summered by the sea, with vacation homes a quarter mile apart along a Cape Cod beach. Those seaside visits had been as close as our families ever managed to be."

That is, until the wedding forced old-money

American blue bloods to share a Manhattan banquet hall with the hodgepodge of Sir William's progeny. Gareth and Gwyneth had been thirteen, spoiled rotten, and delightfully beguiling. Viv, still unmarried, hadn't yet emerged from her shell. The token outsider among the siblings, she had been more likely to talk business with their father.

When Alex learned Josiah Todd had threatened Mamie on the morning of their wedding, demanding that she call it off . . . The man deserved what he got. He had attended the ceremony with a busted lip and a hideous black eye. Alex had emerged without a scratch, satisfied that he'd finally said his piece. Without words.

"You must have loved her very much to commit to her at such a young age."

"I did. Our marriage was quiet. Worthwhile."

"Worthwhile?"

Alex couldn't help but hear her confusion. For a woman as vibrant as Polly, his relationship with Mamie would likely seem too reserved, but at the time, he hadn't given it a second thought.

"I walked side by side with her in protests against unjust laws. We organized petitions and lectures and the like. In a way, it was the heart of our relationship. She was adamant that women be able to make choices for themselves. We shared many things in common—hobbies, tastes, our educations—"

He broke off. Polly stiffened at his side, as if she, too, understood the implications of his words. He had practically declared her less than his equal. Alex wanted to kick himself.

Whatever her thoughts, she only breathed out through her nose. "I'll stop asking questions," she said softly. "I'm so used to knowing everything about everyone. They like to share details with me, because often I can help."

"I saw that at the meeting hall, and at the church banquet. You considered every entreaty with the whole of your attention. And for so many people. Your interest in their circumstances is admirable."

"I don't do it to be admirable. I *like* it. Not only can I help, it gives me a sense that I'm not the only one who's made sacrifices. So many have it far worse."

Worse? Alex had seen the state of the tenement she called home. On occasion he had seen corrugated tin shacks that exuded a greater sense of solidity. In that way, if no other, Polly reminded him of Mamie. Both were essentially selfless creatures, who thought beyond their own suffering. Perhaps aiding others helped ease their personal pains. That went a long way toward explaining his protective instincts toward both women, even if other feelings were diametrically different.

They fell into silence as the streetlamps became more sparse. Alex gave instruction to stop the carriage, and they emerged into the night. "Wait for us here," he told Griggs. "Inside the cab if you're too chilly."

Alexandra Park had been founded by the city to improve conditions among the working poor, but it was located far north of the worst neighborhoods. This open-air preserve was far preferable to the one just west of town, owned by one of the University of Glasgow's largest donors, where Alex had been invited by the dean during his first week in town. That estate sported every hallmark of new money: Greek-inspired columns, ostentatious topiary, gilt accents in every conceivable location. His father would've judged such creations the "reward for a life well-lived." Alex had thought it tacky and embarrassing.

He and his father had indulged in no small number of such squabbles. Now it just seemed petty. Mamie's death, Edmund's poor heath, Mr. Todd's threats all held sway over Alex, as did Polly, who walked beside him into the darkened park. Very little else mattered. Perhaps that narrowing of priorities changed him so drastically. No lofty distractions. Just the fundamentals.

Such a humbling realization, and yet he felt more powerful and decisive for it.

"You're very trusting," he said, forcing lightness into his words. "Do you truly have any idea what I've planned?"

"I assume it can't be any more perilous than what we've already chanced."

"I hadn't meant to . . . ah, damn. Never mind."

"Breathe, Alex. Don't worry about the rest."

They climbed a steep slope that angled up from Cumbernauld Road. The trees gave way to an open copse at the top of the rise. The land here was far too irregular for buildings, which made it the perfect scrap of wilderness to donate to a grateful city. Not that Alex harbored any cynicism about the seller's motives—just an honesty about how such decisions were made.

"Here we are," he said.

He unfurled a blanket over a large, flat rock. The grass would've been softer, but the evening dew had already soaked his trouser cuffs. Polly thanked him and perched on the rock, hugging her knees.

Only then did her eyes widen, catching sight of the fat, quiet duck pond far below. "Oh my. That is some view."

"I thought so, yes."

"How did you find out about this place?"

"I visited the university and inquired after its head of astronomy, Professor Netherfield. He recommended all manner of places around the city for making unobstructed observations. This spot is my favorite so far. Business has meant far fewer excursions than I'd hoped."

"The Green suits well enough for me."

"I would've enjoyed a place like the Green when I was a child. Familiar and natural. Manhattan was always such a bustle."

The springy curls she'd unbound caught a light breeze and snagged across her face. She smiled, tucking the strands back behind her ears. "You'd only believe that from the outside looking in. I'm convinced of it."

"Then how do you see it?"

"Sometimes it's all I ever want. And sometimes it's a cage. More of the latter, of late. But I don't like to think on it."

"No?"

"I should be grateful."

He lay beside her on the blanket, resting on his elbows. "'Should' is a difficult word."

"Yes," she said with a lilting laugh. "That's right, exactly."

"You know what you *should* do?"

"What's that?"

"Just look up."

Polly shot him a wry grin, as if she didn't believe something so simple would make a whit of difference. He knew better. Because when she looked toward the clear, open sky, she gasped.

Smiling to himself, Alex settled back on the blanket and pillowed his hands behind his head. From that vantage, not a single speck of outside light played tricks with his eyes. Only the heavens remained, made brilliant by streamers of iridescent color.

Another amazed sound from Polly. "What in the world is that?"

"You've not seen the northern lights?"

"No."

"I just assumed . . . that is, the latitude means it's not uncommon to see them during periods of high solar activity."

Rather than take offense, as he feared she might, Polly only chuckled. "Lord, Alex, you've seen my home. It's like living in a brightly lit well."

"Well said."

Greens and an eerie purple danced high in the atmosphere, far off toward the Arctic pole. He'd seen the aurora borealis from Nova Scotia and once from Greenland. Those vantages had been better, but he'd never liked to leave Mamie alone for long. Now, this moment with Polly wove into each of his veins and promised to remain just as bright. She made it so. A ribbon the color of an unripe pear faded upward into space, where it transformed to orange and deeper red. His eyes would only just focus on a strip of color before it moved and shifted once more.

She squeezed his hand. "But what *is* it?"

"No one really knows. Some theorize it has to do with Earth's magnetic pull, or wind storms in space. All we know is that they occur around the equinoxes—spring and autumn—and they're more prominent in the northern half of the world."

"So what we're witnessing is mysterious and special?"

"Absolutely."

"Never would've imagined such a thing in Glasgow."

Alex turned. He needed to see her face. So many emotions were difficult for him to interpret—those little clues others read, but which served only to muddle his thinking. Seeing her face helped erase that confusion.

"How do you do it, Polly?"

The green and gold in the sky chased washes of color across her pale skin. "Do what?"

"Keep your spirits up. For example, at the meeting hall. Had anyone else given the speech you did, I would've thought them terribly naïve or even manipulative. But you meant every word, and everyone there knew it. You want the people in your union to fare well."

"Naturally. Others might have different motives, but I'm not so complicated."

"Oh, I don't believe that." He touched her cheek, where loose curls tickled and teased. Her skin was cold. He edged closer on the blanket, and their bodies traded heat.

"I love my people," she said at last. "I'm very proud of them. This isn't an easy life. Maybe that's why I have such pride and ambition for them, often more than they do for themselves."

"But how have *you* managed to survive here? It's dirty and poor and violent. Yet, you keep smiling. How?"

She grew quiet, making Alex wonder if he'd stepped past some invisible boundary. But she was still Polly, and that meant taking him by surprise. "You want to know the secret?"

"Is there one?"

"Of course. Otherwise I'd have gone mad a long time ago." She rested their twined hands on her stomach, looking up. "You make shields. A half dozen or so. You stake them all around, all overlapped to keep out the pain and disappointment. But you leave a tiny crack, right in the front. That's for letting the happiness in."

Alex forgot to breathe. He looked to the sky once again. Being able to name each star held nothing to the way he saw the aurora anew. Through her eyes. He had wanted to show her a natural marvel, to give them both something beautiful to sustain them through what promised to become an ugly few weeks.

Instead, she had given him a gift. He saw color

like a field of flowers and movement like a dancing angel. Science fell away to reveal only beauty. When he could breathe again, he unconsciously mimicked her soft exhale.

She was the most singular woman he had ever known. The scent of her was as clean and vital as the sweet spring grass that surrounded them. He didn't yet understand her motives. She could be the most practiced temptress in history. She could know the identity of every perpetrator and agitator.

At that moment, he hardly cared.

"Polly, will you let me take you home? Stay with me tonight."

Green eyes reflected myriad colors. She traced a finger along one of his suspenders. "Should I fear for my virtue, Mr. Christie?"

This time he managed a wry smile when faced with her teasing. "Yes, Miss Gowan. Very much."

Nervousness invaded Alex's carriage. Polly couldn't remember a time when her body vibrated with such heady anticipation. He had shown her treasures. And with his words, with the closeness of his big, solid body, he promised pleasure. The rest of their troubles would be sorted out later. Just . . . later. She felt a strong premonition that this would be their last time together. Surely whatever he hid about the mill masters' meeting boded ill for the union.

And if he found out she was helping to hide Tommy . . .

So much would eventually wreck their fragile peace. The aftertaste of their brief moments together would be sour. She knew that. But the goodness—she would keep that close for the rest of her life. Tonight was for letting the happiness in. One last time.

"Smoke," he said harshly. "Do you smell smoke?"

Cold iced her skin. Pure fear. "Yes. Oh, God. We're so close to Calton."

The sound of sirens cut through an otherwise clear, quiet night. She slid the carriage open and poked her head outside. Smoke was gathering on the southern horizon.

"The factory district," she gasped.

"Griggs!" Alex's shout carried well. "Make haste!"

The carriage barreled down the tight cobblestone streets. Polly bit her teeth to keep them from knocking together, and clutched the leather bench, digging her nails into the resilient softness.

Not again. Please, be an accident. Please.

Griggs took the corner at a dangerous pace. Alex grabbed her around the shoulder, steadying them both. His mouth was tight, his jaw solid and clenched.

The carriage braked, stopped, shuddered with sudden lack of momentum. Polly was the first out the door to see that Christie Textiles remained unscathed. For now. Instead the fire brigade had converged across the street, surrounding Winchester Fabrics.

The blaze was massive. Heat blasted out from the building in a steady wave that created its own windstorm. The factory would burn. Hundreds of livelihoods would be lost. And the cycle of blame and violence would intensify.

With the mill locked up for the night, there would

be no ready witnesses. Accident or sabotage—a mystery. She had no doubt which option the constables and masters would assume. Even now, glancing at Alex, she found his face as grim as she'd ever seen.

The constables arrived.

"Alibi, Miss Gowan," said Andrews.

A blush rivaled the heat surging from the building as the east wall toppled. "I was with Mr. Christie."

"Is that true, sir?"

"Yes." And yet Alex's expression was not easy.

Polly feared for the future of Calton as she never had. If the masters did not rip the union to shreds, it would be torn apart by suspicion and radical opinions. And no matter her alibi, she would bear the burden of the investigation, as well as the responsibility for making sure no one went hungry. And now, Alex showed her no special regard, no hint of the quiet, amazing moments they had shared at the park.

He stood beside her, but Polly felt entirely alone.

With a booming crash, another wall sank into a swirl of flames. Firemen scampered back from the singed bulge of brick and wood. Polly caught the end of her mother's shawl and pressed it against her nose to keep out the choking flush of smoke.

The police hustled her and Alex off the pavement, away from the blaze. They watched in silence.

George Winchester arrived. The lean, ungainly man's expression darkened as he edged toward his ruined mill and surveyed the wreck of his enterprises. Firemen held him back as the constables converged and conducted what appeared to be animated discussions, with Winchester losing his temper and Andrews signaling for calm.

"Go home, Polly," Alex grated out. "Tell Griggs to take you. I don't want you here."

"I can stay and help."

"No." His eyes were icy and as distant as those of a stranger. "If I'm going to watch these flames crawl across the street and burn down my mill, I'd like to do it alone. Go."

Before Polly could escape his coldness and make it to the carriage, a grim-faced constable whirled her around. "You'll be coming to the station with me, Miss Gowan."

"I told you, I haven't done anything. Mr. Christie is my alibi!" She couldn't help the note of panic in her voice. Her emotions were far too raw.

"I'm afraid that doesn't matter tonight. Now, where are your friends? The rabble-rousers your father looks after."

"At home, sleeping off twelve-hour shifts."

"And six-hour drinking binges. Good. They'll not be hard to find."

Hair whipped across her face. She shoved it back. "But why would we do this? These are our jobs at stake."

"Because you lot are none too bright, miss."

"Oh, I wouldn't say that." Simply hearing Alex's words, invested with so much authority, eased the horrible strain in her chest. But she couldn't depend on even that scant relief, as Alex growled, "In fact, she's rather too bright for her own good."

"Alex—"

"Constable, Miss Gowan will be taken to my home, where I will question her personally." He glared at the man with the prominent white mustache. "I'm sure you have no objections."

The constable nodded, a stark reminder that the law bowed to the industry masters. "No objections, sir. If you discover anything at all, please do your duty and report your findings. Whoever did this *will* be punished."

Polly heard the words, the threats, but she looked only to Alex. Smooth brows. Placid lips. And detached hazel eyes that reflected an eerie orange. Star charts and the dials on his telescope were more accessible.

Fear blossomed in her stomach. From the first, she'd been able to suss little glimmers of where his mind dwelled. Now, when it was most important, she found the details of his handsome face but no emotion. She desperately wanted to see softness where he had none to offer.

The constable walked back toward where Mr. Winchester still ranted. Polly watched him go, if only to avoid looking at her cold rescuer once again.

"Return to my house and wait there. Do you understand?"

"And if I refuse?"

"Then you won't need to worry about the constables. I'll hunt you down myself."

Fifteen

$\mathcal{A}$*lex* paid the cabbie and entered through the front door, mindful of possibly waking Edmund. There, he finally allowed his mask to slip. No longer the mill master, he was simply a man—an exhausted man whose future was only as certain as his next breath.

Stopping in the foyer, he yanked off his ascot and prepared for what was sure to be an impossible discussion with Polly.

Agnes Doward met him there first.

"Mr. Christie, sir, come with me. Please."

He was about to protest. He reeked of smoke and needed food. But her pinched expression spoke to him on an elemental level.

Edmund.

He followed her down the hall. The panic that clawed up his chest burned like the flames that had consumed Winchester Fabrics. Christie Textiles had been spared. And yet he'd come *that* close to losing everything. Again.

As they rounded the corner into Edmund's nursery, his panic intensified and lodged much closer to his heart, where thoughts of his son nestled. He shoved his fingers through his hair, then drilled both fists into his trouser pockets. It was all he could do to rein in his temper and keep from bellowing questions.

Just inside the nursery, he slammed to a halt. Even gripping the door frame wasn't enough to abate his visceral shock.

Polly sat in the rocking chair, with Edmund in her arms.

"What are you doing?"

She looked from him to Edmund, eyes wide. Maybe he deserved her startled expression because his question had been a full-fledged shout.

But Polly Gowan was rarely powerless for long. Her back pulled straight and tight. "Agnes needed a break. She's been up with him all night."

"That's her job."

"Would you like to feel his forehead? Then maybe you'll realize what a trial she's endured."

The certainty in her voice said he wouldn't like what he found. Sure enough, Edmund's skin burned with fever. The world dropped out from below his feet.

"Jesus. He's ill?"

"Tell him, Agnes."

"Since just after you left, sir. He was fussy and wouldn't take a bottle."

Alex knelt before the rocking chair. He touched his son's brow. The staggering pounding in his chest would not be quiet. "I should've been here. Why didn't you send word, woman?"

The color drained from Mrs. Doward's face.

But it only flushed brighter along Polly's broad cheekbones. "How would she have managed that, you dunce? Quit acting a bully, blaming her. He was safe and cared for as well as could be. She deserves your thanks, not your temper. Do you want to run her off after such a short time in your employ? I'd like to see you manage without her. Agnes, dear, what have you done for the boy?"

After a pause, the woman straightened her spine. "The same as I would for any fevered wee child. Cool cloths to his forehead. Bathing him with tepid water. I made broth. Sometimes lighter liquids are easier on their upset tummies than milk. He's kept it down with no trouble." She met Alex's eyes with much firmer resolve. "You hired me because of my experience, raising four babes of my own. His fever *will* break, Mr. Christie. Even ones as small as this are heartier than you'd think."

Alex dropped his head to the rocking chair's hard arm. She had been a godsend for Edmund. For Alex, too. He'd been freed to pursue all manner of terrible decisions.

He stood stiffly and offered a slight bow. "Forgive me. Of all the people who deserve my scorn, you are certainly not one. I ask that you accept my appreciation, instead."

Mrs. Doward only nodded as if the praise was a given.

Polly began rocking again. "When I arrived here and saw how frazzled she was, I offered to take her place for a spell."

The angle of her neck as she looked down at his son . . . Icicles of fear took a different turn. He wanted her. He wanted her beyond sense and good judgment. And he wanted to see that exact sight over and over—not just holding Edmund, but any number of babes they brought into the world.

"Now it's off to bed with him." Mrs. Doward took the sleeping boy from Polly and gently settled him into his crib. "Mr. Christie, I'll wake you if he worsens. Trust that if he's sleeping, he's on the mend."

"Again, I thank you."

Feeling stiff and dazed, he left the nursery. A drink. He needed a drink.

A half hour later, he sat in his observatory with the lamps cold. The northern lights would be dimming soon, making the Orionids easier to see. But he couldn't think past how fiercely his body twisted and tightened. He was a snake ready to lash out at the least little movement.

Of course, that movement would be Polly. The sound of her footsteps in the corridor should have been more tentative. They were not. As sure and exuberant as ever.

With a sharp flick of his wrist, he downed the last of his tumbler of whiskey.

Across the previous few weeks, the man he'd known had been replaced with a greedy creature. Curiosity compelled him to discover exactly how

hard she would push his crumbling boundaries—
and just how hard he would push back. What,
exactly, would it take to make a woman like Polly
Gowan run?

He needed her to run. To leave him alone before
he did them both an injustice.

"Alex?"

"Go away."

"Edmund's asleep now. I told Agnes to try to rest
for a while."

"Good. Now do as I say."

But she kept coming. First it was her silhouette in
the doorway, outlined by charcoal shadows.

"This is the last warning I'm giving you," he
growled. "Get out."

"What about the fire? You were the one who told
me to come here."

"Circumstances have changed. Go sleep on the
parlor settee. I'll talk as rationally as I can in a few
hours."

She stepped closer. Alex tightened his hand
around the crystal tumbler, but the jagged facets
didn't bite deeply enough into his palm. "Things
have changed. You're worried about your son."

"Don't do this."

"What? Offer my sympathies? Or my assurances?
Outside yourself, you have the most attentive person in the world caring for him right now. He's a lot
stronger than you credit him."

She crossed the floor and stood behind him. The
beat of her body pulsed against the back of his neck.
He wanted them both stripped bare, to feel her heat,

skin to skin. Clamping his back teeth together, he prayed for strength—strength to behave as a man ought.

"If we'd been able to return here, with no fire to interrupt—"

He flinched. "Again, circumstances have changed."

Gentle fingers brushed the hair back from his ears. She placed her hands on his shoulders and stroked, slowly, deeply, working out the tension. It was all he could do to keep from moaning. "But if they hadn't, what would you want from me? Right now?"

"I'm not playing this game, Polly."

She kept up her steady massage. Clever fingers dug into his aching tendons and impossibly tight muscles. The rhythm of her caresses didn't increase, but the intensity did—until she was slightly out of breath, and the huff of each exhale gusted against his nape. Alex was stretched between anger and the most exquisite erection he'd ever known. All he could do was hold still. Perfectly still. Lest he haul her to the ground and pound away his frustrations.

She leaned in closer and brushed a kiss on his ear. "Tell me. What do you want?"

"You," he ground out. "Between my legs."

Her hands stopped. Alex's heart stopped. Every caution he'd ever known burst to nothingness.

He'd wanted her to go, and that must have been the perfect thing to say, because she stepped away.

Only, she didn't leave.

She simply walked with measured grace to stand before him. Her knees nudged his apart. He wanted light, to better see her expression, but that would mean breaking the spell. Instead he reminded himself to continue taking in oxygen and exhaling carbon dioxide. He was capable of nothing but that control—a gift to them both.

Polly pried the tumbler from his clenched hand and set it on the desk. She sank to her knees. Any blood remaining in his brain fled south. That rush was like downing shots of whiskey until the stars spun, fell, crashed.

A glance of moonlight from the window caught her profile and illuminated her soft half smile. "I like that you told me."

"Polly."

"And you'll just have to believe me that I've always been . . . curious."

She undid his trouser buttons. One after another. That she was going through with this was destroying his mind.

Slim, cool fingers encircled him. Alex hissed a sharp curse. This was wrong in so many ways. He clamped his hands around the armrests. He wanted and wanted until she must have been able to feel his lust, as it seeped through his pores and ignited in the sharp electric air.

"You're thinking," she whispered.

"Yes."

"Stop. Or I'll have to."

Christ, that lovely neck. She was sturdy and strong in so many ways, but her neck was a picture of elegant perfection. Regal. Proud. And utterly depraved as she bent low to his groin. He stiffened at the first brush of breath against his heated skin. His toes curled in his shoes. His mouth had dried to the point where he couldn't speak, even if he still felt compelled to.

But he didn't. Not anymore. Not so close to bliss. He only craved Polly right there, on her knees, as her lips parted.

Polly took her own advice. She stopped thinking. Every other concern could wait, because she belonged exactly where she knelt.

They deserved this. Both of them. Something raw and stupid and memorable—a moment in time that wouldn't be lost among so many others, before the dawn came and the worst happened. The premonition she'd felt that this would be their last night together was now fact.

Oh, but she had no idea what she was doing. All she followed was a desire to unwind him. Unhinge him. Beneath his many layers, he harbored a darkness she had become obsessed with knowing. She'd sampled so many delicious tastes and only wanted more.

He throbbed where she gripped him fully. Beneath the lingering haze of smoke they both still wore, she caught the scent of a more erotic perfume: his skin, made potent in arousal. She rubbed her cheek along his shaft and gloried in how his thighs tensed.

Just you wait.

With a deep breath for courage, she touched her tongue to his swollen head. The skin was incredibly smooth and slightly salty. Needing more, she licked with quick, wet sweeps. If he held himself any more rigidly, constricted inside that big, tense body, he was going to explode. That made her grin.

"What's so funny?"

"You're supposed to be enjoying this," she whispered against his taut stomach.

"I am."

"Doesn't feel like it. Feels like you'd scamper like a rabbit if I even blinked."

He groaned and laid his head back. "Good God, you're teasing me at a time like this."

"If not now, then when?"

Smiling more broadly now, she resumed her exploration of his manhood. The shaft was lined with veins that pulsed a steady reminder of his excitement. Without much light, she used her sensitive tongue to trace every furrow and ridge. Slowly she learned him, coming to know exactly where he was most sensitive.

Soon tracing and tasting weren't enough. She'd thought this would be all for him, until restless energy settled between her legs. It was a low throb, an ache that needed to be satisfied. She had experienced the same greedy pulse when he'd teased her with his elegant fingers—fingers free of a workingman's calluses.

She had just permitted him entrance past the barrier of her lips when his pelvis thrust. Just a bit. It was enough to give her hope. He wasn't going to fight this forever. An unexpected thrill of competition powered her as surely as desire. After a few experimental tries she found the rhythm that imitated what he'd done to her in their private alley sanctuary. When she needed a breath, she slid her lips off the head and goaded him with languorous strokes of her tongue.

His breathing sounded almost pained. Labored. Edgy. Always through his nose, still holding it in.

She flashed him a playful look. "I'm convinced your cock is the only part of you that isn't lying."

"Christ, Polly, what do you want from me?"

"Your participation. There's no way I'll let you think I did this on my own. Come morning you'll think me some wicked seducer sent to drive you mad."

A ghost of a smile peeked out. "Oh, but you are."

"I do rather like it when you put it that way. But I mean it. Show me exactly how much you're enjoying this."

In truth, she'd expected more resistance. But, as his long body relaxed on an exhale, the stiff muscles of his thighs let go of their strain. He slowly released the armrests, then flexed his fingers as if working them back to life.

Fascinated, she watched as he moved to touch her face. First with his fingertips, then with his knuckles, he outlined her cheeks, chin, nose. She turned to nestle her lips against his palm. After smoothing his thumbs over her temples, he dipped around to cup the back of her head. He threaded his fingers through her curls, down to her scalp.

Polly still gripped his member. His expression was even softer now, lulling her with intent eyes filled with wonder. Lulling, because she was taken by surprise when his hands tightened in her hair. She felt every intention and every wish in that strong hold.

"You're beautiful, Polly."

"I'm not."

"Woman, you'd argue with a tree stump. Believe me—on this score, I win." He reinforced his words with a slight tug on his fistful of hair, proving the full extent of his grip. "But I hate that you stopped. Don't do it again."

She smirked. "Of course."

She resumed, only this time, she had Alex to guide her. The pressure of his hands cupping her skull, guiding her, was unbearably intimate. She knew each lick and nip he enjoyed, and every time she pleasured him just so. They dissolved into a silent call and response. His sensations became hers to command, just as his wishes were hers to grant. The arousal of that trust was as unexpected as it was intoxicating.

She accidentally dragged her front two teeth over his firm head. Rather than pull away, he groaned. "Again," he whispered.

So, very carefully, she obeyed. Just tiny, nipping scrapes. His hands flexed. Lean masculine hips pulsed. Shortened movements. She encouraged him to give in with every stroke of her palm along his shaft.

"Polly," he choked out. "All the way now."

Her insides melted on a hot rush. Wetness slicked her feminine core. He hadn't found his release yet, but she had won.

She relaxed her jaw and took him deep.

A low groan rumbled down through his torso. He shifted slightly, changing the angle, encouraging her to take even more. She swirled her tongue, bobbed an even pace—until he was too deep for even that.

He stilled her head and his hips took over.

Polly closed her eyes, braced her hands around the backs of his knees. And she opened to him.

His rhythm wasn't fast or violent so much as intent. He took his time with every thrust, pushing as far as she could take. She sucked him, followed by long, slow withdrawals. That sensual lethargy helped her relax. Only his merciless grip on her hair and the gasping sound of his breath gave him away. He wanted more. And still, he wasn't taking it.

So Polly fought back.

She tossed her head back, completely off him, and clamped her lips shut. A quick glance at his expression revealed bewildered surprise, like a petulant boy who hadn't gotten his way.

"Do it, Alex. All the way, or we stop now."

He jerked. Closed his eyes. And brought her face back down.

Polly braced herself, because there was no softness left in him now. His hips did the work. He set a pace that matched the beat of her blood. Fast. Hard. Unyielding. She managed to keep still despite the ache her own body clamored to have satisfied. She wanted his hands on her. In her. Everywhere. Instead she took out that frustration on his thighs, scoring his skin with her nails.

He hissed, drove deeper, and groaned her name as the proof of his release hit the back of her tongue. She swallowed. That simple act of necessity pulled another moan from his chest, followed by a long, quiet curse.

Her jaw ached, but the throb between her legs

was far stronger. She slipped off his softening shaft with one last lick. His hands loosened their relentless hold. She was unmoored. The room spun. She rested her forehead on his thigh as he stroked the back of her neck. Thought was gone. Only need remained.

Alex grasped beneath her arms and dragged her up. She winced a little as blood rushed back to her knees and toes. He draped her over his lap, holding her close. The way he buried his face in her hair, right at the curve of her neck, brought unexpected tears to her eyes. He was shaking. She felt it, despite her own unsteadiness.

"I have no words," he whispered.

Polly had expected to find contentment. She'd won, after all. She'd proven what sort of man he could be if he finally gave himself permission to let go. But she was far from content. A pounding rhythm still beat in her belly.

"I have words, Alex. Would you like to hear them?"

He grunted an affirmative.

"It's my turn."

Sixteen

*A*lex never failed to feel a little dizzy and awed when looking up at the stars. The impossible vastness of the universe humbled him, but it also left him eager for more. More to learn, more to investigate.

Holding Polly, he relished that same surge of possibilities.

And, like studying the sky, there were facts he knew without context. He knew the contours of the moon's surface, but he would never travel there. He knew the anatomy of a woman's body and the mechanics of the sex act, but he'd never found success in applying what he learned from medical texts.

Mamie had been too . . . *damaged*.

But Polly. She wasn't simply amazing. She was a gift—someone to put right those years of heartbreaking failure.

He smoothed damp, curly hair away from her neck and kissed her there. Softly. In thanks.

For now.

He kept kissing, then added his tongue and teeth as he traveled down the length of her throat. Feeling her supple feminine limbs, tense yet trembling, he recognized the rock-hard anticipation he'd only just suffered. It was her burden now. Her joy.

"I want to take you to my bedroom."

She released a frayed exhale and pulled away a little. "I can't stay here. You know there's too much between us now."

"And not nearly enough. Put it off until morning, Polly. Let me give you this."

"I don't need too much convincing," she said, tracing his lips. "I just wanted to see if you meant it." Her sneaky grin had returned. She was restless and eager but, such a wonder, she still managed to find the humor in everything. "So what do you have in mind?"

"You don't want surprises?"

"Well, a *few* surprises. Anticipation is half the fun." She pinched his ear. "For someone who doesn't fight it so much."

Alex relaxed into the chair, head back against the leather. His smile felt . . . *right.* Exhausted, yes, but excited by the unknown. After what he'd just done, what she'd just given him, he wanted to play dirty, too. "Do you know what the labia are?"

"No."

"The clitoris?"

"Are they more comets? Because, to be honest, that wasn't what I expected right now."

He laughed loudly. Maybe it was the final release

of all the sensation he'd just experienced. Maybe it was just Polly. That blend of natural cleverness and artless innocence was almost more than he could handle.

"I'll cuff you, you brute," she said with a kitten's snarl.

Without replying, he hefted her in his arms and stood from the chair. Only a little wobble of his knees—then he was stable again. She giggled, despite the confused expression she still wore. Looping her forearms around his neck and snuggling close, she rested her cheek against his chest. Alex's heart seized over that small measure of trust.

After setting Polly on the floor beside his bed, he lit the lamp that softly illuminated his bedchamber. He had yet to care about this leased house. His disinterest was reflected in spare furnishings and a complete lack of decoration. The truth cut far too close—it looked like a monk's quarters.

Able to see Polly's face clearly now, he cupped her cheeks and kissed her mouth. Those beautiful lips were slightly swollen. A surprising tightness in his veins said his body was not yet finished. That tightness would become arousal if he let it.

He would.

"Alex? It's all very pretty, the gentleness and the sweetness." She caught his chin, then kissed him with fierce intensity. "But it's rather unnecessary right now."

He licked his bottom lip. "You enjoyed that."

"Sucking you?"

"Jesus, woman. Yes, that."

"I did."

"And it made you ready for me?"

"Oh, yes. Now do shut up."

With steady, precise movements, he unfastened the buttons of her gown and bared her creamy shoulders. She helped him past some of the trickier barriers until she stepped out from a puddle of brown fabric. He wanted her in silks and satins, in an aurora of color that proclaimed she would never need to work again. But even more, he wanted her naked.

She stood before him in corset and undergarments, already one of the most enthralling sights he'd ever seen. The blush on her cheeks united her freckles and spread down her neck, across her collarbones. As if hearing Alex's silent assessment, she continued to remove layer after layer. He watched, hungry and eager, till she bared her body to the soft lamplight.

Her simple clothing had concealed her like an oyster hiding its pearl. Nude, she was . . . astonishing. Pale, freckled skin rounded over sleek curves. She had wide hips and perfectly-formed breasts. Her stomach tucked inward beneath the curve of her ribs. Graceful, petite legs and dainty toes, which she wiggled in the plush rug—her only outward sign of impatience.

Alex swallowed thickly. This was for him. All for him. Virgin territory, even if she was no longer a virgin in fact.

"Lie down."

She complied, nibbling on the cuticle of her thumb

as he undressed. The avid way she absorbed every movement—intoxicating. He was the most powerful man on earth. How was he so excited, all over again? The proof was undeniable. Her gaze skated down to his thickening member and she grinned.

"I thought I put that to bed," she said.

"And then you took off your clothes."

"You can be very cheeky when you don't stop to think about it."

"Think about what?"

"Holding it all back."

Alex was entirely nude now. That feeling of power returned in force. He controlled every mystery the universe had stubbornly refused to divulge. And he could pleasure Polly Gowan. That much he knew.

"I'm not holding anything back tonight."

At that, she opened her arms. "Then come here. I'm cold."

He stretched beside her on the bed. His mouth found hers without hesitation. The path he traveled down her body was slow and sinuous. He licked along her throat, dipping his tongue into the notch at its base. Polly threaded her fingers in his hair. Her gentle noises encouraged him, calmed him, and kept him so bloody eager.

The tips of her breasts were the palest pink, with tight, small nipples. His mouth watered and his heart hammered. Smoothing his palms over her flesh, he cupped her and brought one nipple to his lips. A simple kiss. Then a deeper one as he sucked and teased. Polly's hands had slipped to his shoulders. It seemed her sharp, ragged nails would flay the skin right off his back. That thought jerked his arousal up another notch.

He was tempted to stay there, feasting on her breasts, but he owed her the release she deserved. He simply wanted her to feel as good as he did.

With firm hands, he spread her knees until she was bared to him. Her legs quivered beneath his touch, as if she fought her reflexes in order to stay in that vulnerable position.

"Christ, Polly. You're incredible."

"I told you, I'm not."

"And I told you, I won't have any arguments on the matter."

Her breasts lifted on quick breaths. "Shut me up, then."

"Just what I had in mind."

He positioned himself between her legs and kissed her inner thigh. That delicious quiver would not cease. Delicately, he touched the curls that hid her womanhood. She flinched just a little before relaxing on a giggle.

"These, Polly, are your labia." He stroked those swollen lips, breathing in the scent of her arousal. "The outer labia, to be precise."

"How do you know?"

"I'm a man of science."

"They taught you women's parts in school?"

"No," he said against her skin. "These constituted a portion of my extracurricular pursuits."

"Hm?"

"I studied it because I wanted to."

Parting those delicate folds, he licked upward

from her glistening center. She shuddered. One hand cupped the back of his head, grasping, keeping him there. Although he'd been sure of his course, Alex enjoyed a new wash of relief. She was so eager. So enthusiastic. Her responses were a drug he wouldn't be able to resist much longer.

Deeper now, he tasted her salt and her honey. He ground his renewed erection against the mattress. He'd never known his body could be so resilient.

He slipped two fingers inside, gratified when she squirmed and called him a name he didn't recognize. "I'll assume that's a Scottish obscenity."

"You're right."

"You'll make me lose my place. I'll have to start all over."

"Damn you."

"Hush." He continued to pulse in and out of her slick channel, harder, more deliberately. "Now, the clitoris is the subject of much debate."

She arched her hips. "Alex, please."

"Would you like to know why?"

"Why what?"

"Why it's the subject of debate."

"You're a beast."

"It's because many men and even most women argue against its existence. Can you believe that? They think it's a myth—a trick of history based on rumors spread by Romans or witches or some such." He paused, right above where her tight bud tempted and shimmered with wetness. "You'll have to tell me what you believe."

He closed his mouth over that nub. Polly gasped,

and her rear lifted off the mattress. He used both hands to squeeze that full flesh, then held her cheeks apart as he indulged. He sucked, licked, circled, until his name became her breathless chant. She grabbed at his hair. Alex looked up her body to watch her face, drunk on how beautifully pleasure suited her features.

Not only was the female orgasm possible, it was glorious. She cried out just before her release flooded his tongue. Alex lapped at the proof of his success. Right then, he was a potent, incredibly smug man.

He levered himself over her. "Well? What side do you take in the debate?"

"It exists."

"I'd have to agree. Learned men of science can be incredibly dense."

Alex rightly counted himself among that lot, but he needed to get smart. Quickly. This was too good to give up.

"Polly? Do you know whose turn it is now?"

"Yours," she said with a contented smile.

"No, my darling. This is for both of us."

Still reeling from Alex's amazing lesson, Polly was again taken aback when he positioned his cock against her opening. "That's possible?"

He offered a smile that was almost shy. "We're about to find out."

Eager now, she grabbed his face and pulled him down for a spicy kiss—one flavored with her own taste. He didn't hesitate, simply invaded her mouth with the hard sweep of his tongue. Their teeth clicked together when he pushed between her legs.

Inside her. So deeply that her eyes rolled shut on a groan. A harsh shudder chased up her back. He nudged her face to one side with his chin and suckled her throat, where the sharp bristles of his stubble scraped delicious pain across her skin. She grabbed the tense muscles of his upper back, as if clinging to the sturdiest ladder. Sleek and powerful, he thrust with measured strokes that edged ever closer to the madness they both craved.

Sweat slicked their upper bodies. Needing to touch him, to feel more of him, she slid her hands down along his ribs, then licked behind his ear. That must've tickled because he momentarily lost rhythm, and tensed over a strangled laugh. She did it again, on purpose.

"You are impossible," he growled.

He snatched her hands, one at a time, and hauled them over her head. His fingers were so long that he encircled both wrists and pinned her there, supporting his weight on his other arm. Polly struggled at first, out of instinct—the reflex of being trapped. But the flare of his nostrils and ragged desire in his eyes restored her composure. He held her down, but Lord, if she didn't feel like the one running the show.

She arched to show off her breasts.

His eyes widened, darkened.

Yes, that would do nicely.

His hips returned to their delectable pace. He put force behind each stroke. His features took on a determined cast, grim with shadows. Polly was almost disappointed after how near she'd come to helping him enjoy himself. They were back to the beginning, with him fighting something she couldn't understand.

She tried to enjoy the needy quest of body and body, but now the bleak turn of his lips wouldn't let her go.

No.

She was going to have him on her terms. That was just plain fact.

Angling her mouth, she took hold of his earlobe with her teeth. He hissed as she applied sharp pressure. "Let go of my wrists, Alex."

He slowed slightly. "Why?"

"I want to tickle you again."

"Request denied."

"You're terribly overbearing. I liked you better with your mouth on my pussy."

His hips stopped altogether. "What . . ." He swallowed. "What did you say?"

"Which part?" She batted her eyelashes, trying not to laugh. "About you being overbearing? Because you are, you know."

"No. About . . . the other."

"My pussy?"

"Yes."

"My quim?"

"Polly, don't. It's obscene."

But oh, that's not what his body said. Not at all. He was harder than ever. His arms shook and each breath seemed to cause him pain.

"You're not the only one who knows words for those places. Only I didn't learn mine from books." She snagged his earlobe again and bit. His pelvis flexed, so deep. "Let go of my hands so I can squeeze your taut arse."

With a choked groan, he complied. In fact, he shoved her hands down behind his back. Polly had barely grabbed hold of that tight, muscled backside when he started again. Head bowed. Arms stiff. Working her slick sheath.

The bliss he'd given her with his mouth was a memory now. Her present pleasure was even more incredible, as fire built low in her belly, right where his shaft reached its deepest point. She wrapped her legs around his upper thighs.

"Are you close, Alex?"

"Yes."

"I am, too. It's right there—right there. Ah, God, fuck me."

"Say it again."

She smiled against his neck and dug her fingernails into his buttocks. "Fuck me, love. I want all you can give."

She arched, twisting beneath a burst of pure sensation. Light blazed behind her eyes, more concentrated than the sun. Her skin flashed hot and cold. Every muscle tensed.

"Polly—" Strong hips jerked a final time. His gasped release sounded as beautiful as it felt. "Ah—goddamn it."

His arms gave way and his wide shoulders slumped. Polly swiped damp strands of hair back from his forehead as he rolled off. He never let her go, simply tucked her there along his side. With one forearm flung over his eyes, he breathed as quickly as she.

Polly knew she should be exhausted and completely drained—and she was. But with no notion of how often she might be able to enjoy such a sight, she edged onto one elbow. Possessively, she snagged an arm around his tummy where his skin was still damp and hot. He was rather scruffy when naked. A beautiful, masculine trail of hair climbed up from his groin, then flared across his chest. She petted upward, smiling at each new texture, until she reached his smooth, defined shoulders and upper arms.

He made a contented noise, which only encouraged her to keep up the soothing caress. It was especially nice to be gentle after how forceful they'd been. She didn't like thinking about why it was important that they be capable of both. Too dangerous.

But there it was. A truth she couldn't deny.

"Can I ask you something?"

Alex only grunted, his eyes still hidden. His breathing, however, had returned to a near-normal pace.

"You seem like most of this is . . . well, new to you. But you were married."

"I don't hear a question yet, Polly." His words were tight. A quiet warning she would not heed.

"That's because you're being stubborn on purpose. Shall I say it? We know it'll embarrass you more than it will me."

"You want to know why a man who was married for six years acts, on occasion, like a virgin lad."

"Yes. Yes, I do."

Alex removed his forearm and shifted to face her. The lamp still blazed. Golden warmth bathed his carved features. Oh, how she adored his eyes. So clear and expressive. He could lose the ability to speak and still tell her exactly what was on his mind. At that moment, he was again thinking that their tryst was a mistake. But some greater need pulsed out from his bones. She felt it jittering beneath her hands on his stomach—the need to confide. Her job was to listen. She wouldn't like any answer he provided, because part of her already wanted him happy.

And this wouldn't be a happy story.

"My wife, Mamie, was abused by her father. He was and remains a disgusting human being. The worst sort of entitled bastard. That entitlement meant hurting his daughters. At first it was both, but Mamie did what she could to protect her younger sister." He shivered and punched his eyes shut. "For ten years, maybe longer, she bore the brunt of his . . . perversions."

"Alex, that's sick."

He nodded stiffly. "My father refused to let me marry before I graduated. His reasons were sound, that I would need a reliable occupation to keep her safe. Plus, her family is powerful. I needed his support. So we waited. Each summer when we met again on the beaches there at Cape Cod, she looked even more sunken." Shoving his free hand through his hair, he choked back a thick swallow. "We married the day after I graduated from Harvard. I took a lesser teaching position in Philadelphia to keep her far from her family in Boston."

"Jesus." Realization eased over her in a slow wave as she watched the pain he still concealed. "Oh, God.

You kept trying to help her, didn't you? Learning all those things about women's bodies."

Another rusted nod. "It didn't help. She never . . . She couldn't, I don't think. Eventually we just stopped trying."

"But what about Edmund?"

He reached down and grabbed a blanket from the foot of the bed, draping it across them both. They were hiding from the world. She wanted to do more than that—to keep him safe from these memories. But this was one of Alex's mysteries. She wanted it solved.

"Mr. Todd, her father—he didn't like losing. That's the only reason I can imagine for his doing what he did. We had cut off all contact. For years we lived as we wanted in Philadelphia, away from her family but closer to mine. Mamie organized charity functions and campaigned for female suffrage. I worked to earn my tenure. We didn't have . . . We slept separately, but sometimes she liked to be held. We made it be enough."

Polly kept still, kept her mouth shut. *Enough.* It was a hideous word when compared to what she had just experienced with Alex. To imagine him living that way year after year, constricting his passion into an ever tighter corner, seemed excruciating. No wonder he had been so reluctant—maybe even unable—to let loose. Long habit born of necessity. And that explained why he always appeared so surprised when he did.

"Mr. Todd threatened to force an annulment through the courts, claiming our marriage had never been consummated. It had been. Technically. But our wedding night had been awful. Mamie and I never discussed it, but we never repeated it either." He shuddered. "I don't find it arousing to make a woman cry."

Her heart aching, Polly touched his brow and drew his head down to her breast. To her surprise, he didn't resist. He simply folded into her and held on.

"Mamie was determined to have her proof. So we made Edmund. Not the most joyous or pure reason to conceive, but she'd never been more adamant about anything. I think . . ." He sucked in a long breath. "I think she wanted to prove that she was free of her father, even if she never would be."

"That wasn't easy either, was it? Making your son?"

"No." His tone stopped her questions. He had given plenty. And she had heard enough.

She shut her eyes against a prickle of tears. What a torture that must have been, with Alex trying so desperately to make it right for his wife. He had done what she wanted—gave her a child—even though it had hurt them both. And eventually, it had taken her life.

Honor and sacrifice. Duty and determination. Even his love for Edmund bore the distinctive stamp of Alex's impression of love. He was no more suited to being a mill master than she was, but he would never back down. This piece of his past laid bare his reasons for fighting so hard.

"Oh, Christ, Polly. We—" He sat bolt upright. "I didn't stop."

Seventeen

What?"

"I stayed inside you," Alex rasped. "There could be a baby."

Polly's eyes went wide and she clutched her middle, where a child might one day grow. The thought was nearly strong enough to steal the strength from his legs. Making those babies. What a joy it would be.

He turned away, utterly dizzy. Frazzled. Wanting to hit something until this confusion ran away screaming.

"I'll make it right by you. Whatever happens. With or without a child."

He grabbed his trousers and kept an even pace as he dressed. Not too fast. Nothing to give away the panic that numbed the ends of his fingers. He knew, logically, that one mistake was not necessarily the end of the world. Conceiving Edmund had required four dedicated, difficult months. Chances that Polly might get with child after this lone incident were slim.

But the possibility remained.

The last hour, on top of an impossible evening, was simply too much to process. He needed time. He *always* needed time to step back from quick or unsettling events and fit them into an order that made sense. Without that opportunity to collect himself, he was left to the mercy of emotions. Right then, looking at where Polly remained, nude and stretched atop his duvet, the emotion he most staunchly battled was possessiveness. He wanted her to stay.

Yes, a factory girl.

Good Christ, a factory girl who had made him feel like a *man*.

Finally dressed, with his emotions roughly under control, he looked upon her face—which had contorted around unmistakable anger.

"Make it right? That's what you'd do."

"Yes," he said with a frown.

"And if I'm the saboteur or the ringleader you and the other mill masters seek? If I'm as bad as they suspect? If I'm in *jail*, Alex?" She pulled the blanket over her breasts. "Or maybe it won't go so far. I'll just be the same weaver I've always been. You'll 'make it right' in the most shameful way possible. Because you're not talking marriage, are you? You'd keep me."

"Polly, you're being ridiculous."

"Answer me."

"Yes," he said tightly. "I'd like you to be my mistress. You'd never want for anything, I swear to you."

She grabbed her rumpled gown and climbed into its dull fabric. Her underthings remained scattered on the floor. He had actually smiled and joked with her as they shared intimacies, a mere hour before. Now the glib, unguarded words were gone, as were any teasing feelings.

"I'd hoped to keep the memories of this grand, naughty adventure till I'm old and gray," she said in a rush. "Little chance of that now."

"What the hell does that mean? What is so wrong with my wanting to care for you?"

"Oh, but there'd be no stopping you then. Soon enough we'd be haggling over costs. Trading favors. You'd buy my parents coal, so I'd feel obligated to suck your knob. I just did it for nothing, you fool!" She jerked her chin up, mouth compressed into a line. "Don't make such an offer again."

Rejection turned his body back into rock. He had survived for years by shutting down any stronger emotion, any more delicious sensation.

"Then forget I did."

She was dressed now. They stood across his bedroom like enemies across a boardroom table. "If you want to question me about the fire or any other blasted thing, get it over with. I'd like to go home. And you need to check on your son."

"It doesn't have to be this way."

She stared at him, any trace of tears gone. She would do more than glare when she found out what he'd agreed to regarding the weavers' wages.

"All right," he said wearily. "Maybe it does. I'll take you home."

"Don't be ridiculous. You need to stay here with Edmund."

"It's after two. I'm not letting you walk back at this hour. Your neighborhood—"

He froze when Polly did. "It's my home, and I'd appreciate it if you stopped your insults."

"Then I'm calling you a hackney. Otherwise I'll be forced to wake Agnes when I escort you there myself." The words came out too forcefully. Like a threat.

Her auburn brows drew down. "That's quite a statement, master."

Alex forced back a flare of temper. They deserved better than they could permit each other, which almost excused her curt tone,. but that didn't mean it grated less harshly on his nerves.

She adjusted the bodice of her gown and swept one last loose strand of hair behind her ear. Anyone looking at her afresh would assume she was what she presented to the world: a respectable if poor young workingwoman. One without cares and without a wicked, teasing sexuality ready to burst loose. But she'd flattened Alex as surely as an earthquake.

Pelisse over one arm, she smoothed any sourness off her features and licked her lower lip.

"What if there is a child?" he asked.

"He'll be raised in Calton. You'll go back to America in eighteen months." She glanced at her undergarments but made no move to collect them, as if she couldn't stand to touch them now. "While I'm going back to the home I know and the family I love. It's my life. You're not part of it." She moved stiffly toward the door. "Good night, Alex."

"You mean good-bye, don't you?"

The light gleamed across her eyes. Her smile was the saddest he'd ever seen. "We'll meet again, I'm certain. There's too much unresolved between us. But not like this. Never again like this."

What she hadn't told Alex was how very much she wanted to be rescued.

Even that notion turned her stomach as she settled into an open-air hackney. The story he'd told about his wife chipped away at the reserve holding back her emotions. Mamie had needed a champion to sweep in and protect her from unimaginable evil. Polly had no such need. To wish for something so utterly foolish would mean turning her back on the traditions that made her life whole—and leave her disappointed when dreams of freedom died.

The cab bumped on along Gallowgate with a grating rhythm of wheels against cobblestones, the driver cursing the entire way. She pressed her head back. Alex's bed, his house, his strong, needy body over hers . . . She knew her place, and it included none of those indulgences.

Her da had always warned her about men who might want to possess both her and her influence. Surely, desiring a man so far above her station wasn't the alternative. She didn't want to be rescued. She wanted to be adored. Given Alex's history, she couldn't imagine that he knew the difference.

The cab lurched, then jerked against a hasty application of the brake lever. She sat upright. A jolt of fear tingled down her spine as two constables appeared on horseback. Her hand ached from holding on to the bench so tightly.

"You're coming with us, Miss Gowan." Constable Utley, the same who had obeyed Rand Livingstone with unfailing compliance, jerked the hackney's door open, grabbed her beneath both arms, and wrestled her out onto the cobblestones. "No Mr. Christie here to protect you now."

Polly screamed, fighting with fists and heels. The man bellowed when she caught his earlobe and yanked hard. She scored a second victory by catching the flesh of his neck beneath her gouging fingernails. Illuminated by the dull orange streetlamps, he snarled foul curses and shoved her to the ground.

With her shoulder blades pressed against the curb, and cold water seeping into the fabric of her gown, she pushed up, but her limbs were drained of strength. Utley had the advantage of position, as well as four stone in body mass. He kicked her sideways. Her spine cracked against the wheel of the carriage. A sob choked out of her chest.

"Don't move." Blood oozed down the constable's neck as he stood over her. "I won't hesitate to kick you in the gob."

"I just want to go home." Her cold, exhausted body shook like an undercooked pudding.

"Not a chance. Not this time. We'll finish our own interrogation at the station."

"I'll go no such place," Polly replied. "You've accosted me on a public street, with no cause or charge. I had an alibi for tonight and you know it."

Utley hauled her off the wet cobblestones. He nodded to the other constable. "Recognize that?"

Polly peered through the gloom. Her tartan.

"Actually, the charge is prostitution. Or can you deny soliciting an unknown man's attentions at Old Peter's last week."

An unknown man. Oh, God. If they didn't know it was Alex . . .

No, they would never know.

"I won't deny or confirm anything."

The detective wore a heavy mustache in the style favored by his professional brethren, which completely obscured his lips. Polly had never realized how much she relied on watching people's mouths when they spoke. "And then we'll talk about the witness who saw your union cronies light the fire at Winchester's."

"That's a lie!"

"Save it, miss."

He yanked her toward a wagon that pulled along the curb. Polly's guts dropped. This was such a stitch-up. But after all she'd shared with Alex since sundown, she could hardly distinguish reality from a sick, sluggish nightmare. She glanced down. A heavy cake of mud stained her skirts. She did her best to right her bodice where it gapped at the neck. The detective missed nothing. His mustache twitched in apparent amusement.

"I've never doubted it of you, you know. Filthy. It'll be Lock Hospital for you. We'll deal with that travesty of a union later."

Her cheeks heated with a shame she had not earned. Lock Hospital was a notorious old beast of a place where so-called unfortunate females were housed. Some never emerged from the menacing building that served as part prison, part institution.

Yet she would not let this arrogant bastard see her cower. She drew her shoulders back to an excruciatingly proper pose. With such bearing, she was actually tall enough to look the short detective in the eye. "Do as you will."

The stately grandfather clock in the corridor struck five o'clock. Alex padded on bare feet toward the foyer. With Griggs still abed, he had no butler to answer the summons. Thus he was the ignoble new-money pretender who opened his own front door.

"Mr. Christie, sir?"

"Yes? Wait, you're Heath Gowan."

"Yes, sir. Polly never came home." The young man's face flushed a vicious red, but he never broke eye contact. "My parents would like to know where she is."

The early dawn air became infinitely colder. "She's not here."

"Did you see her last night?"

The boy's eye was surprisingly astute—and critical. Alex kept his expression neutral. He was not proud of some of the things he'd said, but he would defend what he and Polly had shared with his dying breath. Behind his back, he cracked a thumb knuckle. "Yes, she was here. She left for your home in a hackney, about two o'clock."

Rather than berate Alex, Polly's older brother only nodded. "She'll be with the police, then."

"How do you know?" After their argument, Alex had suspected she might want time alone. But her last words had been a reaffirmation of what her family meant to her. "She has no other place she likes to go? To think or find a moment's peace?"

"We've already checked our friends' houses. No one's seen her. After the fire last night, we can't help but think the police got impatient."

"I told them to leave her to me."

Heath shrugged. He was nearly Alex's height, but as thin as a colt. He would be a big man when he filled out those long bones with a man's brawn. "As if they listen. We don't want to check the station on our own, sir, if you get my meaning."

"Wait in the foyer."

Alex roused Griggs and ordered the carriage readied, then he informed Mrs. Doward of the situation. She nodded from the rocking chair in the nursery. Edmund slept, still feverish, but not with the same frightening heat.

Within ten minutes, Alex changed into his best approximation of a gentleman's dress—just enough time to process his thoughts. And for his fury to grow into something fierce and stormy. The ascot he'd grabbed was barely tied and he couldn't find two socks that matched, but he stormed back downstairs, walking stick and top hat in hand.

The drive to the constabulary seemed far longer than it likely was. A mile or two, at most. With Heath as company, Alex stared out the window, his head swimming in a stew of violence. He nearly wore a hole in the top of his shoe by spinning the tip of his formal walking cane against the leather. What he really wanted to do was crack a few deserving teeth, starting with the constables who had likely embarrassed or even hurt Polly in ways that could not be forgiven.

His cane across their faces and against their kneecaps wouldn't be enough.

Upon arriving at the constabulary, he stormed inside and grabbed the nearest lawman. "Who are you and where the hell is Polly Gowan?"

A slender young constable blanched. His words chopped out in a stammer. "I'm Plimshaw, sir. She's being held until we can arrange transfer to Lock Hospital."

"Was she injured, man?"

"No, sir."

Heath leaned nearer, his voice hushed. "It's not that sort of hospital, Mr. Christie. It's more for . . . well, for women of a certain profession."

Plimshaw nodded, as if relieved of the necessity of revealing that particular detail. "As mandated by the comprehensive Glasgow System for the Repression of Vice." He recited the words as if from a manual on city policy. Maybe it was.

That didn't mollify the rage gathering like molten rock beneath Alex's low ribs. "I sent a woman in my employ home in a hackney cab in an attempt to safeguard her well-being, and she was arrested for prostitution? Is that what you're telling me?"

"And assault on a police officer." Plimshaw consulted his notes. "Her shawl was found at a pub by the docks. There were witnesses. The constables who arrested her were only doing their duty to protect the city."

Choice curses bounced around Alex's brain. "Let me see her. And someone find Constable Andrews. I don't care if you have to kick down his door and wake his children."

The thin, officious constable led the way through the station. Alex truncated his strides lest he overtake the shorter man. Another officer behind a desk found the logbook. More fastidious attention to detail, without producing any answers.

"There's no record of her, sir," the man said. "Perhaps she gave a false name?"

"She was likely arrested because she *is* Polly Gowan. Why would she give a false name?"

"I cannot find the paperwork, sir."

Alex slammed his fist on the desk. Pencils scattered. Even Heath looked taken aback.

"I don't give a good goddamn about your paperwork," Alex growled. "I've journeyed to this stinkhole to prevent an innocent woman from being locked up as a prostitute. Find me Polly Gowan. Now."

"Sir," Plimshaw began. "If you would—"

Keeping his temper was no longer an option. All Alex managed was not to use his walking stick as he'd imagined in the coach. Instead he pounded the tip against the wooden floor and stalked toward the holding cells. Heath followed with an equally determined stride, while Plimshaw sputtered without effect.

The women's cell stank of urine and enough

cheap perfume to make his eyes water. The hairs on his nape and along his wrists stood on end. Woman after woman stared at him from behind the iron bars. Most were filthy, with brassy hair over dead eyes, and some wore the remnants of lip paint or rouge.

One buxom young chit presented her assets. "You can have your pick of us, master, but why not me?"

Alex ignored her words, as well as the implication that he was there to shop for flesh. The idea was reprehensible. More searching. More vacant stares. None of them revealed the lustrous red hair he would know from across a crowded room.

"This is worse than holding them in a latrine," Heath said, hand over his mouth.

Rage gave strength to Alex's voice. "Polly! Polly Gowan, show yourself!"

A muffled struggle from the far corner of a cell caught his attention. He grabbed Plimshaw's lapels and dragged the man with him to investigate. Polly was pinned by two larger, older women, both in the process of stripping her lace-up boots.

Alex smacked the head of his walking stick across the bars, back and forth, until he had the attention of every inmate and constable.

Polly's expression had frozen around a mask of terror. She breathed his name.

"Unhand her. Now. Or I'll be forced to learn whether the bones in your hands are as sturdy as these bars."

The pair of prisoners backed away from Polly, who scrambled to her stocking-clad feet and met Alex at the bars. He saw only a woman who needed him. Over the years he had come to expect such a stripped, beseeching look from Mamie. Seeing it from Polly put an end to the logical foundation of his life. He felt it go. And he didn't fight to get it back.

"I'm getting you out of here," he whispered.

"Someone found my shawl at Old Peter's."

"I heard. But say nothing more. Understand?"

She nodded. "Heath, dear God. What are you doing here?"

"Aiding your avenging warrior." He shrugged. "Not that he needs much by way of aid."

"And what of Edmund?"

Alex clasped her fingers where they gripped the cell bars. "Mrs. Doward has him. Griggs is waiting for us outside to take us home." He straightened to his full height, channeling every measure of his father's arrogance and authority. "Constable?"

"Yes, sir?"

"Listen closely and pray to God you get it right." Polly watched him with expectation, Heath with awe, and Plimshaw with fear. Alex's voice never wavered as he issued the command that would change everything. "I want you to procure whatever paperwork, keys, and officials you require to set my fiancée free."

Eighteen

Are you mad?"

Polly kept her voice low as they fled the hideous police station. She had been brought in for questioning before, and had always walked away without charges. She'd never been there without the protection of the union men. Tommy, Hamish, Les, and especially Da when he was well—they had intervened when the law thought to offer a little harassment. But to be attacked by desperate female strangers was more upsetting than Polly could comprehend. The shock was enough to render her momentarily dumb.

She had always done her best to lighten the burdens of others. This night was proof that some people didn't want to be helped. Why was she so surprised? She even felt somewhat . . . betrayed, as if her good works might not amount to much.

To be accused of prostitution was even harder to face.

The line of Alex's proud jaw bunched. "I got you out of there."

"And now this ends, Alex. Enough of your bullying. I'm not a constable to be ordered about."

Heath had already departed for home, to relieve the worry Ma and Wallace must have suffered all night. Polly walked with Alex toward his carriage as the pastel light of dawn began its gradual rebirth. He grabbed her upper arms and hauled her close.

"Do you still work for me, Miss Gowan?"

She swallowed. "Yes."

"Then you'll step just as quickly as those corrupt bastards."

"*You're* the one acting like a bastard."

"So you'd like to return? To see how the judicial system here treats poor, unmarried women?"

She sneered. "Blackmail, is it?"

"No, this is intimidation. Blackmail is when I say that I'll inform your parents of our dalliances if you continue to protest. Shall we learn your father's opinion about our marriage?"

"Do I get no say in this?"

Grim lines cupped either side of his mouth. "None at all."

No emotion. No acknowledgment that they had tempted the potential for more—a deeper connection. He seemed unable to consider the options he'd stolen when he barged into that jail.

"I knew you were a master," she said with a sniff. "All along, I knew. But I let myself be fooled by your differences. You actually seemed ready to listen and help and . . ."

Care.

But she held that word back. Barely. It had no place in between them now.

He yanked open the carriage door. Griggs already sat atop his bench, with the horses hitched, their necks bowed low. Polly could relate. She was exhausted. No thought stayed in place long enough for her to catch hold.

Alex practically shoved her in with a hand on her rear, and then climbed in to follow. "You insist on behaving as if survival in such a world is the same as thriving. When, Jesus, Polly—you could be so much more."

"That's what you think. Fine. Your opinion. But thank you very much, I'm what I want to be." She exhaled, hoping to banish her outrage and speak rationally. Alex was so cool, so calm about what felt to her like a catastrophe. "I appreciate what you did. I can't imagine the gossip to follow, but we can salvage most of the situation. Maybe I can convince everyone this was just what is was—a sham, to get me out of a bind."

"It wasn't a sham, Polly. I *am* going to marry you."

A secret place inside her went very quiet and very still. Then it burst to life, fluttering like a bird frantic for flight. She backed into the bench, as far from Alex as she could. But she couldn't escape the finality in his unyielding expression.

Clear of the stink and the wretched eyes of the jail, she welcomed back the quick return of ordered thoughts. "That's absurd."

"We'll marry. That will be the end of all this confusion."

Her jaw opened but no sound emerged. The fluttering sensation intensified, becoming the fast, hard whip of a thunderstorm's first winds. Marry Alex Christie. It was too strange to even imagine.

But that secret place whispered, *What would it be like to have this man as my husband?*

"Confusion?" she croaked.

Alex waved his hand. "This disorder. I'll give you a safe place. I'll ensure that your family is cared for. And in return, Edmund will have a stepmother and I'll have a marital partner."

He didn't even blush at the latter. No heat in his eyes. The man she'd made love to was nowhere to be found. He was capable of a great deal of passion and even honor. He obviously loved his son, too.

But his words held no promise of affection for *her*.

She'd always hoped, quietly yet fervently, that she would be lucky enough to marry for love, as had Da and Ma. Alex made it sound like nothing more than a business transaction. They were pawns to their respective causes. The totality of his loyalty was to Edmund, which would never be enough for her. Wasn't it the role of a husband to be loyal to his wife, too? Did he not see how this would steal the respect she'd earned? It would be more than a loss to her pride; it would mean the loss of herself.

And she was still hiding Tommy's whereabouts. A marriage built on intimidation and lies? No hope in that.

Yet if he insisted on talking logic, she could, too.

"Do you have any idea what this will do to your

reputation when the masters learn of your proposal to a factory girl? It's wasteful and foolish."

"What business is it to them?"

"Are you really so naïve? The influence you've earned as a newcomer would become suspect, if not wiped out entirely. As for me, I'll be labeled all manner of turncoat, with my motives suddenly suspect. 'Has she always been a social climber?' they'll ask. 'Was her plan to entrap the first gullible master?'"

"Won't they see the benefits, just as you have, in associating with me in the first place? Union and mill masters working together will be advantageous to everyone."

He kept his posture distant and strict. Apparently the walls disguising his deeper self could be rebuilt in an instant. Polly wondered briefly if he taught his astronomy classes so formally, or if he would show more passion for the subject than he did toward her.

"Those on both sides who harbor more resentment than sense will see no such thing," she said.

"They cannot be that stubborn."

Polly laughed, but it wasn't an expression of joy. "Good Lord, Alex. You're not a dumb man. Look at this with your damned logic! Da could never convince *everyone* to see the bigger picture. Sometimes food in their bellies and medicine for their children took precedence over pay decreases in hard times. With prodding, they rarely see that sticking together means the advancement of all. As their equal, I have a trustworthy voice—one they might heed now. Hamish or Les will take my place, and they haven't the patience or temperament to keep that optimism alive. I'll be relegated to the edges of all I've helped build."

Alex's expression hardened. Flashes from each gas-lamp they passed made his features more intimidating. With staunch, sharp cheekbones, he frowned with the severity of a stern parent. And he was behaving as one.

"You expect to continue with the union after we're wed?"

Her heart stopped cold. "You expect me to stop?"

His shrug made her want to scream. The one hint of humanity he'd shown during their carriage ride was one of condescension. "You'll be my wife. I'll support your politics to the best of my ability, but I will not abide by the dangers you court. And I will not see my business fail."

"I courted plenty of danger in that alleyway with you, but I didn't hear you protest." Anger burned her face and chilled her limbs. "Did you plan all of this?"

"Plan what?"

The accusation took on more strength in her mind. "Tonight. You didn't want me to return to my family. So you set the constables on me with little hints about our relationship. Suddenly they pounced on me with ready-made charges of prostitution. Now you think I'll be your wife. Just like that!"

"You're courting madness, woman." He leaned forward, bracing his forearms against his thighs. "I saved you from that infernal place, and this is the thanks I get? You live in a city where hundreds of people die of cholera because of poor living conditions. Girls with access to free elementary education work instead as piecers and apprentice weavers before they can tie their own boots. And you refuse the opportunity to get free? I cannot believe you would be so stubborn. Not even you."

Polly crossed her arms to hide her fists. "Did you thrust this sort of decree on Mamie, too?"

His hand tightened on the head of that intimidating walking stick. "*What* did you say?"

She realized that she'd stepped over some invisible line. But she was too spitting angry to back down now. "You told me you'd made plans for years to get her away from her father. I wonder if she had any hand in that decision, or if you simply barged in and whisked her away."

"You know nothing about what we endured."

"Only what you've told me. That's more than enough to suspect history repeating itself."

He slid across the carriage's small space and dragged her close. Violently. His deeply expressive eyes—eyes that had reveled in the colors of the aurora, and had revealed so much emotion during their joining—were as lifeless as marble. The warmth of his breath against her cheek only made her shiver. She turned her face, but he cupped her jaw and brought her back to his unrelenting gaze.

"Feel whatever you want, Polly. But know this. I answered my door this morning only to learn that you'd been arrested. It was difficult enough to let you go last night. You cannot assume I'd be fool enough to do that twice."

The kiss he claimed was fast. Deep. Aggressive. It pushed past her defenses just as surely as his tongue forced open her lips. He pushed inside with the confidence of a man who always got his way. For just a moment, she permitted herself the enjoyment he gave, and the memories of how much more they could conjure.

But only for a moment.

She pushed against his chest to edge a scant few inches of space between their mouths. "This isn't gallantry or even some decision made of logic. This is you being selfish. You've finally let yourself indulge in something more than duty. Not even the most pigheaded man would want to give that up."

"I have never been so insulted." A lock of gleaming blond hair traipsed onto his forehead. Although a gentleman, his skewed ascot and that single lock of hair revealed what she'd always known: his power and potential for rough, almost brutal impatience. He looked like the villain she needed to believe he was. "I'm giving you a future you never could've achieved on your own."

"And now who's been insulted? Shut your mouth, girl, and be grateful?"

A grimace twisted his lips. "You make it sound as if gratefulness is so terribly demanding. You won't have to worry about any of it now. You'll be free to live above it all."

Maybe her shudder finally put him off. He let go of her shoulders, where his hands had been clamped like vises. "When you think to force me into this so-called marriage, consider how unkindly your future wife will respond to your methods." She looked him up and down with raised brows. "Do you ever expect a repeat of what we did last night? Not from me."

Alex turned away. Silence claimed the vehicle as they rattled through the night. She wanted to keep railing, to argue until he saw sense and released her from the temptation to simply . . . go along with his plan. He was the master of Christie Textiles and could, by right of fortune and influence, marry whomever he chose. Few new-money industrialists cared much about class or proper station. It would be an easy thing to turn her back to the depriva- tion—the crushing responsibilities—and live as a rich man's wife.

Easy, if she were a different person altogether.

That would mean thinking herself better than her family and her upbringing. How could she con- template such an offense to those she loved? She would live and die in Calton, although the renewed thought of that hardship tightened her stomach into a fierce little ball. When compared to the soft, envel- oping luxury of Alex's bed, her meager pallet seemed a punishment on top of her sacrifices.

The carriage stopped, jostling their knees together. Polly sucked in a shallow breath. Alex didn't even blink. His face remained in profile, half shaded in orange and gold. She found herself tracing the line of his jaw where it angled back toward his earlobe. That light growth of evening stubble against her skin had been a revelation. Beneath his rumpled ascot waited his prominent Adam's apple and the firm tendons of his throat. She'd sunk her teeth into his strength.

"It's your decision to make, Polly," he said quietly. "Outside that door is your family's tenement. I'm coming in with you. You decide what we say to them."

"I won't do it."

She scowled, trying to break the blunt spell he cast. Alex Christie had the entire world figured out. She hated that he was stealing her choices, one by one.

"If you want to go through with this," she said, "you'll do the talking. Will you barge into my family's home like you did that police station? Go, then. Tell Da how it will be."

He only offered a barely-there ghost of a smile. "I won't be deterred in this. And one day, you'll see that I'm right."

He opened the carriage door and stood waiting for her hand. She stared ahead, her heart galloping. To herself she whispered, "A cold day in hell, Mr. Christie."

Sitting at a rickety table in the kitchen, Alex offered Polly's family a truncated version of the evening's events. He was only glad her brothers had already left for the docks. The little tenement was no bigger than his bedroom, although neat and organized to make use of every inch of space.

Her ma offered to serve him a plate of breakfast. One look at how little they had to share among five people and Alex gave voice to a polite refusal. Besides, he could not eat. Not after so much unchecked emotion. The tiny room felt like a noose choking off his air. Lust, fear, indignation , disappointment, hope— they stirred a toxic cocktail in his stomach.

Polly wanted to remain there, when he offered so much more?

No. Her stubborn pride was forcing his hand.

She offered no contradiction or clarification as he spoke, but sat with her hands wrapped around an earthenware mug of milky tea. Occasionally she picked at a crevice in the wood of the scarred table. The proud curve of her neck caught his attention, as always.

"Which is why we wanted to speak with you, so that you know fact from fiction," he concluded.

Her father, Graham, shared many of Polly's features, including the shrewd glint of intelligence in his vivid green eyes. He had yet to say anything, but his rough cough had punctuated every third minute of Alex's recitation.

The man leaned back in his chair and rubbed an idle hand across his chest. "So you're here to put right the wrong you've already committed against my daughter."

Inwardly, Alex blanched. He'd behaved with less decorum than a tomcat. Being reminded so bluntly was no easy thing to hear.

"Several times," Graham continued, "if I were to wager by how late she's dragged in these past weeks. Any chance you could be with child, girl?"

The color leached from Polly's face. Alex fought the impulse to touch her—her back, her thigh, her palm. Anywhere. Just to acknowledge that he was equally culpable. But she would snap off his hand with her teeth if he tried.

Tension glinted off her body in hot pulses. "Yes."

"And what do you have to say about that?"

She straightened, pulling her hands into her lap. The defiance Alex had come to admire turned her posture brittle. "I'd say it was a mistake that we shouldn't make worse."

He could only watch as the two squared off, stare for stare. Polly's mother, though the picture of robust womanhood, seemed not to factor in at all. She continued with the morning's chores, obviously listening, but this was a contest between father and daughter. He knew so little about Graham Gowan, other than by reputation, that he couldn't begin to guess the outcome.

The man turned his attention to Alex, studying, probing. In the scheme of intimidating fathers, however, he had faced tougher opponents. William Christie. Josiah Todd. For Polly to have grown into the woman she was, full of dreams and principles, she would've needed to be raised by compassionate parents—stern, yet benevolent and determined that she should have a chance at happiness.

Alex was that chance.

"Make your case, young man."

No deference or false prostrations. To Graham Gowan, Alex might as well be Tommy or Les—a no-good bastard who wanted his little girl.

Yes, Alex wanted her. He admitted it freely now. How that desire would mature through the years remained beyond his ability to see. All he knew was that she would slip through his fingers if he didn't grab hold. And she would leave him forever if she found out what business secrets he kept.

"I want to marry her, Mr. Gowan. I'll give her a good life." Daring to catch a glimpse of Polly's profile, he found no hint of encouragement. True to her word, she was leaving this to his conviction.

Graham's fit of coughing obliterated the tense silence. His wife fetched another cup of tea and a hot, damp towel, then placed it over his mouth and nose, softly encouraging him to breathe the humid air. Alex could only watch with sympathy. Skulking fear took up residence in his heart.

Polly's father was dying.

Was that the real reason she hadn't wanted him to see her home? The good name of the union rested on the reputation of Graham Gowan. His death would leave only Polly. She would be targeted by police and by those wishing to take power. As a woman, she would be even more vulnerable. A wrongful charge against her would ruin her forever. She might even face prison time.

That thought squeezed Alex's veins. Everything throbbed. He would not see her broken.

By the time Graham's fit had passed, Alex cleared his throat. He met the man's eyes, which were bloodshot and pinched at the corners. "You'll live out the rest of your days in comfort, sir. Your wife will be provided for when you're gone."

Polly practically jumped up from her seat. She hauled her skirts out from the clutch of chair and table legs, then whirled on Alex. "How can you talk that way? Right in front of him? Do you think any of us want to be reminded of a future without . . . without . . . "

A sob choked off her sentence. She braced her hands on the tiny kitchen counter. Although she made no sound, her back heaved between deep breaths while her ma whispered softly against her temple. It was the closest Alex had seen Polly to giving in to hopelessness.

"Forgive my bluntness," he said to Graham.

The man waved a hand. "The women don't like to admit what's staring us all in the face. I have weeks. Maybe less. Breathing is like swimming through tar." He shook his head slowly. "It's Polly's fate if she continues working," he said, glancing toward her. "Conditions are better now, but they're not gentle on even the heartiest bodies."

With measured movements, Graham slowly stood from the table. Alex rose with him, offering his arm for support as the older man walked toward the fireplace, then settled into a well-worn armchair. Alex took the stool across from him.

"You're a right bastard for taking advantage of her."

Alex swallowed the impulse to set the record straight. He hadn't behaved as a gentleman; that much was a given. But Polly had been a full participant in their risks. Perhaps that's why he felt her reluctance so keenly now. How could she revel in their dangerous adventures but refuse the security he could provide?

"You have my apologies, sir," Alex said. "My intention was never to do her harm."

"Oh, I believe that. You two will have a horrible stitch trying to unwind all these mistakes. But I want her honored."

Alex was doing this to save his business. And, most selfishly, to keep Polly close. She'd turned him inside out with incomprehensible passion. By the way her father so shrewdly peered into Alex's soul, he likely knew that, too.

"I can honor her, sir. And I will."

In the kitchen, Polly had recovered her spirit. Arms crossed, her expression was mutinous—and aimed straight toward her father. The Gowan family expression of abject stubbornness was unmistakable. But her father had made up his mind.

"Then you have my permission, Mr. Christie. The sooner the better. I won't meet my Maker with unfinished business."

Nineteen

Polly waited in the antechamber of the Presbyterian church—the same church where she had introduced Alex to her people, only a few weeks ago.

Now she was marrying him.

She wasn't pacing or fidgeting, although the nervous energy rustling inside her skin made her eager to do both. Instead she stood before a floor-length mirror that Reverend McCormick also used to check his appearance before facing the congregation—with perhaps a bit of human vanity beneath his righteousness. She ran a hand down the pale blue dress her mother had worn more than two decades previous, when Ma had recited vows to the man she still adored. Although outmoded, it had been carefully preserved, and remained the best garment in their household.

The dry skin along Polly's palm snagged on the smooth, fine muslin. Ma had said its blue had been much brighter on her wedding day, but that the brightness of memories ever since more than made up for a little fading.

Polly sniffed back her emotion. The whole day would be that way, she feared. At least Alex hadn't demanded to replace her gown with something finer.

He had refused contact with her in the few days since her arrest and his unconventional inducement of marriage. Perhaps hasty arrangements had consumed his time, or consultations with George Winchester as the police still tried to determine the culprit behind the latest fire. Whatever his dealings, Alex had communicated only once: a note bearing the date and time for their wedding. The same note had indicated that her employment with Christie Textiles was terminated.

She'd been fired by her fiancé. First the union, now her potential for financial independence. That he assumed he could take those from her so blithely was even worse. It was hurtful.

God, fate, and the universe she'd seen through Alex's telescope—all had played a role in turning an ordinary Saturday into her wedding day. She would be joined to a man whose idea of love was saving a lady fair. All logic and duty.

What would he do when, one morning soon, he regretted the chivalry that had bound him to a common girl? What manner of friendship, let alone affection, would remain when the loss of her family and community soured her entirely?

It hadn't yet happened, because their nuptials remained a secret. But soon the whole of Calton would know what she'd done. No explanations would be able to varnish her apparent betrayal. She would be cut off, practically confined to Alex's home. To be beholden to him for the rest of her life would ruin the miracles they'd already given one another.

Yet that private, frightening need for more—more of Alex—had only grown. She wanted his affection. Maybe even . . .

Privately, in her own mind, she would no longer deny what she felt. She wanted his love.

He already had hers.

Yet how could she reveal that aching secret to the man who'd charged into her life with so little hint of his feelings? If she had some slight assurance that he returned her new, tender, raw sentiments, she wouldn't be so nervous. She was a tough girl, and he was a strong, fiercely intelligent man. Surely they could make *something* work. Given time. Given patience.

Had he asked rather than demanded, he might have won her acquiescence. The image of Alex down on one knee was enough to shock her breathing into a lopsided rhythm. She pressed her hands between her breasts and fought to steady her ragged pulse.

That he had closed himself off even more tightly only accentuated the difference between what she wanted and what he seemed prepared to give. All logic aside, all motives aside, he had placed so many concerns above her happiness. Had she no good example to draw from, with her parents' love now stronger than ever, she might have been able to settle.

Settling wasn't in her blood.

She picked at the cream lace hem on her cuff until it lay flat around her wrist, then repeated the idle task with the edging of her bodice. Ma had done a lovely job plaiting and arranging Polly's hair. It twined and curled like a bright auburn halo. She rubbed her eyes, which felt gritty from lack of sleep.

A knock at the door startled her, and she scurried away from the mirror. Alex would marry her out of sheer mulishness, even if she wore a sackcloth and ashes. The lay of lace against her skin didn't matter at all.

Upon opening the door, she found her father. "Da, what are you doing here?"

"Come to talk to you, girl. Shut the door so as your husband won't see."

"He's not my husband yet."

"Still steaming, are you now?"

"Of course."

"Well, that's why I've come. I want you to ask what you've been dying to."

She didn't need to pretend. For years, she and her father had shared similar notions on so many topics. Da was her mentor and friend. Her biggest champion. It pained her that he'd given over to Alex's high-handed ways without so much as asking her opinion. He'd never before failed to take her feelings into account.

"Why, Da? Why do this?"

"You heard me when Mr. Christie was there that morning. You heard him, too, girl. I haven't got much longer in this world."

She started to protest but he held up a hand. He

no longer looked merely ill, but genuinely *old*. A merciless fist squeezed her heart.

"You need to accept this, girl. You can't fight time or the will of God. Not even you, though I don't doubt you'd try." He sat wearily on a padded leather stool. "I never thought you were a saint, but what you dared with Mr. Christie—it was a fool risky thing. I'd like to say you were due this comeuppance."

"Da!"

"But I won't. What you do deserve, my girl, is a life free from the gutters. And even if you're willing to argue with that small truth, think on your dear mother. What of her later years, once I'm gone?"

Guilt struck her hard. Polly bit her lower lip, yet she never denied the truth once it leapt into view. "I haven't wanted to. That would mean . . ." She swallowed tensely. "That would mean admitting you won't be here much longer."

"I can excuse that, because it's a hard thing for me to accept, too." Watery kelly green eyes found hers. "A man doesn't want to let his family down. I've relied on you too much, especially these last few months. It wasn't fair to encourage you to bear the burden of the union, all on your own."

"Don't you take that from me, too!"

He shook his head. "Not taking it from you. Just wishing, for my own pride's sake, that I'd been there with you—if only to see what a wonder you've become."

"Da . . . I had no idea."

"Hush now. I love my girl and you know it." She knelt before him when a cough stole his breath. He gasped. His face purpled. She rubbed his back and murmured nonsense sounds until the spell subsided. The obvious pain he suffered drove home what she'd only just been able to admit. He was dying. Her mother and her brothers would soon be on their own. The obligation that fell to Polly was as weighty as bricks across her shoulders.

Funny how caring for the welfare of the whole of Calton had never made such an impact. Maybe because that responsibility had always been voluntary and less personal. Less inevitable.

"Tell me what to do, Da," she whispered against their clasped hands.

"What we always do. We make the best of a situation. I won't call it bad, because I'm not convinced it is." He caught her chin and stared into her soul. "Tell me, girl. Do you care for him?"

Oh, how she wanted to protest. She wanted to find the words that would change her father's mind and unbind her from this mistake, and all the turmoil yet to come.

The steps from marriage to childbirth to old age were clearly defined among her people. Countless feet had already worn the grooves on that pavement.

This was uncharted territory. A poor girl marrying a man of such status. A man who had traveled, who'd watched a son born and a wife die. A man whose deep reserve and explosive desires kept her awake with curiosity. A man who would do his best to provide for her body, her welfare, her family, but might never be able to voice what she longed to hear. She'd be left sitting idle, holding her breath for the rest of her life.

That didn't change the truth.

"I do care, Da," she whispered. "I love him."

"Then promise you'll make this happen. Put that stubborn streak of yours to work on shaping something good for yourself."

"When it comes to stubbornness, he's as bad as I am."

"I doubt that. You're under his skin already. I saw it when he watched you. He's a besotted fool. Just twist him this way and that, like your ma's always done me." He stood with a smile and leaned heavily on the nearby table. "Now give your old da a hug before Mr. Christie takes you from me."

Polly choked on her emotions and held her father's frail shoulders. He smelled of tobacco and wood smoke from their tenement fireplace, as well as the plain lye soap he used for washing. She breathed him in, trying to stanch the premonition that this was the final good-bye she didn't want to make. But if it was, she would absorb every detail: the sound of his breathing as he labored over gasps, the way his gnarled hands petted her upper back, the buoyancy that remained in his voice, even now.

"Let the happiness in, my Polly love."

Tears spilled down her cheeks. She held on tighter. This was her wedding day, and she'd never been more heartbroken.

"And if I can't, Da?"

"Then you're not the young woman your ma and I raised. You have the vision to see a better life for yourself, or you wouldn't fight so hard." He pulled back and wiped the tears from her cheeks. "Always for other people—and I know that won't change. But it's your turn. Fight for your own happiness. I wouldn't be standing here if I didn't believe this man Christie will come around. Give him a chance to love you back. A gift to you both."

Polly soaked up his words like sand at low tide welcoming the return of the waves. She inhaled, pressed her hands against her stomach, blinked back the last tears. Rarely had she seen her father's dear features so adamant and so gentle at the same time.

"I'll do my best, Da. I promise."

"No need to give me the promises. Save those for your husband. Now, show him how a girl from Calton stands up to a challenge."

She released the last of the tension that had bound her so tightly. Alex was a good man. She knew that. And she also knew that the transition from his employee to his wife would be fraught with hardship. The rewards, however . . .

When placing a kiss on her father's weathered cheek, she made her own silent vow. Alex hadn't allowed her a choice, but she'd be damned if he determined the tone of their marriage. She was not his late wife. She had ambitions that his status made possible. And she would not hold her breath, waiting for the day when he might open himself to the love she wanted to give.

She would give it and demand it in return.

She'd threatened to withhold marital pleasures,

but that rash, frankly furious threat made no sense. He might expect retaliation along those lines. Instead she would head straight for the weakness she knew was there. She would do her damnedest to remind him whom he'd chosen. No prim miss.

He was marrying a woman with appetites and an infatuation for seeing him come undone. His passions and his feelings would not remain divided for long. She would weave them together, as surely as she'd spun cloth for the better part of fifteen years. She could do just the same with their separate lives.

Reverend McCormick entered the vestibule and signaled that the ceremony was beginning. On her father's arm, Polly gave herself one last look in the mirror.

Alex Christie didn't stand a chance.

Alex hadn't expected her to meet his eyes, let alone smile when she did. Polly practically floated down the aisle. Her father walked beside her with plodding steps, but Alex hardly noticed. His attention was reserved for his bride.

How different, his two weddings. The day he'd taken Mamie as his wife had been a lavish affair, no matter the animosity between their families. For appearances, the Christies and the Todds had invited half of New England. Flowers, champagne, delicacies of all kinds. Their parents had undertaken a secret war, each intent on outspending the other. He remembered having been surprised by his father's generosity. Only later did he realize that the uncharacteristic loosening of the family purse strings had been to spite Josiah Todd's snobbish blue blood ways.

He'd appreciated that about his father.

As he stood awaiting Polly, however, Alex counted fewer than a dozen witnesses. Her family. Agnes, with Edmund in her arms. The clergyman. No one else had been invited. The difficulties of announcing their union would be saved for another day.

Now was the time to ensure that Polly would be his. Safe and protected—the honorable thing done. And on the most primal level he'd ever known, he wanted her for his wife.

When had possessing her taken precedence over every other concern? He needed to keep his perspective, to remember his reasons for marrying her at all. But how could he? She glowed like a shooting star— an ethereal princess with a crown of fire-gold hair. Her eyes were impossibly vivid when the church's stained glass cast rainbows over that precious green. Alex read turbulence there, despite her fixed and serene expression. Equally was his attention diverted to her mouth, particularly her lush lower lip. What she had done with her mouth, to him, for him . . .

Polly reached his side on a waft of light floral scent. He noticed the lack of factory smells—the dry-dust tickle of cotton and the petroleum stink of machine oil. She had left those behind because they were necessities no more. *He* was her future.

That made him stand a little straighter, proud and determined. Soon she would see the advantages in accepting him.

Reverend McCormick looked up from his prayer

book. "Dearly beloved, we are gathered here today . . ."

Short and plump, McCormick continued the customary words. Alex, however, was beset by a redheaded demon. Rather than keep her eyes forward, Polly turned toward him and fixed a cool stare on his face. The reverend noticed, as a tight frown marred his brow. But she never wavered. She studied Alex with the dedication of a scholar on the verge of the century's biggest scientific breakthrough. He was tempted to stare back, if only to see how long she would persist.

He already knew the answer. Despite her apparently calm expression when walking down the aisle, she had yet to forgive him. But something more curious had taken the place of her anger, as if she were lit with inner bonfires that made her eyes spark a sharper, clearer green. His heart beat like pagan drums.

Just what spell was she casting now?

"Will you, Alex Christie, take this woman to be your lawfully wedded wife?"

To have and to hold.

From this day forth.

Through all the days of your life.

He realized too late just what had been brought to bear. Another wife. Another potential for untold worry and pain. He had been thinking with his chivalrous instincts and, to be brutally honest, with his cock. Something so groundless, based on caprice— no matter how wonderful—could not be trusted. The flurry of his attraction had only added to the logic that seemed so clinical and sound. His reliable system of assessing the world had been nothing more than a tool for making Polly his.

The words formed on his tongue anyway. Deep, potent desire gave them voice. "I will."

Polly's lips tipped in that smile. Did she think this was a joke? Did she assume that married life was a lark? He knew better. He knew it required serious work.

"I will," she said, still watching his face.

He couldn't help it. He faced her directly, accepting her unspoken taunt. Just as he'd suspected, he regretted it almost instantly. Christ, she was beautiful. The gown was likely a hand-me-down, but it suited her curves as well as if it had been designed by a talented dressmaker. Pale blue was just the shade for her personality, like the sky before sunrise—all possibilities made real. Cream lace contrasted with her thick auburn hair. Her expression was that of unexpected warmth. He hadn't earned it, not with how she resented his actions.

"You may now kiss the bride."

She tilted her chin. Quiet challenge blazed across her flushed cheeks. Her grin took on a lopsided humor, as if she could burst into laughter at any moment.

"If not now, then when?" she whispered.

Alex tensed. She had said those exact words when he'd accused her of teasing him—only, she'd been on her knees at the time. There in the church, she not only read the deepest secrets of his mind, she was making toys of what she'd discovered.

He cupped her face in his hands and kissed her. Quickly. No lingering sweetness, despite how his body made greedy demands. He straightened and offered his arm. Polly scowled briefly, the only time her smile slipped. But as she faced her family, she tucked away any frustrations. That false serenity had reclaimed her mouth, as if she were a perfectly happy bride.

Alex couldn't find it in himself to wish otherwise.

Across the span of only two pews, her brothers clapped her on the back—heartily, as if congratulating a teammate after a well-struck goal. The younger of the two boys, Wallace, handed her a flask. Alex watched in stunned silence as she unscrewed the cap right there in church. And drank deeply.

Ah, God. That throat. He couldn't look away from the way her muscles constricted over each swallow.

Perhaps she knew he watched. When she finished, she handed it to Alex. Grinning. Licking her lips. At least this was a dare he could accept. He took two hearty gulps, which helped offset the burn that had invaded the rest of his body.

Married. A wedding night.

Yet she had spat such furious words, threatening no such privileges. Was this behavior some elaborate means of revenge? Taunting him with sensual prospects, only to drop him cold when they were alone? He steeled himself to that possible disappointment.

A more resilient corner of his soul refused. To seduce his own wife. No guilt or worry or thought to the reputation their vows now protected. Such a gift. Such a challenge.

Such glorious rewards.

What had he been thinking? Walling off that passion? Little else seemed important when she looked at him as if he were the biggest mountain she would ever climb. She was an opiate. Like throwing a punch, or riding a colt barely broken—one as likely to kick as to obey. This woman, the new Polly Christie, was the personification of his lost control.

Alex couldn't wait for the sun to set.

Twenty

Such profuse reward.

What had he been thinking? Waiting, off that
pretend...

look...

...she would...

Polly didn't return to Calton that evening.

Instead she accompanied Alex, Agnes, Edmund,
and Griggs to Dennistoun, with her few posses-
sions stacked at her feet. Her mother had packed
them into two carpetbags borrowed from a neigh-
bor, because their family had never required luggage. They were the sorts to live and die within the
span of a few streets—boundaries as sure as any
holding cell. Alex hadn't just fetched her from the
police station. He'd dragged her out of a far more
cozy prison.

That traitorous thought shot a shiver up her back.

She would not let circumstance change who she
was. She would remain the same girl.

And yet, Polly Gowan now longer existed.

The silent, stern-faced man sitting across from her
in the carriage was her husband. She was stepmother
to the infant asleep in her arms. Some strange sense
of new loyalty had compelled her to hold Edmund

on their journey to her new home. She would be his mother from that day forth.

At least it seemed an easy task—not that she held any mistaken thoughts of motherhood being easy. Loving the child that looked so much like his dear father would be as simple as breathing. She did just that, breathing the scent of his downy blond hair. So soft and warm, he smelled of the milled milk soap Agnes insisted was best for his tender skin. The vitality of Edmund's small body against hers made her heart swell. He would be a man someday, and she would see that happen. She would help Alex make him strong and honorable, and likely rather stubborn. That made her smile, and she kissed the boy's head once again.

Already she had been altered—transformed into Polly Christie with the recitation of a few simple, powerful words. She had no idea who that woman was.

Throughout the subdued festivities that followed the ceremony, she'd felt Alex's gaze on her at unexpected times. Never coy. More like he was suddenly struck with the notion that she was the only person in the church, and that no one would notice his attention. *Polly* noticed. When she lifted her eyes now, she found Alex staring once again. He appeared as if he'd just witnessed a miracle. Awed. Stricken. Almost agonizingly hopeful.

She would dig inside of her new husband until he spoke that hope aloud. It would take time and then a little more time, until she could trust him with the love she no longer denied. The barest concessions would make him the center of her world.

That was the scariest, most daring thought she'd ever had.

First, before he learned what a mistake it was to begrudge her what she deserved, she needed to keep control. Keep the pace. The easiest way to do that, of course, was to take advantage of what their encounters had taught her. Her husband was a man with needs he thought he could deny. But he was no monk. Polly smiled a very different sort of smile, in anticipation of ensuring she had his complete attention.

"You're staring, Mr. Christie," she said softly.

He bit his back teeth together and answered with a nod. Lord, he nearly looked apprehensive. She wanted to shake him by the lapels of his fine, deep charcoal suit until his secrets rattled out.

The carriage rolled to a stop. Griggs opened the door and affixed the step. Agnes offered to take Edmund, but Polly politely declined. She used Griggs's proffered hand as balance and brought the boy out into the gathering twilight. A warm, humid breeze promised summer days would return eventually.

But the nights . . .

She could no more predict the outcome of their first night as husband and wife than she could chart the paths of the planets. Perhaps Alex could do so, but if he fancied he possessed any more certainty about the next few hours, he was only deceiving himself. They were an experiment the world had never seen. Explode. Melt. Fizzle. No telling.

He followed them out of the coach and assisted

Agnes. Griggs started on the luggage. Alex maintained his odd silence, wearing it like a blanket around his proud shoulders.

The next few hours were filled with familiar routines of evening, yet everything was made new. She made tea in Alex's kitchen. She watched, taking mental notes, while Agnes bathed and fed Edmund. Polly offered to rock him to sleep.

"Tonight of all nights?" Agnes gave her a playful scowl. "Go now. You've tiptoed around long enough."

"Tiptoed?"

"Deny it, girl, and I'll get *really* testy. Off to bed with you."

Agnes walked toward the nursery with Edmund and a burping cloth over her shoulder. Griggs had taken the bags upstairs. All Polly had to do was climb the stairs to meet her future.

Where had Alex ordered her established? In his room? In another? All her life she'd wanted a room of her own, a place of privacy for quiet thoughts and quiet breathing. Did she still want that? Truly? The answer was as fleeting as ribbons of color dancing across the sky. Alex had shown her that. Yet the aurora was more stable than her excited, confused emotions.

Desire added gunpowder to the mix and only made it worse. She was crawling out of her mind and completely out of her skin. The brief climb up the stairs pacified her not at all. Each step pinched with tension.

Through an open door, she saw that her bags had

been deposited in what appeared to be a guest bedroom. It was made up with dark drapes that would block the light of morning, and more curtains of the same midnight-blue wool lined the bed. The candle she lit made it seem like a somber cave.

The glorious dream of a room of her own looked very, very lonely.

Damn him. She damned him for the tears she blinked back. Whether done maliciously or with respect for her privacy. This felt like banishment.

Rifling through her carpetbags, she found her best nightgown. It was the closest thing to a luxury she owned, having sewn the garment using cotton and thread purchased with her tiny savings. After completing the finishing touches, she'd fought the notion that it was too showy for a girl in a tenement. Only when in need of a special moment of luxury had she worn it to bed, just for herself. That it was three years old barely showed.

She had carefully washed and ironed it when Ma and the boys were out of the flat. Da had been sleeping. No matter her lingering resentment of Alex's methods, she wanted to appear beautiful for him. She touched the snow-white lace she'd knitted herself. Little had she known then that she would wear it on her wedding night—or maybe she *had* known, harboring secret hopes.

After unwinding the plaits from her hair, she brushed until its auburn color shone, even in the modest candlelight. Almost reverently, she unfastened the ties of her mother's wedding gown—now Polly's wedding gown, too—and laid it across the bed. She smoothed the fabric just so, knowing even as she did that nervousness was the root of her fussing. With her resolve in place, she took one last look at the gown that held such meaning, then removed her undergarments. The nightgown was a cool breath from heaven against her skin. She shivered, imagining Alex's hands running along the smooth fabric before diving beneath.

But first he would see her in it. In his bedroom.

If Alex wanted a wife, he would get one. He would get the only one she knew how to be. That meant being strong enough to set her own terms. No docility when better, happier, more satisfying days glowed on the horizon—or, in this case, in the intimate darkness of passion's greatest night.

Satisfied with the result of ministrations that only added more fire to her belly, she nodded to herself in the mirror. He wanted her. She wanted him. Nothing simpler.

She pulled her laundered tartan around her shoulders and crept out of the guest room on bare feet. She knew the location of his study, there at the end of the corridor. A faint sliver of light stretched out from beneath the closed door.

Having reached his bedroom, she assessed it with a keener eye than on their first foray into that intimate place. The space was nearly as stark as the rest of his home. A washstand occupied one corner, and a plain wooden chair sat in another. The dressing screen and wardrobe were as austere as possible. For such a wealthy man, he lived with incredible simplicity.

Yet, it was Alex. The scent of him. The resonance

of the air. She breathed deeply, and clasped her hands against her breastbone. This was where she needed to be. She would stake her claim as thoroughly as he had forced his demands on her.

The bed seemed his only concession toward high living. Bed curtains the color of summer leaves at twilight created a refuge for the large, plush mattress. A matching duvet and pillows sent a little dance up her spine. She would lie with him again, wrapped in that place of softness and warmth. That they were married only added to the excitement pooling low in her belly. They would awaken there, together as husband and wife, with no fear of consequences.

If only he would give her a sign. Something. Anything to nurture this unexpected new faith. Then she could imagine waking in his arms for the rest of their lives.

She sat on the bed, with her lips still curled into a smile.

Alex finished his whiskey. Not that it cleared his mind. The enormity of what he'd wrought would not let him be. He had never given thought to walking down the aisle again. He had mused, on occasion, that Edmund would benefit from the tenderness of a woman. But for himself? Not once.

Not before Polly.

Even the idea of taking her as his mistress hadn't been enough to assuage the hunger to possess her. *All* of her. She would never know the touch of another man.

Only his—his hands, his mouth, his body joined with hers.

The excitement of those images was undeniable. He shoved up from the chair behind his desk and paced. He could've used his influence to negotiate or even threaten the police. Diminishing the rumors about her arrest would've meant the application of a few bribes. He had little money to spare, but he would've been able to do that much for her. His sense of duty was an unshakable thing.

He fought his arousal and his misgivings with the science he loved: star charts, his telescope, thoughts of the aurora that had faded with the coming of spring.

No, Polly had invaded even those calming places. He shoved the telescope and watched it swivel away.

Her freedom had not required marriage. His *need* for her had.

How else would he have claimed such a fiery, stubborn, incredible woman? She could not be bought. She could not be coerced. Even earnest seduction would've bounced off a shell honed of determined sacrifice, coupled with her insistence that their stations were unequal.

Fear and want had determined his actions, while he remained dizzy and weighed down at the same time. The man he'd become in Glasgow was as unfamiliar as life under the sea.

But he *was* that man, whatever that might come to mean.

Now, his wife awaited him.

He was stripping his ascot even as he strode down the corridor toward the guest bedroom . . . which was empty.

For an instant, his heart seized. She'd gone. She'd

resented his heavy-handed behavior so much as to simply flee. The shock nearly doubled him over.

As his vision cleared, he saw her wedding dress. It had been laid out with care, not flung aside in disgust. He stepped forth and touched the lace along the bodice. His eyes caught on Polly's bags, which had been ransacked. A hairbrush rested on the tiny vanity.

Confused but resolute, he stalked with greater anticipation toward his bedroom. Of course she would be there. He should've expected no less from his indomitable girl.

His heart seized for a very different reason when he opened the door.

Polly slowly arose from his bed, bathed in the light of two tapers. Silken red hair draped in heavy curls around her shoulders. In his entire life, he had never encountered its color, its texture, its equal. That glorious, shimmering beauty had first caught his eye, but the graceful sweep of her features had entranced him ever since—the wide arch of her cheekbones, the laughter that shaped her guileless smile, and the dancing fire in eyes like enchanted pools.

And her body. Good God, he could barely look on its perfection. Pert nipples stood out in relief against a fine cotton nightdress. Her breasts were unbound, full, luscious. The barest hint of hair between her legs waited, dark and tempting, beneath the pale fabric.

Her smile turned teasing. "Took you long enough."

His swallow was more like a gulp. "I was thinking."

"About?"

"How to keep up with you tonight."

"You tell pretty tales, Mr. Christie, but I can hear right through them."

"Fair enough. Would you believe me if I said I regret having installed you in the guest room?"

She held out a hand. "Yes, and I expect an apology."

He walked toward her as if his body had been forged of iron and drawn by a powerful magnet. The doubts he'd tussled with for hours fell away in a rush. Lust took its place. Lust—and a caring he could not deny.

"I'm sorry, Mrs. Christie."

Her eyes widened. The delicious softness of her lips parted. Their hands touched.

Entwined.

Flame shot through Alex's body. She was in his arms before thought, with her warm curves pressing against his chest. She kissed him with as much passion as he'd come to expect from this amazing woman. He licked the seam of her lips, and she opened to welcome his tongue. Hers was hot and textured in that fine, exciting way, as if their plunging need could create a friction strong enough to sizzle and light.

He did not take. She did not acquiesce. Instead they matched one another, kiss for kiss, touch with ravenous touch.

Polly tugged at his clothing, which had become almost painfully constricting. He needed air. He needed room to move. Most of all, he needed her hands on his bare skin. Their fingers tangled as they stripped his coat, collar, shirt. She yanked open his trousers, which made him laugh a giddy release of pent-up energy. He kicked off his shoes, shucked his trousers. Her gasp was more fuel for his raging fire.

"Oh, I remember that," she said, taking his phallus in hand.

Alex groaned. He clasped his hands around hers. The pulse of his hips was involuntary but unbelievably *right*. An eternity had passed since they'd last touched—if a week could be an eternity. His mind bent the laws of physics, insisting that it was indeed possible.

He needed more, and more still. After releasing her maddening fingers, which continued to steadily stroke his hard prick, he grabbed at her delicate nightgown. Flesh and curves. Breast and stomach and waist. Those secret curls. His hands felt clumsy and rough against the finely spun cotton.

"It's the best garment I own." Her breath feathered over his collarbone just before she pecked tiny kisses across his pectorals. "Don't rip it," she said with a voice full of teasing.

Alex stilled, inhaled deeply. He removed her hands from his aching body and deliberately raised them overhead. "Hold still."

After a rush of pure emotion at seeing her happy trust, he knelt. He still felt clumsy, but at least his hands had purpose. Undress her. But don't hurt her beautiful cotton creation. He hadn't expected her to wear something so lovely. It was simple and pure, whereas his Polly was cunning and devilish. That contrast was everything he'd come to need from her.

As Polly stood trembling, he traced his fingers up

her calves. The cotton pooled around his forearms and gathered as he caressed up, past her knees, past the sleek strength of her thighs. When he reached her backside, he kneaded and squeezed. Every touch became rougher, more demanding. He slid around to her stomach, which bared the apex of her legs. With two thumbs he parted her folds and licked inside. Her gasp sank low into a moan as he tasted, teased, drove her higher.

But even there, he didn't linger. Her moan returned—this time with disappointment. "Patience," he whispered against her damp flesh. "Wouldn't want to be too hasty."

"You're going to get yours."

He gave the silken skin below her belly button a single kiss. "Oh, yes."

Up and up he trailed. The nightgown was almost entirely caught along his forearms. Still she waited with her hands overhead. Bared breasts offered another temptation he could not resist. He swirled each nipple with untamed aggression. Her body was a feast. A treasure. He could spend the rest of his days and nights learning every beautiful inch.

God, they were *wed*. They had a lifetime.

Blood beat in his ears and his erection was furious with want. A little shimmy and one last delicate tug freed her from the delicate cotton. Polly scampered onto the bed. For a brief, breathless moment, she was on all fours with her rounded arse his to admire. Admire? Hell, *drool* over.

She turned to sit against the pillows, then crooked a finger. "Come and get me."

"That seems to be the theme of the evening."

He stalked onto the bed. She backed a little tighter against the pillows. Perhaps she felt the animal hunger building inside him, threatening to burst free.

"You want me," she whispered with a sly smile.

"I do." She pointed her toes and gave a little wiggle, as if she, too, could not contain the pulses of want. He grabbed her calf and pulled her to the middle of the bed, completely flat. "Yet I had a misguided notion of taking this slowly," he said. "I wanted a proper seduction on your wedding night, Mrs. Christie."

"Removing my nightdress was slow enough. Give me your strength now, Alex. You want to."

"Yes," he growled.

"And *I* want you to."

The animal claimed him just as he claimed his prize. Arms around her, legs entwined, he pressed his throbbing shaft against her belly.

She smiled. "Mm, that's mine."

"Yours." He took a rosy nipple into his mouth again, and grazed his teeth against her sensitive flesh. Small, elegant hands tunneled deep in his hair and scraped down to his scalp. Her restlessness moved with his. Whether she opened her knees or he did was no concern.

"Prove it, Alex. Prove what's mine."

He positioned his swollen head against her opening, which was slick and hot. His mind was gone. He thrust home. Deeply. She took every inch, even grasping for more with taut fingers digging into his flanks. Alex levered over her and supported his weight on his elbows. He bowed his head against her neck. Every thrust proved how much his muscles could give to her and take from her. Polly crossed her ankles at the base of his spine. The position drew them even closer, but she still managed to slip a hand between their bodies.

"Touch yourself," he gasped. "Between your legs."

"Oh, *yes*."

"Bloody hell."

Her eyes rolled closed on a quiet exhale.

"Look at me," he rasped. "I want to see it on your face. I want you to see it on mine."

Each time he thrust to the hilt, he felt her fingers working. The desire in her eyes was a fire he stoked higher with every rough movement—until her release choked out on a little scream. She arched into him. Her pelvis ground against his, seeming intent on making blissful seconds become infinite.

The sheen of her flushed exertion was beyond arousing. Alex sipped at her temple, then roughly claimed her mouth once again, hips and tongue questing.

She cupped his cheeks and held his gaze. "So hungry. So close to what you need. You wanted me to see it. Now show me."

The tide of his pleasure was too much to contain. He shuddered, groaned, and drove into her hot, soft slickness one last time. "God, Polly," he gasped, neck arching back. "My Polly."

Boneless, he sank into the bed. They wound together in sighs and contented stretches. Her smile was just as wicked, but satisfied in a way that made his chest ache with pride. Pure masculine pride. He snuffed the candles, pulled her beneath the covers, and gathered her close.

Sleep claimed him nearly straightaway. He was simply overwhelmed. Caressing her hip and waist soothed him like no thought ever could. The perfect symmetry of man and woman. Through the fog of that lassitude, the words Polly whispered against his shoulder barely made sense.

"That was just the proof I needed, Mr. Christie."

Twenty-one

Married only two weeks, Polly left Alex's house without telling him, which felt like a betrayal, especially because she did so with the intention of seeing Tommy.

Meet me.

Those were the only words on a note delivered by post that morning. Tommy had signed it.

She told only Agnes that she was going. Checking in on Edmund had become habit. The little boy was fast melting her heart. His fever had long passed, and Edmund was making his first forays toward eating solid foods. When Polly peeked into the nursery, he'd been happily smashing porridge around a plate set on the hardwood floor. "Easier cleanup," Agnes had said with an indulgent smile.

Polly tied on her bonnet and grabbed her tartan shawl, which Alex had later retrieved from the constables' station. Spring had fully taken hold of the city, using its annual might to beat back winter.

Warmer air. Rain, but with moments of sunny brilliance. The weather didn't match her mood. She was jittery and apprehensive, not only about visiting Tommy but about Alex's reaction if he discovered their secret meeting. Just when she and her husband had found a measure of happiness, however tentative, she was going against his explicit demand. His *unfair* demand. But she needed to. She was bored, restless, and in need of her old sense of purpose.

She couldn't simply abandon her old life in favor of a new one.

And Alex had been acting strange of late—more than usual. George Winchester and Julian Bennett had each been by the house several times in two weeks. Their discussions behind the locked library doors turned heated every time. Once Polly had heard Mr. Winchester shout her name and call her "an ambitious piece of gutter trash."

It had warmed her heart when Alex threw the man out, even as she worried about the repercussions. "I won't open this door to you again until you apologize," he'd said, cool and calm, before slamming it in Mr. Winchester's face.

All the secrecy coincided so closely with the upcoming renegotiation of the weavers' contracts, and he hadn't brought up the topic of Jack Findley again . . .

Polly's nape prickled with dread and suspicion.

She had been kicked out of every circle. That knowledge left her at sea. She might never be involved with finding out who'd sabotaged Christie

Textiles, let alone the identity of the arsonist. How would she bear being so excluded?

Holding Alex through the night was a consolation, but even the warm temptation of his embrace didn't reverse his demand that she leave the union and stay off the factory floor. Nor did it stave off the inevitable. A showdown was gathering, with their interests on either side.

She arrived at a tenement block even more ramshackle than those on her street and knocked on a door. Of all the people she knew, she most wanted Tommy to understand how she'd wound up married.

The door burst open. He hauled her inside.

Polly slugged him in the arm. "Let go of me! You're acting like a rabid dog."

"You deserve worse."

"What I deserve is your thanks! I've worked to find out what really happened, and the first thing I get from you is scorn? That no one's come looking for you has been my doing."

"I'd have laid low just fine."

"Living like a gutter rat. Don't give me that bollocks."

He nodded curtly toward a wicker chair in the small kitchen, then took a chair opposite around the solid wooden table. Mrs. Larnach's late husband, a carpenter, had made almost all of the furniture in the tiny little flat, but he'd been gone five years. The place was slowly deteriorating.

Crossing her arms, she leaned away from her childhood friend. "Go on, then, Tommy. Make your accusations."

He snatched her left hand. The simple gold band Alex had bestowed shone on her finger. "Married the master, have you? How could you turn against us like that?"

"Turn against you? Good God, Tommy. Think of the advantages!"

"Explain them to the assembly on Friday. I'll drag you there, if you like."

"I'd like to see you try." She paused. "Wait—*Friday*?"

That no one had told her of a new meeting meant she was truly done. A complete exile.

"Yes, not that you'll be welcome."

"Oh, I'll be there. And if you make trouble for me, I'll tell them where you've been hiding and how we should've turned you over to the constables a month ago. None of them will care about the truth. No one wanted this lingering over our heads when it comes time to negotiate our contracts. They need a scapegoat so everyone can get on with business as usual." She pointed a finger at her chest. "*I've* kept that from being your fate. So don't you dare threaten me."

He looked chagrined for a moment, then his shoulders slumped and his youthful yet haggard features pinched into a scowl. "Say your piece, then. Why did you marry him?"

"He gave me no choice," she said, her tongue dry and thick. "What's worse, *Da* gave me no choice."

"Tupped you, then, did he? Did you laugh with him after? Telling stories of our simple ways?"

"Shut your filthy mouth and see reason. He's had nothing to gain by mingling with our people, or learning the names of everyone on the mill floor. At least he's *tried* when no one else has."

Tommy's dark hair looked like tousled shadows even when lit by the spring sunshine streaming through the kitchen's only window. "Is that how he caught your eye? Or was it the other way around?"

"I'm certain he came to Glasgow with no intention of marrying a penniless factory girl. Had he any sense, he'd have taken after a local debutante with money and connection." She forced a breath of calm. "Can't you see? This is our chance. Finally, someone with influence and an interest in hearing me out." She pushed away from the table. "And I dare you to say I shouldn't do what I can to keep Ma safe and secure. Look me in the eye and tell me I don't have that right—bloody hell, Tommy—that *obligation*."

"You're a whore, then." So calm. So devastating.

She banked a shudder. "Think what you like. But he didn't need to marry me. Had he just been looking for a quick go, he'd have left off without a backward glance."

Said so bluntly, and said to another person—not rattling inside her addled mind—she realized just what Alex had done. He was arrogant, stubborn, and occasionally blind to emotion of any kind, but he was *good*. She believed that, just as she believed he would be the one to bring change to their forgotten little corner of the city.

"Then tell me why he's thrown in with the other masters, eh?"

Her ribs felt tight. "How so?"

The leer Tommy sported left no room for doubt. He believed what he was going to say. "Mr. Alex Christie, your new husband, has entered into an agreement with the rest of their lot. They want to reduce wages this year—reduce costs to make up for the sabotage losses."

"No. I don't believe you."

"Why else do you think we're having this meeting? Rob Callaghan heard it from the overseer at Bennett's."

"Jack Findley? He's the one pointing the finger at you! There's no reason to trust his word."

"It won't matter once Hamish starts talking strike." He smacked his fist into his palm. "About time."

"You'd have everything undone. Now, on the verge of being able to get what we deserve?"

"How can you believe that so blindly, when your husband's a liar?"

The room dipped and swam before her eyes. He wouldn't. Not with his principles. She couldn't imagine Alex Christie harboring such devious motives. He walked in a straight line and thought in a straight line. That he could've been using her to undermine the union was not only an entirely new fear, it was too hurtful to contemplate.

"I'll find out, Tommy."

His dubious expression was at least a change from the violent twist of his lip. "Find out what?"

"What he knows. What he's agreed to. If they intend to provoke a strike just to break us down, they must have plans to bring in workers from the Highlands or Ireland. That sort of arrangement can't be concealed, not down on the docks. And if they believe we'll sit idly by, they're dead wrong." She met Tommy's gaze head-on. "You know how hard I've worked, when no one else thought I should. Trust me, just as I trusted your word. I can be the ally we never thought we'd have."

With his thin, rugged features still dubious, Tommy nodded. For a second she caught a glimpse of the boy she'd grown up with. They'd shared the scant treasures life afforded. Now he seemed willing to share a little bit of belief.

"You're a mad girl. You know that, right?"

"Says the devil himself. And Tommy?"

He scuffed his toes against the bare wood floor. "What?"

"What do you know about the night I was arrested?"

"That it happened. Something about prostitution? I assumed it was just gossip started by the pigs or the masters. But you were with him, weren't you?"

"Yes. Trying to find information about Jack Findley." She ignored his look of disbelief. "The night I was arrested, the constables had my shawl. I'd left it by accident at Old Peter's. Someone turned it over to the police as evidence against me. I need to know who that was. Maybe it was a master or the police, as you said. But maybe . . ."

Feeling as if she were being watched by a thousand eyes, as if the walls had ears, she whispered a name. She shouldn't trust Tommy either, but when it came to steering clear of another stint in prison, he might have just enough sense to be tenacious.

"And what will you do in the meantime?"

A tremor of foreboding settled at the base of her spine. "I'm going to find out what my husband's hiding."

Alex awoke in the middle of the night, his heart racing. He sat up and fumbled for the lamp's wick to check the time. The clock on his bedside table read half-past three. With an arm over his eyes, he flopped back onto the bed. His heart still thudded at a tremendous rate, as he searched through wisps of sleep to catch the remnants of the dream that had shocked him to wakefulness.

Nothing came. He may as well have blamed a plain white wall for his anxiety.

Polly was not in bed beside him. He kicked out of sheets and tugged on his dressing robe. The floor was cold against his feet despite being early May. He'd been in Scotland for three months. Disconcerting that it seemed so long. And he had another year and a half to go.

Not that he thought it likely he'd last that long. Winchester and Bennett were primed to ruin his chances. If their all-or-nothing strategy of revenge against the union went ahead as planned, they would destroy more than Alex's chances at earning his father's bequest.

A whole community stood poised on the verge of collapse.

As did one very new, very precarious marriage.

He shoved a hand through his hair, wondering why he hadn't smacked Bennett across the mouth when afforded the chance. First he'd reminded Alex of the masters' unanimous agreement to decrease wages. At the first hint of Alex's hesitation—because, Christ, he was more uncertain than ever about that decision—Bennett had blamed Polly. Insulted her.

Alex regretted his restraint, no matter how disastrous it would've been.

He needed a drink. He needed the stars. Awaking long before dawn hadn't been a burden when working for the university in Philadelphia. The most fascinating constellations could be seen when the world slept. Glasgow conspired to take a great deal from him. His sanity, chiefly, because with the industrial smog and the bright streetlights, both gas and electric, he could never get a clear view of the sky.

And he needed to find Polly. The bed didn't feel right without her at his side.

Padding downstairs, he poured a whiskey at the sideboard in the library. Bennett had sat in that wingback by the fireplace, his fat jowls wiggling like sacks of egg yolks. "Eat or be eaten, Christie. That's something you apparently didn't learn from your father."

Such an attitude had steered Alex away from capitalism and its fortunes, which turned like a gaming wheel. Yet William Christie had done good works when he'd been able. He'd been a hard old bastard, but he'd never been heartless. Compared to men like Bennett and Winchester, his father had been able to chart a narrow path between profit and morality. Perhaps trade wasn't as clear-cut as Alex had always assumed.

After downing the first whiskey, he poured another and thought to check in on his son. Agnes remained in their household, assisting Polly now that she stayed home, but Alex needed contact with Edmund. His son was the reason he jumped through hoops like a trained dog.

Only, his boy was not alone.

Alex stopped in the doorway. The heart that had only just slowed leapt forth as if powering a flat-out run. He'd witnessed this scene before: Polly in the rocking chair, with Edmund in her arms. Both were asleep. The last remnants of a fire slowly died in the nearby fireplace. Yet the image never failed to steal his breath away, along with any rational thought.

He loved his son. And he dearly loved his wife.

The realization hit him in waves. Cold at first. Then burning hot. He let the truth of it cover him like a new skin. Swallowing past a hard lump in his throat, he gathered every detail of that timeless picture. He was a scientist. His imagination needed such fuel. He needed the wrinkle along Edmund's cheek where it pressed against the swaddling, and how his knitted cap overwhelmed his brow. Alex needed the slack angle of Polly's neck, with her head cradled by the back of the rocker, and how her arms protected his son even in the throes of sleep.

Keep them. Keep them both. Safe and happy.

The pressure of those simple, needful impulses constricted his chest until he needed to sit. Hand shaking, he found a nearby chair and eased into its embrace. At least they were both with him. For now. It was an unhealthy purgatory.

He sat watching them and nursing his drink until the fire ebbed to near-darkness. The first shades of dawn tinted the backs of the nursery's drapes. He could've sat there forever. There was no peace to be found when faced with the oncoming storm. Somehow he'd thought he would have more time. More time to change generations' worth of prejudice and mistrust. More time to convince them of a beneficial agreement and earn his fortune.

More time to win Polly's heart.

Once she learned what he'd agreed to . . .

She stirred. Alex's heartbeat roused once again, as did the taut, hungry body that remained so greedy for her touch.

She blinked, then rolled her neck. Her eyes found Alex. "Oh!"

He touched his forefinger to his lips, signaling for quiet. On silent feet he arose and lifted Edmund from her arms. The warmth from that tiny bundle grabbed him in deep, primal places. So much potential. Gently, he laid his son in the crib. After a massive yawn and a few smacks of his gums, Edmund quieted and returned to slumber.

Without thought, he took Polly's hand. He left the nursery door open when he led her into the corridor and up the stairs. Upon reaching the landing, he whispered against her temple, "Next time, wake me. Or Agnes. You need rest."

"I do nothing strenuous all day. Besides, I like holding him. He enjoys it."

He pressed his forehead to hers. "I enjoy it, too."

Her eyes shone radiantly where the first rays of

sunshine crept through the nearest window. "Take me to bed."

They kissed each other down the corridor. Arms tangled in clothing until they were locked in his bedroom and stripped naked. Alex sucked in a sharp breath. Christ, she was amazing. So beautiful of face and form. A piercing passion swept over him like the blaze of a comet. His limbs worked with jerky precision as he pulled down the bedcovers, urged her to lie down, and followed her into that blissful refuge.

Again, her smile. Eyes wide and blatantly appreciative, she raked her gaze from head to toe. She was as cheeky as she was sensuous. "That sight never gets old."

"Never say never."

"Don't doubt me, master. I know when I speak the truth."

He stretched along his wife's lithe body. "You insist on calling me that."

"You react to it." Her hands slid around to hug his waist. "Not much seems to affect you. I've needed to be creative."

He wanted to touch her everywhere, *now*, but started with her face—the curve of her cheek, the fullness of her wide, soft lower lip. "You're too creative for my sanity."

"Bollocks to that."

He shook his head, grinning. "What if I responded to different provocation? Would you stop then?"

"What do you have in mind?"

"Let me think on that," he whispered against her mouth.

"We've already established that you think too much."

She grazed her thigh along the outside of his. He was close—very close to where they would be joined. Breath to breath, belly to belly. He pressed his lips to hers. Softly at first, then he delved inside to challenge her in a rough duel of tongues and teeth. Air became a precious commodity. His lungs heaved. He wished the dulling pang of whiskey wasn't so cloying, because he wanted more of her taste.

Fingers that had been gentle now dug into the flesh of his hips. She found the place where he throbbed and ached. Alex groaned, thrust, clutched her buttocks. Her resilient female flesh felt indescribably perfect in his hands. He kneaded deeply and drank deeply and kissed deeply. With his arms tight, he turned her onto her back. Dawn was crawling across the bed, brightening the red of her hair and the challenging green of her eyes, illuminating the freckles on her pale, flawless skin.

Only that radiant sight held the power to restrain his passion. He just wanted to look at her.

"When you call me 'master,'" he said softly against her mouth, "you put us back on different levels. I never set out to be anyone's better."

"Too bad the way the world works."

"I never would've thought you resigned."

Although one hand remained maddeningly tight around his erection, she lifted the other to brush the hair back from his temples. Sexual and sweet—both.

"Hardly," she said. "But we don't have to let it in here. You remember what I said about happiness?"

"To let it in."

Frank appreciation deepened her smile. "That's right."

He nudged between her legs. With a long, sensuous caress, he traced the line of her inner thigh and found her center. She was wet, hot, open for him.

"Polly?"

She batted her lashes, appearing almost innocent. Almost. "Hm?"

"Let *me* in."

Twenty-two

Polly sighed as he pushed inside. Being filled, being covered by his lean bulk—every time, she edged closer and closer to simply letting him make her feel good. He could pamper her for the rest of her days, but the woman he cossetted and doted upon would not be *her*. The real her.

That didn't mean she could keep from going weak when their bodies locked together. She moaned, her eyes rolling closed.

He let go of his hesitation a little sooner each time, as if he was beginning to trust how good they could be. His hand found her breast. He palmed her sensitive flesh and ducked his head toward her chest. She gasped when he took her nipple into his mouth. Wet and warm, his tongue slicked over and over in sensuous circles, even as his hips pulsed. He found a deep, lingering rhythm with both. Sensation spiraled heavenward.

There remained so much she wanted to do to

this man. With him. But for the moment, this was enough. They were tender and passionate, both, as the sun bathed them in gold.

She grabbed hunks of pale hair and held him at her breast. Arching toward his patient attentions, she let her body reveal unspoken thoughts. He slid his hand down her ribs, as if taking note of every individual bone. Such a patient man, he'd probably learned the name for each—as if he could catalog what made a body unique, what made its heart beat and its mind strive for new ideas. Emphasizing his patience even in the midst of his hunger, he switched to her other breast and started anew. First kissing. Then a nibbling touch of teeth. Finally he drew her into his mouth, sucking deep.

Polly spun away. She writhed against her pillow and twisted her hips up to meet his steady invasion. So hard. So long. He bared his teeth yet pumped with precision, hitting a spot that turned her hot and mindless.

Sweat shone on his brow. The muscled press of his torso stretched heavily over hers. His ribs and pectorals shifted with each gyration. She should've felt crushed, even trapped. Instead she clasped her hands around his lean waist and drew him closer. He responded with a faster rhythm.

She moaned against his ear. "I like that," she gasped.

"I'm sure you do."

"Because I'm wicked?"

"Because I can never surprise you."

Taking his earlobe between her teeth, she bit

harder than she'd intended. He grunted and shoved her against the mattress with a hard thrust. "I dare you to try," she said.

"You so enjoy pushing me."

She bit again, then gasped his name when he moaned. "You're just learning that?"

Alex suddenly laughed. His shoulders heaved. The delicious muscles lining his chest and stomach tensed as his hips faltered in their steady rhythm. His mouth bent into a precious, boyish smile. "Slow learner," he whispered.

Before she could respond, Polly found herself flipped. She squealed before joining in his laughter.

Alex stretched flat beneath her. With his arms behind his head, he ground up into her body—his prick still filling her so deeply. That beautiful grin took on a salacious edge she'd never seen. "Surprise. I win."

"Oh, you do?" Polly balanced with her palms on his chest, quickly giving over to giddy delight. "I beg to differ."

"Begging does not suit you."

"No, I don't believe it does. Taking, though . . ."

She dug her fingertips into his thick muscles. Never had the bronzed gold of sunlight draped across a more handsome man. Shadows defined the curve of his powerful chest, the neat lines of his tense abdomen, and the sweeping, elegant strength of his ribs. He swallowed thickly, then parted his lips on a sensual intake of breath. Indulging her desires, she stroked upward to his wide, solid shoulders. Luscious hair tickled her palms. A contented purr shook beneath her palms. She leaned near and scraped her teeth over his heart. His gasping breath and tight hips told of his pleasure even before he murmured her name.

Using her thighs, Polly discovered just the right angle and just the right rhythm. She realized the power she held—the power he'd given her. She could accept as much or as little as she wanted. She could set the speed that suited her needs. Even more than when she'd been pinned beneath his solid weight, she reveled in setting the terms.

"You're understanding now, aren't you?" he asked softly.

"I am."

"Then take me, Polly."

A surge of responsibility thrilled her. Challenged her. She drank in the sight of his naked need. Hazel eyes darkened. She bit her lower lip on a naughty grin. Slowly, anticipating this more than she could've imagined, she retrieved both his hands from behind his head. And placed them square on her arse.

"Hold tight. Don't let go."

His eyes rolled closed on a long "Yes . . ."

Polly arched back until she could rest her palms on his taut thighs. Just the right spot. She liked being able to find it again so quickly. With Alex holding her firmly in place, she began to move. Deliberately at first—only a tense, tight slide of her sheath. She felt every ridge and each hard inch, learning him as intimately as she had with her tongue.

She pulsed faster. The muscles in her thighs sizzled with the decadent burn. Alex gripped her buttocks harder, opening her in new ways. She felt vulnerable, but held with such strength. The fullness she'd come to associate with intense pleasure began to build between her legs and deeper, just below her belly.

He joined her now, pumping up as she dropped down. She tipped forward to brace her hands on his chest. But that wasn't enough. She wanted to be closer. With her forearms looped around his neck, she pressed her breasts against him. The hard points of her nipples ground into his chest hair.

"You do this to me." She bit the stiff tendon that climbed his neck. Sparks dashed behind her eyelids when he grunted. Each press of teeth pulled a different noise from him. She feasted on skin and sound. "Alex, you drive me mad when you fuck me."

"Bloody Christ," he gasped.

"I want everything you can give me." She shook, so near to her release. "Now, my love. God, *now*."

He rasped a strangled sound. His hips stiffened on a deep drive. He shook from thigh to shoulder, and ground his head back into the pillow. Polly thrust two fingers between her thighs. She closed her eyes and took the image of his bliss with her into the dark. Her body jerked, a long sigh eased clear of her lips, and the dark exploded into a brilliant field of white.

As full morning lit the ceiling, Alex lay still, remembering the myth of Helios riding across the sky in his chariot. The ancient Greeks had believed him the personification of the sun's blaze from east to west. Alex had never put stock in mythical explanations of how heavenly bodies moved or how they were created. But he'd read stories from the Greco-Roman, Norse, and Egyptian canon to his younger sister, Vivienne, when she'd first arrived at their father's New York brownstone. Barely eight years old and half wild, speaking only French, she had surprised them all by quieting for Alex when he read.

So he'd learned myths for her. Their power was in binding him to the sister he adored.

With Polly curled against his side, her breathing quiet, he wondered how Viv fared in Cape Colony. Or Gwen, his little ray of sunshine. Or Gareth, so full of potential and mirth. Alex missed them dearly and owed them all letters, even as he awaited news from them. Only to Vivienne, however, would he confide the wonder and uncertainty of that morning.

I've married, Viv. She's penniless, mulishly stubborn, occasionally vulgar.

Burying his nose in Polly's hair, he breathed deeply. The tightness that had been lodged in his chest since childhood was no longer so easy to find. He had to search for that reflexive morbidity. He wanted to be free of it now. Polly had given him a gift and a goal he'd never knew he needed.

But, good God, Viv, she's beautiful and terribly clever. And how she makes me feel . . .

Polly stirred gently. Her hands gripped his waist, even though her eyes remained closed. She hummed a contented sound as she blinked to full wakefulness.

Alex kissed her forehead. "Good morning."

"Mornin'."

"Your accent is almost impossible when you're groggy."

"Och. No teasin' now."

But she was smiling already, as if daring him to do just that. To keep teasing until nothing mattered other than gathering more and more of her radiance.

Viv, you really must meet her.

I love her.

He touched two fingers to his lips and smelled Polly's scent. On his skin. Threaded through the sheets and in the air. Oh, yes, he loved his new bride.

Yet why did he hesitate in telling her? Perhaps because he had forced her to wed. He had taken her from her home, and had taken from her the calling that defined so much of her life. And through it all, he kept the secrets of the mill masters. She would not forgive him for that.

More time. He needed more time to set everything to rights. Then he could confess the emotions that banged so fiercely in his heart. He would say it out loud and turn this capricious union into a lasting one.

She sat up and stretched. The pose offered him a breathtaking view of her back, where lush, vibrant hair trailed down to just below her ribs. Tempting twin divots marked the tops of her buttocks. With her arms over her head, she arched slightly, reminiscent of the way she'd arched while riding him. In three-quarter profile, her breasts stretched upward, too. Her nipples were pert and upturned, just like the tip of her nose.

Alex traced his hand up her side. He barely touched that soft flesh before she collapsed in a heap of giggles.

"So there's your ticklish spot," he said.

Pulled tight into a ball, she peeked out from beneath the shield of her hair. "Impossible man. I didn't know what sort of monster I'd awaken."

"Never poke a bear while it's sleeping."

"A bear?" She giggled again, then flipped her hair aside. Hands interlaced over his chest, she rested her chin atop them. Magnetic green eyes—eyes he'd been lost to for a long time—looked up at him with lurid delight. "You do rather remind me of one when you take your clothes off."

"Excuse me?"

She pushed her fingertips into his chest hair. And scraped him. She smiled at his soft hiss. "No one would ever guess you hide this lovely body beneath your business suit. So strong. But you'll give yourself away if you let that beard grow."

Alex rubbed a hand over three days' growth on his chin and cheeks. He'd never been lazy about his appearance, but other concerns had eclipsed his regular priorities. "I'll shave."

Polly frowned slightly.

"What?"

"I wish you didn't have to," she said. "It felt . . . wonderful."

"Where?"

She blinked, seeming aghast. Only for a moment. "On my tits, love."

Alex grabbed her around the waist. "Foul-mouthed temptress."

"Or you could always call me your wife. That works, too."

Both of them went still. Their gazes locked. They hadn't spoken about *any* of it—just went about their separate days and joined in breathless passion at night. Two married people lived under that roof, but they had yet to acknowledge the fact.

He sat up. "I'll look like just another Scotsman if I keep the stubble. Seems my father passed on a touch of ginger I hadn't known was there."

Polly wasn't letting him go. Up on her knees, she curled along his back. Breasts, stomach, hips. All for him. He felt the urge to shout for joy—and run to hide. He'd never known a woman more bent on having what she wanted. Clever hands mined the hard, tense places along his upper back. He remembered that long-ago evening at Idle Michael's when she'd tended to his scrapes and cuts. How could he have known what pleasure yet awaited them? The groan she pulled out of him was completely unavoidable.

"But I *like* Scotsmen. They look burly and strong, like I'd be protected forever." She pressed her lips down along his nape. "Isn't that what you've offered me, Alex? What you promised my da?"

He turned his head and caught the back of hers. They kissed like that, as if they couldn't even wait to face each other. Desire he'd thought thoroughly sated swelled so suddenly that he forgot to breathe.

This was what he'd been missing. All he'd never had.

"Yes," he said against her wet lips—that lovely wide mouth with its teasing mischief. "It's what I promised."

She mussed his hair and climbed off the bed with

the enthusiasm of a girl half her years. But she wasn't smiling anymore. A sense of foreboding he couldn't ignore gathered like a cloud over his happiness.

"Polly? What is it?"

"I've spoken to Tommy," she said. "Since the wedding."

He froze in the motion of sitting up. That meant she'd ventured into Calton, while he'd been arguing with men of business or bending over the journals that blur into lines of ink. He'd just . . . *assumed* she would stay home. His instructions had been for her own good, but he'd been a fool to believe Polly would give it all up. Knowing her history with Tommy added a surprising edge of jealousy.

"Why?"

Green eyes flashed before she hid them away, looking out the front window. She still wore no clothes. Was she doing it on purpose? The effect was undeniable. He traced the line of her buttocks even as his mind burned with a hundred terrible possibilities.

"He wanted to meet me because he'd heard we were married. I needed the chance to explain myself."

"Who told you where to find him?"

"I've known where he was."

"*What?*"

"I wasn't about to hand him over to the police, now was I?"

She finally grabbed his dressing gown. If she'd planned to hold this conversation while nude, she thought better of it now. Yet Alex did not breathe easier. He pushed off the bed and shoved his legs into a pair of trousers.

"I had no need to tell you," she continued. "I'm not a prisoner here. And besides, it wasn't your business."

"My mill nearly burned to the ground. You've been hiding the prime suspect. Then you sneak out of my house like a fugitive, to meet a man who *is* one. Jesus, Polly, you make it damned hard to keep you safe when you run through Calton looking for trouble. So tell me. How the hell is that not my business?"

"Your mill. Your house. Your business. And now I'm *your* wife. I'm to be dragged along with no say in anything! There's a difference between being protected and being claimed by a tyrant." She tossed her hair back. That God almighty stubborn chin volunteered to lead her resistance. "Speaking of tyrants, you might be interested in something he heard. Something about how the masters are set to decrease wages to compensate for recent losses."

This was it. She knew.

Alex ran his hands through his hair. Feeling dangerous and barely in control, he stalked across the bedroom. He wanted to shake Polly until she begged and apologized—for what, he didn't know. For turning him inside out? For making him regret the decisions he'd needed to make?

"Tommy's not wrong," he said at last.

Her laugh was a ragged, pathetic thing. "But not you. I told him that you're different. Give me that much, Alex."

She looked at him with a hope he could not honor. Just as he'd feared, he was out of time. He shoved his surprising, amazing desires into a box and closed it. Locked it. Buried it.

"The decision was unanimous," he said soberly. "For the sake of the mill, I need to stand with the other masters."

"You *sided* with those bastards?" Hurt registered so plainly across her dear face. Skin illuminated by the gathering sunlight pinched around her mouth. She pulled into herself, tightening the robe, hunching her shoulders. "For how long? How long have you been pretending to give a good goddamn about finding out the truth? Or about helping the weavers?"

He stared her down. She was as angry as he'd ever seen. *Good.* Because he was about to explode. "Since the morning before we saw the aurora. I agreed at the meeting that followed."

"So tell me, was spending time in Calton just a lark? You shouldn't have been an astronomer or an industrialist, Alex. You should've been an actor, because I believed you actually cared."

Alex snagged her chin and held fast, even when she tried to jerk away. "And you, *wife.* I actually believed you wanted to learn the truth about the fire. How long have you been hiding Tommy?"

"Weeks. And a good thing, too. He'd have been hanged before being given a chance to defend himself. You saw what the police did to stitch me up. I dare you to argue he would've been treated fairly." Alex felt her teeth grind together beneath his fingertips. "In the meantime, you lied just long enough to twist me into this bloody marriage."

He grasped her upper arms. "Tell me you didn't enjoy this morning and I'll call you a liar right back."

"Let go of me! You don't like being called a master, yet look what you've become. You've taken everything from me! I *trusted* you."

"I can understand relenting for the sake of your family. Marrying me would protect them. Christ, I even encouraged that." His mind rebelled against the memory of her daring words and how eagerly he'd drawn them in, like a lad with his first filthy fantasy. He clasped his fists at his side, standing silent and still in the bedroom that shared their mingled scents. "But did you marry me for the union?"

Those beautiful lips, still swollen from his kisses, tilted into a sneer. "Had I wanted anything from you that badly, I would've jumped at the chance to marry you. I'd have tattled to my da after our first fuck."

"No, you knew exactly how to play me. Sex and innocence and prying under my skin."

She slapped him. The shock banged through Alex's skull. "I don't recall dragging you into a factory office and forcing a kiss. Yes, I talked with Da about approaching you, getting to know you better. We needed that opportunity, just like you needed information from me. So don't you dare tell me this was some sordid trickery."

Polly rubbed her palm while Alex rubbed his cheek. "To think," she said, breathless now, "I defended you! To everyone! I told Tommy outright that you wouldn't side with those fat cats and their greed. You believe you've been taken as a fool, but that worthless honor is mine. You thickheaded *idiot*. I fell in love with you! I've sat in this house like a prisoner. Waiting. I've shared your bed and your body every night. Still waiting."

Breath seared inside his chest. "For what?"

"For you to say *anything*. Anything to make me feel like more than some refugee you pulled out of the slums." The flush of her cheeks had turned as pale as milk. "I've turned myself inside out in the hope you might see me as more than a lover wearing a wedding band—or the means to some industrial end. Turns out I've been blind to how far a master will stoop to add to his riches."

Alex shrugged, as if their disagreement was no more devastating than being unable to agree on a wine to serve with supper. "That cannot be true because I am not a rich man. I'm worth little more than my largest telescope. To earn my inheritance and keep full custody of my son, I need to make this wretched company profitable by the end of 1883."

She nodded curtly. "That year and a half you mentioned."

"That's right. And I'll do anything—*anything*, Polly—to make it happen. Don't believe for a second that your union is exempt."

"I've shared so much with you. Tried to make you happy. Hoped you'd make *me* happy. You've treated me no better than gutter trash. Gutter trash, Alex."

He'd thrown Winchester into the street for leveling that same insult at Polly. She looked just as he felt, as if ready to vomit.

He could tell her, *I love you, too.* He could tell her how wrong she was, that he respected her more than any woman he'd ever known. But his honesty would only muddy the situation. The mill and the union, his son and his wife—he needed to choose, just as he'd sacrificed passion for Mamie's sake.

No one could have it all.

Cold. So cold. When had his room full of sunlight and love turned into four walls stuffed to the ceiling with ice?

"If you can't live with the decisions I've made, then an annulment is for the best."

The spark in her eyes faded. A layer of cloudy gray shaded their bright green beauty. She nodded. Stiffly. But her shoulders no longer bowed. She stood regally. "Have it your way, master. I'm used to that by now."

The door to his bedroom shook. Agnes knocked roughly, her words raw as she shouted through the wood. "Mr. Christie? Where's the missus, sir? Come quick. It's her da."

Twenty-three

Polly pinned her hair back in a severe bun, using the looking glass above her mother's Georgian porcelain basin—one of her family's few treasures. It had been passed down from mother to daughter, just like the genuine tortoiseshell combs she brought out for the funeral. Her hair finished, she donned the black she'd worn for her grandma's funeral three years before.

She was wearing her own clothes, not the ones Alex had ordered made for her. And she was back in the home where she'd been born. Her old pallet had held her, not his strong arms. That she shared the tiny space with her mother and brothers was no longer such a dire concern. That she succumbed to random fits of tears . . . she tried constantly to hide that truth.

Her da was dead.

Hours later, after the somber service at the church, the mourners arrived at the graveyard where her father would be laid to rest. Flanked by her brothers, Polly supported Ma and worked to keep her steps even, slow, determined. She would not let the weakness in her knees get the best of her. They were as soft as the veil whipping across her line of sight. May leaves rustled on that breeze. Such a beautiful spring day. But black lace darkened her view.

Ma had never appeared older or more haggard. Whatever grief Polly felt paled by comparison. Maybe, in some odd way, she was lucky. The loss of her father competed with other gut-twisting emotions. A raging, red anger. And heartbreak. Both burned in her chest.

Dozens of people—maybe as many as a hundred—crowded around the gaping mouth of his open grave. Heath and Wallace joined Hamish and Les as they carried the coffin out from the church. Even Tommy was there, protected for a time by a community bound together in mourning.

Polly said nothing when the reverend paused in his recitation to allow last words from family members. Instead, fingers numb, she held her mother's hand as they each tossed a clod of dirt into the grave. The pale pine of his coffin no longer gleamed. That beautiful wood had seemed such a waste, but the union membership had pooled donations to buy the finely crafted piece. The ground would own it forever. But, swallowing thickly, Polly was grateful now that they had insisted. It was a final measure of respect for a man few, if any, outside of Calton would remember.

No one said a word about her marriage. Her

father's final gift had been to shield her from talk on this, her first day back among her people. But she would've borne the worst whispers to have Alex at her side. She loved him. She *needed* him. That he remained at home flayed her down to muscle and bone. Her face hurt from holding back screams that yearned to come blaring out. She remained a married woman standing alone at her father's funeral.

"Ashes to ashes, dust to dust," Reverend McCormick intoned.

He dipped his chin and led that final service for Graham Gowan. Every disagreement and grudge was set aside. Everyone wore the same drab black—for most, the best clothing they owned. They prayed the same prayer, which Polly could only mouth. Her throat hurt too badly to speak.

She supported her mother through the rigors of the day. The church food churned in her stomach as she endured best wishes from those who'd idolized her father. Soon, most of the men would slip away and raise a pint in his honor. She wished she could join them.

Shoulders aching, she pressed her back against an elm that stretched its newborn leaves high over the football pitch where she had watched Alex compete, seemingly ages ago. Some boys and young men did so now. Sunday was their only freedom from the workweek, and no one—not even those grieving most deeply—begrudged them an hour of play.

Hamish Nyman joined her. The expression he wore was nearly . . . sheepish. She hadn't expected that in the least.

"Here to offer your congratulations on my wedding, or your condolences for my loss?"

"He was a good man," Hamish said, skirting her question.

"That he was. I wonder what you'll do with the mantle you'll pick up in his stead. Wear it or burn it?"

"Depends on you." He hadn't argued against her assumption. Hamish intended to make a play for the leadership.

"On me? Hardly. You'll move on without me, and with good reason. I wouldn't trust me either."

He added a noncommittal noise, then worked to roll a cigarette. "You did what you had to. Only the worst of this lot would begrudge you that."

She shook her head. "Don't talk bollocks to me. I know better. And I know exactly what I'd be calling a girl like me."

"You've never been just any girl." He lit the cigarette and drew in a deep breath. Silvery smoke caught the breeze as he exhaled. "More than that, you're still Graham's daughter. If we want this strike to hold firm, we need you. Your support. Your blessing."

Strike.

It was exactly what she'd hoped to avoid. The masters were planning to punish everyone for the actions of a few, whose identities remained unknown. They wanted to destroy the union her father had worked decades to forge. The wage decrease would cause an internal split—accept it for the sake of hungry children, or risk worse by fighting for more.

But no. They'd hold the line together. No one would take advantage of them.

"No violence, Hamish. We can't have it."

His shoulders slumped, as if relieved. "I didn't think you'd agree at all."

She pushed away from the tree. The weakness that had invaded her joints upon learning of her father's death was nowhere to be found. "Just where do you believe my loyalty lies? After all these years? Don't be absurd."

"You could lose everything."

"No worries on that score." A single word repeated as a droning chant in her mind. *Annulment*. "I have all that I need when I stand with my kin."

He faced the setting sun. His beard obscured the set of his mouth. "Well, well. Seems one of the masters thought to pay his respects."

Eyes narrowed, he nodded to the walkway leading to the church.

Polly knew whom she'd find, even before she turned.

Alex Christie wore a suit that cut close to his lean hips and flared across his shoulders, accentuating their breadth. He didn't hesitate but strode forward, face straight ahead. The eyes that followed him up the walkway did not alter his focus. With his top hat in place and walking stick in hand, he played the part of the mill master to a most convincing end.

Only, now she knew it wasn't an act.

Curses bunched on her tongue, but she kept silent. He greeted the reverend. He bowed respectfully to her mother where she sat among dear friends. He shook hands with her brothers. Polly squished her sense of disloyalty. Her family couldn't possibly know that she and Alex had fallen out. Coming home to comfort her mother for a few days didn't imply permanence.

Hamish touched her on the shoulder. A conspiratorial gleam in his eyes filled her with a dread she couldn't name. "We decided to move quickly. The meeting's tonight. Eight o'clock at the old Gorman warehouse."

"Why not the meeting hall? We've held our assemblies there for ten years."

"We can't trust anyone from outside our circle to make plans. Understand?"

"Hamish," she said, trying to stay composed. "It's a bad precedent to set. The meeting hall is available to any peaceful organization in the city. It's one of our few claims to legitimacy. We'll look like anarchists!"

He flicked his small green eyes back toward the church, where Alex still mingled with the mourners. That he remained, offering his condolences, constricted a place in her chest that had flared hot and greedy at the mere sight of him.

"Make your choice," Hamish said. "Eight o'clock."

Polly swallowed. Her father was dead. Hamish was not the man she wanted to take his place—or even *her* place. But she knew where his loyalties were. Maybe with a little luck and the right words, she could keep him from pushing the membership toward disaster.

Alex had taken his side. She would take hers.

"I'll be there."

"You're your father's daughter, girl." He snubbed

his cigarette out in the grass. "Now, I think I'll leave you two alone."

"Hello, Polly."

She closed her eyes. Breathed in. When she faced daylight once again, Hamish had walked away to rejoin the congregants. Alex took his place.

The setting sun burnished his sandy hair. Hard lines radiated from his eyes toward his temples, and deep grooves dug around his mouth. His expression was rife with sympathy that made her knees weak. The unrelenting cleverness that shone out from his green-and-gold eyes admired her every feature—as concentrated as a caress and as eloquent as a thousand questions.

Kissing. Touching. Making love. He'd ruined all of it.

Even declaring her love hadn't been enough.

She wanted to hate him but found only sadness. How could she feel any grief beyond what was due her da? Yet it was right there, pounding out from her bones. She mourned for the marriage she'd been forced into accepting, and for the loss of the man she'd only just come to adore.

"Hello," she said quietly.

"I'm glad so many people are here for you and your family. That support must be reassuring." His mouth drew downward in an even deeper frown.

She wanted to shout at him. *I don't have your support! My own husband!*

But her heart went out to him, as it always did when people suffered. Maybe all those years, letting the happiness in, she'd been holding the ugliness at bay by reaching out to others. At that moment, no matter their differences, she sympathized with a fellow human being who had also recently lost his father. Six months on from Sir William's passing, and eleven months on from Mamie's, Alex appeared weary from the grief she'd only just been forced to bear.

"Did you have . . . support?" she asked.

He looked down to where his walking stick dug into the soft spring loam. "Many people attended his funeral."

"That's not the same thing."

"No, it's not. But my siblings were there. We've always had one another."

Polly smoothed her hands across her stomach. Inside crocheted black gloves, her palms were damp with sweat. "I'm glad you came."

He faced the sun easing toward the western horizon. She'd always admired the strength of his profile, the aristocratic surety of it. Beautiful, yet stalwart and capable of great passions. The thought of passion, so recently shared and so recently lost, was particularly devastating. "I'm sorry for your loss, Polly. I wish I could've come to know him better."

The line of his back seemed especially straight, his shoulders square and stiff, as he turned to walk away.

A mistake. One of them was making a mistake, but she could no longer tell who or what. His name was on her tongue when he stopped. Returned. His nostrils flared, as did some unspoken emotion in his hypnotic eyes.

"I'm asking you, Polly. Come home."

Polly backed against the tree. There was nowhere else to go. All she could do was stare and try to breathe. He stole her reason and her pride, only to replace it with selfish, youthful urges—and to sweep it all away when they'd stood on the brink of happiness.

"You told me once that you thought yourself a progressive man," she said. "You drafted petitions and marched alongside Mamie. Now you're ready to throw all of us into a fire as big as Winchester's. Whose side will you take when the constables come to arrest Tommy? They will, you know." Polly shook her head. "Can't have the truth get in the way of profit."

"That's not fair."

"None of this is fair. So tell me, Alex. What happened to the man you were?"

He didn't flinch, didn't drop his eyes. "I became a father. And I learned how to fight."

"Not hard enough. You're settling all over again. I was taught that settling was no better than failure. If you'd learned that, we might still have a chance. But I bloody hell can't do it on my own."

She might as well have been talking to the tree at her back.

The grim line of his mouth fit the day's mood. He tipped his hat like a stranger. "Good evening, Mrs. Christie."

Alex walked away. He climbed into his carriage and didn't look back.

Once inside, he leaned against the leather. His head weighed a hundred pounds. His heart weighed more.

What happened to the man you were?

The drive home wasn't long enough to escape the echo of her question. He'd given her an answer—a true answer. But it wasn't enough.

He played games of chess with business possibilities. The weavers would strike. Polly had all but said so. Many started peacefully enough. He had witnessed them in the United States, avidly following their progress in the papers. For every one that was amicably resolved, another ten ended in violence. Decreasing wages would fan hot tempers on one side, while the damage done to the mills made the masters implacable. A strike now would mean bloodshed.

Could he carry that on his conscience?

He knew the answer. It would mean being wed to a woman who hated the man he'd become, just as he would hate himself. Assumptions that he would have more time to pick through the threads had come to naught. His deliberations and reason had little place in Glasgow.

Evening crept up on him as he worked in his study. He lost focus for minutes at a time, as if sleepwalking between duties. Numbness had pervaded his body, his mind, ever since making love to Polly during that early dawn. Nothing else held the same intensity.

He shoved away his ledgers and penned the letter he'd been dreading. Each word scraped across the paper as if made indelible by a tattooist. The petition for an annulment. Once he had satisfied the terms of his father's will, he would do what he could to aid

Polly and her family. In the meantime he would give back her freedom. It hadn't been his to control.

When that dreadful missive sat drying on his desk, he found that the light had nearly gone. A gentle rap on the door pulled him back to reality.

"Mr. Christie, sir?"

"What is it, Agnes?"

"I'm putting Edmund down for the night. Would you like to say good night?"

This had become a ritual. No matter how exhausting his day, he always made time to see his son off to sleep. Edmund would be walking soon. Already he was making sounds that approximated words. The idea that he would, very soon, become a fully functioning little boy dragged thorns across Alex's heart.

What was worse, he and Polly had taken to saying good night to him together. She'd hummed some Scots lullaby as she kissed Edmund on the head, smoothing his hair. Now she was gone. She hadn't come home after the funeral, nor did he expect her to.

He shoved those pains aside as rocked Edmund.

Agnes folded a blanket. "Have I ever told you about your father when he was a lad?"

Alex frowned. He'd never heard the woman speak so informally. Beyond that, the subject set him on edge. His father? As a boy? Part of him didn't want to know. Thinking of William Christie as a stern old bastard was much easier. Clearer.

Yet reminders of his goodness would not accommodate Alex's mood. What man would feel obligated to rescue the daughter he'd sired off a French dancer? After Viv's mother died, their father had done just that. She'd became inextricable from their little clan because of his quiet kindness and implacable will. And always, his love for dear Catrin had been the bedrock of their family. The Welsh girl and the millionaire magnate. He had made choices out of love, when many in his place would have weighed expenses and aggravation.

The realization knotted Alex's stomach.

"I don't believe you have," he said quietly.

"His da was a drunk. Died in a fight where someone brought a busted bottle." She paused. "Does it hurt or help to hear it, sir?"

"Both. Go on, please."

"His ma slipped between the cracks, if you take my meaning, sir. Left him on his own to grow up wild. He used his fists to start, making money from bare-knuckle fights. And one day he just disappeared."

Alex shifted Edmund to better cradle him. "Disappeared?"

"He hopped a schooner to America. A decade later, his name showed up in the papers from London. He'd become quite the success." She smiled in a way that, oddly, made her look far older. "We're not the English, you know. We don't hold people back so much by order of rank and birth. Some may have been jealous of his success, but most were proud of what he'd managed."

She exhaled heavily, looking quite tired. "Once all this fuss dies down, no one will think any less of Polly either. We're proud of our girl and always will be. She's never been wrong about people. Trusted the right ones. Suspected the guilty ones." She shrugged. "I thought maybe you'd like to be told."

"She isn't an easy woman to know. Neither was my father."

"Nor to be raised by, I'm sure. But doesn't that make the undertaking all the more important?" As if closing a book, Agnes resumed her customary polite detachment. "Now, to get this young man off to bed."

He let her take Edmund and watched as she bundled and shushed him. Alex needed air. Room. Answers. None of those would be found in the small nursery. More curtly than he intended, he kissed Edmund and bid Agnes good night. "I'm going out."

Some power he couldn't explain added vigor to his limbs as he climbed the stairs three at a time.

What happened to the man you were?

All he knew was that a tantalizing future beckoned, just beyond his reach. Polly was strong, determined, and one of the best people he'd ever known. Certainly the most selfless.

And he'd walked away. Like a stranger. Like a man who didn't care.

He fisted his hands in his hair and pulled. He cared so much. Did anything else matter beyond the future they could make together?

If Alex had any say in the matter, and he certainly did, he would find the right balance. From the start he'd known that cooperation would yield better results. A heavy dose of strong emotion had stolen that clarity.

But he was clearheaded when he tossed the annulment into the fire. All doubt disappeared by the time that hated document shriveled to ash. He grabbed his coat, hat, and walking stick. She would be at her parents' house. No, he thought with a pang of sympathy. Her *mother's* house.

He'd only just stepped outside when a shadow moved among nearby shrubs. "Who's there?"

"You know who I am, master," came Tommy Larnach's sneered reply.

Alex hefted his walking stick like a weapon. "Tell me why I shouldn't smash your brains in right now. You little shit, you started this by blowing up my factory."

"Keep insulting me, and I won't say what I came to say." Wiry and sleek, Tommy lurched into the faint light that shone from the parlor window. Blood had dried across his nose and upper lip. A nasty gash slit the top of his right cheekbone. He looked down at his shirt, then lifted that worn cotton. "Besides, Livingstone already had his way with me. He's the man you want."

Despite shadows that colored him in shades of midnight, his bruises were obvious. Cuts peppered his thin chest.

"Bloody Christ. Livingstone did that?"

"I was following him."

"Why?"

"He's never been clear of suspicion in Polly's mind. We all have too much history with the bastard. Turns out one of his men tipped off the constables on the night you two were at Old Peter's. And no coincidence Livingstone gave her tartan to the police."

Tommy shuffled forward, more clearly illuminated by lamps in the front parlor. "He caught me tonight as he came out of Winchester's office. And there was another man. Well-heeled. Don't recognize him. Some agreement between them—laughing together like chums from a pub."

Alex had gone numb from neck to hip—the whole of his guts. Just frozen. "Nothing to do with Jack Findley?"

"Bennett's man? No. He's more likely to wind up in a doxy's bed than be traipsing around causing trouble. I learned what he'd been saying about me and we . . . Well, we had a little chat." He grinned fiercely.

"Why should I trust you?"

"You can't, I suppose. But we can start with something simple. I know where your wife is tonight." The young man's mouth pinched into a flat line before he exhaled. "I don't want to see her hurt."

Alex held back a flash of panic by will alone. "Tell me."

"The union is voting to strike. Polly still thinks she can persuade them to keep it peaceful." Although he still held his injured arm, Tommy stood up straight and looked Alex square in the eye. "She'll fight for it, master, but she won't win."

Twenty-four

The temper in the old Gorman warehouse was already ugly. Polly sat beside Constance Nells on a pair of moldy crates that shouldn't have been able to hold their weight. Companies with healthier bank balances had moved from the docks to the Woodlands, then farther west across the Clyde. Whatever enterprise used Gorman's must be in desperate straits. She shivered although the air trapped in that squat, dilapidated stockroom was hot with sweat and the fervor of too many raised voices.

Only invoking her father's memory had permitted her in the door. Walt Nells had never appeared more intimidating as he let her pass. Neither had he ever looked at her with more scorn. He was there for Connie's sake, and for her protection.

Polly had only herself.

Hamish stood at the front of the mass of workers. A broad smile shaped the curve of his beard. "We've been here before," he said as the angered voices quieted. "We've been in dire situations, with no clear path to take. We've been betrayed by our own over the years. Although those slights won't be forgotten, we can and must move on." He stared pointedly toward where Polly sat on the crate.

Her face burned hot. So many words of defense leapt into her throat, but she swallowed them back. She had been too hopeful in believing that Hamish's civil words at the funeral would continue after he took control.

"Now a strike is our only choice. The masters have been unable to find the perpetrators of the sabotage and arson, so they're intent to blame us. And why not? They always have."

Shouts from the crowd threatened to overwhelm his speech. His own fault, Polly thought. Because whipping them into a frenzy was his intent, nothing rational would be said that evening.

What should have been a quiet meeting of no more than a dozen key leaders—including the best, most levelheaded negotiators—had swelled to more than forty people. All believed that they knew the way clear. Polly doubted whether they even understood the extent of the troubles they faced. The union her father had labored to make effective was in tatters. They sat in a dockside warehouse like fugitives, wailing like children deprived of promised sweets.

"Now, to pay for the burned mills," Hamish continued, "they plan to reduce our wages and cut benefits. Anyone who doesn't agree to the decrease will be sacked. What are we going to do about it?"

"Strike!" came the sharp reply of dozens of voices.

Hamish raised his voice to be heard above the muddled roar of conversation—some of which spiked toward argument. "We need to make them see we won't be bullied. We need to hold together!"

"But what are we to live on until then?" a woman called.

"The union has resources to cover the basics. We can do this if we stick close and stay intent on our demands."

Les stood, lanky as ever, his clothing in disarray. "But what *are* our demands? Do we even have a consensus, or will the union devolve into a group of autocrats as bad as any masters? I will not support an organization that favors the dictates of a few! We must be in agreement or the center will not hold."

"That's why we're here." Hamish's weariness was beginning to show. "To reach a consensus."

Polly indulged one brief, selfish thought. *Now you know how difficult it is, my friend.* But that was all she permitted. Sadness and dread urged her to jump to the front of the room.

Another voice chimed in. "Are we even agreed that a strike is necessary?"

Shouts of disagreement drowned out Hamish's reply. He raised his hands, joining in the fray of voices, before dropping his arms. The cocksure man appeared lost.

"I should go home," Connie whispered. "We both should, Polly."

The tone had changed so drastically that the meeting more closely resembled the last moments before a pub brawl broke out. Polly could stand it no longer. "I won't let it end this way."

Her feet propelled her toward the front of the sweltering warehouse. She was halfway there when one particular shout proved just how close they were to ruin.

"We'll take it to the masters! Take it to their homes and families. See how they like it!"

Her guts clenched when that call for violence wasn't met with censure—but with cheers of approval.

She hurried forward, more determined now.

"Polly, don't!" Connie pleaded from where Walt stood by the exit.

Her shout was, by far, the most sensible offered that evening. And it was the only one Polly chose to ignore.

She shoved past a score of angered men and women. Her elbows connected with ribs and the meat of shoulders. Some cursed her, but most parted, wearing looks of surprise. Persevering meant holding on to her patience, her courage, and her sense of right and wrong. So many considerations—but she was certain of each one.

She broke through to the front of the gathering, suddenly undaunted by the bodies. She caught her balance and stumbled into place beside Hamish. Perhaps she appeared as some pratfall stage act, because some of the shouting quieted. Well, at least she had surprise on her side.

"That was harder than it should've been," she said with a forced grin.

Hamish's cheeks were an unhealthy white along

the top of his beard. Sweat matted the bright red hair against his forehead and turned his neckerchief limp. He appeared as if that fight in a pub had already taken place, with only a few bruises and cracked teeth missing from his air of defeat.

"Do you mind, Hamish? I couldn't keep quiet any longer."

He nodded, almost dumbfounded. Good. More surprise.

And there she stood, surround by a crescent of expectant faces, with the north wall at her back. Every voice quieted. She made a point of making contact with each set of eyes in the front row. Look. Hold. Connect with scared souls and angered hearts.

The room was hers.

"I saw my da buried today," she said quietly.

Those words hadn't been planned. She flinched, in fact, as if someone else had spoken of her father's casket being lowered, how that shiny pine had dulled with the first fistful of dirt from Ma's hands. Her eyes watered and her throat closed around the punch of grief. She had nothing left but what could be wrested from the stubborn, frightened, hopeful hearts of her fellow weavers.

She couldn't stop. Not now. Da would've been standing there in her place, had he been well and able. Instead she stood for them both.

"Men still take their hats off as a sign of respect, don't they?"

Pointedly, she locked eyes with Les. He had always been her most reliable deputy. True to form, and thankfully so, he slid his flat cap off his head. Other blokes followed suit. Hope rose in her chest—hope that she still dealt with civilized men and women, rather than the crazed animals the masters believed them to be.

"He would have had worthy insults for the state of this place," she said, dubiously eyeing the ceiling. "But probably, he'd hold more pity for the poor sods who work here."

That got a smile or two. Although she hadn't spoken at his church service or at his graveside, she felt as if her next few words were the eulogy her da deserved.

"Few of you have any notion of how often he plotted and schemed for our little rabble. He and I sat at our kitchen table, and by the fire when his life was slowly ebbing. All the while, my dear ma sat knitting lace at pennies apiece. She never agreed with dragging me into this rowdy lot. But Da . . . he was as stubborn as me."

A few more smiles. Quietly reminiscent. The older men and women, especially, shared that humor because they'd worked alongside him for tens of years. Maybe those elders would be able to hold the peace.

"More stubborn, even, because he never once thought about how strange it was to have a girl standing before you. He never once said that he'd wished I was a boy, or that it would be easier if I were a man. I thought that strange more than once, even as I started in. He'd only tell me, 'Smile for them, girl. No one can think past your smile.'"

The one she wore at that moment felt less forced,

more as if she were simply telling tales down at Idle Michael's.

"Now, I don't know about that," she said ruefully. "Because he talked a load of bollocks as often as he talked sense. You remember, Les, that time when he wanted to trade Colin Potts for a pig?"

"Said a pig would've worked the looms with more grace," Les replied. "And would've better satisfied Colin's wife!"

Laughter—nervous at first—changed the mood in the warehouse. Polly wanted to keep that momentum on her side. "And the time he swam across the Clyde after losing a bet with Hamish here?"

"I beat him fair and square," Hamish said smugly. His white-faced fear was receding. "I finished my quota first."

An unexpected lightness came over her as she spoke. "Sure you did. Da knew you would, too, just like he knew the bet was good for morale on a day of low spirits—that day, eight years ago, when a quarter of Bennett's workforce had been made redundant. I swear he laughed the whole way across, just like the rest of us did while watching from the riverbank."

"There was a lot to laugh at," a woman called. "Palest arse I ever did see!"

Polly grinned. "It was either swim nude or face Ma with the muddy washing. I know which one any of you would've chosen!"

More laughter now, good honest laughter. This was grieving, she knew, just as much as it calmed frayed tempers. She was saying good-bye in ways she hadn't been able in the cemetery.

"But he would've been upset, and rightly so, at this discord. You cannot know how it pains my heart to hear us tonight. This fear. *I'm* fearful, too. I'm fearful that everything he worked toward will be bowled under by anger and burnt to a crisp by hot tempers." After a deep breath, she lifted her chin. "I'm here to ask for your patience. Your wisdom. Your ability to compromise. Otherwise we'll be consigning ourselves to the will of the masters—and consigning my dear da's life to that of just another dreamer."

"Please, let's sit," Hamish added. "Sit and we'll take this as civilized people."

Slowly, so slowly, the forty-odd workers began to take seats on the stacked crates. Les started them off. Polly passed him a grateful nod, and smiled at Connie when she rejoined them, dragging Walt by the hand. The soft rustling of fabric and the occasional scrape of wood against wood replaced the clamor of the previous half hour.

"Polly? If you would?" Hamish gestured toward the lectern, formally giving over his place.

Then he, too, found a place among the crowd. Left alone, she was once again in charge of her people. She'd wanted it all along—purpose, connection, acceptance. But the hollow in her chest could not be ignored. Buoyed by the strength of her da's memory, and looked upon with glimmers of hope amid so many expectant eyes, she still felt incredibly alone.

Shut up and get in," Alex told Polly's brothers. "She's at Gorman's warehouse."

Although Wallace was built to proportions more suited to a man, he was still but a lad. Both boys shared their sister's coloring, all whiskey and flame. "That place is a shithole."

They barreled into the hackney beside Tommy.

As the horses jerked forward, Alex stared down all three young men. His grip on the head of the walking stick threatened to pop his knuckles right out of his skin. "She's on her own in Glasgow at night. How could you let her venture out on her own?"

"Let her?" Tommy's laughter had a hard edge. "No one's ever *let* that girl do anything."

Wallace lifted his chin in a way that reminded Alex of his sister, Vivienne, always challenging the world to think less of her if it dared. "And begging your pardon, sir, we're not her husband."

"No, you're not."

If Polly really was in danger . . .That evening, he carried a deep, untapped capacity for violence.

A few dockside shops still spilled light onto the wharf—pubs and less-reputable hotels. Certainly not the sort of place where upright citizens ventured after hours. The lads spilled out of the cab with graceless enthusiasm, and Alex tossed the driver a few coins.

He raced ahead of Tommy and the Gowan brothers. Moisture stained each inhale with the rot of the busy harbor, where petroleum slid alongside mold and dead fish. A light fog blurred every line until even the corner joints of brick buildings looked as soft as hair. Through a narrow walkway and up a climb of stone steps, he came to a rise, where a low building dominated a blind alley. In the receiving yard on its south side, a winch and several broken-down wagons waited like shadowy spiders. What should've been a lifeless building shone a pale glow.

God grant me another chance. I'll make it up to her.

Voices in disagreement echoed out from the warehouse and bounced down the tight dead end. He slowed and moved with the darkness until he found a crack of light. A door was ajar.

Inside, Polly was surrounded.

"Thirty, maybe forty people," Alex rasped as the others caught up with him, "Jesus, what was she thinking?"

He took in the lay of the warehouse's interior. What he should've done was round up the constables, but the union—and Polly in particular—had already suffered menace enough from the authorities. Alex would simply need to wade into that lot as if his name adorned Christie Textiles.

A lucky thing.

But the assured cadence of her voice gave him pause. How calmly she could command people's respect. How easily she eased even the most restless natures. No wonder he'd fallen for her. She had the power to charm dozens at a time. To find himself the center of her attention was like being hit by lightning. Only, he didn't hurt. He wasn't suffering. She had freed him in ways that would take him years to fully understand.

"Now," she said evenly. "The first thing we need to do is consider our options. As it stands—"

"I have a question, Mrs. Christie."

Alex saw Polly's shoulders draw back. In that place, the use of her married name wasn't a compliment or a show of respect.

"Who said that?"

Rand Livingstone pushed into the semicircle, followed by two men wearing silvery scars across rough faces. "I did, lassie. Tell me, why should anyone give a rot's toss what you have to say?"

"I'll put it right back to you, Livingstone. You've never stood with us, not like Howard McCutcheon has. He's been overseer at Christie's for ten years, but he still sees the path to justice." She appealed to the crowd. "But has anyone at Winchester's *not* felt the weight of Livingstone's bullying—bloody hell, even his fists and truncheon? Women, tell me you haven't been pressed to accept his hands on your bodies."

A fierce undertone attested to her truth.

"That bastard." Tommy Larnach wheezed and sagged to his knees. The brothers helped by propping him beneath his arms. Thick black hair covered his forehead as he slumped forward. "He's going to set them all off."

For the first time, Alex could see why Polly defended this unlikely lad. Fierce and unkempt, sly and menacing, he worked hard to hide a sense of fairness as stern as Polly's.

Inside the warehouse, Livingstone's voice lifted to a shout. "There is no Winchester Fabrics now! We need to give Tommy Larnach over to the police and end this." He turned to sneer at Polly. "And we need to know how willing you are to aid your precious cause, Mrs. Christie. Perhaps you can share information gleaned in the master's bed? *That* I'd like to hear. Give us the secrets of the scheming whore who sold out all of Calton."

Angered cries filled the warehouse. Polly's magic evaporated, just as molten slag replaced the blood in Alex's veins.

He slammed open the warehouse door.

Twenty-five

Alex and Polly locked eyes. For that brief moment, they shared every fear and every hope.

Then Rand Livingstone fired a gun.

"You son of a bitch!" Alex bellowed.

Before he could reach the human scum and his hulking bruisers, the scene melted into chaos. Workers in the rough clothing of the poor scattered toward far corners. Men sheltered women behind crates or machinery, while others hurried toward the exits. Alex jumped aside to avoid the crush. He glanced back to where he had seen Tommy, lying between Polly's brothers, but he could no longer see the lads. He only hoped they would stay together and protect one another from the stampede.

"Polly!"

Like a fish fighting its way upstream, he shouldered past fleeing bodies and called again for his wife. He broke through the crowd but she was gone. He spun in search of her auburn hair.

A crack of fire surged through his jaw. Thought was blown from his head. Reeling, as pain raced like a bullet from skin to bone to brain, he staggered backward and caught his balance against a crate. Another blow smashed the base of his skull. The crate beneath his hands gave way. The whistle of another descending blow gave him a blink of warning.

He flipped onto his back and swung his walking stick. The wood slammed against a man's forearm. With his attacker doubled up, cradling the wrecked limb, Alex lurched to his feet. To his surprise, he was gathering details with uncanny sharpness. His opponent was one of Livingstone's cohorts, some ungainly troll with carrot-orange hair and huge shoulders. And the walking stick in Alex's hand was a much less satisfactory weapon than a nearby pipe.

He snatched up the hollow length of steel. "Where is she?"

"You broke my bloody arm, you bastard," the brute said with a snarl.

Something grated behind Alex's left ear when he spoke. So he wasted no words—simply hefted the pipe in one hand and the walking stick in the other. "Where?"

"That man's bodyguards have her. I was only supposed to scatter the crowd."

"What man? Livingstone?"

"No! Some Yankee."

Alex slammed the stick across the man's upper back, then raised the pipe. "Where is she?"

"Out to the north docks, with the lightweight craft." The troll's words were squeaky with panic.

"Us and Livingstone were supposed to follow. We'd be paid then. To a schooner called the *Mamie*."

No.

Throwing the weight of his frustrations behind it, he jabbed the pipe into the man's ribs. His stumpy opponent groaned in agony and slumped to the floor.

Alex met him there, grabbing his collar and giving him a shake. He ground the toe of his boot between the man's legs. "Who has the gun?"

"Livingstone."

Heath burst into the warehouse. "We saw them!"

Alex shoved the troll's head against the planks and snatched up the makeshift weapons. Fear like he'd never known made his heart shake like a terrified animal's. No coincidences. Not now and not like this. Threads of information laced together, weaving a funeral shroud for Josiah Todd.

He left Tommy with Polly's younger brother. "Wallace, rouse the constables. Invoke my name and send them to the north docks. Make it happen."

Then he and Heath shot down the alleyway. The young man had found a jagged piece of wood, which he hefted over his shoulder like a cricket bat. Their footfalls slapped against the moist cobblestones, straight toward the docks. Each pounding step crushed pain up through Alex's jaw and the base of his skull. He focused on his aches rather than fears.

So many times he'd led with his brain, as if his body was just a container to carry his thoughts from place to place. Now his body was his most important asset. He'd beat Josiah Todd into oblivion with his bare hands. If Livingston or anyone else was stupid enough to intervene, they'd get the same.

"Here!" Heath tore around a corner, Alex on his heels.

A dozen yards later, they burst onto the main walkway that ran parallel to the docks. Ships of all shapes and sizes cluttered the River Clyde, maybe a hundred in all.

"A schooner called the *Mamie*," Alex grated out.

Heath hesitated, concentrating. Then he nodded. "This way."

The lad worked these docks. If anyone could help find Polly, her brother would make it happen.

"It came into port in April," Heath shouted over his shoulder. "Big vessel, for a pleasure craft. I don't remember it unloading cargo, which is why I remember it at all."

Alex had believed his former father-in-law a despicable but ultimately cowardly man—one more apt to use stealthy, backhanded means rather than overt action. Had Todd truly descended to the point of madness, intent on taking revenge on Alex for having married Mamie? For taking Edmund?

Just how far would he go?

Polly clutched where a stitch jabbed under her ribs. The corset beneath her funeral garb was laced too tightly. She'd hustled to keep up with Livingstone. He hadn't let go of her wrist since dragging her bodily out of the ramshackle warehouse. Once up the ramp of a schooner and through the hatch, he threw her down against the inner hull. Only thick carpeting cushioned her landing.

Livingstone spoke to a lackey who descended the ladder into the hold. "Stay with her, Hollis. I'm going to find the others."

Then he was gone.

Hollis sat on a leather-padded bench that curved along the port side. Polly sat half propped on her elbow. She had smashed her knee against a crate during the mad flight from the warehouse. Blood seeped through her stockings. She shoved tangled hair out of her face.

The posh interior of that small schooner made Alex's residence look fit for paupers. Decorated with elegant paintings and even a foot-tall marble bust, it more resembled a palace than a boat sitting in industrial Clyde Harbor. The scent of flowers was too absurd to believe, until she spotted a beautiful glass vase filled with freshly cut blossoms. A sideboard next to Hollis's bench was full to bursting with crystal decanters, delicate wineglasses, and even a tray of ripe strawberries.

Trying for calm, she flicked her eyes to where Hollis sat leering. He smirked, then licked his lips. Polly hid the shiver that slunk down her spine.

"Where are we?" she dared ask.

"Shut up."

Fine. No sense talking to a man who made a living beating up innocents. He sported a number of scars on his face, and his nose jutted at a strange angle toward his left cheek. Livingstone was a bully, but he'd always been clever enough to strut through town with bigger men at his beck and call.

Her thoughts kept jerking back to that warehouse and the fear she'd battled. Livingstone, Hollis, and that other, stumpy hunk of ugly muscle. All of them threatening the workers she'd only just reassured, rousing them against Polly's entreaties for calm.

With one bullet, Livingstone had scattered her people as if they were terrified sheep.

And Alex. She'd met his gaze across that sea of fear, before he, too, was swallowed by the chaos.

She shouldn't indulge thoughts of him or why he'd barged into the warehouse. To break up the meeting? Had he brought constables with him? Perhaps he'd really taken to such extremes. Now that she knew the pressure he faced to make Christie Textiles profitable, much of his obsession made sense.

Yet Livingstone was now her most important consideration. What game was he playing? What "others" had he gone to find?

The wail of a baby shocked her from her musings. She recognized that cry.

Edmund!

Although her first reaction was to distrust her own brain, her instincts were stronger. Edmund. With both the baby and Polly on board that schooner, Livingstone—or whoever was funding him—had gathered two of the few people on earth who mattered to Alex Christie.

A place in her heart sank in on itself, slowly, like an apple rotting from the inside. Alex would die before letting anyone hurt his son. She knew it like she knew that she loved him.

She wouldn't sit by and watch that happen.

Turning away from Hollis, she faked a hard cough until her eyes watered. "Please. Water. Anything."

The man sneered. But another round of hoarse, heaving coughs left her gasping. Blinking past wet lashes, she saw his frown of concentration. Lord, he looked dumb.

Come on, you pillock. Be just dumb enough.

She almost laughed when he stood and trudged with giant feet toward the sideboard. He opened a decanter of clear liquid, but Polly didn't wait long enough to find out what he poured. Leaping up, she grabbed the marble bust off its plinth. It was heavier than she'd estimated, like lurching with a boulder. Her arms burned, and her back nearly bowed.

But she would not be deterred.

Hollis turned. She heaved the bust into his abdomen. He doubled over. Not waiting for him to recover, she grabbed the decanter. Rather than shatter, the glass thumped heavily against his skull, almost bouncing out of her hands. Another sharp blow, this time to the marble sideboard, splintered the decanter into shards. Its slender base fit neatly in her hand—an impromptu knife of jagged glass.

She attempted to jab his face, but had to skitter away from his sloppy attempt to grab her legs. She thrust the wicked decanter down again, this time connecting with the top of his spine. Blood spurted from his ragged skin. She kicked him in the kidneys, one boot after the other. He gurgled and slumped forward.

Part of her shook with the fear that she'd killed him.

Part of her wanted to kick him again.

But Edmund needed her.

She searched the long, narrow room in the belly of the ship for a better weapon. On the wall behind a wide oak desk hung a series of daguerreotypes. The sepia tones revealed unfamiliar hunting destinations. In each photo, a man with white hair and a full white beard stood over dead animals—elephants and tigers and a whole menagerie's worth of wildlife. Whoever owned the boat was quite the hunter.

Now Polly was, too.

Because at the center of that pictographic arrangement hung a sword, a ceremonial pistol, and a small machete.

She grabbed it. Lord knew if she'd be able to use it without hurting herself. No matter. She adjusted her grip on the engraved silver handle.

Passing the sideboard, she grabbed the drink Hollis had poured and tossed it back, gratified to find it was liquor. The sudden blast of alcohol fired her brain—just what she needed. She couldn't climb the ladder in her skirts while holding the machete. So, with the knife clamped in her teeth, she grabbed the rungs. Nerves made her swift. Years growing up defending herself against brothers and a neighborhood of curious young men had made her strong.

At the top of the ladder, she paused. The hatch remained open. Cautiously, so slowly, she peered into the night. The sky was murky with cloudy shadows, stealing her sense of perspective. But the men who stood there were easy to identify. Livingstone. Winchester. And the white-haired man from the photographs. Another figure caught her notice. Huddled nearby, with her back against a crate, sat Agnes. Edmund was in her arms, quieter now and wrapped in a blanket that glowed white in the strange evening haze.

Their gazes met.

Agnes's eyes opened wide. She shook her head minutely.

Polly took the knife from her teeth and raised a finger in what was probably an unnecessary gesture for silence.

Three men. Winchester was a nasty old tycoon, but Livingstone was tough, muscular, and still had his pistol. The other man obviously had a penchant for killing innocent creatures. Polly didn't like her odds. Not at all.

"You *owe* me." Livingston sounded even more angry than usual. More importantly, he sounded betrayed. "I did everything you asked—the looms, the fire, the charges against the girl. She's in your hold because I threw her down there. I deserve what you promised."

Livingstone. This whole time. Everything had been his doing. The rumors about Jack Findley had been a ruse—whispers in the right ears, playing on who she would trust and suspect. The wild-goose chase had wasted valuable time enough to let the union rip itself open, and the masters would never be blamed.

The man with white hair snarled in that polite way gentlemen were best able to manage. "I paid you—both of you, goddamn it—to ruin Christie Textiles. I won't pay up until that happens, and last time I checked, it's still open for business. "

"You've got his wife and his son," Winchester said. "Isn't that enough?"

"Not by half. I want him broken."

Polly's feet were growing numb on the rung. She needed to make a choice. Hide. Go to Agnes. Charge like a wild warrior woman.

"Josiah Todd!"

The three men turned their backs to Polly, but they didn't obscure her view.

Alex!

Her husband stood at the top of the gangplank. He appeared ghoulish, like a burly Celtic warrior of old. Fierce and fiery. The suit he'd worn to the funeral, the one she'd so admired for its cut and quality, had been dragged through hell and back. His top hat was gone. His sandy hair was a rugged mess in the twilight. He carried a metal pipe in one hand and his walking stick in the other. Both weapons paled next to the grim determination that fixed his expression in stone.

"Ah, Alex. Good of you to join us," said the man with the white beard.

My God.

He was Josiah Todd. Mamie's father. For Polly, everything fell into place. This was the fiend who had ruined a woman's life—his own daughter, no less. The monster whose callous perversions had driven Alex to take such desperate steps to save her.

"I'm here for my wife." Alex's voice was devoid of inflection.

Polly gasped. He didn't know about Edmund. Not yet. Instead he was doing battle to save yet another woman. Chinese fireworks sparked in her blood. She had resented him when he behaved like a stubborn mill master, but that tenacity had forged him into an avenging warrior.

"You can't have her." Mr. Todd's voice was just . . . *odd*. Up and down. Too loud, and then too quiet. Maybe that was how he always spoke, even in the face of imminent harm. Because Polly knew without a doubt that Alex was going to do him harm.

Her husband shifted the pipe in his palm. "Hand her over or endure what comes next."

"I have no time for you now, Alex. Maybe later you can have your pretty whore of a bride. Maybe not." He turned, grinning, toward where Agnes sat cradling Edmund, who started to cry. In Josiah Todd's grin, Polly saw the soul of a living, breathing demon. "Either way, I'm keeping my grandson."

Twenty-six

Josiah Todd had the power to drop the world out from under Alex's feet with just a few words. Always had. For years he'd threatened to send Mamie away to a Swiss boarding school, just to taunt Alex. He never had, of course, because that would mean he, too, would have to give her up. Just the threat, however, had stolen many nights of sleep.

Now the monster had Polly. And dear Christ, he had Edmund. The twist of sleepless nausea in Alex's belly was long gone. In its place burned fourteen years of heartache and loss, and a man's determination to save his family.

"Winchester, what did he promise you?"

The capitalist sneered. "Why should I tell you?"

"Because I'd like to see if it outweighs the lengthy sentence you'll receive when all of this is over."

"I won't go to prison."

"Oh, but you will. There was a witness, George. Your man Livingstone left Tommy Larnach alive.

He's with the constables as we speak. And that boy sings like a canary."

Winchester turned on Livingstone, his face darkened in rage. "You said you got rid of that nuisance!"

"Gutter slime like him can be tough to kill, sir." He grinned. "They're like rats."

Alex made a point of ignoring him, despite the overwhelming urge to turn Livingstone's face inside out. And where was Polly? Fatherly instincts demanded that he charge toward his son and hold him close. He could not afford to indulge any of those distractions. Instead he focused on Winchester. One less opponent to take by force.

"I doubt the other masters will be pleased that your greed meant running me through," he said. "So you stooped to sabotage. And arson against your own factory? Where was the sense in that, man?"

"Mr. Todd has promised compensation. I was to— what was the phrase? Divert suspicion."

"That won't change what the masters will do to you. They'll cast you out. 'Strike' is a dirty word, one that hasn't been spoken here in many years. You've turned a ghost story into flesh-and-blood reality. No one will forgive you for breaking that peace. So tell me, what compensation did he promise?"

"One hundred thousand dollars," Winchester said with a pinched voice. "And all of the inventory remaining when Christie Textiles is dismantled."

Livingstone appeared ready to do murder. Not against Alex, but against Winchester and Todd. "Fuck that," he growled. "One hundred thousand for this pig? I want the same."

Todd only ignored him, as did Alex. He'd deal with the bully later.

"I hope it's worth it, George. But if it isn't, feel free to step right past me." He hefted the pipe, gratified when Winchester's eyes widened to the size of eggs. "You don't need to suffer what these two have coming. Stay with them and it will destroy your reputation. You're a fool to think you'll be able to buy it back. Leave now and I'll offer what protection I can."

Winchester appeared ready to vomit and scream and faint at the same time.

"I said *now*!" Alex bellowed.

With slow but inexorable steps, Winchester backed away from Todd and Livingstone. "It's all gone off the rails, you see."

"You walk away," Todd said tightly, "and I'll have your head on a pike."

"I'm sorry, gentlemen."

Alex stepped aside as Winchester hurried past. He descended the gangplank with his head and shoulders bowed. His fate would be decided later.

Heath waited just out of sight on the dock. As soon as Winchester hurried down the street, the young man crept up the plank on his hands and knees. It was the best plan they could come up with on short notice, and with no idea who was aboard the schooner.

Now Alex faced two men instead of three, although Livingstone still had a gun.

He couldn't help but glance toward his wailing son. There was Agnes, holding Edmund. The bow of her body over Edmund helped alleviate Alex's fears only a little. The woman was endearingly loyal but no match for these beasts. Although his heart seized at the sight, he fought to calm his frantic pulse.

Then . . . another movement. Though shrouded in black, her pale skin still glowed a soft white in the evening gloom. The figure silently padded toward where Agnes huddled against a stack of crates.

Polly. Good Christ.

Although he tightened his fingers against a flash of dread, he did not waver. She was unharmed. And he had two more opponents to take down.

"And you, Livingstone? What did he promise you?"

"Five thousand. And Polly to do with as I pleased."

Alex swallowed bile. "Seems you already tried that with her, and she came out the victor."

"That won't happen again." The man drew his pistol out of his waistcoat. "Maybe what I want to do tonight is put a bullet through her pretty little face. She hasn't been worth all of this."

He strode back toward the crates, as if he, too, had seen Polly's movement. Heard her. Sensed her. Because he found her without difficulty. He placed the muzzle of the pistol against the side of her head.

"Better yet," he said, "let's talk about what we really want. There are three men on this ship. And three prizes: Polly, this mewling brat, and money. Both of you fine gentlemen have more than enough to spare. Did you really think you could offer Winchester so much without me getting wind?" He shook his head at Todd. "Too bad Christie laid all your cards on the table. Had I learned later, I'd have shot you in your bed. Would've enjoyed that."

"You'll regret this." Todd's silver beard shook with pent-up fury.

"Like you made Winchester regret his decision to walk away? Hardly. You hired me for a reason, Mr. Todd. Because you're too much of a coward to do the dirty work yourself. That's not a scruple to dog me." He cocked the pistol and waved it at the huddled trio. "Let's see what you'll pay to make sure I don't pull this trigger."

Todd stepped toward him. "Put that gun away, you cretin. Don't you dare hurt my grandson! He's *mine!*"

"Get back." Livingston turned the pistol on Todd. "I don't care who I have to shoot, but I'm not leaving this bloody boat without compensation."

A glint of metal snaked up from where Polly knelt, as she stabbed Livingstone in the side. Even from the distance of a dozen yards, Alex heard the squish of flesh being ripped open. The man howled and dropped to the deck. The pistol discharged a plume of smoke and sound, but the bullet flew wide of any target. Edmund began to scream.

Alex bolted from his place on the gangplank. He swung the pipe low across the backs of Todd's knees, then struck twice more at the base of his skull. The sick crunch gave him far too much satisfaction. The old man fell to the deck.

"Heath! Hurry!"

He didn't stop to see if the lad obeyed. With his eyes fixed on his final opponent, he raced forward and kicked the gun away. Polly straddled Livingstone where he sprawled face-first on the deck. She held what was perhaps a machete. Blood appeared black on the blade she pressed to the back of his neck. A nasty gash in his side was visible even in the dim light, bleeding profusely.

"Get Agnes and Edmund off the ship. I'll hold him here."

"Mrs. Christie, as you are wont to say, bollocks to that." He yanked her off the man's back and hauled her up, over his shoulder. Polly squealed. Paying no mind, he shoved the tip of his walking stick into the gash in Livingstone's open gut. The bully gnashed out a pain-laced scream. "Mind you, I also have this steel pipe. Move and I'll shove it up your arse."

In the distance came the sound of police bells. Wallace had done his job. *Good lad.*

"Livingstone, I hope you live long enough to tell the constables what you know about Todd. If you do, I'll pay for your treatment, recovery, and a ticket out of Scotland. Agreed?"

Livingstone groaned and nodded.

"Alex," Polly shrieked, "let me go!"

"I'm not letting you go again. Just watch what you do with that knife." He jerked his chin at Agnes. "If you would, Mrs. Doward. We're leaving."

Agnes struggled to her feet. In her arms Edmund still writhed and screamed. It pounded Alex's heart to see his son so distressed, but distressed was far preferable to harm. He'd make it up to the boy when they were safe. He'd make it up to Polly, too, even if she hammered his spine to pieces.

"Heath, how are we—?"

The blast of another gunshot ripped open the night.

Alex flinched. He watched as Heath cupped his arm and slumped against the side of the schooner. Todd was lying on his back, arm outstretched and holding a small caliber pistol that spewed smoke.

"Heath's here, too?" Polly's voice neared hysteria. "What happened?"

The good man who'd spent years repressing his inner beast gave over to a rage so great that Alex thought nothing of shrugging his wife off his shoulders. The way she cried out her brother's name only added more fuel. He strode to where Livingstone's Colt had skidded to a stop. He picked it up and aimed it at his father-in-law.

"You deserve no less than torture," he growled. "I should take you apart a piece at a time with that machete. I should tie you to a bed and keep you a defenseless prisoner for the rest of your life. I should let some soulless animal climb on top of you, night after night. Strip your soul. Destroy your mind. Drive you mad with pain and betrayal. I *should*." Alex cocked the pistol. "But I won't."

Todd coughed. The back of his head gleamed with a sickly wetness. "I hope your new bride fares even more poorly than my Mamie did under your care."

"Burn in hell, you sick bastard."

And he calmly put a bullet through Josiah Todd's heart.

Polly couldn't stop shaking as the hackney sped them toward the hospital. Her hands, her legs, the whole of her guts—everything quivered. His head braced against a carriage window, Heath had lost most of his color. He clutched his shoulder, where she pressed his wadded-up shirt against the bullet hole in his shoulder.

"Polly, quit fussing." Although he likely meant nonchalance, he delivered it through clenched teeth.

The cab bounced down the streets at a pace that her logical mind knew was obscenely fast. But not fast enough.

"It'll be all right," she said, a little breathless. "I won't let go. The blood loss isn't too great. Just through the meat, you see. Nothing serious."

"Sis?"

Her throat constricted. "Yes?"

"You're babbling."

"Oh, you hush, you cheeky bastard." She blinked past the tears she'd fought since leaving Alex on the schooner. There hadn't been time for a quick kiss or a desperate hug, let alone talking. They had parted within seconds—she for the hospital with Heath, while he stayed behind to sort matters with the police.

The carriage pulled to a jerking stop that nearly tossed her from the bench. A few moments later, she watched as a doctor and his assistants helped Heath down the steps. He walked of his own power into the hospital, with his eyes turned squarely toward the nurse who held his hand.

At least he seemed to fare well enough for that. The lad would be fine. Polly took a deep breath and let it out on a whoosh of relief.

But exhaustion threatened to overwhelm her. The stress of the entire day crashed on her like stones tossed from a bell tower. Her eyes felt lined with crushed shells. Every blink grated. The heavy drag of her funereal skirts pulled her earthward.

Inside, a nurse led her to a private room to wash up, then to a tiny chapel where she could wait. Polly nodded and let the nearest pew take her weight.

Alex had wanted an annulment. She'd been the one to protest their marriage so staunchly, but she'd also declared her feelings. Her *unrequited* feelings, it had seemed. Maybe the unknowns that yet stretched before them had been too intimidating. So many missteps cluttered the path leading from their wedding day. Her pride had caused some of those stumbles, as had his defensive reserve. When exchanging heated words, she hadn't been able to see the matching uncertainty woven through his sharp accusations.

She knew differently in her heart, and perhaps she always had: Alex Christie was capable of so much emotion.

She wiped her eyes. He would not keep denying her. Their passion—their *love*—was too important. The reward of his devotion was worth the trouble of wresting it out of his heart. He had wielded a pipe to help save her life. She would use the same against his thick skull if he kept behaving like an ass. Timidity didn't suit Graham Gowan's only daughter.

The chapel door opened and closed behind her. A man's hand appeared in her line of sight. He extended a handkerchief.

She looked up to find Alex standing beside her, in the aisle between the pews.

But he was not the determined master or even the contemplative stargazer she'd met months earlier. That man hadn't known his true desires, his true potential.

That man hadn't been her husband.

She took the handkerchief. It smelled of his body—warm and soapy, but tinged with the sweat from his fight. Pressing it to her cheeks and mouth, across her nose and eyes, was beautifully intimate. She wanted to be close to him.

"The doctor said your brother is already out of surgery. I think you could've sutured him just as well."

The gentle admiration in his voice was almost as healing as the news he shared. She took another breath and let hope flourish.

"What about the police? Will there be any charges against you?"

"No." His lips flattened and his hazel eyes blazed— what she'd come to think of as his mill master's expression. Tough. Resolved. Unrelenting. "I . . . *convinced* them of the truth. Winchester and Livingstone added their testimony, but I'm not through with either of them. Just because they made sensible choices on the schooner doesn't mean they'll escape their crimes so easily. The masters and the union wouldn't be at such odds without their selfish ambition."

"And Todd's family? You said they were important."

"So is mine. I'm worth very little, but lawyers for the whole of Christie Holdings won't back down in defending me." He smiled tightly. "They can't afford to. Scandal and share prices don't mix."

Polly felt optimistic enough to laugh. "You sound like a right bastard."

He blinked. Cautious amusement replaced the tightness straining his mouth. "That shouldn't sound like a compliment."

"It was meant as one. Where's Edmund?"

His quiet smile looked entirely depleted, but it was still a smile. With any luck, it would become easier each time, until *her* Alex returned. "Agnes has him, back at the house," he said. "She badgered one of the young constables until he had no choice but to accompany them in a hackney."

Now came a real laugh. Locked places in Polly's chest were opening to the future. "I should've liked to see that."

"You know, he's alive because of you."

"Agnes had more a hand in it," she said with a shake of her head. "Not me. And I wouldn't be alive either had you arrived any later."

"Then you both would be . . ." He blinked a few times and looked away, then nodded curtly. "The authorities will need to speak to you as well. They're curious what happened to the man they found in the hold."

She shrugged. "I hit him with a marble bust and stabbed him with a shattered decanter."

"Good girl." Obvious pride shone from his eyes. The skin at their corners crinkled with shared humor. "The rest of those at the union meeting will be asked to give statements as well."

"Some won't come forward. They fear the police too much."

Rather than sit, as Polly might assume, he knelt. He took both of her hands, but surprisingly, hers were steadier. "What if you asked them to? They respect you, Polly. They would listen to you, especially if it meant putting all of this behind us."

Her skin flushed, then chilled. "You didn't want me to have anything more to do with the union."

"It's as important to you as the stars are to me. I want to keep you safe, but not at such an expense." His lopsided grin made her heart tremble. "Is a mistaken man allowed to change his mind?"

She scooted closer, right to the edge of the pew. On a fit of daring, she kissed the end of his nose. "Absolutely. Much simpler that way. But I won't lie to them, Alex. I won't be a mouthpiece for masters who keep secrets and make no concessions in return."

"They will have guarantees from *all* of the masters regarding fair wages and working conditions."

She laughed outright, which sounded too loud in the tiny chapel. "Oh, and what woodland sprite will make that happen?"

"Me. I swear it."

"Are you magical now?"

"Not only have the weavers rebuilt our mill practically from scratch, but production is up more than ten percent from last year. I've run the numbers. I know their businesses inside out. None of them can compete with our growth." He kissed their interlaced fingers. "Besides, someone I know has shown me the merits of being stubborn."

"*Our* mill?"

"You're my wife," he said nonchalantly. "What's yours is mine."

Oh, he wasn't playing fair at all. And she didn't want him to stop. "What about your inheritance? The prize money?"

He sat beside her and pulled her into his lap. Polly gave a little gasp. He was so strong, so unyielding. The horrors of that evening had folded into his skin. New lines. New burdens to wear on his face. He looked drained, but with determination layered over every dear feature.

"It was never about the money," he said, voice thickened. "It was about keeping Edmund safe from that monster. And tonight—God, I almost lost you both. You think I give a damn about the money? I'd hand it over in a heartbeat."

He smoothed his hand along her temples, sweeping back her tousled hair. She must look a fright, but his reverent expression said he didn't see her that way.

"Our fathers taught us the same lesson. We *can* have it all if we fight for it. Only, you learned that lesson a lot better than I did. This new version of myself . . . I didn't know myself until tonight. Now I refuse to compromise. I want safety for my family, success in my business, validation in my studies. And if you're willing, I want to know I'm your husband—as surely as I know that I love you. Let me be that man, if no other."

Joyful tears gathered in her eyes and made swallowing difficult. "Go back," she whispered.

"Back?"

"To the part about loving me."

His eyes moved over her face as if trying to memorize every line, every tiny hair. Everything she'd hoped to find in those fascinating hazel depths shone without reserve. She had never been so cherished.

"I've loved you for so long that I can hardly think back to when it wasn't true." He heaved out a heavy breath. "But I was wrong in marrying you. I gave you so poor a choice as to make it no choice at all. I wanted you. As simple as that." A smile flashed across his mouth. "I should've known that forcing you is the worst possible way to get you to agree."

Polly bit her lower lip. His words were so much. Almost too much. But they were exactly what she'd longed to hear—everything she'd desired from the man she loved so much.

"How should you have done it, then?"

He didn't hesitate. He simply stood and urged her to her feet. Mischief glinted in his eyes. What would it be to see this man happy all the time? Could there be a greater gift in the world?

At the front of the chapel, standing before the tiny altar, he knelt. "I'll marry you all over again, if that's what you want. Or . . ." He looked away. His throat worked over another swallow. "Or we can continue with an annulment. I won't keep you if you want to go. But I won't compromise anymore. I need all of you—stubborn and fierce, caring and clever. Be my woman for all times."

Slowly, knowing this moment would last with her

for all time, she knelt, too. And kissed him. Their lips touched tentatively at first, and then with more assurance, more fire.

Her husband in more than name. They were bound, heart to heart.

"I don't want to get married again," she said against his mouth. "And I certainly don't want that bloody annulment. I love you, Alex. So very much. You're my gentleman and my warrior. My husband in all ways." She cupped his cheeks in her hands, kissed him again and again. "I shouldn't have hidden what I knew. Maybe if I'd have trusted you, but I couldn't risk—"

He held her tightly against his chest. Words rough with emotion tickled along her throat. "Enough now, Polly. It's all in the past. We'll let the happiness in, but nothing else."

"Oh, Alex." A tremble of absolute joy shook through her. "That's the vow I'd have wanted to exchange on our wedding day."

He only held on tighter, kissing her neck with a delicious combination of desire and tenderness. "Then let this be the start. Right now. What say you, Mrs. Christie?"

"I say, I do."

Epilogue

New York City
January 1, 1883

The carriage stopped in front of the Christie family brownstone with a jarring finality that ended Polly's quiet humming. Alex watched his wife with a steady eye toward her gathering tension.

That humming had awoken him at daybreak. Only, at that hour, he had assumed it simply a sweet accompaniment to her morning toilette. She'd dragged a brush idly through rich auburn curls draped over one bare shoulder. *All* of her had been bare, with not even a dressing gown. Softly padded hips and fine-spun ribs. The graceful spine and elegant neck that had fascinated him from the start. Softness and tenacious strength. Her catlike smile had said that she knew exactly what the impropriety did to him, and that she loved it as much as he did. He always, always awoke ready for her. And they enjoyed that fact as no two people ever had.

He smiled at his own whimsy. Yet he couldn't

deny that it felt like the truth. There were wealthy men, lucky men, and men who were loved unconditionally.

With Polly by his side and the mill a robust success, Alex was all three.

Now he suspected that the songs she'd unwittingly hummed throughout the day revealed disquiet. She had behaved much the same way in the week leading up to their daughter's birth. Granted, she was an armored valkyrie compared to him. Oily, stomach-sick worry had been his companion for those endless days. To lose frail Mamie had been difficult enough. To lose Polly . . .

Yet, as doggedly as ever, she'd cursed her way through the whole ordeal. Alex had come through with an expanded Lowland Scots vocabulary and a renewed appreciation for his wife's resilience. His relief had quickly been replaced by hope. Yes, he could be happy now. Anything they faced would be easier because they shared one another's strengthening love.

Three-year-old Edmund's baby sister, Catrina—an ode to his departed, beloved stepmother—sat on Agnes's lap. The patient old woman was as much a part of their family as blood relations. Her children grown, with lives of their own to fulfill, she'd declared her desire to see new lands. New York was the first city other than Glasgow she'd ever visited.

"No sense letting the wee girl wrinkle your fine gown," she had said, offering to hold the babe.

Looking upon Polly's fretful expression, however, Alex guessed his wife might have enjoyed having little Catrina to hold. Her fingers tangled and untangled in her lap, as if jerked by a puppeteer.

Even Edmund, handsomely dressed in the only set of clothes he hadn't outgrown during the transatlantic crossing, fidgeted with noticeable energy. "We here, Da?"

"Yes, we're here," Alex said.

Polly stared out the carriage window toward the hulking brownstone, which was oddly drained of color by the pale, snowy light of the winter afternoon. Once, the structure had intimidated him. Now he knew better. He knew where his father came from, and how hard he must've worked to achieve such success. The mansion was a small part of the legacy Alex was proud to accept.

"Agnes, please go ahead with the children. Get them settled while Mrs. Christie and I attend to business matters in the library. Afterward we can make introductions."

"Of course, Mr. Christie."

A footman from the mansion opened the carriage and assisted Edmund to the pavement. As Agnes followed, Polly bid their daughter a silent farewell by gently touching the infant's bright red curls. With the rumble and thud of boots on the roof, the coachmen unloaded the luggage. Perhaps Alex might eventually see his family decamp to a hotel, but he needed a few days among his siblings. Sparse communication and bare snippets of detail left him hungry for news. The final answers—whether they had succeeded—had not yet reached him.

With the carriage to themselves, Alex considered

taking Polly's agitated hands in his own. But coddling her had never been the right approach. Instead he leaned across the scant space and grabbed her waist. She squealed as he hauled her onto his lap. Some manner of female witchcraft meant she knew how much resistance he needed. A token protest, surely, but she wiggled and squirmed just enough to make him feel he'd brought her to heel. That thought, no matter how much fantasy, aroused him like no other. That he could tame and take such a woman.

But as he looked into her eyes, he knew better. He was the one who'd been tamed, taught to love and need, and to trust in both.

"Are you with me, my love?"

She tried a weak smile. Her thighs were tense across his. "You've given me little choice, Professor Christie."

He grinned at her use of his new title. Officially, he wouldn't take his position at the University of Glasgow until they returned in March, but ever since learning of the pending appointment, she had insisted on using it whenever she felt like teasing. Which was often. At least it was a better moniker than *master*.

Except her quiet words were shadows of her regular self.

"Tell me," he whispered.

"Your family . . . what will they think of me?"

"I've never heard you doubt yourself."

"I've never been minutes away from meeting the rest of the famed Christies."

"The *notorious* Christies would be more accurate."

"But my deportment lessons and tutoring, all my new clothes—what if they don't matter? What if they think managing the mill while you teach isn't respectable for a lady of my new standing?"

"Don't belittle your role. I won't have it. You do far more than manage the mill. You're the linchpin to the whole operation, where the union meets the masters. And the school was your idea."

He smiled at the memory of her reaction to Julian Bennett's accusation that the weavers were all illiterate. A polite snarl had shaped her lips, and she'd sworn on the spot to prove him wrong. Of course Alex had supported her decision to begin mandatory schooling for the factory's young people. He refused to simply *take* from the people of Calton. He would give back to the small community that had given him the joys of his life.

Yet a line of worry cut between her brows. "The last thing I want is to be looked upon with embarrassment by the people you love. Lord, Alex, I couldn't stand that."

"You remember what I told you about my stepmother, and about Viv. For pity's sake, she's a viscountess who's been running a diamond brokerage! They'll respect you all the more for the responsibilities you've assumed so diligently." Slowly, he stripped her white kid gloves, which were edged with exquisite silver thread embroidery and lace. Bright green eyes watched as he pressed her bare palms to his cheeks. "We're not a family of saints. Only one generation separates us, my love. My father was a child of Calton, just as you are. He belonged here," he said, nodding toward the brownstone. "And so do you."

"I belong with you."

"Then you're in the right place." He nuzzled her cheek, her neck, and down to the delectably soft flesh pillowed above her bodice. "My family will adore you because you're a good woman. You bore me a beautiful daughter. You love Edmund as your own. And you've utterly transformed me into a man worth knowing and loving."

"You were worth loving before," she said with a hint of laughter. "You were just . . . tightly wound."

"The word you're looking for is 'broken.' I didn't know it at the time, but I was."

"And now look at you. As filthy-minded as the next red-blooded male." She dragged his face up from between her breasts. Her smile had widened— a return of the teasing he'd grown to adore. "I can hardly believe you stand before successful capitalists and wise scholars and keep a straight face."

"I wouldn't be able to if you were there to smirk at me."

"I smirk out of love."

"I'll remind you of that next time you speak before the union. Turnabout is fair play."

She reached around and pinched his bum. "The worst part is, I believe you would. Not that it'll matter when we get back home. I could address them wearing nothing but bloomers and a bonnet, and they'd only care about the size of the bonuses you'll hand out."

"Everyone on that factory floor deserves a share of the Christie fortune. They made it possible."

"They'll name parks and important buildings after you—you wait and see."

He shook his head. "I told you, Polly. It was never about the money, nor winning my father's last challenge. It was about claiming the life I wanted, even if I didn't understand that at the time. Others deserve a chance at so much happiness. Your brothers, your ma, even Tommy and Les and the rest. They're part of you. In a way, they're part of me, too."

"Back to where the Christies came from. Going home."

Feeling almost bashful, he smiled softly. "Something like that."

She flung her arms around his neck and pulled him down for a quick kiss. The tip of her tongue pushed past his lips, infusing him with another jolt of masculine pride. He loved that he could do that to her, repeatedly, whenever they wanted.

"But believe me, Mrs. Christie, the bloomers and bonnet would still take precedence."

"They might at that. Now in we go, before the coachman suspects our activities."

After one last hot kiss, he whispered, "He'd be right to."

Alex descended from the carriage and held out his hand—to be gentlemanly, for certain, but also as a means of admiring her radiant appearance. The midnight-blue gown had been custom-made in London before their departure for New York. The shimmers of brilliant silver and gold threads woven into the fabric reminded him so much of stars against a dark, infinite sky that he had flatly refused to heed her protests over the cost. The sweeping neckline accentuated her bosom, while artful tucks, pleats, and a subtle bustle hinted at the mouthwatering feast of her curves. Matching blue and glittering silver ribbons adorned her bright auburn hair and trailed between shoulder blades swathed in a fur-lined winter pelisse.

She wore the gown effortlessly, as if born to such finery. Alex knew better and admired her all the more for it. His wife was infinitely brave. She would fit in just fine with the Christies.

With Polly on his arm and a heart near to bursting with satisfaction, he escorted her up the steps to the brownstone. They clung to one another whilst traversing little patches of ice and slushy snow, past clinging ivy vines withered by the cold, and into the soaring marble foyer.

"Alex!"

Viv practically ran out of the library and into his arms. Despite his surprise at his sister's uncharacteristic jubilation, he held her with all of his strength. In a rush of words, she explained that she had indeed prospered while managing a diamond brokerage in Cape Colony. But the most surprising revelation occurred a few moments later when, joining her in the library, Alex watched her tuck along her husband's side. Blocks of ice had been warmer when last he saw the pair.

Viscount Bancroft, weathered and tan and resplendently dressed, held out his hand. "Good to see you again, Alex. Glad you made it through in one piece."

A little dumbfounded, Alex flicked a questioning glance toward his sister. She only smiled, as joyfully as he could ever recall. The letters she'd penned from the Cape had hinted at her happiness, but this was far more than he'd dared hope.

Alex shook the man's hand. "And you, my lord."

"Call me Miles. Please. We're past all that nonsense," he said with a deprecating grin. His gaze shifted toward Polly. "And who is this magnificent creature?"

With more pride than a man should have the right to feel, Alex introduced his wife. Polly accepted their congratulations with grace and aplomb. Then her eyes alit on the portrait of Sir William above the huge fireplace aglow with a crackling fire.

"Well, well," she said cheerily. "If that isn't the very image of a man from Calton. You look a great deal like him, Alex."

Viv laughed. "She's not wrong. Now, you simply must tell me how you came to be married. My brother pens letters as if writing a scholarly treatise."

Alex exchanged a grin with Polly but decided to save the topic for later. "We all have stories to share, I suspect. But where are the twins?"

"They haven't arrived yet."

"And Delavoir? I want to conclude these legal matters."

"He stepped out briefly." Viv glanced at her husband with an sly smile. "Something about giving us privacy?"

"Hush," said the viscount. "You'll embarrass the new Mrs. Christie."

Polly giggled. "Oh, hardly."

"Anyway, he said this letter is for you." Viv's

mischief receded. A glimmer of far deeper emotion wet her eyes. "It's from Father. I received one, too. Just . . . prepare yourself."

Alex nodded. His fingers were numb as he took the letter. "In that case, if you'll excuse me."

Polly followed him into the corridor, which was dim with long winter shadows. Briefly, he touched her face. She leaned into his palm before finding her bravest smile of the day. "Get on with it, then. I want to hear more about the Cape."

He kissed her forehead, which she tucked against his shoulder. "I knew you'd find your feet."

The hiss of gaslamps and his thudding heart were far louder than the rattle of servants in the kitchen. Polly kept her body pressed against his, but without needing to be asked, she kept her eyes discreetly lowered. In doing so, she offered both the stability and privacy he needed.

He opened the envelope.

My Alexander,

Circumstances both left us widowers with young sons. Whereas I fled the hardship of facing fatherhood on my own, you persevered. You do our name credit by raising Edmund with such devotion. No matter how you look back on the mistakes I regret, know that I love you both.

I am continually humbled by your intellect, just as I envy your faith in the permanence of this earth. You look at its solidity with assurance. I do not pen such words as a slight, my son, but as a confession of my amazement.

Always, I have craved proof of my success, while you possess the confidence to look sky-ward with a limitless imagination, to transcend these mortal bounds.

In Calton, I hope you've learned to better appreciate my origins, as I've endeavored, rather imperfectly, to appreciate you. Keep your fearless heart, my son. I wish you success in your undertakings and, perhaps one day, a love to see you through the rest of your life. My material wealth and your distant stars are naught but dust without the love of a bonny lass.

Your father,
William

Alex chuckled despite the stunned, humbled tension his father's words had built beneath his chest. "He's right, you know."

"How's that?" Polly lifted her face, full of silent questions.

"I'm a lucky man for having found a bonny lass." He gathered her petite body in his arms. To hold her was to breathe and to hope. "I love you, Polly."

She stood high on her tiptoes and kissed his lips. Even better was the soft way she whispered, "And I love you, Alex."

No teasing now. Just the truth he carried every day in his heart. He threw a quick prayer of thanks up to where he hoped his father might hear. Then he led the woman he adored back into the library.

Continue reading for an exclusive excerpt from

The Christies, Book One

One

*A*lthough Miles stood well back from where the *Coronea* had docked, the push and crush of humanity threatened even his studiously crafted calm. Hordes of disembarking passengers wrestled with their belongings as they forged toward land.

The ripe stench of coal fires, harbor rot, and hundreds of bodies overpowered the clean salt of the ocean. Seabirds circled and swooped in a chaotic dance. Miles touched the back of his neck where a light wind teased his hair. The cool seaside air reminded him of Southampton.

I watched thee on the breakers, when all was storm and fear.

But Lord Byron's words offered Miles no comfort, only an odd sort of foreboding.

Viv had left him a note. Yet another elegant, prissy note to say she was leaving.

So he'd sobered up. And made a decision.

After catching the first steamer back to England,

he'd evaded his father long enough to gamble his way into a bit of ready cash. Then it was off to Cape Town.

Vivienne Bancroft would come back to him. Willingly.

With a hand to his brow, he looked toward the luxury clipper's topmost deck. Viv would be up there among that tangle of people, along with the manservant he'd sent to intercept her luggage.

Intercept . . . and then hold hostage.

Miles found himself twirling his wedding ring. That little hypocrite—all decorum and indignation until her mouth met his.

Had beastly Sir William given his daughter a plump dollop of cash, she would've had the financial means to end their marriage. Miles would've gone back to London, alone, solvent enough to keep the family estates intact. But little else remained of her dowry.

Instead, the challenge of Old Man Christie's bequest offered a one-million-dollar reprieve. *Damn and blast.* Far, far too much money to ignore.

His scant head start aside, during which he'd secured accommodations in Kimberley and completed banking transfers, he and Viv would need to learn quickly: every major player, every aspect of the diamond trade, and even the bloody weather. They were starting near to zero. He should have been terrified but a sharp thrill sped the beat of his heart.

The crack of a whip snapped his attention toward a man sitting atop a heavily laden wagon. The road leading away from the docks, clogged with dark bodies, permitted no room for the vehicle to pass. Burly and dough-faced, the wagon master wasn't directing his whip at donkeys, but at people.

"Get off there," the driver shouted. He threw his weight into the next strike of braided leather.

With relentless clarity, the Cape's autumn sunshine illuminated every face twisted by concentration and fear. The donkeys continued to bray. The wagon master raised his arm again. Leather sliced through the air, this time striking a tall shirtless man whose dark, scarred back had already suffered the bite of a whip.

"Out of the way, you kaffir scum!"

Across three months, the colony had subjected Miles to many such scenes. Perhaps the difference, on this occasion, could be traced to the bitterness Viv churned in his blood. His arms ached with the need to pummel his fretfulness into submission—or pummel *someone*. The lawlessness of the colony, the other-worldliness of it, gave him permission to do what his tedious title had never permitted: take matters into his own hands.

"Oh, bloody hell."

He strode into the crowd, abandoning his role as a mere bystander. Fully a head taller than most of the scrambling people, he fixed on the wagon master. Every crack of the man's whip filled Miles with sizzling indignation. Like most of the British Empire, Cape Colony hadn't permitted slavery in almost fifty years. That didn't stop some colonists from treating Africans as they would the lowest animals.

Miles didn't consider himself a do-gooder, but such a flagrant abuse of power assaulted his most basic principles. It wasn't sporting and it simply wasn't British.

He elbowed his way through the throng until the wagon master loomed above him on the bench. Miles quickly climbed aboard, senses centered on his target. The wagon master turned just as Miles balled his fist and let it swing. A satisfying crack of bone rewarded him as his opponent's nose gave way.

Blood streaked the man's mangy beard. Narrow-eyed anger replaced his stunned grimace. He reared back the butt of his whip and brought it down like a cudgel. Miles used his forearm to deflect the blow, then retaliated with jabs to the gut.

Foul exhales accompanied the wagon master's grunts, but his flab seemed to absorb the impact of each punch. Winded, he tottered slightly. His guard dropped. Miles snatched the whip. When the man's expression bunched around the need to continue the fight, Miles jabbed the butt of the whip against that broken nose. The wagon master clutched his face.

"Are we quite through?" Miles demanded.

His opponent sank onto the bench and nodded once. Rage still flared across his expression but his shoulders caved forward.

"Good." Miles slowly coiled the whip. "Now, I suggest you notice the situation here. Too many people, for one. Laughably poor engineering. But that's no excuse for whipping people."

"They're bloody kaffirs," the man said, his voice muffled behind his hands. "Beasts like these donkeys."

Miles glanced across the sea of faces, more dark than light, and wondered again at the state of the

Cape. Ripe, raw, it perched on the edge of violence. He tasted its bitterness in the air and felt it itching under his skin—a shocking sort of awakening.

"No more beastly than the rest of us," Miles said.

He hopped down from the wagon.

As the immediacy of the fight seeped from his body, Miles shivered. He eased back into the crowd on legs just shy of steady, intent on returning to the machinery crate. Surely Viv had found her way off that damned clipper by now.

He bumped into a solid wall of ebony flesh and found himself looking up at a man—a rare occurrence. Before him stood the same shirtless African who'd taken one of the wagon master's cruel strokes. His shaven head gleamed.

"Thank you." The African's deep bass was melodic, like the notes of a bassoon. "Boggs is a scourge."

Miles raised his eyebrows. "A scourge? Nice word."

"I speak the truth."

"And I believe you. My hope is that I won't require his services."

"Hire a wagon," the man said. "I'll drive for you instead."

Miles studied that dark African face. Every feature was as he'd seen in caricatures and even so-called scientific journals: the wide, flat nose, the large lips, and the fathomless black irises surrounded by white. Those demeaning illustrations hadn't captured what it was to look upon such a man. Miles found intelligence and a rugged, hard-edged dignity—a refreshing change from the feckless gentlemen who'd comprised his social circle in London.

"You need a work pass," Miles said.

"Yes, sir."

Without a work pass, Africans could be subjected to police harassment or expulsion from the city. In Kimberley, the threat of diamond theft tainted all manual laborers, regardless of skin color, but Africans bore the heaviest burden of suspicion.

"Good, because I need reliable workers. I'm returning to Kimberley, if you're interested." He held out his hand. "Call me Bancroft," he said, omitting a significant part of his identity—namely, his title.

The man stared at Miles for a long moment, then shook hands. His grip was strong, his expression intent. "I'm Umtonga kaMpande. But you English seem to find that a challenge."

"No argument here."

"Because you have shown the kindness of a friend, I ask that you call me Mr. Kato."

"That is a kindness in itself, Mr. Kato."

With nothing more by way of niceties, he turned and strode back toward the *Coronea*, toward Viv, glad to know that the tall African would follow.

Viv brushed a gloved hand across her forehead and pinned the porter with a hard look. "What do you mean they've been *taken care of*?"

The short man, bulky and rippling with menacing muscles, simply shrugged. "Your baggage has been taken care of, ma'am."

Fear brushed up her spine. Had her things been stolen? Hardly on African soil for five minutes and already a snag. She took a quick breath. "By whom?"

"He said he was your husband. Lord Bancroft."

She locked her knees against the impulse to sink onto the foot-worn planks of the dock. "My husband," she whispered.

Of course he would come. She'd been willfully naïve in believing her trip would signal her intention to remain separated.

She needed her belongings. Every last item would be necessary if she were to endure the twenty months that remained of her contract.

She wouldn't dwell on the immensity of her task, choosing instead to relive the lessons of her father's many successes. One day at a time. One foot in front of the other. Piece by hard-earned piece. In doing so she would find the strength to survive this trial. Deep inside, she would rediscover the tenacity of an urchin who'd once stolen a dying vagrant's dinner just to quell her own aching hunger—and the resilience on which that quiet girl had depended when her mother was jailed and hanged.

But at present, she needed to find her husband.

She signaled to Chloe Tassiter, her maid, who handed the porter a shilling. "Can you take me to him, please?" Viv asked.

"This way."

As nimble as a rabbit, he ducked into the crowd, navigating passengers, porters, and incalculable bags and trunks. He jostled to clear a path. The same foot journey without his aid would've been terribly difficult, two women consumed by bodies.

Unlike her siblings, Viv had endured the grueling burden of an impoverished youth and the secret knowledge of her illegitimacy. That meant balancing the strictures of good society with the example of Sir William Christie's limitless ambitions. She never failed to appreciate when her way was made easier by the privilege she now enjoyed—privilege she would labor ceaselessly to keep.

Good heavens, a million dollars! She'd be able to return to her home in New York, to her life. And she would finally be free of the title she'd learned to wear like a horse harness across her shoulders.

Viv bumped a coop full of clucking hens and bruised her hip. She and Chloe didn't so much walk as gush toward some unseen destination.

Chloe took Viv's upper arm and offered a reassuring squeeze. "Courage, my lady."

Although a servant since her youth, Chloe had never lived as roughly as this.

Viv, however . . . Her body ached with deep recognition. She had once hidden in the shadows of a similar world, her days marked by stealth, fear, and hunger. She breathed its filth and knew its secrets.

"My lady, do you know where we're going?" Chloe asked.

A shudder wiggled through Viv's stomach—that sudden, queasy feeling of being taken advantage of. The porter could be leading them anywhere. Suddenly, her husband's volatility held more appeal than those beastly unknowns.

"I say." Viv lifted her voice above the din. "Where are you taking us, man?"

"Just there." The porter nodded toward where a wagon waited along a footpath.

Viv stopped short.

Miles, Lord Bancroft, leaned against one large wheel. Only, she'd never seen him in such a state. Gone was the snide aristocrat, preened to perfection. In his place stood a taut, muscular man whose waist-coat gapped open along a lean abdomen. His neck was bare. He'd rolled his shirtsleeves. A coiled whip dangled from his belt and rested against his hip.

Blinking back the grit and sunshine, Viv struggled to assemble the jigsaw of new impressions. Thick hair he normally tamed with pomade stuck out in spiky disarray. The coffee-dark color was streaked through with lighter strands, kissed by bright midday. Every indecently exposed inch of flesh had assumed a lus-cious caramel shade. Too much time spent in the sun, her mind argued. But the color suited him—much bet-ter than the pallor of genteel boredom and too much time spent in gambling halls.

A taunting grin turned him from merely handsome to maddeningly so.

Miles . . . wearing a whip. He'd turned positively heathen.

Viv tried to tell herself that she didn't want to see him there, obviously pleased to have taken her by surprise. Yet she could not deny a flush of relief. Confronted with the stomach-sick shock of the Cape, she realized that her will alone would not be enough. Never had she felt more gallingly female.

She needed him. He knew it. And her pride would suffer.

For the sake of that bonus, however, Viv met him at the wagon. "My lord," she said simply.

"My lady." Miles bowed, more sarcastic than respectful. "Surprised to see me?"

The hard emotion in his eyes tempted her to recoil. Yes, she'd left him. Her reasons remained strong and valid. No glare, no matter how intimidating, would change her mind.

A fine spray of dried blood formed a ghastly constellation across his rumpled white shirt. That he'd already found trouble was hardly a surprise.

Her attention returned to Miles, to his shirt, to his tanned neck and forearms. To the vigorous width of his shoulders and the ready strength of his thighs. This version of her husband was new. All new—at least on the outside.

"We have tickets for the train to Kimberley," she said, banishing her fascination. "Can you take us to the station?"

Miles's grin returned. "We're all yours, my lady . . . for a price."

Tender skin chafed beneath her gloves and between her breasts. Better than anyone, she understood that apparent courtesies from her husband would be met with a reckoning. The gleam in his eyes told Viv that the last thing he would demand was money.

Continue reading for an exclusive excerpt from

Diva

The Christies, Book Three

One

*A*very Palmer's feet hit the frigid wood floor. Only the sound of the dreaded siren could propel his movements so swiftly in the pitch darkness. His heart imitated a locomotive's chugging rhythm. He grabbed everything by rote. Trousers and shirt. Coat and boots. Gear to protect against the stinging cold.

He pounded on Ollie's door. "Get up, old man! You hear it as well as I do!"

Another quick smack made the hinges rattle. At the sound of boots thumping on the plank floor, Avery turned from that unpleasant chore. His uncle was the only family he had left. Though a drunk and a wastrel, the man knew grapes. He also knew the valleys of the Rhone Vineyard intimately, just as a husband would have memorized his wife's curves.

Avery stuffed his wide-brimmed hat atop his head. Although he aspired to Ollie's gifted understanding of the land they both nurtured, he had no intention of learning a woman so thoroughly. In Singleton, his obsession with the Rhone Vineyard was legendary—as were the measures he'd taken to keep it. That unpleasant renown made him a candidate for no more than a sweaty romp.

He grabbed three day-old biscuits from the tin on the kitchen counter and shoved them in his coat pocket. Coffee would've been nice, but when the siren blared, there was no time.

"Ollie, get along!"

He stalked through the parlor and out into the brittle night. August in Australia. Nothing was sharper, colder, more beautifully sparkling.

And utterly deadly to the vines.

His second, Max Kovalev, was supervising the field hands in lighting bonfires at the ends of each row. Avery hustled to where the big, weathered pirate of a man lit another torch.

"How bad?" he asked.

"Bad enough to kill, Boss."

The snap and damp in the air had already told him the worst. Maybe he just wanted someone else to be right for once. "Get those torches lit!"

Avery's crew was comprised of former prostitutes, criminals, and orphaned youths—none of whom had compunctions against working for a man of his reputation. They had nowhere else to go.

But their fate was not his concern. Every one of them had made bad choices. Only keeping the Rhone mattered to Avery.

He clapped his hands to warm numbed fingers and rouse his troops. "Children over the age of six—out of bed. Anyone who doesn't work loses their pay, and I will personally escort you the hell off my land."

He snatched the nearest torch and dipped the head into a bonfire's crackling heat. Fire sizzled to life. He strode toward the farthest row, lighting each bonfire he passed. Soon flames blazed across the landscape in pin-pricks of orange and yellow. A score of workers did the same along the interminable rows.

The vines appeared no more alive than rock. Their winter-pruned cordons were only stumps, like a man with his arms hacked off. But unlike a man, the vines kept their vigor under the soil, stored in roots so deep that they held the Rhone knitted with underground stitches.

But any extreme could be deadly. If the frost settled into the veins . . .

Avery reached the end of his row, where the young-est children waited with arms full of fans. Despite the frigid air, he stripped out of his coat and shirt. The work would soon turn blisteringly hot. He strapped suspend-ers over his long underwear and accepted a pair of fans. He paused to eye Max's oldest son. Ivan was only ten, but his broadening shoulders and thick neck already attested to his father's sturdy build.

"Pass that armful around, but keep a pair for your-self," he said to Ivan. "You're old enough to join us."

The boy's frown transformed into a beaming smile. Children tended the fans, stood at the ready near sand buckets, and brought water to the adults. Ivan was no longer a child, not by any standard Avery kept. He'd been even younger when his parents died.

Time for Ivan to earn an adult's keep.

Avery strapped the fans to his arms and led the procession back toward the main house. Four dozen torches stretched between his body and that destination. Hefting the cloth fans, he used them like a bird used wings. Precious heat wanted to escape into the night, but he dragged it down toward the vines.

Muscles honed from years of labor tingled at the halfway point. Smoke and cinders bit his skin. He glanced across the hundreds of rows. His eyes glazed in a moment of panic. A third of the vineyard remained unlit. His pace far outstripped the others who wielded fans. What began as lightweight wings made of balsa and linen would soon weigh heavy on weary limbs.

"Pick it up!" he shouted over his shoulder. "Every minute counts!"

An hour later, the last of the bonfires and all of the torches sparked skyward. Tendrils of silver and charcoal blended into a hazy mass above the vines. Even that would help blanket the rows and trap the heat. Miles distant, smoke from other spreads proved that every vintner in Hunter Valley fought the frost.

The children skilled in more dangerous chores were tasked with refueling each station. More wood for the bonfires. More petroleum for the torches. Avery finished his third complete pass and accepted a dipper from Lucy Kilgore, a girl barely six years old.

"What are you doing out of bed?"

"Ma said we need to save the vines."

"Your ma's right."

He swigged one more gulp of water, then soaked his hair and face. Soot washed down his skin. Lucy's mother was out in the fields, laboring with the fans. In keeping with her sordid history, Beatrice had offered her company to him on a number of occasions—and with increasing regularity.

He handed the dipper back to Lucy. The last thing he needed was to entangle himself in the girl's future. He was not a surrogate father, and that was exactly what Beatrice desired.

Midway down another row, he knelt in the dirt. A layer of frost skated the surface. He clawed the earth, needing to know whether hope remained. The soil was chilly four inches down, but not strewn with ice crystals. A cutting from the nearest plant revealed what he needed to see: life. The vines yet pumped vital juices to their vulnerable extremities.

He glanced up to where Max had paused two rows over. "Keep at it," Avery said. "We've got this."

He broke off half a biscuit and shoved it in his mouth. Then back to the fans. By the time the first hint of dawn began to change the sky from fathomless black to deep, deep blue, his chest ached and his back screamed. Two hours later, the sun peeked above the horizon. Rays of pink and gold shot across the valley. The last snaking fingers of frost glittered briefly under that bright assault, then weakened. Only harmless dew.

"Fires out! Save the fuel!"

His crew rushed to obey his command. They doused the flames with sand, water, and caps for the torches. Acidic tinges of spent fires surged into the dawn air. Avery stank of smoke, and his long underwear was soaked through. He'd get cleaned up later. Just like he'd eat later and sleep later.

Back at the house, he found Max and another

overseer, Lucas Hoffer—a hearty Prussian with a keen sense of taste. His fair hair was almost white, yet he had the smooth skin of a man in his twenties.

"Everyone's on frost chores after breakfast," Avery said. "Replenish the fuel stores and sand buckets. Repair the fans. No one sleeps until the work is done, but no one works past three."

Max and Lucas nodded and strode off to disseminate the orders, leaving Avery to take a deep, smoke-stung breath. He had survived another night. The sun was poised at the base of its arc across the sky. In summer, that same sun would be his enemy, but for now they were allies.

He blinked. The silhouette of a carriage materialized on the horizon. The mail coach wound down the snaking trail from the top of the valley toward his home.

At least he hoped it was the mail coach. The men from the bank weren't due for another two months. Avery would have good news for them by then. The alternative, that his creditors would follow through with the threat of foreclosure, was too infuriating to contemplate. He could defend his home with fists and drawn weapons—and he sure as hell had. Fighting bankers, however, was like fighting phantoms.

Yet no businessmen emerged from what was, indeed, the mail coach. It was piled high with luggage, as if someone intended to stay awhile.

That someone was a stunning blonde. She tilted her wide-brimmed hat against the dawn as she stepped down from the carriage. A haughty glance assessed the smoke-grayed vineyard with one sweep. She wrinkled her nose. That anyone would look on his night of hard work with such disdain made him feel like punching a hole through a wall.

She walked toward Avery as if strolling through immaculate gardens. Instead, loosened earth kicked up along the woman's blue-and-cream day gown.

Who in the devil's name was she?

"Excuse my arriving unannounced this morning," she said. American? Maybe. "I'm looking for Mr. Avery Palmer."

"That's me."

"Very good. I'm Gwyneth Christie. My late father was Sir William Christie."

Avery tensed. Every muscle became as fixed as the unyielding vines he'd been so desperate to save. Desperation of another sort fused his fingers into fists. "Then you can get the hell off my land."

Gwen tried not to stare at the heathen man, just as she attempted to minimize the offense broached by his single harsh sentence. To no avail. She had never received such a discourteous welcome.

"I'm afraid that's not possible," she said.

Briefly, she wished she had as much natural, jovial tact as her twin brother, Jonesy. Ever the stickler for fashion, even Jonesy might've been at a loss when faced with the disheveled Mr. Palmer.

No use dwelling on the impossible. Her brother was half a world away and she needed to do this on her own. If this man was intent on behaving like a boor, she would do her best to charm him. Surely he could be no gruffer than the great Sir William.

"I believe my father's attorney apprised you of my arrival. You know the nature of our situation."

"You're here to try and run my vineyard."

"Hardly." The idea of her *farming* was worthy of a genuine smile. "I'm sure I don't know a thing about making wine or growing plants."

The coldness of his expression banished any comparisons to her father. She had never known eyes of such a pale, icy green. Sunny brown hair poked out from beneath his hat. It was so in need of a trim that it curled at the base of his nape. His jaw and upper lip were lined with pale morning stubble, which lent him the appearance of someone half wild.

He narrowed his eyes in a squint that hid their distinctive color. His hard assessment from head to toe left her feeling judged—and found wanting. Gwen had been the object of adoration and male appreciation for so long that his obvious contempt rendered her breathless. Maybe charm wouldn't work after all.

A sneer edged his finely shaped mouth. "I'd wager you know very little. About anything."

He turned and trudged toward the main house. Sweat slicked his back. His long underwear clung to sharp shoulder blades and the long, strong column of his spine. *Muscles.* Good God, she couldn't remember witnessing such a display of unpolished brawn. Aggravation and a twinge of fear mingled with pure feminine curiosity.

"I'm here," she called after him, "because the vineyard is in arrears. Something about spoiled vintages? Tell me that isn't the case and I'll be on my way."

Mr. Palmer stopped mid-stride. Those robust shoulders tightened, as if pride could fuse bones. He inhaled. Gwen did, too, matching him in that moment. Waiting.

Mr. Palmer stalked back to where she stood. "I would appreciate if you kept from bellowing the details of my financial affairs."

Gwen hoped her flinch was disguised by a heavy thump, as the driver deposited the last of her luggage onto the ground. He looked to Mr. Palmer with dread. She would've thought it laughable to imagine a burly coachman cowering before a man who tended grapes. She recalled similar expressions in town when, in seeking accommodations and transport, she had mentioned the man's name.

Scorn. Loathing. Fear.

The truth glared down at her with icy green eyes. Mr. Palmer was very, very intimidating.

However, she had no intention of letting a bully dictate the terms of her stay. Sixty percent of the Rhone Vineyard belonged to the Christies. For no reason was she leaving Australia without earning her million-dollar bonus. She had put her career on hold just when she should've been performing every night. Singing. Receiving the applause of sold-out crowds.

Nothing but success would make that sacrifice worthwhile.

"Answer me," Gwen said calmly. "Then I'll know what sort of man you are."

"Will you, now?" His voice was impossibly low, as if a thunderstorm could form words.

"I already know you're hardworking." She squelched the urge to add *if unsuitably dressed*. "I only ask that you do not spoil my impression by lying."

He closed the distance between them. For a moment, all considerations fell away. Gwen found his bearing . . . *menacing*. He carried himself with such arrogance. Brawn added to his daunting appearance. Sturdy, thick shoulders, a flat stomach, powerful legs. He stood before her with his arms crossed over a chest indecently outlined with damp cotton.

Muscles, she thought once more. Good Lord.

No other man, no matter how tall, had made her feel so petite, so tiny—verging on completely incapable. She did not care for that feeling. Not at all.

"You presume to know what sort of man I am, Miss Christie?"

"I presume nothing, but I do expect an answer."

A tic along his jaw brought her attention to the deep hollows beneath high, sharp cheekbones. His golden stubble glittered as the rising sun washed across his face. Yes, he was intimidating and gruff.

He was also a singularly handsome man.

She chose to focus on his lack of cooperation.

"You'll be on your way no matter what."

"Not unless you can demonstrate its viability as a business."

Mr. Palmer flipped an ash-covered finger under a tuft of lace adorning the shoulder of her gown. "What would you know about that? Coming here in such frippery?"

"Kindly keep your hands to yourself, sir."

He did not.

One of the galling side effects of being the youngest Christie was her family's loving yet stifling tendency to treat her like a porcelain doll. Such vulnerability, however, would give Mr. Palmer permission to tread all over her for the duration of her stay.

She swatted his fingers away, and made a show of rubbing the ash marring her gloves.

"I've done my research, Mr. Palmer. I know your creditors are out of patience. They will assume control of this vineyard next year when your loan comes due."

She could ensure his cooperation by telling him about the million-dollar prize she stood to earn. But later. His behavior was not worth a crust of bread, let alone such an incentive.

"Christie Holdings needs no such dead weight dragging down its profit margins," she continued. "The land will be sold at auction."

"I told you to keep your mouth shut."

"No, you said to keep my voice down. I've been practically whispering."

Forcing a smile, she turned to hand the driver a crown. "I appreciate the ride. Good day."

"You're staying?" The driver kept his words hushed.

"I am."

Heavy coats and a fur hat gave him the silhouette of a bear. "Your funeral. Just try to keep on his good side."

"Was that his good side?"

His caution did not ease. "You're still alive, miss."

The carriage jerked to a start. Matched black horses snorted hot breath into the cold morning air.

Haggard workers trailed in from the fields. Their clothes blackened with soot, they appeared as a regiment of sleepwalkers. Curious glances toward Gwen were to be expected. Only one woman, with lush dark hair and a little girl by her side, skewered Gwen with a chilling stare.

"So tell me, Mr. Palmer," she said despite a tiny bout of nerves. "Where shall I keep accommodations?"

"You assume I'll give you a room."

"If not, I assume I'll claim one."

"You think you're quite the grand lady."

She quirked a smile. "More like, people often make the mistake of believing I'm just a pretty face."

The ferocity in his expression did not ease. Poking a circus tiger would be safer. "We have no need for pretty faces."

She interlaced her fingers over the handle of her parasol. "If your creditors appeared right now, demanding their money, would you be able to fend them off? Looking and behaving as you do?"

She held his hostile stare, although the sweat-slicked notch at the base of his thick throat kept tempting her to stray. Perhaps rumors were true, that he was born of criminal stock. If so, more unsavory rumors might hold merit as well. She was quite proud of herself for holding her own against a purported murderer.

"Come with me," he said at last. He flicked his attention toward the stack of luggage. "But carry your own damn bags."